20/20 PERFECT VISION

A NEW WAY OF BEING

SHARON VELISEK

GOOD INTENTIONS PUBLISHING

ISBN: 978-1-9991928-1-5 (Paperback)
Good Intentions Publishing

Interior & Cover Design: STOKE Publishing
Cover Photo: Digital Dean Photography

CONTENTS

PRAISE FOR 20/20 PERFECT VISION

Sharon Velisek takes us into a world where the universe might just be working to put us where we need to be. This is a thought-provoking book about the meaning of life, about how fate might be encouraging us to be our truest self, and the ways in which we might have spiritual guides that can help us live the life we're meant to live. A powerful and meaningful read! - **Cara Lockwood, USA Today bestselling author and editor**

Finally, someone has taken Seth and Jane Robert's complex channeled principles of conscious living and woven them into a fictional template for thriving. The non-physical colorful "helpers" that guide the main characters to discover a deeper meaning to their lives are there for all of us, if we but stop to listen. Readers are gently directed to uncover the purpose of their own reality – to find meaning and passion in their lives. Those who are curious, and those already on the metaphysical path will have difficulty putting this re-energizing and thoughtful book of uncommon wisdom down! – **Julie Larsen, Thought Energy Practitioner**

20/20 Perfect Vision changed how I think about my life, relationships, family circumstances and personal experiences. Let this inspiring story help you discover the truth about your own beliefs and decisions...and create the living experience that you dream of! - **Eva Hlavackova, Holistic Nutritionist and founder of Epicholistic.com**

I dedicate this book to those with a curious and open mind!
I hope this is you...

INTRODUCTION

In 1995 a very traumatic event etched itself forever onto my life. I'd been shot in my driveway by an ex-boyfriend who was stalking me at the time. After several years of recuperation, I wrote the book *Stalked & Shot: A True Story of Survival and Change,* which told of everything that happened before *and* after the shooting. But there was more: while lying on my driveway, profusely bleeding and very close to death, I experienced several phenomena I was driven to find answers for. I had an out-of-body discussion with myself, heard voices in my gut that gave me the important instructions that kept me alive, and I became mesmerized by the pulsating golden circle of loving energy that surrounded me. And then there was the fact that I did not die, even though I'd been shot twice at close range by a sawed-off shotgun! What was going on? I needed to know. So, I began a two-decade search for insight into these burning questions. This book is the result. It's a motivating and imaginative story that describes the way I now think the world works. If it helps in any way, my aspirations will be well rewarded.

The personality I am will forever reside within these pages. Please, join me!

1

GOING ON A TRIP

"There is no logical way to the discovery of these elemental laws. There is only the way of intuition, which is helped by a feeling for the order lying behind the appearance." **Albert Einstein**

"The map says go two miles to the north, then turn west at the junction and go one mile till you reach the next junction, and then turn north again for eight miles. Ah, just keep driving, Malcolm - I'll let you know when to turn," Crow directed, as he leaned forward in the passenger seat scanning the horizon for clues. Such adventure!

We'd been driving most of the day already. The landscape through the mountain ranges had been incredible, but we were gob-smacked as we descended the last mountain and found ourselves plummeted into the staggering, enormous, eternity of the prairies. The land rolled on like an ocean before us. And the colors! The sky was such an intense and penetrating blue. Squares of lush, vibrant green crops waved in the wind, and oh...my...gosh...a brilliant mustard yellow field was dancing next to the delicate mauve of another field. It was stunning everywhere I looked. Enormous cloud sculptures sailed along in the sky. I was leaning out the window taking picture after picture: I couldn't stop taking them. I'd never seen anything like it before as I'd never travelled beyond the mountains. From the moment I laid eyes on the prairies, I felt that everyone needed to see them. They were *that* magnificent.

We drove on and should have been getting close to our destination, but for some reason we saw no sign of the large barren dinosaur park we were heading to, even though the land surrounding us was as flat as a pancake. Then suddenly the narrow gravel road turned into a large parking lot. Ahead of us, we could see the end of the earth! We all scrambled out and ran to the edge - and gasped when we looked down on a completely different world in all its strangeness and glory.

"I think we're here," Crow softly declared as he gazed in awe at the incredible landscape that lay below us, all the way to the right, and all the way to the left, as far as the eye could see. "In my wildest dreams," he continued, "I could not have imagined anything like this!" Malcolm and I were speechless and could only nod in agreement. What an astonishing place!

We got back in the van and followed the winding road down into a different time frame, and a different reality. It was NOTHING like our home in the suburbs. It was so quiet - yet it exuded a strength that was deafening. "I don't know about you guys, but I feel like there's something special going on here," I pointed out. Little did I know how right I was.

IT WAS ONLY A SHORT WEEK BEFORE THAT MY HUSBAND, MALCOLM, and I had been sitting around the supper table discussing our mutual discontent with our city lives. Neither of us enjoyed big city living anymore - too much coldness, everybody wearing blinders in their struggle to keep separate the more crowded they became. Malcolm suffered the monotonous effects of riding the giant wave of commuter traffic every day - going to, and coming back from work, over and over. But we had a hefty mortgage, and many other monthly payments we couldn't ignore.

"Why," I asked despairingly, "are we living a life that neither of us enjoys anymore? Somewhere along the way, I think we blindly followed the herd and moved to the big city - bought a house that won't even be ours till we retire, plus all the toys and bills that come from living like this. The only time we really seem to relax and enjoy ourselves is when we get into the country. Is that how we want to spend the rest of our lives?" We owned, along with the bank, a comfy home in the suburbs, and we had great friends, but I was starting to feel claustrophobic and trapped - like I was being unwillingly forced in the wrong direction.

"Then you're really going to like what I'm about to say, Julie," Malcolm teased. This is one of the things I loved about my husband – he was always able to lift me out of my doldrums.

"I'm all ears! I hope it's good news."

"Well, I was talking to Crow at lunch today. He's been itching to get out of the city and into the country too, so he started searching the internet and found a place in Alberta where the prairie drops away to reveal a surreal landscape that looks like it could have been Jurassic Park eons ago. Now it's a barren park full of fossils and weird rock formations! And it's huge! They've found all kinds of dinosaur bones there already, and they're still finding more. They've got campsites too, so it wouldn't even cost much to go. What do you think? Would you be interested in spending a week checking it out - breathe some fresh air - walk on trails without traffic and crowds - cook on the camp stove - wake up to the sunrise - and end your day watching a magnificent prairie sunset? I've heard they're exceptional with no mountains in the way. We could drive out next week in Crow's van – take the tent, and just relax in the land where the dinosaurs once roamed. How about it - do you want to go?"

I was certainly not going to say no to an offer like that. I was very interested, especially since there would be no buffets, hot tubs, pools, or swim-up bars. And since there were none of those attractions, the other campers were probably more my kind of tourist, too. "Heck, yeah! Let's go! I'll just have to see if I can get time off on such short notice, but it shouldn't be a problem."

"You know, ever since Crow told me about this place, I've felt this nagging desire to go. It's like we're *meant* to go. I know I've felt like this before, but never to this degree. This time is definitely different. Call me crazy, but I feel like we need to do this together – you, me, and Crow. I'm beyond excited about it. I'll call Crow right away and tell him." Malcolm picked up his phone to call.

I loved seeing Malcolm so excited. "Following our intuition will be good for us," I told him. "Let's see where it takes us." I wanted a stress-free vacation, but more than that, I wanted to leave my duties and responsibilities behind and go exploring into something unknown, something where my imagination would be allowed some freedom.

Crow was able to reserve a campsite for the following week, and when the time came we packed his funky old purple van with our tents, sleeping bags, camp stoves, food, water, flashlights, sunscreen, bug spray, and all the paraphernalia we could think of. It was going to be a full day's drive, so we planned to take turns driving.

We got together the night before leaving, and confided in each other that we felt like *something* was going to happen this trip – it was going to be a game-changer somehow - we just knew it, but none of us could put a finger on how or why or what. It was like going through a door with no idea of what was on the other side, but you knew you had to walk through it. You also knew that once you did, there was no turning back. Your life would be forever changed.

And we were oh-so-right!

2

THE DINOSAUR PARK

"Biological diversity is messy. It walks, it crawls, it swims, it swoops, it buzzes. But extinction is silent, and it has no voice other than our own." **Paul Hawken**

Our campsite was fairly large and quite private as it was the last one in the row. It was pleasantly nestled between two large poplar trees, which not only provided us with necessary shade, but also the beautiful rustling sound of the wind, and plenty of loud birdsong. We'd arrived in the evening, giving us just enough time to set up our tents and unpack our gear before we were able to lean back on our comfy camp chairs to watch the incredibly large ball of sun get swallowed up by the horizon. Then we made a campfire and sat around talking while staring into the flames. We still had that overwhelming feeling that something was special here - something was waiting for us. And with those thoughts on repeat, we attempted to drift off to sleep. It was a glorious first night.

I woke to see Malcolm coming into our tent holding two steaming cups. Through the open tent flaps, I could see the early morning sun poking through the mist. The air was still crisp and cool though, so we sat up in our tent, sleeping bags wrapped around us, and enjoyed our campfire coffee - the best you'll ever get in my opinion.

Later on, over a tasty breakfast of bacon and eggs devoured in the fresh air, the three of us discussed the plans for the day. There were a few choices, but in the end, we decided to venture onto the walking paths by ourselves, just to get acquainted with the peculiar and exciting rock structures. After lunch, we planned to go on one of the tours, which promised to bus us into the restricted areas of the park. And then to just relax after supper, making sure to get ourselves back onto the rocky cliffs with our cameras to catch the sunset this time. With our decisions made, we washed the last bits of breakfast down with one more cup of java, slathered on the sunscreen and sprayed ourselves from head to toe with bug spray. Then we headed off to find the trails, which actually began fairly close to our campsite, we discovered.

It didn't take long to be hit by the realization that this was an extraordinary landscape indeed. There was no visible end to the strange rock columns of every shape and size. Some even had enormous flat pancake-like rocks precariously perched on top of them, often at odd angles, which gave the impression that they could fall at any moment. The winding path between these monolithic structures, otherwise known as *hoodoos*, was very granular and quite slippery when wet. It seemed relatively easy to get lost too, as the trail often disappeared. So, we stuck together and carefully ventured farther and farther into this bizarre terrain. And, of course, as with most things, we became increasingly comfortable as we went along. We allowed ourselves to relax and become part of this new world around us.

As I followed along, I got to thinking that this is what we'd done in our city lives as well. It dawned on me that a familiar formula existed: most people were a bit apprehensive of allowing something new to enter their lives, while at the same time being attracted to it out of curiosity, but once they were in it for a while they become at ease with it, and the original feelings of apprehension and attraction changed to acceptance and comfort. However, I didn't think comfort was supposed to last forever. It struck me that we were at this point in our city lives. After attaining all the comforts we originally strived for, and finally feeling like we fit in with the crowd, a little nagging voice had snuck in the back door - pushing us to move on, try something new, branch out, explore possibilities, show some creativity, get out there and discover our potential! Maybe that was the reason underlying our mutual discord with city life. But how could we change our current life when it had tentacles attached to so many different areas? It's not like we could just roll up our tent and sleeping bags and move to another spot and say, "*Okay, here we are. We're ready for another adventure.*" We had a house, payments, jobs, friends, and responsibilities to others. But, I liked *this* reality so much more. Our city life felt like a massive weight on my shoulders, while camping out here felt so light and free.

I figured it was probably time to quit my daydreaming, but I planned to discuss my new revelation with Malcolm and Crow later. Right now, however, I needed to bring my attention back to the present and enjoy where I was at the moment. Just in time, too, as I saw a scorpion on the path directly in front of me! We'd read that we should watch out for these creatures, along with rattlesnakes and black widow spiders. Apparently, they would *most likely* not hurt us as long as we gave them adequate space and time to move away. I sure hoped the pamphlet was right. I stopped dead in my tracks. It did, too. I slowly backed off to a what I hoped was a respectable distance, watching as this little creature decided the threat was gone and scurried off to a hiding place in the rocks beside the path. Best to keep my attention on the present, I thought to myself, and make sure I was looking down. A scorpion was one thing, but a rattlesnake was another matter.

After a few hours of hiking, we went back to the welcome shade of our campsite for lunch and talked about what each of us discovered on our morning hike. What amazed me was how different our perceptions were. How could three people go to the same place, see the same things, and come out with entirely different perspectives and stories to tell? Malcolm and I had some similarities, but our good friend, Crow, was on another planet, which was actually fairly typical for him. His nickname suited him so well, not only because of his untamable jet-black hair, black eyes and slim crooked nose, but because he was highly intelligent and forever curious.

"It's like I was wandering around on Mars." Crow was too excited to stay sitting as he began to describe his feelings. He jumped up and acted out what he was saying. "All my senses were on high alert. I didn't know what surprises or dangers were lurking nearby, whether I was being watched, or if something or *someone* was going to jump out at me from behind a rock. I was focused on every step and present in every moment. My nerve endings were tingling – more with anticipation, but there was fear there too. I don't think I've ever felt so alive. I'm still vibrating."

Amazing! While I'd been daydreaming, Crow had been on Mars! Two different people, two different experiences. Turns out, Malcolm was somewhere in between.

"I was paying attention for sure. I remember reading about rattlesnakes and scorpions and didn't fancy a surprise encounter with either," Malcolm cautioned. "But I was still in this reality – not like you two. And I definitely recall wishing I'd remembered to wear my hat. That sun was brutal on my bald head!" He winced as he rubbed his hand over his rather sunburnt head. "But in all seriousness, I felt a great sense of comfort being surrounded by these bizarre rocks. Maybe because I've always liked collecting rocks and have a connection to them? I'm not sure, but I do know that I was here on earth with my two feet on the ground. I felt very peaceful and contented amongst these strange surroundings. I felt like I'd come home somehow, like I was right where I needed to be. It was a really good feeling."

That was just our first hike. Maybe our senses were heightened because we were in a strange new environment, or perhaps we had a deep attraction to this very ancient landscape? We didn't know, but we found ourselves all quite eager to see what the tour would present to us.

The bus slowly took twenty tourists on a bumpy restricted road several miles into the badlands. Here the hoodoos were much larger and even more sculpted, likely because tourists weren't allowed to freely climb all over them. How extraordinary when you do a complete 360° and all you see are odd looking structures. It must have been such a sacred place for the indigenous prairie people. It certainly felt sacred to me.

Our guide took us to a rather large hoodoo that a horseback rider discovered many years ago: the head of a dinosaur stuck out one side, and its tail out the other side. You have to admit that's pretty cool. Now here we were, examining it – like visitors from another reality. It was so interesting to be looking back at the remains of an era of dinosaurs that roamed over lush tropical vegetation, on the very spot we were standing! It was hard to visualize, but here was the proof - a dinosaur frozen in time in a rock! Questions erupted in my mind. Was this going to happen to our time on this planet? Were people, or some new unknown creatures thousands of years in the future, going to be looking at our way of life frozen in time? And why did the dinosaurs die out and humans take over, anyway? I felt like the dinosaurs did a better job of taking care of the planet than we do. They certainly didn't pollute. They just wandered around, living their lives - eating and being eaten. We definitely have not shown ourselves to be good stewards of this planet so far. The dots are connected for us to cause our own extinction if we aren't careful. Questions, questions...I always had so many questions.

Back at camp after the tour, we grabbed a beer, sank into our camp chairs, and proceeded to discuss what we'd seen and how we felt about it. As before, it was different for each of us. And as before, Crow was far out on his own personal perch.

"It really opens your mind when you're in an environment like this. It brings up so many things to ponder. Like the past, present, and future. They're like three buddies that never leave each other's sides. The dinosaurs are in the past, we're in the present, and a big fat question mark is in the future. And what was before the dinosaurs? Who roamed the earth then? Maybe in the dinosaurs present, they came across bits and pieces of spacecraft, or fossilized bones of giants, or signs of an advanced human civilization! Who knows? Being dinosaurs, they would just step aside and continue looking for their next meal, which you'd think would make for a happy dinosaur future. They were ruled by their stomachs, not a constant quest for discovery like us humans. We're not just looking for our next meal. We have to figure things out. We want to *know* what happened. And when we do discover some actual proof, we're driven to piece everything together. But what about what comes after us? What about our future? Just look around you," Crow demanded as he teetered on the edge of his chair. "How do we use this dinosaur past to help us in our human present to create a better future for the world? We can't act in the past, and we can't act in the future - only the present. That's *all* we got! That's where the action is, that's where the power is – only the present! And that's right now!"

No doubt about it, Crow was on a roll. There was no stopping him. He got up and started to pace, and our eyes followed his every move. "We're sitting here on top of a bunch of old bones from creatures that don't exist anymore. That changes things for me. I don't want to join them and become extinct. I don't want the warring nations to annihilate us all with their bombs and their chemicals. I don't want to add to warming up this the earth. I don't want to spread pollution and plastic to every single part of the world. I know extinction could be out of our control, just like for the dinosaurs. After all, I've heard the earth does wobble on its axis, and meteorites and asteroids are flying around that could crash into us at any moment - and let's not forget the natural disasters like earthquakes and volcanoes that the earth can deliver. Now, if one of those things happens, well, so be it. But *I* don't want to contribute to causing my own extinction! That would be plain stupid!" Crow was visibly upset as he took a moment to breathe and calm himself. He looked directly at us, and straight into our souls as he said, "So - I say again. How can we use this past around us to do something in the present - *right now-* to make a better future for us – for everyone?"

Crow's look was begging an answer, but both Malcolm and I were still caught up in the enormity of what he'd just said. How does this guy take something as simple as a guided tour in dinosaur country and come up with the big questions affecting mankind? We'd always thought of him as a visionary - not that Malcolm and I had closed minds - on the contrary. We liked to question everything, too, and maybe try out new theories. Still, it was usually Crow that led us in directions we would never have thought to go ourselves.

"Well, maybe the fact that dinosaurs didn't know they had a past, present, and future is the reason they died out," Malcolm said, taking a crack at it. "Maybe the 'powers that be' thought they had enough kinks worked out with the earth's systems to try a life form that was able to comprehend a past, present, and future. Maybe, just maybe, it was decided by whoever or whatever it was that started this whole universe to begin with, that it was time for another experiment. Something along the lines of…ahh…*'Let's give them a brain that can analyze, and we'll throw in a good dose of creativity so that they can create things. Of course, they'll need to do this all on their own free will, or it would be like us doing it for them. Let's hope they go in the right direction and make themselves a paradise to live in. But I suppose if they don't and it gets too bad, we could always shut them down with another extinction and try again.'*" Malcolm looked up at Crow. "How's that for an answer?"

Crow was quite surprised, as was I. "Where did that come from?" Typically, Malcolm was the sensible one that preferred staying in the norm.

"I'm not sure, actually. I just opened my mouth and out it came. Truthfully, I'm a bit surprised at what I just said too. But it is interesting, you have to admit. Maybe it's this place. Look at that huge sky up there. It gives a mind room to soar."

“It does give you lots of room to feel comfortable, that’s for sure,” I said as I looked up. “I think I’m going to contemplate what you two have said while I put together a delicious camp supper for us to devour.” I liked cooking, and I really enjoyed cooking outdoors. I thought the two of them would continue on with their conversation while I started supper, but instead, they both leaned back in their chairs, sipped their beer, and went wherever it was their thoughts took them.

3

ENCOUNTERING AN ENERGY PORT

"Never doubt that a small group of thoughtful, committed citizens can change the world; indeed, it's the only thing that ever has."
Margaret Mead

When I cook, they clean – that's my rule. While Malcolm and Crow busied themselves cleaning up the considerable mess I'd made making our supper, I plunked myself down onto the chair, put my arms behind my head, and leaned back to look up into that big beautiful sky. I watched the clouds streaming by, and let my thoughts float along with them. Where did we come from? Why were we here? What were we supposed to do with our lives? Was this life all there was, or was there more after death? All questions I'd asked myself many times before but never finding any satisfying answers. After we'd bought our house in the city and got full-time jobs to pay all the bills, I never found much time to sit and ponder like this. There was always something to do or some commitment that had to be kept – someplace we had to go – somebody we had to meet. But not out here. There was lots of time and space to let myself go. I felt a noticeable sense of freedom, and I have to say that I loved it. I'd have been happy to stay in my chair exploring my thoughts the whole evening, but we'd made plans to get a comfortable spot on the hoodoos to watch the sun melt into the earth this evening. So, when the dishes were done, we grabbed our cameras, and off we went.

Wow! I had no idea! The brilliant sun created very distinct shadows against the hoodoo formations. There was no end of excellent photo opportunities. Crow's long skinny legs, topped by his crazy hair sticking out at all angles, coupled with Malcolm's bald head and slim muscled body, plus my short frame and ponytail hair made for some incredibly distorted shadows that we managed to paste onto the rounded rocks, and then photograph. We could have easily been taken for aliens from another planet. I had plans for one, or maybe even several, of those photos to go up on our fridge when we got home. When we tired of that game, we gave ourselves glowing halos with the sun directly behind us, making us look like angels this time. We were even able to squish the sun between our fingers, or pretend to jump up above it. We had a lot of fun with it, but after a while, we just wanted to quietly sit and watch the final disappearance of that gorgeous golden globe.

We stayed on that spot for quite a while, talking about life in general and our place in it, and the persistent theme of not feeling fulfilled in our present situation in the city. We all felt we had more potential but didn't know what it was or how to get at it.

"I think I feel more stuck than trapped," I said. "It's like I'm coasting in neutral, and I want to step on the gas but I've got nowhere to go. You know what I mean?"

"Yeah, I get you," Malcolm acknowledged. "I got to say, though, that I feel both stuck and trapped. I guess because it's my high paying job that pays a majority of our bills. There's a responsibility there for me, but let me tell ya' – my work no longer excites me in any way, shape, or form. And that's the sad truth!"

"I hear you guys," Crow added. "I didn't consciously feel this way before we came here, but now that I've seen the openness and freedom of this place, I'm feeling completely trapped by my old life. Go figure, hey."

But in all seriousness, how accessible was this freedom? We were on holidays, after all. We couldn't stay here day after day for the rest of our lives. Obviously, the novelty was going to wear off, and we all knew better than to make rash decisions. We did come to one conclusion, however, and that was to do *something* different with our lives. What that was, we weren't sure, but we knew we had to make some changes somewhere, somehow, when we got back to the city.

By the time we headed back to camp, it was starting to get dark, so we made sure to keep an eye out for the creatures that scurry around at night. Malcolm led the way, with Crow in the middle. And as usual, I was a bit of a dawdler and lagged behind.

A slight motion caught the corner of my eye. When I glanced over to see what'd moved, I was stunned - it looked like the earth was splitting open! Yes, a crack was definitely forming and moving at an astonishing speed - straight for me! With no time to think, I quickly jumped back as it furiously sped past me, heading to who knows where. My heart was pounding. It all happened so fast! My first thought was that ground doesn't normally split open like this. Was I hallucinating, or was this really happening? Maybe it's an earthquake! Oh, no! I finally found my voice and yelled to Malcolm and Crow. They turned and quickly ran back, but stopped dead in their tracks when they saw the threatening crack that now separated us.

"What the...!" Crow started to say but never finished as the crack began to glow.

"Look at these lights shooting up from this crack!" I gasped from my side. Mixed streaks of gold, green, and blue light beams were darting up out of the crack. Within seconds they seemed to spread all the way along the split for as far as we could see. We watched, mesmerized, as they quickly grew stronger and higher, like mini northern lights rocketing out of the earth. Not only were these lights getting taller, but the crack was getting considerably wider too, which really scared me. I didn't know what this crack was the start of, but I *did* know that I wanted to be on the same side as Malcolm and Crow, and to get the heck out of there. Feeling there was no more time to waste, I decided to jump over. The last thing I remember hearing was Malcolm and Crow yelling, "DON'T JUMP!" But it was too late.

Something took hold of me and lifted me up higher and higher. When I finally stopped, I was suspended in mid-air. Then some sort of golden energy started to swirl all around me and even flowed through me. I became dizzy and rather disoriented.

Then suddenly I was propelled upwards again, but very quickly this time, till I came to a complete stop. I slowly looked around. I had no idea where I was or what was going on. I was surrounded by a beautiful intense blue color, but as far as I could tell, I was alone. I looked down at myself. My body was there – hands, feet, clothing. I seemed to be intact, but I felt extremely light, like there was no weight to me at all. I tried walking, and that seemed to work okay, although I wasn't walking on anything but blue air, which was a rather odd sensation, to say the least. What on earth is going on here, and where on earth am I, I wondered, although I was quite sure I wasn't on earth at all.

"You're visiting us for a while," a voice behind me said.

I whipped around and saw *something* standing there - about ten feet away - looking directly at me! It had the shape of a person, but seemed to be transparent, and it kind of glowed. I thought for sure I must be hallucinating. How else could I explain this? But, I couldn't tear my eyes away from it. The more I stared at this shape, the clearer its features became. It was indeed a person, but here's the weirdest part – it looked a bit like me, but much taller and definitely masculine! Where'd he come from, I asked myself? What was going on? Should I be trying to run away? Would he chase me if I did?

"You're actually not hallucinating at all," he calmly explained. "You've entered our vibrational reality. I heard your entrance, and thought I'd come to greet you."

I can't say I was scared, because surprisingly I wasn't, but I did feel unsure and somewhat threatened, which brought out my defiant side.

"How did you know what I was thinking?" I demanded. "And what do you mean, 'you heard my entrance'?"

This being graciously smiled as he spoke. "To answer your first question, I know what everyone is thinking. None of us here need to speak, although we can if we want to. We communicate with thoughts or images, not words, but I'll use words for you as I realize you do not know how to use your telepathic attributes yet.

"And for your second question, I can feel even the slightest change in our vibrational reality. Your entrance created quite the change, and I felt that. This is a rather delightful place," he said, glancing around. "It's peaceful and of good intent. No harm will come to you here, so you needn't feel threatened."

"Okay." I decided to play along with this dream I was having. And this being did indeed have a peaceful manner about him, so I started to relax a bit. "Can you tell me how I got here? And why I'm here?"

"Why, you encountered an earthly energy port. These show up from time to time at various coordinates on your earth. When you jumped over this particular one, you were caught up in its electromagnetic energy waves, and they propelled you here. Although, you did have to be suspended for a while so that your density and frequency could be altered slightly. Humans are generally too dense to enter our reality. That is *how* you got here. As for *why* you are here, that is a question only you can answer. But I can tell you that only humans of a particular mindset, and with a frequency somewhat similar to yours can be affected by an energy port."

"What kind of 'mindset' are you talking about?" I asked suspiciously.

"An inquisitive and curious mind that is searching for answers. That's a necessary prerequisite. You and your friends have those qualities. You're all searching for answers. Not to worry, you are not our first visitor, nor will you be our last."

I *knew* this was happening to me, but at the same time I had a hard time *believing* it was happening, even if it was just a dream.

"You know about my friends?" I questioned.

"We know about everything. Nothing is ever hidden from us."

Holy! I'm not sure I liked the idea of that. "Who is this 'we' you keep talking about? Are there more of you?" I looked around for them, but saw nothing but blue air. I couldn't stop myself from being curious, and certainly hoped the saying 'curiosity killed the cat' wasn't going to come into play.

"Yes, there are many of us here. In that respect it is similar to your earthly dimension. As you begin to learn more, you'll come to understand the various dimensions of existence. We simply live in a different one than you do."

Begin to learn more! Does he mean I'm going to have to stay here now and learn in their classroom? But no, wait - he said I was only visiting, so there must be a way to go back home. I was about to ask when I realized that he already knew what I was thinking, which I was beginning to see was quite a handy thing - certainly much quicker, and definitely more precise than words.

He was smiling such a kind and reassuring smile. For the first time I noticed that he was now clearly wearing some sort of glowing robe. It was a soft blue-green color and seemed to sparkle – like when the sun shimmers all over the water of a lake on a sunny day. "You would not want to stay here with us at this point. You're living a physical life - a rather significant life, in fact. However, you can certainly visit any time you want. It's the wanting that will bring you here. We can offer you great help with your earthly existence. As for going *home* as you put it - all you need to do is ask, and you will be back."

That seemed awfully easy. "Well, if I can come back, can my friends come with me?" I asked, as I wanted them to be part of this.

"If you're talking about the two you are camping with, the answer is yes, they can. We would welcome it. They only need a strong desire and a mind that is open to possibilities, and they both have that."

I was beginning to see that he did indeed know a lot about us. I wanted to go back to Malcolm and Crow and tell them all about this experience, but I also wanted to ask more questions. By now, I was feeling safe and comfortable with this being. He was fascinating. I wasn't ready to end my visit yet.

"How do I come back with my friends? Do we need to find another energy port? What do we do about our frequency?" I was trying to sound intelligent, but the truth is I had no idea what he meant by frequency.

I could see he was trying to suppress a little smile. And then I realized that he knew exactly what I *knew* and didn't *know*. He shook his head. "An energy port will not be needed. You can come here by desire alone. Do not worry about your frequencies. They will self-adjust with the depth of your desire."

"Then why the energy ports in the first place?"

"Hmmm...the answer might be more than you can absorb right now, but I'll try to explain. You see, energy ports exist in many different areas of your earth, and in various forms. In fact, more and more are opening up all the time. We are concerned that the human species could be heading for trouble, so we work with people to help them discover their consciousness, and their abilities so that they can hopefully create a better future for themselves, and all of mankind. There are many different futures available after all. Our purpose is to help."

That definitely was more than I bargained for. It all sounded tremendously serious. I'd often felt that our civilization was going down the wrong path, but I had no idea 'beings' in another dimension were watching and trying to help! And I was talking to one of them! I was excited, but also a bit bewildered, and somewhat disoriented suddenly.

"Your disorientation is signaling that it is time for you to return. You'll be able to remember this, but your memory could be somewhat distorted upon entering your physical plane again. This is a skill you will be able to improve on with time. Now close your eyes, be calm, look inside, and imagine yourself returning to your time and place on earth. Do not worry. We will meet again."

"Wait! I don't know your name. I assume you use names here?"

"My name is Omar, and it is indeed a pleasure to meet you, Julie." I swear I saw him wink. "Now, off you go."

I nodded and did as Omar instructed, but felt only emptiness inside. Doubt, and a bit of fear, crept into my mind. But then in the next instant, I felt a whoosh inside me. Very slowly, I opened my eyes, truly hoping I was going to see Malcolm and Crow, and not Omar.

"Julie!" Malcolm yelled. "Look at me. Can you see me?"

Why would he be asking if I could see him? Of course I could see him - his face was only a few inches away from mine. "Yes, yes, I can see you," I said as I tried to sit up. I still felt disoriented.

"Thank God, you're back," Malcolm cried out as he hugged me tightly. "That beam of light must have knocked you right out when you jumped. Your body landed here in a lifeless heap, and we've been trying everything to get you to open your eyes and talk to us again. You had us so worried!"

The look of relief and joy was undeniable on both of their faces as they helped me up. It was such a good feeling to be loved and to feel safe with my feet back on solid ground again. The three of us stood there in the dark, hugging each other with tears flowing freely for what seemed a long time. Each one of us had experienced, in our own way, a powerful emotional event.

In the soft glow of the moonlight, we carefully found our way back to the campsite. This time they made me walk in the middle, just in case. There was so much I needed to tell them. They had no clue what'd happened to me. I planned to explain everything, but I wanted to be inside our tent when I did, as I did not want to take the risk of rising up into thin air again while telling my story. When we got back to our campsite, we found our flashlight and set that up in the middle of our big tent. Then we got comfortable on top of the sleeping bags.

"Let's go back to the beginning of this whole thing," Malcolm said, looking at me. "We're not sure what that crack was, or that colorful light, but it had enough force to knock you right out! What do you remember?"

Omar said my memory might be distorted, so I made an effort to recall the details as best I could. "I might have appeared knocked out to you, but I was very much awake. In the middle of my jump, I felt something grab hold of me and lift me higher and higher until I stopped in mid-air. I could feel some sort of energy flowing into me from this swirling circle that was around me, until I felt dizzy." I hesitated. "Look guys, this is weird stuff. It seemed okay while it was happening, but now when I'm telling you I have to wonder if my mind was playing tricks on me. It's just so out there."

"I think you need to get it out, Julie. And we need to hear it," Malcolm instructed. "Just go for it, and then let's see what we can make of it in the end."

"Okay," I sighed. "That's only the beginning. I hope you can hold on to your disbelief and judgements till the end. I *know* it happened. I was there. It was very real, but I'm beginning to wonder if it wasn't just a dream or some type of unexplainable hallucination."

"Dreams don't knock you out like that, so it couldn't have been a dream. You have our complete attention and interest. Plus, we know you too well to judge you unfairly," Crow said. "You can feel safe with us."

"Thanks, you two. I think I needed to hear that." Self-doubt had indeed been creeping in. I truly did not want to be branded as a crazy lady, especially by these two. "Okay. Here goes. After getting energized I was propelled upwards again, until I came to a complete stop. There's no other way to describe that place except by saying that it was a beautiful blue color, everywhere I looked. It wasn't actually a place, though – it was just this stunning color. I appeared to be alone. I was in one piece, but I felt very light. I was able to walk, but found I was walking on nothing but blue air! I started wondering where I was, and then I heard a voice behind me, so I quickly turned and found myself a few feet away from a transparent, and somewhat radiant being, looking straight at me."

"No way!" Crow gasped. "That must have scared the dickens out of you!"

"It was definitely a shock. But for some strange reason, I wasn't scared. However, I did feel a bit threatened until he started talking. His smile and his manner were very calming, and he assured me that I was in a peaceful place, and that no harm would come to me. That made me feel better." I smiled as I remembered the feeling.

"Go on, Julie," Malcolm urged. "This is absolutely fascinating!"

"Well, then I asked how he was able to answer my questions before I even asked them. He told me they know everything there, and that in their reality they don't use words, but instead communicate telepathically with images or thoughts. I have to say, it made things so much easier and quicker. And that's not all," I was getting excited now. "He said that I might be able to develop this ability too!" I really liked that idea. "Can you imagine if we could read each other's minds? You wouldn't be able to smile on the outside and hate on the inside – you'd be found out right away. We'd all have to learn to be careful what we think! And even acknowledge what it is we think!" I was starting to get sidetracked, just realizing the implications of some of the things I'd learned.

"Let's talk about that later," Malcolm said. "I want to hear the whole story first."

"Right," I continued on. "I asked how I got there and he explained that the crack I jumped over was actually something called an energy port! Apparently, there're lots of them on earth! When I asked why I was there, he said only I could answer that question. But listen to this – he said that only humans with a similar frequency to theirs can be affected by these energy ports! Plus, you need a mindset that is searching for answers. That's us! He knew about you guys too, and he said you had the right kind of minds as well. I wanted to know if we could all come back, and he said we could without even using an energy port – just by desire alone!"

"No way! I'm in!" Crow exclaimed with his eyes shining like

black beads in the glow of the flashlight. "I want to see what this place is like and meet this guy. Does he have a name?"

"Wait a minute, wait a minute," Malcolm interjected, holding up his hands. "Let's think about this a bit more before we go traipsing willy-nilly off to another dimension. I know Julie came back and seems unharmed, but there's a lot more I want to know before I'm on board with this. Plus, the doubting part of my brain is wondering if maybe Julie unknowingly ate something that would cause hallucinations, or maybe she touched one of the plants around here and it got into her system somehow and created this experience? I don't know, but I think we need to look at this from a skeptical point of view too."

"You're probably right, Malcolm," I agreed, nodding my head. "I know it happened, but we should probably take a step back and look at it from all angles as to *why* it happened. Afterall, it is quite mind-blowing, so you gotta wonder. Let me finish my story first, and then we can pick it apart and make a more rational decision about returning or not."

"Okay, you guys," Crow sighed. "But I still think it's real and that we should try to go there. Anyways, keep going, Julie."

"You asked about his name. It's Omar, which is a name I happen to really like. I knew an Omar once and always thought that was such a cool name to have. Anyhow, I asked Omar why energy ports were needed to begin with. He told me there are many possible futures available for our world – some definitely happier than others. The energy ports help bring important knowledge to our species to help us develop our abilities so that we can make conscious choices about going in the best direction." I paused to think about the words that had just come out of my mouth. "That does make it sound more like a hallucination, doesn't it? Maybe you're right, Malcolm."

"It's definitely my first reaction," Malcolm confessed.

"I got an idea," Crow interjected. "You're going to like it too, Malcolm, because it's sort of safe and scientific." Crow hesitated - his wheels were spinning – you could see it in his eyes!

"Well, don't keep us in suspense. What is it?"

"If we threw caution to the wind and tried to go back," Crow began, looking at us intently, "we would know if it was real or not. If it was a hallucination that Julie had, for whatever reason, then we will have no luck getting to that dimension because it only exists in Julie's mind. If, on the other hand, we are successful, then we will have opened a really big can of worms. And, if you remember, we did say that we all felt like *something* was going to happen on this trip. Maybe this is the something." Crow looked at Malcolm and I hopefully.

"Hmmm...I don't know," Malcolm started. "It might be the solution. Let's think about it tonight and see how we feel in the morning."

"But think about this too," I quickly added. "If we do try to go back, any kind of doubt is going to be a problem. We'll have to suspend our idea of this being an experiment if we want to generate the kind of desire required for success. I suppose all we can do is do our best and see what happens." I didn't think I was going around the bend, but more proof one way or the other would help set my mind at ease, so I was all for Crow's idea.

"One more thing," Crow threw in. "Keep in mind that there is also the possibility of actually being successful. We do have to think of that outcome as well."

"That would be startling to say the least! But wait a minute. Here's something that's just struck me," Malcolm said. "From what you told us, Julie, you must have been in that other dimension for ten or twenty minutes, at least. But you were knocked out for less than five minutes, tops."

"That doesn't sound right. I was there at least ten minutes, and it took a while for me to get energized and propelled there. How could that be?"

Not surprisingly, Crow came up with what sounded like a plausible explanation. "I remember reading in some scientific magazine that time as we know it only exists on earth, and not in the rest of the universe. Like if you lived on Saturn, time would have to be different because it spins on its axis at a different rate than earth does. So, it couldn't run on a 24-hour clock. Maybe this other dimension doesn't have time, or has a different sort of time."

"That actually makes sense!" Malcolm was surprised. "If you think about it, time really is a strange thing. When we drove out here and came to the place where you have to set your clocks ahead an hour - well, what happened to that hour? Did it just disappear? So maybe it's not so weird after all. We can think of it as a *time extension* - extra bits that can get put in between the seconds and minutes we register on our clocks."

"How did you actually get back anyways?" Crow asked. "You never told us that part."

"Omar told me to simply close my eyes, relax, and imagine myself being back. It didn't seem to work at first, and I got a bit worried, but then I heard this whooshing sound inside me. When I opened my eyes, I was looking at your faces, right close to mine! And, I have to say, I've never been so happy to see the both of you."

"Us, too, Julie," Crow confessed. "We were frantic when you buckled at our feet. Nothing we did seemed to bring you back, and we tried everything we could think of. It was a bizarre experience for all of us."

"Hey, what happened to the crack and the light after I collapsed?" I asked.

"I don't know. I was so focused on you I didn't think to look. I have no idea what ended up happening to it," Malcolm explained. "What about you, Crow? Did you notice anything?"

"By the time you came to, it was gone from where we were. But I do remember seeing a glow heading off to the north."

"I guess we're never going to know," I said, looking at their faces, glowing so softly from the dim yellow light in our tent. How wonderful to have these two compassionate and intelligent people in my life, I thought. However, I was starting to feel very tired. "I think it's time to call it a night, guys. I'm suddenly feeling exhausted." With that said, we all went off to bed.

This bizarre, unexpected experience consumed our thoughts

that night. When you have an experience that is entirely out of the ordinary, upon which shelf in your mind do you place it? How do you fit it into your normal familiar everyday structure? How do you even begin to make sense from it? I wondered what, if anything, would come of it?

4

TO GO OR NOT TO GO

"All of science is based on information passing through our consciousness, but science doesn't have a clue what consciousness is."
Robert Lanza, M.D.

The three of us sat nestled in our camping chairs under the canopy of poplar trees the next morning, warming our hands on hot coffee mugs. We'd begun a discussion of yesterday's events. I'd played the whole scenario over and over again in my mind trying to fall asleep. There was definitely a part of me that questioned if it actually happened. However, there was an even bigger part of me that knew, without a doubt, that it had. It was quite the dilemma. Thank goodness I had Malcolm's positive, logical mind and Crow's inquisitive spirit for support. Not to mention the unwavering trust we all felt for each other.

"What you told us last night Julie has really got me thinking," Crow said. "If we discover that this other dimension actually exists, then you gotta wonder, where is it?"

"That crossed my mind too," Malcolm admitted. "Where are the structures that allow for the existence of another reality? They certainly haven't been discovered by our scientists yet, because if they had, we'd definitely all have heard about it by now. It'd be quite the discovery. But then I had to wonder if scientists were even looking in that direction, as it strikes me as being way out of their accepted field of research."

Just then, a gust of cool wind blew through the trees, sending a flurry of leaves and debris swirling down on us. I pulled the hood of my jacket over my head and drew the zipper up as far as it would go. We had to cover our mugs to keep bits of leaves from falling in.

"But hang on here Malcolm, just because we don't know about the existence of other realities doesn't mean they don't exist," Crow declared triumphantly. "Our civilization doesn't know about a lot of things, even though we might think we do. If you remember, there was a time when humans didn't even know there was such a thing as bacteria or viruses, but they existed, and managed to cause a lot of sickness and death, whether we knew about them or not," Crow said while trying to pick bits of fallen twigs out of his disheveled morning hair.

"That's a good point," Malcolm agreed. "But I think getting anyone, including me, to believe that we can just hop over to another dimension will be difficult. It will definitely require some kind of proof. Afterall, we do live in a civilization that has come to rely on facts with proof to back them up."

"Yeah, but I bet weird things happen to lots of people. They just don't talk about it because, in our society, you get branded as being a bit *strange* if you do have the guts to tell others. We might not burn people at the stake anymore, but we certainly do not take them seriously," Crow argued. I watched Crow as he vehemently defended anything *strange* or *weird,* and realized, as would anyone who saw him, that he'd probably be branded as being a bit strange himself – or maybe eccentric would be a better word to describe him.

Another gust of wind, and another downfall of twirling leaves. Where was our sunshine, I wondered? I'd been listening to Malcolm and Crow go back and forth. Somewhere in behind their conversation I heard a bunch of noisy magpies having their own discussion, and a part of my brain was curious what they might be talking about.

"You've been very quiet, Julie," Malcolm said. "What do you think?"

"Well - I have to say that I definitely felt uneasy telling even you two about my experience – my supportive husband and my trusted friend. It sounded so bizarre and impossible as it came out of my mouth. But here's the stickler - I *know* it happened. I don't believe I was dreaming or hallucinating. Plus, I highly doubt I was on some unknown drug induced trip either, and I know I'm not crazy. Which leads me to ask what the heck happened then? That's going to bug me for the rest of my life if I don't follow it through and find out more – one way or the other."

"Yeah, I see your point, Julie," Malcolm nodded slowly. "And I think you're probably right. I also have a lot of questions I want the answers to. Plus, it'd be next to impossible to try to forget about this experience, or pretend it didn't happen," Malcolm paused as he looked at Crow and I, who were looking right back at him. "Weird as it might be, are we okay with attempting to go back then?"

"Yes, yes, yes! Let's go!" Crow said with so much enthusiasm that he knocked his chair over as he jumped up. "Right on!" Malcolm and I both laughed. Crow's free spirit added so much excitement to our lives.

I think we all knew we had to at least try, but I certainly did not feel nearly as eager as Crow. What had me worried was *how* we were going to do it. I knew Omar said I could bring them back, but I wasn't sure if our doubt would hinder the desire that was apparently so necessary. Plus, did we have to wait till dark? Did we need to be meditating – something I'd never even done before? Maybe we were supposed to hold hands to keep us connected? I didn't know. Quite frankly, I hadn't been given much in the way of helpful instruction from Omar, and I was uneasy about jumping into the unknown, especially trying to take others with me.

"I have no idea how to make this happen," I confessed to them. "We're going to have to make some sort of plan as to how to proceed. Can you imagine the three of us sitting solemnly on top of a rock in the twilight, eyes closed, holding hands, and hoping to disappear? And then someone on the path below spotting us and reporting us to the park ranger as some crazy stoned campers out on the hoodoos. Then a rescue party would come, shining their flashlights on us – all concerned and wanting an explanation. That would be downright embarrassing!"

"We don't want that! Look, we're here for three more days. Why don't we mull it over today and see if we can figure out when to do it, and where. Maybe even how," Malcolm suggested. "You brought up a good point, Julie. We don't have a clue what'll happen, or if anything will happen, so we certainly don't need to draw attention to ourselves, or answer someone else's questions at this point in time."

"How about in your tent?" Crow suggested. "It's big enough, and we could sit on our sleeping bags so that we won't hurt ourselves falling off of something if we do collapse?"

"That's actually not a bad idea, Crow," Malcolm nodded in approval as he thought it over. "Since we have no idea what's going to happen, we can't even be sure we'll come back – that is if it works to begin with. But let's hope we do; otherwise someone is going to find three collapsed bodies in our tent! That would make for interesting headlines, don't you think?"

"Enough thinking!" I declared as I got up. "Let's go for a walk. I'm sure our minds will keep churning while we're walking."

By now the warm sun had chased away the clouds, and the gusts of wind seemed to have died down. It was a pleasant temperature so we took off hiking on the well-travelled public paths behind our campsite. We'd walked in this area before, but this time we were in for quite a surprise. We noticed it right away, but none of us could put our finger on it well enough to describe it, except for Crow, who was always willing to take a stab at everything and anything.

"Are you guys picking up on what's going on here too? I feel like my feet are connected to the earth, or like the earth is supporting me in some comforting way that it never has before - like I'm part of it somehow. And I'd swear it's sunnier, but I know the sun can't get sunnier. The rocks seem to be gently glowing too, or pulsating with energy – I don't know. Help me out here you guys? You feel it too, don't you?" Crow asked hopefully.

"I do feel it, Crow," I said. "But I couldn't figure out how to describe it. You did a pretty good job, though. To me, it feels like I've sunk into the surroundings – like I'm a part of everything around me. It's so cool!" We looked over at Malcolm and could see by the serene look on his face that he knew exactly what we were talking about.

"Well, if we're going off the deep-end, at least we're going together!" Malcolm declared.

We continued walking for the rest of the afternoon, just so we could soak in all the good feelings we were experiencing. We were in hoodoo wonderland, and did not want to leave!

When we finally arrived back at camp it was fairly late, and our stomachs were letting us know that it was time to eat. I started making supper, and the guys made the evening campfire while discussing how and when to attempt our dimension shift. I listened in.

"I don't see any reason to keep ourselves in suspense," Crow said. "We've agreed to try it, so why wait? Why not try it tonight after supper? We've established that your tent is the best place for it, so all we really need to do is figure out how."

"You're right," Malcolm agreed. "I'm finding it hard to put it out of my mind, so best to try it and get it over with. Then we can go on, one way or the other. Tonight, it is. Are you okay with that, Julie?" Malcolm called over.

I was making homemade hamburger patties. I put down the one I'd been shaping before answering. "I think tonight is perfect. I don't want to live with this indecision and uncertainty any longer than I have to. I feel like my integrity and my sanity are at stake. So, let's do it and see what happens," I said as I grabbed up another bit of hamburger meat for the next patty. "But, think about this – what if we are successful? What if we do meet up with Omar again? Then what? Do you guys have questions you want answered?" Who was I kidding? For Crow that was like asking a little kid if he wanted candy in a candy store.

"I've got so many questions running through my mind - you have no idea! I think I'm gonna write them down. Did anybody bring paper?" Crow asked excitedly.

"I don't think paper's going to travel with us, Crow," I explained. "But your mind is. If it's anything like when I was there, all you need to do is *think* your question and Omar will answer it for you. See how handy that is?"

"Okay, then. Let's talk about our questions and that way those thoughts will hopefully go with us. I'll start," Crow said. "I want to know *why* – why are we here, and why are they there, and why do we have such dense bodies? Why can't we read thoughts, and why can't everyone see other dimensions if they do exist? And then there's *what* and *how*. I could go on and on, but I guess I should narrow it down, huh?"

"Yes, Crow. You definitely need to narrow it down. You're even confusing me! Maybe have a couple on your mind," I suggested. I couldn't help wondering what I'd gotten myself into.

"Okay. So, my most important first question would have to be why are they there, while we are here? What's the purpose behind having two different realities existing at the same time? Why is it like that, and how does it work? That's what I'd like to understand. What about you. Malcolm?" Crow asked feeling quite satisfied with himself. He grabbed another beer, and leaned back in his camp chair. This was his kind of conversation.

"Let's see. I think it would have to be - what are we supposed to do with the information we get, if we manage to get some? Is it for our own personal benefit, or are we to share this with others even though we might become the butt of everyone else's jokes? It seems to me that if you get hold of *special* knowledge, what good does it do to keep it all to yourself? Isn't the definition of a good life one that gives back?"

The fire had died down to the perfect size for cooking burgers. I rearranged the hot embers, and then listened to the marvelous sizzle of the hamburgers as I placed them one by one on the hot grill. "I think you're right, Malcolm. We can't keep knowledge from another dimension to ourselves, unless we want to drive ourselves crazy. But on the other hand, we don't want to be labelled as the batty trio when we try telling other people about our experiences. It would be a fine line, I'd think." Those hamburgers were starting to smell really delicious as they cooked away. I heard someone's stomach growling – actually I think it was mine. "On the other hand," I added, "we don't even have any knowledge yet. We first need to get that, and I'm not sure our attempt to go back is even going to work." I got up to go and slice some pickles and tomatoes to go with the burgers.

"You're right. That's the first step. Nothing's going to happen if we can't manage that," Malcolm agreed. "But, in case we do manage it, what would you want to ask, Julie?"

I stopped slicing as I thought about Malcolm's question. I was comforted by the fact that Malcolm was with me in this venture. He'd always been my main source of support, and I loved him dearly for that. I smiled at him. "I would like to know how to read people's minds. That would be a skill worth having, don't you think? How interesting conversations with others would be. We'd know if they were saying what they were actually thinking, or if they had something to hide. Maybe we could get rid of the legal system as everyone would know if someone had actually committed the crime or not. Salesmen couldn't lead us on with promises they never planned to keep. Advertising would change too because no one could get our attention by stretching the truth and playing with our minds. Politicians might have a hard time of it, as they couldn't fool the unsuspecting public anymore by making promises they never planned to keep in the first place."

I came around to the campfire to flip the burgers. Man, they smelled good! "Think about it," I continued from my crouched position. "Our world would completely change: no lies to hide behind, no secrets, no cover-ups, no excuses, no bluffing. What a difference this one ability would make. Everything would become known to everyone. The game we all play would be over. We'd have to learn to relate to each other, and ourselves, in a totally different way – an honest way!" I was feeling more enthusiastic than worried now.

"That would be super cool," Crow beamed. "I wonder what my boss thinks of me? Or what my co-workers think? Do you think it would work if I tried this when I got back?"

"Who knows? It might be worth a try. But I think it would be more important to figure out what *you* think of others," Malcolm challenged Crow. "If everyone automatically knew what everyone was thinking, don't you feel like you'd want to make sure you knew what *you* truly thought, *before* they did? Just in case you wanted to change some of your thoughts?"

"I have to admit this is pretty interesting stuff, but I'm going to interrupt, as supper's ready," I announced. "Let's eat! Who knows – it could be our last meal!"

We all dug in and stuffed ourselves. Without a word of a lie, those were the best tasting burgers I'd ever eaten, and from the sublime look on Malcolm and Crow's faces while they chewed away, I'm pretty sure they'd agree! Good thing I made as many as I did! When we could eat no more, we sat there for a while, enjoying the satisfying feeling a full belly gives a person. I think we were stalling a bit too. However, time was ticking, so Malcolm and Crow eventually got up to clean the mess I'd left for them in the camp kitchen. There was no denying that our nervousness, and excitement grew as the witching hour approached.

5

THE VISITORS MATERIALIZE

"The physical senses allow you to perceive the three-dimensional world, and yet by their very nature they can inhibit the perception of other equally valid dimensions." **Seth & Jane Roberts**

Dishes were done – everything was spotless. We couldn't put it off any longer. It was time. We filed into our large tent. Malcolm hung the light from a hook.

"Are you guys okay with me zipping everything up tight? I know it sounds silly, but I feel like I need that sense of protection."

"Sure," they both said.

"Whatever makes you feel comfortable," Malcolm added. Then we settled down on top of the sleeping bags, getting as comfy as we could.

"I'm finding this a bit nerve-racking," Malcolm confessed, as he rubbed his bald head back and forth a couple of times – a habit he'd developed for whenever he was nervous or worried. "We're attempting something we know nothing about. There's a part of me that's screaming to forget about it and play it safe. But, I feel an even stronger compulsion pushing me forward." I looked at him, nodding, as I felt that way too. But then Malcolm added, "I have a confession to make to you guys. I know I'm thought of as the *safe practical one* of this group, but ever since you've told us what happened to you Julie, an obsession has been creeping into me. I've been trying to repress it, but it's getting the better of me. I *do* want this knowledge. I *do* want to find out more. My old ideas of living safely are being pushed aside by this growing desire to learn the greater truths about reality. I feel like I have two personalities, and that one of them is getting out of control!"

"Ahhh, that's why we're friends, Malcolm. I always knew there was a visionary inside you," Crow joked. "But seriously, try to relax with it if you can. We'll all go together, and have the biggest adventure of our lives." Crow gently patted Malcolm on the back.

Just then the campfire outside our tent made an explosive cracking noise. We all jumped! Talk about tension! "I think in our excitement, someone forgot to put the campfire out," Crow said, pointing to himself. "Wait here and I'll go douse it."

While we waited for Crow to return, Malcolm and I held each other's hand, and tried to give whatever reassurances we could muster. After a few minutes Crow was back. "It's all good. The fire is out. Now, let's see if we can start one in here."

I swallowed hard. Okay. No more delaying. I looked at Malcolm and Crow, cleared my throat, and said in my most solemn voice, thinking that would be an appropriate tone, "I once saw a movie where a bunch of people were trying to contact a dead person. Since I have no other reference point for something like this, I think we should start by doing what they were doing. Afterall, Omar has to have been dead at some point to be where he is, so it might give us our best start."

"Yeah, I guess he would have to be dead, wouldn't he? I never thought of that." Crow said. "What did these guys in the movie do?"

"Well, they sat in a circle, like we are, and held hands," I answered, trying to exude confidence. We took each other's hands. Now what, I asked myself? I wasn't about to start chanting like they did in the movie, but I did think about what Omar had said. "Let's see if we can create a great feeling of desire in our minds. But we have to remember to get rid of any doubt," I was careful to add.

"That would make for a good start, Julie. I think you're going to be good at this. Maybe we could also add imagination to our desire by mentally picturing ourselves being there," Malcolm said, but then he laughed. "And you know what's going to happen? We're going to be successful and find ourselves completely tongue-tied because it worked!"

"I could see that happening," I said. "But don't forget, we actually don't need to speak - just to think. And we all do that, no matter what state we're in. I think our biggest hurdle could be coming up with enough desire to change our frequency to what's needed."

"Well, we're never going to know unless we give it an honest try," Crow offered. "We don't really have anything to lose - nothing ventured, nothing gained." He turned to face me. "Are you ready to guide us to the other side, Julie?"

"Sure. Let's see how good we are at venturing." I tried to sound confident and adventurous, but I was trembling inside.

We tightened our grip on each other's hands. "Now, close your eyes and take a few deep breaths and clear your mind." I got that from my yoga class, but this was definitely no yoga class. We each did a deep breath in and a deep breath out, twice. I wasn't sure where to go from there. I knew I needed help, but there didn't seem to be anybody to help me. I continued on as best I could, silently praying for some sort of guidance, or sign, or anything.

"Let's bring into our minds a deep desire to meet Omar. A *tremendous* desire. Believe he is real. *Believe* we will be successful. Try to let a picture of him develop in your mind and think about how much you'd like to meet him." I wanted to pat myself on the back, as I thought that sounded pretty good. We waited a few minutes, but nothing happened. I quickly snuck a one-eyed peek and saw that we were still sitting there, eyes shut tight in wrinkled up faces. Darn! No pat on the back for me. What was I supposed to do now?

Then out of the blue, I heard a voice very clearly in my mind repeating *let go of the fear – just let go of the fear*. Where did that come from, I wondered? But I went with it as it seemed quite sure of itself.

"I think we'll try that again, but this time, we need to let go of the fear we have of actually being successful. Let's try to replace the fear with approval. Feel a sense of joy and happiness as we increase our desire for this meeting. Think of it as being a fun adventure. Let go of any thoughts of failure and focus *only* on success. Ready…begin," I said. I seriously was not sure where I was getting these instructions from. I heard them in my mind, but I knew it wasn't me who thought them.

We waited for what seemed a long time. In fact, I was ready to sneak a peek again when I heard, "It's good to see you again," spoken softly behind me.

My eyes shot open. I saw that Malcolm and Crow had theirs open as well, as big as saucers, which meant they'd heard Omar's voice too. Thank goodness! They were staring over my right shoulder, but I was staring behind them as two pulsating 'beings' I'd never seen before started to take shape. "Who are you?" I blurted out. "How'd you get in our tent?"

"Let me explain," Omar took charge of this rather unnerving situation as he quickly stepped around to where we could all see him. "Why don't you two come over here as well so that I can do the introductions," he motioned to the other beings. We were speechless - this was not at all what any of us imagined would happen.

"We decided to come to you, as it's much easier for us to travel to your density than for you to come to ours," Omar explained. "When you visited me, Julie, you asked if there were others like me, and I answered that there were many of us. I brought along two of my colleagues for you to meet. They were curious to meet the three of you. I hope it wasn't too much of a shock."

Malcolm and Crow were tongue-tied and continued to stare, mouths hanging open. Mentally they wanted this to happen, but in their heart of hearts, they didn't believe it was really possible. They were genuinely stunned.

"It's quite the surprise, I have to admit," I answered. "I had no idea you could come to us. I guess none of us thought of that. Quite honestly, there was a part of us that didn't think we'd be successful in meeting you at all."

"Yes, we've been watching. I don't want you to feel badly, but it gave us some amusement to watch your attempt. However, your desire was indeed very concentrated, and with a little bit of help, here we are."

"Was that you giving me those mental instructions, then?" I asked.

"Yes, it was. You just needed a little nudge in the right direction, which is more than understandable as you've never done this before. Now, let me do the introductions. Perhaps that will set everyone at ease," Omar said, looking straight at Malcolm and Crow.

"Malcolm and Crow, this is Bluedon and Griffin. And I am Omar, as you already know. I'm sure I can speak for all of us in saying that we are very happy indeed to meet you."

All three beings were taking on more and more visible features, although they still looked somewhat transparent.

"I can't believe what I'm seeing," I said, completely astounded. "I knew you looked similar to me, Omar, but Bluedon is starting to look like Malcolm, and Griffin looks like Crow – even the crazy hair! How do you do that? And why? Are you guys replicas of us?"

"No, not at all. We simply want you to feel comfortable with us, so we're taking on a look that will hopefully help you feel that way. We realize that beings appearing from another dimension create anything but feelings of comfort at first sight. But I believe you will all get more accustomed to us as time goes on."

I could see their cloaks forming now too. Omar's was once again that beautiful shimmering blue-green color, but Bluedon's cloak was a pristine white color that shimmered with soft yellow lights when he moved. Griffin's cloak was a rich glorious golden color –

like silky sunshine radiating everywhere. "Your cloaks!" I gasped. "They're magnificent!" Their beauty was hypnotic - I couldn't tear my eyes away.

"Oh, these," Omar said as he raised his arms in the air and slowly turned around. Light was shooting out of the material in all directions as he did so. "These cloaks are made of light energy, and that's the reason they're so spectacular."

"They truly are wondrous to behold!" I exclaimed. Malcolm and Crow were still staring and still speechless, but they'd managed to at least close their mouths.

"Perhaps your shock might lessen if you said a few words," Bluedon urged Malcolm. I noticed Griffin was watching Crow very closely.

"Ah...hello, Bluedon," Malcolm managed to say. "You're definitely right about being in shock, and I sure hope you're right about feeling more normal in time too. How about you, Crow?" Malcolm elbowed him without taking his eyes off Bluedon.

"Me too," Crow mumbled, still looking quite stunned. "I'm happy to meet you all, very happy," Crow slowly nodded, but not able to take his eyes off Griffin. This was definitely not Crow's normal exuberant self. What was going on in his brain, I wondered?

"It's so cozy with the six of us here in your comfortable tent," Griffin offered as he looked around. "I've visited your reality many times before, but it's been a very long time indeed since I went camping. Earth is truly an incredibly beautiful place! Could we sit down?"

Crow hesitated. He was trying to sort out how transparent people wearing light energy cloaks could actually sit. "Sure," Crow said slowly. "Make yourself comfortable." We all moved back a bit to make room for them in our circle.

They had no trouble sitting down at all. They simply sat down cross-legged, as though they had normal bodies, although I noticed they seemed to sit on top of the sleeping bags rather than sink in like we did. I was still amazed that they could visit earth! How do they do that, I wondered? And why would they even want to come here?

Omar spoke up. "I believe Julie has told you that we can read your thoughts, so words are not necessary for us. But since you do not currently possess this ability, we'll answer your questions, if you have any, by speaking. Julie's just been wondering how we manage to 'go on trips,' and I think Griffin might want to answer this one."

"I sure do," Griffin jumped right in. Not only did he look similar to Crow, but his personality seemed to have the same style of exuberance that Crow's normally had. "And from the looks on your faces, I can see that I have your full attention, as none of you have been able to take your eyes off of us since we got here! Makes me feel kind of important," he said with a pleased look on his face.

"Let's see – how do we travel? Well, we just *think* of where we want to go. It's a simple process, really. But then again, we don't have the mental restrictions your society has, plus, our body is much lighter as you've probably noticed. Travel 101 says understanding and belief are the first requirements for travelling in this manner, which is not a problem for us as it's an accepted fact in our reality. We simply *know* we can do it, and all of us do it, all of the time. We go in groups, or by ourselves. It's our choice, really. We think of where we want to go and voila – there we are. But, we also know that we are only going into other realities as observers, not participants. Does that answer your question, Julie?" he looked at me inquisitively.

"It answers one of them, but I have so many more," I said. No surprise there. "*Why* do you want to go? Isn't it nice in your own dimension?"

Bluedon joined the discussion now too, "Our reality is extraordinary! Collectively, we've made it that way. However, to know what you want, it helps to understand what your options are. Sometimes we accomplish this by going to look at other realities. Plus, we like to help others."

"And don't forget," Omar added, "that we've lived on earth several times before, and have fallen in love with many aspects of this truly remarkable place. Sometimes we want to come back for a visit - just to remember and enjoy."

That piqued Malcolm's curiosity and finally got him talking. "What do you mean you've lived on earth many times? Are you talking about reincarnation? Because that's what it sounds like to me, and I don't see how it's possible."

"Then you're one of the many who do not like the idea of reincarnation," Bluedon sighed. "And I can understand why. But let's see if I can shed some light on this matter. First, let me ask you, Malcolm, what does the word reincarnation mean to you?"

Malcolm had to think a bit. "Doesn't it mean that after we die we have to keep coming back for more and more lifetimes until we get it right? And karma means we have to pay for the debts we create in other lives, so we keep needing to return until all the debts are paid. Am I close?"

"Not bad. That does seem to be the most common belief we run into these days. But I want to ask you to consider looking at it from another perspective. Try thinking of it as a personality *wanting* to experience as many different aspects of life on earth as it can, so it uses several different lives to accomplish this. Does that make it sound more palatable to you? Bluedon asked.

"It certainly sounds like a more acceptable explanation. At least it doesn't rub me the wrong way. But if what you're saying is true, then where does karma fit in?"

"Karma doesn't fit in, at least not the way you think of it. Consider this: for every action there are many possible outcomes, or results. Your personality *wants* to know what they all are, from every angle. It *wants* to explore all sides of a situation. And the best way to know what something is all about is to experience it." Bluedon was about to continue when Malcolm quickly interrupted him.

"Wait a minute, here. Are you saying that if I do something nasty to someone else – let's say steal something from them – then I'll have to discover what it's like to have something stolen from me – just to know how it feels?" Malcolm asked incredulously.

"That's exactly what I'm saying, although it's not that you *have* to experience that side of it, but that your personality, at one level, will *want* to know what that feels like. But don't forget - it goes both ways. If you do something nice to someone else, you'll want to experience what it's like to have someone do something nice for you too."

"Well, I like that part, but I still don't get it. What's the purpose behind all of this?" Malcolm looked perplexed, but no more baffled than the rest of us.

"Good question," Bluedon replied. "If you never had to experience the consequences of your own actions, you'd never be able to refine what actions you want to take going forward – and the ones you want to leave behind. There would be no means for growth, or learning, or development of your 'self' otherwise. It's the mechanism used for becoming who you are."

"What if I choose not to believe in it? Then what? I mean, there're so many people that don't think this way."

"It's the way things work, whether you believe in it or not. Those who think it's hogwash are in for a big surprise when they leave this dimension," Bluedon pointed out. "Either way, you have to admit it's not a bad plan to follow – you know, just in case we're right. Be aware of what you do, and don't do, to others! That way, you can't go wrong."

Malcolm seemed to like the idea of that. "I'd never thought of it that way before, but I guarantee you I'm going to be thinking about it a lot now. If what you're saying is true, then I need to really start looking at my actions."

"I have a question," I interjected. "Why isn't this common knowledge in our society? Why do a lot of scientists steer away from the very idea of reincarnation like it's the plague! Why are they not trying to prove its existence?"

"That's three questions, Julie," Omar joked, smiling his brilliant smile at me. He got up to give his answer, and as he did so the lights from his robe shot off in all directions, creating quite the light show in our tent. "It's actually quite simple, really. People living on your earthly plane at this point in time trust their physical senses. What you see, touch, taste, hear, and smell is what you all believe in because that is what's *real* to you – right here – right now," he gestured to the things in our tent and sniffed the air. "And speaking of smell, I'm finding it quite stuffy in here. Could someone unzip some of these zippers and let in the beautiful fresh evening air? I guarantee you none of us will float away!"

I got up and opened the entrance to our tent and some of the window vents too, but all the while wondering if any of these guys could actually unzip the zippers themselves. I mean, they could obviously smell, and see us, so maybe they could unzip zippers too?

Omar took a big breath of the fresh air streaming into our tent. "Thank you Julie! That is so much better. And in answer to your mental question – no, we cannot unzip such a thing as a zipper, but then again, we don't need to as we're able to go right through your tent material!"

Hmmm, I hadn't thought of that.

"Now, let's get back to your question. You interpret the physical world around you according to what your physical senses tell you. Science trusts the senses to a significant degree as well. At this point in time in your society, science has become very prominent. Please understand that I'm not trying to put science down as it has a very important and necessary place in your society, but it does have one prerequisite that narrows its abilities, and that's proof. It's based on finding physical proof. Am I right?" Omar asked and waited until we all nodded. I found him to be a captivating speaker.

"So far, so good. Now, let me ask you another question. How would you *prove* the type of experience you're having right now; transparent beings, dressed in glowing light robes, from another dimension sitting in your tent discussing reincarnation?"

That was a bit of a shocker. How could you prove something like that, I wondered, but decided to at least try? "The only way we could prove it is if others could join us and see you, and listen to you the way we are," I speculated. "But I get the feeling that's not possible, otherwise we'd already be doing it."

"You're right. It's not possible, and here's the reason why: you need *belief* to see us in the first place, you need *curiosity,* you need an *open mind,* and you need *imagination*. We exist in relationship with your mind, not with your physical senses. Science would want to detect us on a measuring device, but you'd need much more advanced instrumentation than you currently have to pick up on our frequencies. At this point in time, we can't be scientifically proven. But we do exist, don't we? Or are the three of you going daft? How are you going to explain this experience to your friends? Or are you going to be brave enough to even try?"

"What a conundrum," I said to Malcolm and Crow. "How *are* we going to explain this? Or are we? I don't want to be labelled as a delusional group of misfits that have gone off the deep-end."

"You're right, Julie. It *is* going to be a problem." Malcolm chuckled, "I can just hear Cliff asking what kind of drugs we were on? It doesn't matter what we tell him - he's not going to ever believe us. I don't know how we're going to handle this. But I *do* know that I'm not crazy. I know I'm seeing the three of you, and I know we're having a terrific conversation that's got my head spinning. It has to be real. I could never have made any of this up on my own."

Suddenly, we could hear footsteps and soft chatter approach our tent. I could feel apprehension grip my chest. How were we going to explain these three glowing beings in our tent to whoever was approaching? Were we being too loud? Maybe this was the camp host coming to tell us to quiet it down? Talk about a sense of looming dread. We sat there in silence, minds scrambling for some sort of plausible explanation we could give, when we noticed that the chatter seemed to be diminishing. We listened intently, and sure enough, whoever it was passed us by. It must have been some campers going for an evening stroll. We remained silent for a few more minutes, just to make sure they were gone. Holy! That certainly brought Omar's question home to rest in a very intense way. What were we going to do?

"Is it okay to speak now?" Bluedon whispered mischievously.

"Yeah, go ahead," I sighed. "I don't think it's going to be possible to simply *forget* your visit to us, so we may as well continue on and hopefully we'll sort out how to handle it in the future." What had we gotten ourselves into, I thought to myself?

"Thank you! I have a little secret that might help put your concern at ease. There are other people, all over the world, that have also encountered energy ports, just as you did. They're learning this information too. So, you see, you're not alone. We hope that over time you'll find ways to communicate with them so that this knowledge can grow.

"I also want to explain that your current humanity was actually designed to focus on, and trust, their physical senses. There's nothing wrong with doing as you have been doing, or as your friend Cliff is doing. Your physical senses help to root and center you in this particular life that you're living. They help keep you grounded in one reality. In fact, they are the reason that you see your reality as it is. They keep you tuned to this channel. But, that doesn't mean there aren't other channels in existence. People have more abilities than they currently know. It's time to start searching other frontiers – inner frontiers, or other channels, if you prefer. You have a consciousness that needs discovering from a fresh perspective. You have a greater self that uses inner senses to reach you, and that needs to be acknowledged and explored. Things are indeed starting to change. Even some of your scientists are starting to look in this direction. As we said before, we're here to help in that regard. Reincarnation is just a start."

"Can you actually see my other lives then?" Malcolm tested, still feeling a bit skeptical.

"Yes, I can," Bluedon easily assured him. "Would you like me to tell you some of them?"

"Yeah, I would. I have a feeling that might help me in some way."

"Then we will honor your feeling," Bluedon answered. "I see numerous incarnations. In fact, you seem to be quite enamored with earth. You've been both male and female in various roles. Once you were a quiet, withdrawn monk, and in another life, a king -

actually, an unfriendly and incompetent tyrant. I see a lifetime in which you were a poor, bedraggled beggar, and in another as a revered woman with advanced knowledge in an undiscovered ancient time. In one life, you were burnt at the stake, which was unfortunate as it created a strong need for secrecy in your personality. These are but some of your lives. Several of your current characteristics are also found in these other lives because they're all a part of *you*, and your greater self.

"Now, if you were able to wrap your head around the fact that time doesn't actually exist - and that all of your lifetimes are happening at the same time, then you might be able to understand that *you* are in a constant state of becoming. There is much more to you than you previously knew. But I know that's asking a lot for you to accept at this point. Just know that this life is for experiencing and *learning* from your experiences."

"That's a lot to take in," Malcolm frowned, shaking his head. "It's going to take a bit to come to terms with what you just told me, but I have to admit it sort of *feels* right, especially the bit about the need for secrecy. I felt that one in my gut when you said it. In one part of my brain, it all makes sense, and in another, it sounds totally crazy."

"I hear you, Malcolm," Crow whispered. He'd been following the conversation intently, but without moving a muscle. "Do all of you know about our lives?" Crow quietly asked.

This time Griffin answered with an incredibly compassionate look on his face. "Yes Crow, we do. Remember, in our reality nothing is hidden."

Crow turned as white as Bluedon's robe at this statement. "What's going on, Crow?" I asked. He got fidgety and looked extremely uncomfortable - like he had something to hide. He couldn't even look at me.

"You don't need to worry," Griffin began in a comforting tone. "There's not a being in this tent, or even in this entire campground, that has not had poor judgment at some point in their lifetimes, including us. We do not judge. We simply observe and try to help. If you've done something you're not proud of, then examine it to learn its lesson, and *go on*. When you bury it, or try to hide it, it will resurface, as you have not dealt with it. Maybe this lifetime…maybe another lifetime. There truly is nowhere to hide anything, so it's best not to cover up your issues, but bring them to light and learn from them. Everyone must face themselves at some point. You're no different; you're no better and certainly no worse than any others. Does that help?"

"Oh, if you only knew." Crow let out a big sigh. You could see the tension in his neck and shoulders melt away. "But I guess you actually do know. It takes a bit of getting used to this idea that you know everything I think and do - and have done."

"We're all working on our development. It doesn't matter what reality you're in, or what stage you're at – it's all a work in progress," Griffin offered. "In our dimension, the fact that we create our own reality is accepted and understood by everyone - absolutely and completely. No exceptions. Whereas in your dimension, this is not understood, nor is it part of your accepted truths about life. I'm speaking of the type of truths the entire human race simply 'knows' and doesn't even question - like the sun coming up in the east and going down in the west. These truths, or unquestioned beliefs, do indeed affect the way the world works, and the way your personal reality works. If every person in your world undeniably believed that they were the ones that created their own reality, what do you think that would do?"

Crow shook his head, "Our world is definitely not like that, but if I close my eyes and try to envision that sort of environment, then it becomes quite obvious that the first thing to be tossed out the window has to be blame. How could you blame someone else for your situation if you were the one that created it?"

"Very true…" Griffin started.

"But wait a minute here," Crow broke in, acting like his old self for the first time that night. "I didn't ask to be born into a poor family, with parents that had no problem beating their frustrations out on me. So, I don't get it. If I create my own reality, explain how I created that," he demanded. "I was just a little kid!"

"It would appear that no child ever asks for the life they are destined to live, especially if it's an unhappy childhood. There are indeed horror stories that can be told by far too many. However, when you keep in mind the structure of life – the bigger picture - these issues take on a different meaning. First, there is no such thing as death. Your physical body will indeed *die* at some point, which is a necessary fact. But your consciousness cannot possibly die - ever! And I do mean *ever*. Look at us. We've lived on earth in physical bodies many times, but do we look dead to you? We're very much alive, and will *always* be. You know that voice inside you - the one that talks to you all the time? You'll take that with you when your physical body dies. You'll still be thinking and talking, even though you have no brain to think with, or mouth with which to speak. You'll also take all of your learned abilities, all of your experiences, all of your perceptions, and all the knowledge you've gathered in this lifetime. Your possessions will disappear, but your knowledge will remain, and keep in mind, I'm not talking only about intellectual knowledge but also about emotional knowledge. Were you able to develop compassion, understanding, empathy, gratitude, love, and courage? There is just so much one can learn in one lifetime in earth's reality."

We were so engrossed in what Griffin was explaining that we didn't hear an owl land on one of the poplar trees above our tent. When it let out it's eerie hooting call, we nearly jumped out of our skins!

Griffin laughed. "Relax, you guys. This is just a friendly discussion. We're not asking you to disintegrate and re-integrate with us!" However, that comment didn't help us relax at all. "Just kidding. But seriously, at least *try* to relax. There's no need to be so tense.

"Let's get back to the situation of a child born into a family that does not treat it well. Since you know that you will still live after you die, you'll be able to understand, and maybe even accept, what happens to you *before* you're born." Griffin stopped for a minute and took a good look at us. I got the feeling he wanted to make sure we were still with him after that last statement.

"You will all spend time *in between lives*, and while you're there you'll discover that there are many choices available to you for your next life. It's you who will make those choices, with a little bit of coaching from your greater self, of course. You might decide that you'd like to try your hand at an earthly existence as part of the human race again, but this time you want to understand, and experience with full effect, what it's like to overcome adversity so that you can discover your strengths. So how will you set this up for yourself? There are many ways to create this scenario on earth, as humans seem to really enjoy drama and have many stage props available to help with this type of script. After deliberation, you decide to pick parents who are not that well suited to parenting, and who will provide you with childhood problems that you'll then have the opportunity to overcome in your adulthood. And there are more choices yet - what culture do you want to be born into - what religion do you want to grow up with - do you want to be male or female and experience the issues that are attached to either gender? You can choose a wealthy, or a poor family, as both can support an unhealthy childhood. I could go on and on, but I think you can understand what I'm saying. It's you who chooses. You cannot blame your parents. You cannot blame your society or your religion. You cannot blame your financial situation because YOU chose it. You are the one creating this reality for yourself.

"Okay, I see where you're going with this," Crow said. "But if I chose it, then why don't I remember choosing it?"

"That's the crux of it, isn't it?" Griffin answered, glancing up at Omar. "We get asked that question over and over, don't we?"

"We certainly do," Omar nodded as he sat back down.

"You're not meant to remember the part where you did the choosing and setting up of this particular lifetime," Griffin continued. "That knowledge is moved to the depths of your consciousness. It's there, but not easily accessible during your physical life, fortunately for you. Think what would happen if it was. It'd be like heading out on a wilderness camping trip, knowing full well that if things went wrong you could always come home to your creature comforts. You wouldn't experience your 'trip' to the same depth as you would if you had no other choice but to undergo all the challenges you are bound to come across living in the wilderness. You're able to truly live *this* life because you know of no other. You need to have the complete experience to truly learn from it. Do you see what I'm saying?"

"Well, when you put it that way, it actually does make sense," Crow confessed, although he still looked perplexed. It was difficult to come to terms with. "But these are such new ideas for me. I feel like an hour glass that's just been flipped right over! Like I gotta look at my life from the beginning to now through a completely different set of lenses. What worries me is that in doing this, I might lose the glue that's held me together all these years. It hasn't been easy, as you know."

Griffin got up and went over behind Crow. He put his hand on the middle of Crow's back and gently whispered in his ear, "Nothing is ever lost, but there is much to be gained." Crow was trying to hold back tears, but failed miserably, which got me all misted up too. I saw a tear sliding down Malcolm's face. Malcolm put his hand on Crow's shoulder to try to give him some comfort too. This was powerful stuff: so much emotion all jumbled up inside.

I could understand what Griffin was saying, but it was something that never occurred to me before. It completely changed the rules I'd grown up with, and my perception of my current life. All this time, I was blaming other people and situations for what was going on in my life, whereas with this thinking, I had no one to blame but myself. Wow! But then I realized that if it was me who chose this, then I was the one with the power to change it too! I liked that realization. I could change my life – I could *create my own reality*, like they said – a reality that I wanted for myself – not what society expected – not what my family or friends expected – I was the one that could choose! I knew I was going to have to try this out to see if it worked. I just had to figure out what I wanted to create.

Omar interrupted our thoughts. "I believe we've given you all a lot to ponder tonight," he said, looking at us intently. "Too much at once would overwhelm you, but just know there is a great deal more to teach you, should you be interested in learning."

"I know I want to learn more. You can't leave us hanging now," I insisted.

"Same for me," Malcolm added.

Crow was still too shaken to say anything, but he did manage a nod.

"We're leaving to go back to the city in a few days. Will we be able to reach you there?" I asked.

Omar laughed. "You can contact us anywhere. We're all connected, so any strong emotion, desire, or need on your part will bring us to your dimension. I'm sure our next discussion will be just as interesting as this one."

Omar and Bluedon stood up and went to stand beside Griffin. The three of us watched in total disbelief as they slowly disintegrated before our eyes, leaving us with the strangest combination of feelings: curiosity, wonder, and an unexpected sense of peace. However, I also noticed in me a sense of dread, along with a wee bit of suspicion. Oh dear!

There were a few seconds of dead silence in our tent. Then Crow found his voice again. "Did that *really* happen?" he asked, still a little shaky.

"I know I saw it, and I know heard it," Malcolm conceded. "But it's difficult to believe it when they're not right here with us."

"Now you two know how I felt after meeting Omar. It's definitely different from anything we've ever experienced before, but I *know* it's genuine. In fact, it feels more real than the life we've been leading up till now, don't you think?"

"It actually does, Julie. That's a good point," Malcolm agreed. "It feels like they already told us so much - I can't imagine what else they have to say."

"Check your watch, Crow. What time is it?" I asked.

"That's weird," Crow answered. "It's only 9:00. It feels like it should be closer to midnight! Didn't we start this whole thing around eight?"

"It was a little after eight when we headed into the tent," I said. "They had to have been here more than an hour. Maybe it's the same as my encounter with Omar. I'm not sure what's up with time being expanded like that, but maybe that's one of the things they're going to explain to us in the future?"

"Maybe," Malcolm agreed. "Speaking of the future, they did give us a lot to think about, so personally, I don't think we need to contact them for a while. What do you guys think?"

It was agreed that, yes, we needed time – probably lots of it to examine this new *we create our own reality* idea and see if it could actually affect our lives. We decided to wait a while before attempting to contact our transparent friends again.

6

CROW'S CHILDHOOD

***"Suffering is not good for the soul, unless it teaches you how to stop suffering. That is its purpose."* Seth & Jane Roberts**

We create our own reality, they said. Huh! I was pondering just how that could possibly work. It was still very early in the morning and I was daydreaming in our tent instead of sleeping. Outside, the birds had a noisy symphony going, seeming to say *'get up, you lazy thing - daylight is here.'* Well, it might have been the beginnings of daylight, but it was most definitely not time to get up - unless, of course, you were a bird. Early morning has always been my favorite time to lie in bed and think; I seemed to do it often. I got my best ideas then, so it never bothered me that I was awake while Malcolm slept soundly beside me.

Just how do we create our own reality, I asked myself again? There seemed to be no 'ifs' or 'buts' in their statement. We were responsible for our lives. Period. We chose it. We created it. No one to blame but ourselves for any situation we were in. But what about all the people who were terribly sick? Or the people starving in poverty? Or all the violence in the world? Do we actually create the miserable situations we sometimes find ourselves in? I can't imagine anyone choosing to do that. It simply made no sense - I could find no logic in it. But maybe, just *maybe,* that was the problem, I suddenly thought. Didn't one of them say that we tend to depend on our logical brains, but that the way things work is not necessarily logical? You have to admit that stepping beyond the sensible and logical rules of our world would be like stepping into an unknown dimension...and that's exactly where our new trio of friends resided, I realized with a start - in a place that was definitely not logical or reasonable in any way, shape, or form that I could understand. When I made that connection, I could see that logic was going to have to be left behind if we were going to be able to grasp what they were trying to tell us! And who said logic was so all-important anyhow? Wasn't it Einstein that said, *"Imagination is more important than knowledge?"* That's not a very *logical* statement for such a brilliant thinker!

And then I got to thinking about when people thought the world was flat. It must have been so obvious to feel that way as anyone with a brain and a lick of sense could *logically* see that if it wasn't flat, you'd fall off! But it wasn't flat! Imagine how long it must have taken for the entire human race to buy into the new idea that the world was actually round. Interesting that it took actual scientific *proof* to eventually end the debate and make it an accepted belief. It would seem that physical proof is definitely hard to dispute, but I was fascinated by the realization that *proof* could actually overthrow *logic*. Maybe, just maybe, logic and reasoning aren't as important as we think they are. Maybe it's okay to step past logic and see what else there is. Maybe we can even step past proof too, as our new friends said it was also limiting. So, what have we got to lose? What are we so afraid of as a society?

"Julie, Malcolm...you guys still sleeping?" Crow whispered softly outside our tent.

That certainly jolted me out of my daydreaming. "I'm awake," I answered as quickly and as quietly as I could. Malcolm was gently snoring away and I didn't want to wake him. I silently crept out of my sleeping bag, grabbed my jacket, and joined Crow around a warm morning campfire. He even had the coffee ready! I must have been utterly lost in my thoughts not to have heard him moving about in our campsite making coffee and a fire!

"I couldn't sleep," Crow said, after I got myself settled in one of the chairs. "I can't get those guys off my mind. It's like they opened a trap door on the top of my head and blasted me right through it - and now there's no going back. I feel like I'm floating in thin air with nothing to hold on to. It's downright scary!"

I looked over at him, somewhat surprised, as normally Crow is not one to admit being scared. I could tell something was still bugging him. "Same for me, Crow," I offered after taking a sip of coffee. "Just before you asked if I was awake, I was deep in my thoughts, trying to piece it all together to make some *logical* sense from what they told us, but then I realized that it actually has nothing to do with logic, and maybe that's why it's so difficult for us to grasp. Plus, I know they said we were designed to use our physical senses so that we could stay grounded in this world - and that's all well and good – but what we experienced last night went way beyond those senses. Obviously, there's more to everything than we previously thought. Maybe that's why you feel like you do."

"I think you're right. We were definitely experiencing a new type of sensation and learning new concepts that have nothing to do with logic, or proof for that matter. It was a lot to take in all at once, and I have a feeling they just showed us the tip of the iceberg," Crow said, but then stopped. He was looking out towards the horizon. The sun was starting to show its early morning face, which slowly lit up our campsite as it methodically crept up into the sky. The birds were still singing their early morning melodies. It was a quiet, peaceful setting on the outside, but I sensed a gloomy cloud surrounding Crow.

"I've been doing a lot of thinking about my childhood and what Griffin said about it - also my adolescent years, of which I am not proud of, and where I'm at now. As you know, my childhood was not stellar. There was a lot of emotional and physical abuse in my family - positive reinforcement was not part of my upbringing. But apparently, according to Griffin, I chose this situation! You know how that makes me feel? I've been blaming my parents for years, but suddenly, I'm not supposed to blame them anymore! It's like I got the rug I built my life on pulled out from under me. If I created my own reality, then *I* am to blame. And then I realized I can't even use the word *blame* anymore because it's been wiped right off the chalkboard with just that one statement - you create your own reality! There is no one to blame because it was a choice I made, apparently with a purpose in mind! I had to wonder then, why did I choose that? What did that kind of upbringing give to me?" Crow looked up at me, but I could tell he wasn't expecting an answer.

"And that's when it all came together," he continued. "Those *chosen* adversities created an opportunity for me to choose what I wanted to be like and what I wanted my life to look like. Had I grown up in a happy environment, I wouldn't have needed to even think about this. But when you're faced with crap, at some point you look at it and ask yourself if you want that crap to continue, or do you want to move on to something better? It wasn't really a conscious decision for me, and it certainly took a long time, as well as a lot more self-induced crap before I had enough, and thought I should head in a different direction."

"I knew you had a rough childhood, Crow, and I've often felt sorry for you in that regard. However, what you've managed to create from a rough beginning is impressive. But you have to admit that creating your own reality has to change the way we think about situations like yours too. I suppose I shouldn't feel sorry for you, now that we know you created it yourself, and for a reason. Still, I'm even more amazed at the good job you did of overcoming your adversities. It puts such a different spin on things, doesn't it?"

"Yeah, I certainly had a knack for creating difficulties for myself, especially after I ran away from home. What's a 14-year-old boy supposed to do when he runs away? How was I going get a place to stay and food to eat when I had no money and only a bitter taste in my mouth from the last beating?" Crow let out a big sigh as he slumped back in his chair. "Julie, I'm going to tell you something I've never told anyone else before. I feel like I need to come clean with this and share it with someone I trust so that I can finally pull it out from under the carpet. Those three knew it without me even saying a word, and I think you've always known there was more to my story than just my messed-up childhood. I don't mind if you share it with Malcolm either. You guys are the best friends I've ever had."

I reached over and put my hand lightly on Crow's knee. "Whatever you need to say, I'm listening. I knew something was on your mind, so best to get it out," I reassured him as I leaned forward in my chair ready to listen.

"Okay - here goes," Crow let out another sigh as he fixed a far-away gaze on a tree across the road. "When I ran away from home, I didn't just go down the block. I ran and ran and ran. Seemed like I never wanted to stop. But when I did, I found myself in a small town with a tight-knit community where everyone was wary of me. I was only 14! Can you imagine – just a mere 14 years old!" Crow shook his head. "Looking back on it, I can see why no one tried to help me. I was an angry, dirty, disheveled, skinny little kid with an attitude and a pimple problem. Pretty hard to warm your heart up to something like that. So, I stayed on the outskirts, rummaging through garbage cans behind stores and residential areas, sleeping wherever I could find a protected spot. I knew people were whispering about me behind my back, and that stung, but I certainly couldn't blame them. I didn't feel good about what I was doing either, but hunger was a powerful motivator.

"Then one day, I ran into a group of other guys who had the same indignant look I did. They were older, but they took me in and made me a part of their group. It felt *real* good to be part of a group and not alone anymore - until I found out what they did and how they got their money. But by that time, it was too late. I was in. And to get out would be dangerous. They started my training with simple auto theft and B&Es, moving me up in time to bank robberies, which according to them I was very good at. I never hurt anyone, but there were those in the group that did. When I finally came to my senses, I realized that I did not want to be part of this lifestyle anymore, but I had no idea how to get out. I knew all their secrets. They would never have trusted me to just leave. So, I bided my time trying to sort out what I was going to do. I didn't want to live my life like this. I wanted to be a better person and knew I was capable of it. I just didn't know how to leap from where I was to where I wanted to go.

"Then one night, I was in the middle of a bank robbery when everything went wrong. Alarm bells were going off, and I was running scared. I tripped on something I never even saw. I went down hard and hit my head on the polished granite floor. Knocked myself out cold. When I came to, I was lying on a bunk in a jail cell with two strange guys staring down at me."

"Holy!" I couldn't contain myself. "That must have really scared you!"

"It did, but being scared was a feeling I'd become quite accustomed to by then. My nose felt like it was broken, and man, did my head ever hurt. At first, I felt panicky – like I had to get out of there and get back to the gang. But then a little voice crept into my head, saying *'this is your chance - you better take it.'* And I realized this could change my life forever. I was guilty for sure. How could I even suggest I wasn't? They found me gripping a bag full of money lying stone cold on the bank floor. Pretty hard to argue against that fact. So, I laid back down and started to think. I knew I wanted out of that group – that was for sure. Anyways, when it came time for me to talk to a lawyer, I asked him if it would be possible to get sent to another prison – somewhere far, far away – and if I could get an identity change. Turns out, that wasn't a problem at all, as long as I told them who else was in the group and where they stayed. That created quite the predicament for me. I didn't want to tell, but I wanted out. It was one of those forks in the road that changes your life forever. After a great deal of soul searching, I told them what they wanted to know. In turn, they sent me to a detention center for minors way up north. It was so far out in the boonies, I didn't think anyone would ever find me. They gave me a new name. And along with a new attitude, a buzzcut, and my new crooked nose, which was never set properly after I broke it, I really didn't look anything at all like I used to. There was one terrific guard there that went above and beyond to help us kids. It was because of him I managed to get my grade 12 and a positive, rather than a negative outlook on life. He gave me hope and a sense of confidence in myself. He also found me a job when I got out, and I never, ever looked back. I liked the looks of the future so much more than the past." Crow looked over at me for the first time since he started his story. "Now, you know. And so far, you're the only one who does."

To say I was stunned is putting it mildly. I'd known Crow for over a decade now, and Malcolm had known him even longer than that. Never was there any indication of anything like this in his past. "Wow, Crow!" I managed to whisper, shaking my head. "I had no idea - no idea at all."

"Well, I am who I am, and I sure hope this doesn't change anything between us," Crow declared.

"It does, though," I blurted out "It does change things. I have even more admiration and respect for you now than I did before! Your story is incredible - and just look how well you've done with your life! It's nothing short of amazing! I'm feeling quite speechless. I wonder what Malcolm will say?"

"I'll tell you what I'll say," Malcolm poked his bald head out of the tent. "I love you, buddy – more than ever!"

"Man, that is so good to hear. You guys have been great friends, but you still wonder what others will think of you should they be told the ugly truth. Thanks for being there for me."

"We always will be too," Malcolm assured Crow as he scrambled out of the tent. "When I woke up and heard what you two were talking about, I wasn't sure if I was awake or dreaming. I had to pinch myself. Then I laid back and listened to your astonishing journey. Your story definitely takes the cake for the worst childhood memories of the three of us. But I know there are plenty of stories out there that are even worse than yours too."

"Isn't that the sad truth," I said.

"You guys got anymore hot coffee?" Malcolm asked as he dragged his chair over by ours and plunked himself down.

"Sure. I'll get you some," Crow offered as he jumped up to find Malcolm's cup.

"It's pretty nice to be waited on like this. Thanks buddy!" Malcolm teased. He waited for Crow to deliver his coffee, took that glorious first sip, and then proceeded to put his concept of the blame game into a nice neat nutshell. "You know Crow, some people cling to their childhood misfortunes for all they're worth. They brand themselves with their memories and then use them to play the victim for the rest of their life. But if what our new friends say is true, then you create and design your own reality – you chose this for a reason – so you can't blame anyone except yourself. The *poor me* character gets written right out of the script!

"I wonder how many people will be left floundering and looking for a place to hide when they realize this? It seems there's nowhere to hide because what you're trying to hide from is yourself. And wherever you go – there you are also - for eternity apparently! When you look in the mirror, the person looking back at you is your very own creation! You are the artist! You're painting your own personal portrait! I find that to be a very liberating concept, but also a daunting one as it instantly heaps a big serving of responsibility onto your plate, whether you want it or not. And I think that, in general, people do not readily warm up to the idea of accepting personal responsibility. I'm curious how you managed to overcome your childhood issues, Crow? How did you keep yourself from turning into a victim?"

"I'd like to know that too," I added, looking over at Crow.

"You know, I never really thought about it before. I guess if I look back, I'd have to say that I don't remember ever feeling like a victim. It just was what it was. As I got older, I began to realize that other kids' families were different than ours. There was a scary vibe in our house – I felt like I was always walking on eggshells - but at my friends' place, I could relax. It's not like my friends never got in trouble either, because they certainly did. But their punishment was never physical or cruel. It was given with the attitude of '*hey, you did something wrong...it won't be tolerated...here are the consequences,*' - that sort of thing. But then the whole family would go on and have good times together." Crow looked at us with a puzzled look, "I don't remember any good times together with my family, although I'd like to think there were some. I just became really good at ducking and trying to stay out of the way. I never really blamed anyone, and I actually don't remember feeling sorry for myself. I sometimes wished it was different, but I knew that was not gonna happen, so life went on. Then when I got older, I'd had enough. I wanted out, so I ran away."

Crow was so matter of fact about it. Did he still have intense emotions connected to his childhood days, I wondered? It seemed he'd come up with a good way of looking at it though. I got up to stretch after such an intense morning conversation. Just then a great analogy hit me, which I needed to share, so I sat back down. "There are so many things that can happen in childhood – some can be pretty bad too - but maybe we don't need to carry them on to adulthood. Maybe they're just meant to be used as a springboard to bigger and better things when we become an adult, and then let them go as we improve ourselves. Like climbing a ladder - once we step up to the next rung, we don't need to hang on to the previous one. It would be better to focus our attention on the rung we are currently hanging onto, and to the rung coming up, don't you think? Blame is pretty normal in our society, but if we all accepted that we created our childhood situation, then we'd also understand that we knew what we were setting ourselves up for. And I'd like to think that we chose it because we thought we could handle the challenge. After all, why would we want to set ourselves up for failure? You certainly passed with flying colors, Crow. You've climbed very high on your ladder, and should you want to, you could always look down at all the rungs you've dealt with in your past, and be pleased with your progress! I bet your ladder continues upwards for a long way."

"I like that analogy! I haven't spent much time looking down, but I can easily imagine climbing all the way into the clouds!" Crow's smile spread across his face as he envisioned this for a few moments. "However, there are lots of people who would have trouble thinking like this. If only they could change their perception about their personal situation, then they'd be able to see it differently - from a position of *personal power* instead of blame. And who doesn't like personal power? We are our own creators, after all. That's what they said, and I'm liking that concept more and more as it gives me a great sense of opportunities for possible achievements."

"You're right. It's such an important concept - it's got to be rule #1," Malcolm added. "I know it's going to change my life. I really like the idea of creating from this point on, and not letting the past interfere with my creation. Deal with it, and then move on. I guess it is true that you can be whatever you want to be. No limitations, except for the ones you put on yourself. I think we're about to start off in an exciting new direction."

"Sounds like it should be easy," Crow cautioned us. "But from my personal experience, I have to say that getting from point A to B swimming upstream takes a tremendous amount of determination, energy, and belief in yourself, and that's not even getting into the terrifying moments that get thrown at you. But with each other's support, I think we can do whatever we choose to do. A little outside help will always be appreciated though, and I think we just found three interesting friends to help us with that," Crow laughed. "In fact, I bet they could teach us how to float downstream instead of continually struggling to go upstream!"

"To change the subject - I'm hungry!" Malcolm declared. His stomach was growling. "Let's have breakfast and figure out what we're going to do on our last full day here. Tomorrow, it's back to reality."

"Jeepers, it seems like we've been gone for months, so much has happened," Crow said. "I wonder what reality back home will look like to us now."

7

THE HERO'S JOURNEY

"The cave you fear to enter holds the treasure you seek."
Joseph Campbell

We devoured a delicious breakfast banquet to celebrate our last full day of camping; all the leftovers were used, and washed down with lots of strong coffee. Afterwards, since we were in no particular hurry, we sat around in the shade and had a business meeting of sorts. We truly did not want to leave this gorgeous peaceful spot, but we found ourselves chomping at the bit to get back home and insert our new found concepts into our old lifestyle. However, we were quite aware that these ideas might look like gibberish when we got back to our old familiar way of living; kind of like the way a dream makes so much sense when you're in it, but when you get up the next morning it makes no sense at all, or even disappears from your memory. We were doing our best not to be naïve, but it was hard to maintain some sense of realism while trying to contain our increasing excitement.

Would we discover something we wanted to change? And if so,

how would we go about doing that? Would our lives actually take on a new direction, or were we going to forget all about this new information and continue plodding on as before? We drew a great deal of comfort from the fact that we were in this together. Before we came on this trip, we were certainly close, but now we had an even tighter bond after all we'd experienced together.

Then there was the problem of how to contact Omar, Bluedon, and Griffin in the city? And would we even find the time to try? Our city life had always seemed so hectic to me.

"Well, we're not going to get any answers sitting around talking about it all day," Crow stood up to stretch. "Let's get those dishes done and head off on a hike." Which is exactly what we did. And what a lovely hike it was. The trails led to areas that seemed so familiar to us by now. It was like saying good-bye to old friends - we didn't think we'd be back for a long time.

In the evening we perched ourselves on what had become our favorite sunset rock, just to relax and savor the moment. We felt a great sense of peace within ourselves and with everything around us. The sun was half an hour from setting, so we laid back on the warm rock, hands behind our heads, looking straight up at that stunning clear blue sky – a color so intense that I was sure it could swallow us whole.

"I can't believe how beautiful this is - it's so perfectly simple – and it doesn't even cost anything," Malcolm declared.

"Isn't that the truth," Crow agreed.

"Wouldn't it be neat if we could just lay here for days, with this serene environment all around us?" I added.

"Well, you know you could if you really wanted to."

"Nice try Malcolm, but you know very well that we have to go back to work. Holidays are nearly over," I answered back.

"I didn't say that…must have been Crow," Malcolm said, quite surprised.

"Wasn't me," Crow said, equally startled.

We quickly sat up and looked around. There were only the three of us on that rock. It was puzzling. We slowly laid back down again, waiting to see what would happen - but nothing did. After a bit, we let ourselves relax again, thinking we must have been hearing things.

"What I meant was that if you *really* want something, you *can* make it happen - and before you go all weird on me again, let me tell you that it's me, Griffin, just joining you for a wonderful evening sunset in this more than ideal earthly setting."

We sat up again to see where he was, but he wasn't there. We could hear him, but we couldn't see him, which was definitely an eerie feeling.

"Where are you?" Crow asked.

"I'm laying right beside you! But don't worry about seeing me - you won't be able to. I left my body back in my dimension," Griffin explained, as though it was no big deal at all.

"What do you mean, you left your *body* behind?" Crow questioned.

"Pretty much exactly what I said - I left my body behind and travelled with my consciousness. I forgot that this might be difficult for you to understand, and apparently accept, as you guys don't knowingly do a lot of that in your dimension. I guess I should have warned you somehow. I was checking in on you guys and saw what a nice place you'd taken yourself to, so I made the quick decision to stop in and join you. I love sunsets, especially spectacular ones like this. Sorry if I scared you," he added somewhat sheepishly.

I don't think any of us knew quite what to say. They came with their bodies before, and that made it somewhat believable. But now Griffin was talking to us without a body! It felt totally unnatural, and even a bit creepy.

"Griffin," I started to explain, "it might seem very ordinary to you to travel without your body, but we don't do that sort of thing here on earth. We have a body that we take with us wherever we go – so it's more than a little shocking to have you in our midst with only your voice, quite frankly."

"I do see your point, Julie, and I'm sorry I didn't somehow prepare you for this possibility before coming. But the fact is that you do indeed go places without your body – pretty much every day."

"No way," I countered.

"When you go to sleep at night, what do you think happens?" Griffin calmly asked.

"Ah…we sleep, our bodies get rested, our brains sort out some of our problems from the day, and we dream," I said. "At least that's my understanding. But to tell the truth, I've never really thought about it much before."

"I know this will sound sacrilegious to you, but your society hasn't figured out very much about how things actually work yet. The truth of the matter is that you do a lot of travelling when you're sleeping - and you leave your body behind, lying on the bed. It's normal - everyone does it, whether you know about it or not. The part of you that goes is your consciousness, and it truly does not want to take your heavy, dense body along with it. Even though it agreed to live in that body for this lifetime, it also remembers the freedom it had without it, before it came back for a physical life. In fact, if it couldn't get out to play at night, humans, as you understand them, wouldn't be able to exist."

"I've heard that before – I think I read it in an article somewhere. But, if that's true, then why don't we remember those nightly excursions when we wake up?" Malcolm asked.

"Oh, there's far too much for you to remember. Your brain, and especially your ego, are focused in your physical life. That's what they're designed to do. If all the stuff from *the other side* was to float into your memory, you'd get pretty confused and lose touch with your current reality. And remember, you created this reality for the learning experience, so you need to be focused here, in *this* life when you're awake, and not drifting off somewhere else."

"Then why are you showing us what else is out there?" Malcolm questioned as it didn't seem to make any sense. "If we're supposed to focus on this reality, then why are you telling us about all these other possibilities? Shouldn't we be staying anchored in the here and now, which, by the way, is becoming increasingly confusing the more you guys tell us?"

I suddenly got a mental picture of Griffin's face, sporting a rather pleased smile. "Well, yes and no. Let me tell you the reason why we've come into your lives. Simply put, we thought you seemed ready and willing to expand your minds and take on a bit more knowledge. Not everyone is, you know. Expansion and growth can't help but happen when you open your mind to how life *really* works - never mind what your scientists have been telling you. Changing your beliefs, your understandings, or your perceptions will change your life. And if we can open your three minds to new beliefs and new possibilities, then your lives will change, and so will the lives of those you touch, and on and on. It's the ripple effect in action. You're not the only ones, you know – we're helping many people. Your civilization needs this right now. It's ready for expansion: a change is in the works. I hope that explanation will do for the moment as I think we should just lay back and enjoy this gorgeous setting sun while it's here. We can talk later."

So that's what we did. Little did we know that as that golden ball sunk into the earth, it was taking our old life along with it: out with the old, in with the new. It was such a quiet, serene moment - only to be interrupted by the ring of some guy's cell phone, of all things! Talk about getting jolted back to reality.

"Griffin, are you still there?" Crow asked.

"Yes, I'm here. Wasn't that a stunning sunset? So much nicer than that guy's cell phone going off, don't you think?"

"Like night and day," Crow agreed. "So, can we ask you some questions before you go wherever it is that you go to?"

"Ask away, my friend. You have my undivided attention."

"What I'm wondering is, where is my consciousness in my body? Is it in my brain, or my heart, my gut, or where? Or does it even have a place?" Crow asked.

I shivered. The light was starting to fade, and without the sun to warm things up I started to feel chilly, but I didn't care, as I wanted to know the answer to Crow's question too. I was glad the other campers had already left to go back to their campsite, though. That way I didn't need to worry if anyone heard *someone* other than the three of us talking! That would be difficult to explain at this point.

"That's a really good question," Griffin said. "I'm impressed! The answer could get a bit complicated, though. I'm going to try to give you a bare-bones description, if I can. However, I doubt you'll believe what I'm about to say as it's quite different from what your current society believes. Here goes anyway. Do try to keep an open mind.

"The *self* that you are is actually composed of several parts. You know of your physical body, but your other *mysterious* parts cannot be seen. They are relatively unknown, let alone understood. They are, however, rather important, as your physical being exists because of them. But I'm getting ahead of myself.

"You see, your consciousness is like a director. It deals with your physical reality *and* is also connected to your inner reality. As we said earlier, before you were born, your *self* decided on what body you would take on, but we never explained how it does that. This is the part you'll most likely have trouble believing. In the inner world, there exists a realm of light that physically you cannot see, and sound that you cannot hear with your ears. It's this sound and light that forms the being that you are, with the help of your *whole self*. Together, they create electromagnetic patterns. You actually exist first as a sound and light *being* that is attempting to become physical. With a great deal of intense focus, you usually succeed.

"Now, what happens to your consciousness once your physical body is born? How does it connect to it? Where does it reside in your body? That was your question, I believe. Your larger identity, or your *whole* self, is indeed a considerable force. A single body could never hold your entire consciousness, but a portion of it does connect with your human brain - a little at first, and then more as the brain grows in its capabilities. Think of a baby and you can easily see how it becomes more *conscious* as it grows up. That part of your consciousness keeps track of your physical world and feeds information back to the rest of your consciousness, which is connected to the inner body of light, sound, and electromagnetic energy.

"There's also another portion of consciousness that stays with your physical body so that it can orchestrate the bodily processes you take so much for granted; like breathing, your heart pumping, muscles moving, and the myriad of chemical reactions required for all of your bodily functions. A portion of your consciousness is doing that for you – let's call it your *body consciousness* – and a thankless job it is, too! Look, I have to say right here and now, that I find it the absolute height of arrogance that your society could actually believe that these most magnificent and intricate physical processes are nothing but a lucky *accident* – a *fluke* of nature! C'mon…seriously? Let's get real, folks!" Griffin let out a big sigh. "Okay, I'm glad I got that off my chest. But seriously, in ancient times people revered the mysterious workings of their body. Some also understood the idea that sound and light, connected with conscious focus, could be put to tremendous use as a source of energy. It's my hope that this will become common knowledge once again. That's a lot of renewable energy going to waste." Then Griffin paused for a moment. "Hmm…I can see by the dumbfounded looks on your faces that I have likely said enough – maybe even too much. Have I at least answered your question, though?"

Malcolm's mouth hung open, and he was silently shaking his head. Then I realized my mouth was open too! Crow looked stunned. We were all trying to grasp what Griffin had just told us about inner lights and sounds - truthfully too crazy to comprehend at first hearing. How could this be? I am a physical body. I can feel me, I can see me. When I look in the mirror, I find me looking back at me. I don't see any of the things he was talking about. But then again, he did say they were parts that weren't visible, so of course I wasn't going to be able to see them. "But Griffin," I said, "why? *Why* is it like this?"

"That's a huge question and will require a really big answer spread out over a period of time. I think it might be more than you can handle right now. I'll give you a hint, though. Basically, you're here to experience and learn lessons for your own personal growth. Something you all seem to be doing, whether you're aware of it or not. You've got lots to contemplate with what I've already said. Why don't you think about it on your own and see what you come up with? Then we'll have another discussion - maybe all six of us."

"Yeah, okay. But to change the subject, we're leaving tomorrow – are you sure we can reach you once we're in the city?" Malcolm asked. This was definitely a fear we had.

"We're accessible wherever you are. We may come one at a time or all together, with or without our bodies. No need to worry about that. Just know we are with you. The only thing that could stop this would be a belief on your part that we don't exist. If you believed that, then we couldn't come, even if we wanted to. So as long as you're open-minded and believing, we will be a part of you."

"Wow…I had no idea beliefs were that powerful," I said.

"They are like the current in a river. As your beliefs go, there your life goes. We'll talk more about beliefs another time. I have perhaps overstayed myself. We'll talk again."

After that statement, I felt Griffin's essence disappear. The air seemed *thinner* somehow. We were left looking at each other - still in shock. Another shiver went through me. This was weird stuff, and getting weirder all the time. What had we gotten ourselves into? Was it real? Or was the life we led before real? They were definitely different. But I didn't feel like we had the option to only *half* believe - or believe only when it was convenient. We either had to jump entirely on the believing train, headed to who knows where, or turn back to our old life and forget what we'd experienced. Which way was I going to go? And what about Malcolm and Crow? How did they feel? I didn't want to go alone, but I knew I'd jump on that train by myself if it came to that. There was no way I was ever going to be able to go back to what I once was.

"Julie," Malcolm was the first to speak, "we need to discover what's going on here, don't you think?" He handed me the old brown sweater he'd brought along. "I can't deny that it scares me, because it certainly does. Plus, I'm pretty sure there's more to come, and none of it is going to make us look *intelligent* in the way society currently describes intelligence. No doubt we're going to be judged by others, whispered about, and branded with an unwelcome name or two - but I'm incredibly drawn to finding out more. It's like a magnetic pull that I can't control. No matter where it leads, I feel compelled to follow and explore. How about you?"

I pulled Malcolm's sweater over my head and instantly felt warm and cozy. "I feel exactly the same. I couldn't go back to my old life even if I wanted to. It seems like we've entered a portal into the unknown, which I find frightening, but I also get the feeling that it's precisely where we're supposed to be. It's terrifying to start down a path not knowing where it'll lead, but I simply can't turn back. I think I'm hooked. I don't know if that's a good thing or a bad thing, but I need to find out." I looked over at Crow. The evening breeze was gently blowing his wild black hair back and forth. I hoped he felt the same way. "What about you, Crow? Are we in this together?"

"I'm in a hundred and one percent! Let's head back to camp and see if we can bounce some of Griffin's new ideas around before going to sleep, although I have a feeling sleep will not come easily tonight."

Back at camp we built our last fire with a sense of reverence. When it was nicely crackling away, Malcolm surprised us by saying, "Would anyone like a nice glass of port for a night-cap?"

"No way!" Crow exclaimed. "You've got port! How'd you manage to keep that a secret?"

"It wasn't easy, but I thought it would be a welcome treat at the end of our trip, so I managed. I am capable of surprises, you know! But never in my wildest dreams did I imagine we'd be discussing beings from another dimension when we drank it. I thought it would go more like - great park, amazing dinosaur fossils, beautiful weather, incredible scenery - something a bit more mundane and harmless than going to different dimensions, travelling spirits, robes made out of light energy, and creating our own reality to boot!" Malcolm said as he poured each of us a substantial glass of port.

"A toast to the three of us!" Crow said, holding his glass high. As we clinked glasses and looked each other straight in the eye, it felt like we were sealing a pact between us. And when a night owl in the tree above gave a long h-o-o-t, we took it as nature's sign of approval.

"I'm so glad the three of us have had this experience together," I said, smiling. "I have a feeling we're really going to need each other for a strong support system. I can't imagine what people are going to say when we tell them about the adventures we've had here. At least the three of us know we're not going around the bend. I'm not sure how we're going to explain it to our friends, though."

"Have any of you guys ever heard of the *'Hero's Journey?'"* Malcolm asked.

Crow and I looked at each other quizzically – neither of us knew what Malcolm was talking about.

"It's when people find themselves on a path they never asked for, or even envisioned going on. Basically, they get thrown into an unknown, and sometimes unwelcome, situation from which there is no turning back. Sound familiar?"

"Very!" Crow acknowledged. "It's comforting to know that others have faced this sort of thing too. This is interesting - tell us more."

"It is comforting, isn't it?" Malcolm agreed. "Well, I heard about it in my English class in University. It was a man called Joseph Campbell that developed the idea. The only direction you can go is forward, with no way of knowing what forward will bring. There are usually battles to fight and hurdles to overcome, but these challenges force you to look deep inside yourself to discover strengths you never knew you had – nor would you ever have found them any other way. I feel like the three of us are about to set off on our own hero's journey as we have no idea where any of this will lead. What do you think?" Malcolm asked, looking at us rather seriously. "Are we ready for something like this?"

I did a quick soul search. It didn't take long. "I'm ready. Admittedly, I'm scared, but I'm also thrilled to the core, which is a feeling my old mundane life hasn't given me for a long time. I can't even begin to imagine where this is going to take us," I conceded.

Crow wasn't scared in the slightest – he was energized. "This hero's journey could be the best thing we've ever done with our lives," he said excitedly. "I have no doubt there's gonna be challenging times, but the fact that we can bounce ideas off each other should help with whatever comes up. So, what happens at the end of this journey - if there is an end - or does it just keep repeating?" he asked Malcolm.

"From what I remember, at the end of the cycle, you're to share with others what you've learned. It's not beneficial to keep knowledge to yourself," Malcolm explained. "You have to give back."

"And isn't that what Griffin was saying - by changing your own life, you help others change theirs too?" Crow questioned us. "This is exciting stuff!"

"It actually is, Crow," I agreed. "Don't you guys find it hard to believe that it was only a few short days ago that we decided to go on this trip. Maybe the discontent we felt with our lives back home was the very beginning of this journey. Afterall, it was the catalyst that brought us here."

"Yeah, I think you're right," Malcolm said.

I continued on, "You know, personally, I think my restlessness came from feeling that time was passing by so quickly, and I had nothing of value to show for it! I used to want a nice house with nice things, but when I got them, it all seemed so shallow and unimportant - more like a ball and chain. Something was definitely missing in my life, but I couldn't put my finger on it. I simply was not content with where I was," I tried to explain. "How about you, Crow? What made you want to go on this trip?"

"I've actually been pondering that very question for the last few days," Crow answered. "I told you about my past...you know, getting out of jail and working very hard to make a new life. Well, what did I do that for, I asked myself? It was obviously the right thing to do, no doubt about that, as I felt a tremendous sense of *rightness* while I was busy developing my new life. I had a strong sense of vitality; like I was riding a wave of potential. And it felt *so* good, *so* right, *so* worthwhile. I remembered that feeling of motivation in my gut Then all of a sudden it hit me - I don't have it anymore! Somewhere along the way, I lost it. I must have taken a wrong turn unknowingly, and ended up at what now feels like a dead end." Crow had been looking up at the stars while he spoke. He paused, took a large sip of port and then looked over at Malcolm and I. "I *want* that feeling back. More to the point, I *need* to get that feeling back. I'm beginning to believe that it's the force that drives life. At least it's the force that drives my life, and I plan on finding it again."

"Now, that was well said," Malcolm declared as he got up to shuffle the hot coals around and throw a few more logs on the fire. We weren't planning to go to bed any time soon as this type of discussion was helping us to discover our thoughts. "I think you're right too," Malcolm assured Crow. "It's the part about finding your potential that struck a chord in me the moment you said it. Recently I've been feeling like I've sold my soul, just to obtain the *look* our society says is correct. But is that *all* I'm capable of? Is that all the potential I have? It seems so shallow to me now." The logs suddenly caught fire and air pockets hissed as our campsite was freshly illuminated. I could see the anxious expression on Malcolm's face as he continued. "I *know* there's more, but what is it? That's the tricky part. When you have a high-powered job, a house to maintain, and all the lifestyle trappings we've managed to accumulate, how do you let all of that go and develop a mindset that moves you in the direction of discovering your potential? Does it mean I have to quit my job and sell the house to do this, or can I do it while still keeping the life I had? These are questions I have no answer to - but I want to ask those questions and find those answers. So I think you were spot on, Crow, when you talked about getting back on the path to discovering your potential. I didn't know it before, but I do now - that's what I want to do too, no matter where it takes me."

"Me, too, Malcolm," I nodded. "I think that's exactly why we both felt out of sorts. In my heart of hearts, I know there's more to life, and I want to go out there and get it. But just like you, I don't know how to do this, or what it is I'm even chasing. How do you start to pursue your own potential, when you don't have a clue what your potential is? Ever since I was a kid I was told to get a good job, find a nice husband, buy a nice house in a nice neighborhood, get some nice friends, and put enough money away for a happy and healthy retirement. That was the understood goal I grew up with. It was supposed to be the good life – but is it? Maybe as kids, we should have been taught to look inside to find out what it is *we* want to do, and to go out and try – mistakes and all. Learn to search for and develop your personal potential, right from the get-go. Wow, that would have been a different childhood, don't you think?"

"That would have been very different indeed. Instead of trying to figure it out now, we would've been looking for it all along. Who knows what our life would be like now if society thought differently back then?" Malcolm declared. "But maybe it doesn't matter when you start your journey, as long as you do it at some point in your life."

"Yeah," Crow added. "I believe that's the important bit. And while we're on this topic, does anyone have any bright ideas about where we go from here? What's our next step on this journey we've agreed to start on?"

"A refill is the first step," I said, holding my glass up for Malcolm to fill. I thought maybe a bit more port would assist in *loosening* my mind to help sort this out. We were primed and ready, but we just sat in silence and stared at the fire. In the background I heard the crickets singing their nightly symphony, and the odd coyote howling its lonely cry. It seemed the perfect setting for a fairy godmother to tap us on the head with her glowing wand, and give us a direction. But no major breakthrough came to any of us. I think it dawned on all of us about the same time that this was *our* journey, nobody else's, and we were the ones who would decide which direction it would go. That was such an enormous, empty, lonely feeling. Silently, we looked up at each other. In the softening glow of the campfire, I saw fear on their faces. And I knew it was on mine too. This was definitely no fairy tale.

"It would be a lot easier if someone just told us what to do - or if there was someone we could follow," Crow pointed out. "But trying to figure out how to begin when the possibilities are virtually endless, and the destination unknown, is a bit overwhelming."

I heard it in my head. "There are no wrong choices." I quietly repeated it out loud, and to my bewilderment and shock, Crow and Malcolm said the exact same thing!

We looked at each other in stunned surprise. "Did you guys hear that in your head too?" I asked.

"Yeah," they admitted.

"So maybe we won't be alone on this journey after all?" I said quietly. "I have a feeling Omar, Bluedon, and Griffin will indeed be with us. But I think it's going to be up to us to do the work. Maybe our first step is to learn how to communicate with them easily. The knowledge they have is coming from such a different vantage point than we're privy to, and I have no doubt we're going to need a lot of guidance from them."

We were all ever so grateful to have their support. Otherwise, it would be like standing at the edge of a cliff, all alone, knowing you had to jump in order to learn how to fly, but feeling so scared because you'd never flown before. That must be what a young eagle feels like when faced with this solitary moment. How does it come to believe it can fly the very first time it jumps out of the nest? It's never tried before. Does it merely trust that it can? Are we going to be able to do the same thing? Will we be able to nurture that same feeling of trust, understanding, and acceptance when it comes to letting go of our safe place and going for it? Would our transparent trio be there to catch us? We didn't know, but one thing I felt sure of was that we were going to jump - all three of us, holding hands. We would do it with vigor, mixed with a great deal of fear no doubt, but we were definitely going to take a flying leap!

And since there was no such thing as a wrong decision, then the first step was not the considerable dilemma we'd made it out to be in our minds. We chose instead to pick a goal and concentrate upon that…hoping that baby steps along the way would eventually get us there. Our goal was to discover everything we could about the new concepts Omar, Bluedon, and Griffin had introduced us to. How could we use them in our world? Then when we felt comfortable with what we were finding out, we would give back, like in the hero's journey, and let others know. We liked our goal. Not just in our brains, but in our entire body. It wrapped itself around us like a warm comforter on a cold night.

With a goal established and settled, we doused the campfire and took ourselves off to bed, thinking about how exciting our lives were to become. We would not live another ordinary day for the rest of our lives.

8

HIDDEN BELIEFS

"Rigid ideas can indeed act as leashes, so that you are forced to circle like a tied puppy dog about a very small radius." **Seth & Jane Roberts**

The next morning, we woke up feeling a sense of purpose, instead of bewilderment. So, it didn't take long after breakfast to take our camp apart and pack everything into the van. We knew we were going to miss this extraordinary place. It would always have a special place in our hearts. We hoped Omar, Bluedon, and Griffin were coming with us, as they'd told us. Once we actually made contact with them in our city life, we'd be able to lay that fear of abandonment to rest. For now, we had nothing to fret about, except the long drive ahead.

It's funny how everything looks different when you yourself are different. How does that happen? The scenery driving out to the dinosaur park had been beautiful indeed, but seeing it on our way back, I'd have to describe it as absolutely astonishing! The crops of every color danced back and forth in the fields, like they were synchronized swimmers. The drifting clouds effortlessly created majestic sculptures with every passing second, and the sun was like a center stage musician, pulling out all the stops in its featured solo. And when we saw the mountains again, we were taken aback by their regal personality: rock solid but somehow as comforting as a mother's gentle arm wrapped around us.

"What's going on here?" Crow asked. "Are you guys getting the feeling that we're in a different landscape than the one we saw coming out here?"

"I sure am," I said, feeling quite in awe. "It's like everything's alive. Take that tree up ahead - it's like it has a life of its own, just like we do, with thoughts, feelings, aspirations and everything! It's not just a big green tree. I can even feel it connecting with me, and I can feel it smile! Have we fallen down the rabbit hole - or are we going crazy?"

"Let's hope not. I can feel it too," Malcolm said. "Even though I'm concentrating on driving, I sense something very different going on around me. The highway itself seems to be carrying the van along effortlessly - like we're cruising a few feet above the road. I'm not sure what to make of it, but if all three of us are feeling it, then it's got to be real...right?"

"I think so. At least I hope so. Maybe when you allow yourself to be less rigid in your thinking, you see possibilities you were blinded to before. Sort of like looking through clear glasses now, instead of the dark ones we had on before. There's so much more to see!" I said, looking everywhere. "Funny thing is, though, it was always there before too. We were the ones that were blind! What else do you suppose we've been missing?"

"Well, I'm not putting dark glasses on ever again," Crow declared. "I like what I see. It's magical. I feel like I've got friends everywhere I look."

It was definitely a great feeling. I couldn't get over the fact that it'd always been there before, but *we* hadn't seen it. If changing our attitudes could do this, I had to wonder what else was in store for us as we uncovered other possibilities.

The drive was beautiful all the way through the countryside.

However, as we approached the suburbs, traffic and congestion started to pick up, and the magical connection we'd felt with nature diminished There was no sense of happiness or contentment from the traffic all around us. Weird - why not, we wondered?

"Nature is nature," Crow offered. "But vehicles are not nature. Could that be it?"

"But we're driving a vehicle, and inside we have, or at least had, a happy feeling that connected with nature. Maybe there are happy people in other vehicles too, but all we see is the car, and not what's inside. Maybe the car is an impervious outer shell that we can't penetrate the way we can with a tree. After all, a tree has no protection or covering - it's out there for all to see, and if you think about it, it's really very vulnerable. It can't even run away when it sees disaster heading straight for it. And maybe that vulnerability is what allows us to connect with it." I carried this notion a bit further. "A car is not meant to be vulnerable. It's designed to be a powerful, anonymous, all-encompassing bucket of safety for us to step into. Of course, we're not going to be able to connect to it like we are to something from the natural world."

"That's probably true, but cars are here to stay. No one's going to abandon them just to get back to nature," Crow pointed out. "Not even me. I like having my van to get around in. It's what I use to get myself out of the city and into nature. So, we're going to have to find a way to work with them, because like I said, they're not going away. They might change shapes or use a different power source as time goes on, but our society expects to be able to get wherever we want to go, whenever we want to go. And a promised feeling of connectedness to nature is not going to make people quit using them."

"I have to agree with you on that one," Malcolm added. "Take global warming for instance. Even though we know we might be contributing to climate change, we still keep on driving. Look at us."

Euphoria drifted away as we realized how enormous some of society's problems are, and how difficult it is to tackle them. We knew there'd be more of this to come as we headed right smack-dab back into congestion and our old life. Welcome home, I thought to myself. This was going to be a challenge!

"Let's go home guys, and see what else we find out," I said, feeling a bit gloomy. We drove the rest of the way in silent contemplation, gazing around us at the trappings of a city life.

When we turned the corner and our house first came into view, my heart skipped a beat. It really did feel like home, and a sense of comfort swept through me. This was my little spot in the world, and that was a good feeling.

We unloaded our stuff, and Crow took off to his place. We'd made plans to meet two days later. Tomorrow was back to work, and back to our old routine, which gave me the odd feeling of trepidation, excitement, and curiosity all rolled into one. I wasn't sure what to expect.

Malcolm and I put everything away, and ordered a pizza for supper, after which we sat down on our comfy couch with our feet up. There was still a bit of port left from the camping trip, so we poured ourselves each a glass.

"What do you think it's going to be like tomorrow at work?" I asked Malcolm.

"I don't know. I've been trying to overlay what we learned on top of what we knew before, and I have to say it's all a bit confusing. I feel like I'm trying to put together a very complicated 3D puzzle. I don't even know what piece to look for because I don't have a finished picture to guide me."

"I know exactly what you mean," I admitted. "I think I'm going to simply pay attention to what goes on around me at work, and try to notice how I feel about it too. Then later on, maybe we can figure out how to merge our new knowledge with our old lives, and hope for at least some improvement. Obviously, we're not going to quit our jobs, sell our house, and go live on a farm and live happily ever after like a fairytale. Although, I have to admit, that doesn't sound half bad to me - except that I don't know much about farming or living off the land."

Malcolm laughed. "Neither do I. But I bet you we could learn if that was our hearts desire. Why not? Both of us grew up in the laid-back atmosphere of a small town, and look how we learned to live in a high-density neighborhood. Why couldn't we go the other way too? High density to quiet farm life? We're only in our mid-thirties, after all – I've heard that's a good time to switch careers."

"That's something I never thought I'd hear coming from you! Do you really think we'd be happy on a farm?" I challenged.

"I'm not saying that's what we're going to do – just that we could if we really wanted to, and not to rule it out. Like Griffin said – if you really want to do something, you *can* make it happen. We've got to learn to be less rigid and more open minded if we're going to make changes in our lives," Malcolm cautioned. "I think you're right about your attitude towards work, though. Let's just see how it plays out and go from there. I can tell you one thing for sure - I am *not* looking forward to the commute tomorrow. I don't see how that could possibly be good for anyone."

I felt sorry for Malcolm. Slowly creeping along for an hour trapped in a car is not my cup of tea. I often wondered why people did that to themselves, but then here we were, doing the exact same thing. Oh well, nothing was going to change instantly, we realized, so we decided to head off to bed.

We both had strange dreams that night. I'd never been one to remember very many dreams; Malcolm recalled even less than I did. So, for both of us to actually have, and remember, a vivid dream on the same night was definitely not our norm. Something was afoot, and we knew it.

We told each other our dreams when we woke in the morning, but had very little time to discuss them as getting ready for work was always a rush.

Mine took place in some sort of complicated mall environment. I was there because my daughter (*I don't have any children*) wanted some help buying flour. Apparently, she couldn't find any. So, I came down to the mall to help her. Then someone she knew showed up, and he told me about a problem one of his friends was having. I thought I had some information that could possibly help his friend, so I sat down at a counter and started writing on a napkin how I would go about helping. But while I was doing this, my daughter and her friend were goofing around, obviously not interested in getting the help I was offering. A few times I said to my daughter, "Hey, let's go," but both of them just ignored me. I finally decided I would just leave, and when I started to walk out, my daughter then came with me. I also made the decision to not give her friend what I'd written on the napkin because he didn't really seem to care about it anyhow. When my daughter and I were walking towards the place we thought would have flour, a frail older lady with white hair tied in a bun, came up beside us and said how much trouble she had in finding the doctor's office in the mall. She said it took a long time to find, and how confusing the layout of the mall was. She told us that if we wanted to find flour, we'd first have to find the city office as they knew where everything was. But, apparently, finding the city office was just as tricky as finding anything else in that mall. And that's when I woke up! The interesting thing about this dream was how real it was. I could feel myself there again, even as I thought about it.

I found Malcolm's dream to be rather interesting. He was visiting his hometown by himself. When he drove in his car down the street where he lived, he found that the house he grew up in was no longer there (*in real life, it's still there*). He drove around and around the area, thinking maybe he took a wrong turn somewhere and just wasn't in the right spot to see his home. Then suddenly he was not in the car anymore – instead, he was in the air - not flying, but moving around and looking down on his hometown. From up above, he was actually able to see his house. He even found himself going inside and checking out his old room. His Mom and Dad were there too, and they all had a friendly chat. Then he was back in his car again, trying to drive to his house. But once again, he couldn't find it. And that's when he woke up, feeling a great sense of frustration. As he left for work, he told me that he still hadn't been able to shake that feeling of frustration.

"This is too strange to be a co-incidence," I told Malcolm. "I'm going to stop on my way home to see if I can find a book on dream interpretation. Maybe *someone* is trying to tell us something!"

"Great idea," Malcolm agreed as we kissed good-bye. "Let's check it out tonight, along with how our day goes, which I have a feeling could be interesting." Off we went in separate directions – him in the car, and me on foot.

I always enjoyed my twenty-minute walk to work. I marveled at how nature managed to exist within the city. Thank goodness too. Something was needed to offset all the concrete, glass and metal. A few birds, a patch of grass, and some trees went a long way to help balance the mood, in my opinion.

There was no time for any sort of reflection when I arrived at work, however. I was met with a fast pace and a need for quick solutions to any and every issue that came up. It was like being thrown into a fast-moving river. Yikes! The contrast between our camping life and our working life was shocking. But I got through the day, as I knew I would.

I was able to slow down again on my walk home. I stopped off at a used book store to find a book on dream interpretation. I was surprised to see how many there were to choose from. It seemed a lot of people did try to figure out their dreams. Why hadn't I, I wondered? I leafed through a few of them but didn't find any I liked. Then I came across one that seemed easy to use, so I purchased it and proceeded on home.

I had to get supper going, so I didn't have time to check the book out any further. While I was mindlessly chopping up vegetables, I thought about how completely different our holiday had been compared to the life we had become so used to. I was afraid of sinking back into our old life and forgetting what we'd learned on our trip. Even though I didn't want that to happen, I could feel the old ways draw me in, like I was required to fulfill some sort of unspoken duty in order to maintain my membership in the club of humanity. It was not going to be easy to resist falling back to old ways. Going against the flow would take guts and determination, just as Crow had warned. Supper was almost ready when Malcolm came home. I wondered what kind of day he had.

As soon as he walked through the door, I knew something was up - the mischievous look on his face gave it away. He wrapped me up in the biggest of hugs, and whispered in my ear, "You will never guess what happened to me today!"

"You got fired?"

"Not even close."

"You got a raise?"

"Nope."

"You found a farm for us to move to?"

"Nice try," he laughed as he released me. "But no, that wasn't it."

"Then what?" I begged him. "You have to tell me."

His eyes sparkled as he said, "Bluedon joined me on my commute to work!"

"No way! How did that happen? Did you ask him to come?" I was eager to know.

"No, I wasn't even thinking about him. Traffic was going along at a slow pace, and then came to a complete halt, which got me cursing a bit. All of a sudden, I heard his voice saying, *'so I'm guessing you find this to be one of the more unpleasant aspects of your life,'* and I just about jumped right out of my seat. I looked over, and there he was in the passenger seat, smiling at me!"

"Are you serious?"

"Yes, I'm very serious. After I got over my initial shock, I told him how nice it was to see him. I asked how he was doing and told him how glad I was that he was showing up in the city and that I had so many questions for him. In truth, I got a bit blubbery," Malcolm explained, looking a little sheepish. "Anyways, after we got over that part, he told me he thought he'd join me on the long commute because it would give us time to talk, just one on one. He said he decided to come with a body after what happened when Griffin showed up without one. After all, I was driving, he explained, and he didn't want to be the cause of an accident!"

"Wow! Let's leave supper simmer and go sit on the deck to talk about this. I'll grab a couple of beers. I want to hear everything you guys talked about."

We settled into our comfy deck chairs. The street traffic had died down, and the kids on the block had gone home for supper, so the only sounds left to serenade us were the birds busily chirping away in the mountain ash tree in the middle of our yard.

What Malcolm proceeded to tell me seemed out of this world, but then again, everything we'd been through the past week was out of our world. I was beginning to question if maybe our world had been too small?

"First of all," Malcolm started, "Bluedon asked me if I liked driving to and from work like this every day. To which I answered, no. How could anyone enjoy something like this? So why do you do it, he asked me? That seemed easy. I do it to get to work, I told him. It's the only way I can get there as there's no public transportation that goes from where I live to where I work, so I have to drive. Then he asked me if that was the same for all the people in these other cars, too, and I told him I suppose so as we always seem to end up doing this at the same time every day. Okay, he said, you do it so that you can get to work - and I nodded.

"Do you like your work, he asked me? I told him I do for the most part, but there are times when it leaves me feeling less than fulfilled and more like I'm a cog in someone else's machine. At that, he just nodded and was quiet for a while. Then he asked why it is that I work? We need the money, I told him. We have a mortgage to pay and other bills as well, and without both of us working, we wouldn't be able to pay for everything and save up for retirement. At that, he went quiet again. My mind was churning...why was he asking me these questions?"

I interrupted. "But he had to know what you were thinking. Remember, how they'd answer our questions before we even asked them?"

"You're right - I finally remembered that little detail. That's when I asked myself what was this guy was up to, because he was definitely up to something. I felt like he was trying to tease certain information out of me."

"That's what it seems like to me too." I shifted around in my chair. "What happened then?"

"Believe it or not, he asked me about the dream I had last night! That was a shocker. How did he know I had a dream - I'd even forgotten about it? But he told me to think about it as it might give me some answers as to what was going on in my life, and that dreams can be helpful in that way, but of course, we need to have that belief before it would work for us."

"Well, that's timely, since we actually came to that conclusion ourselves this morning. I did end up buying a book on dream interpretation on my way home. Let's check it out after supper and see what we come up with."

"For sure. But hang on - that's not where it ended. He went on to explain, in a very serious tone, that it is absolutely essential that I examine my beliefs about what I feel is important to me in life, and how work fits into those beliefs. Apparently, the dream would offer me clues. I was always to remember that we create our own reality, and, for a reason. He said it was the first rule they told us about because it was the most important. Now that we were back in the reality we unknowingly have been creating for ourselves all along, we were getting an opportunity to see it from a conscious perspective, he explained. Then he said something that will stick with me forever - your expectations and beliefs create your reality, and *not the other way around*. If changes are to be made, they will come from an examination of those two attributes. If you're happy with your current reality, then leave them be. If you're not, you better start figuring out where the change in thinking needs to happen."

"Holy! This is going to take some serious contemplation to sort out."

"That's precisely what I said. I wanted to talk to him more, but he told me I had to do some thinking on my own first. When I looked over, he was gone! Good thing traffic was down to a snail's pace because my mind was everywhere except on driving after he left."

"That's incredible! I don't even know what to say, other than, once again, it feels right. You know what I mean? It sits right. Like finding one of the pieces to the puzzle you talked about earlier."

"That's exactly how it feels – not just in my head, but in my gut too. You can imagine how the rest of my day went. I couldn't concentrate on anything. My mind was on everything except the task at hand. All in all, it was both a difficult and an extremely exciting day. I wonder how Crow's day went. Do you suppose Griffin came to talk to him too? And what about you? Did you get a visit from Omar?"

"No, I didn't get a visit, and I'm sure Crow will tell us tomorrow night if something interesting happened to him. But you know, I agree that our dreams are indeed trying to tell us something. Why don't we have our supper and then see what we can come up with? We've got to start examining our beliefs too. Wouldn't it be good if we could discover our expectations and beliefs that have created *this* reality – the one we find ourselves in?" I looked around our backyard; at the healthy mountain ash tree full of red berries and chirping birds, the lush green patch of grass we called our lawn, the colorful flowers I'd managed to grow, the shapely rocks I'd placed here and there. I was quite happy with all that I saw, except for one thing - the traffic on the other side of our tall fence had started up again. That was a sound I knew I could do without.

"Great idea!" Malcolm said enthusiastically, as he stood up and stretched. "Let's embrace it and see where it goes? These guys are for real, and I know they're here to help. I think it's time to start putting their advice to work. I feel like I'm past caring what others might think of me."

Another turning point for Malcolm. I'd had the feeling he was still holding back a bit, but after Bluedon's visit, his attitude seemed to change. I was happy about that too. I was ready to try new things but I wanted a partner who was wholly committed, and it appeared I now had that.

We didn't watch TV that night as we usually did. Instead, we looked at the dream interpretation book and tried to decipher our dreams. It said that dreams are made up of symbols, and that everyone has their own symbols and their own meanings for the symbols. To start with we'd have to figure out what our symbols meant to us. There was no standard formula.

"What do you think the symbols are in your dream?" I asked Malcolm.

"Well, obviously there was the home I grew up in. Off the top of my head, I'd say that would stand for my home base, or my roots to me. Is that the sort of thing the book is asking for?"

"I believe so. What about your car? What does that mean to you?"

"Hmmm...I'm thinking of it as a vehicle, a way for me to get from here to there. I guess I'd say it's like my body, which is kind of like a vehicle too, as it gets me to places. Now what?"

"It says to insert the symbol *meanings* into your dream, instead of using the symbols themselves, and see what the dream is telling you. Give it a try."

"Okay. Let's see - I was in my *body* searching for my *home base* but couldn't seem to find it. However, when I got out of my *body* and looked from above, I had no trouble finding my *home base* at all. Whoa! It's telling me that I will find my home base, or my roots, easier when I'm out of my body and looking from above, rather than cruising around in my body feeling frustrated. I can't believe it! I have been searching for something – even before we went on our trip – but with no luck at all, and now I find out that I just have to look from above without my body."

"I think you're right! But Malcolm, how do you get out of your body to look from above? I don't think the dream told you that, did it?"

"No, but maybe our new friends can help me with that. In fact, I'm sure they can because they seem to have no trouble with going in and out of a body. Or - maybe it means I just need to see things from a different perspective – a higher perspective. I think that makes sense. So now I need to figure out how my idea of work fits into it all, like Bluedon said."

"It's actually pretty exciting, isn't it? Let's see what my dream tells us."

"Should we be writing this down?" Malcolm asked. "Seems like it might be a good idea, don't you think?" He got up to get a paper and pencil and then told me to go ahead with my dream.

"It all took place in a mall, which to me is a symbol for a public place where lots of people gather. That's easy, but I don't get meeting my daughter, since I don't have one. I'm guessing it could mean my responsibilities, as having kids certainly carries a heavy responsibility, in my opinion. And her friend would probably mean even extra responsibility. Flour – why were we looking for flour? Maybe my mind is thinking that from flour you can make bread and all sorts of other sustaining foods. I'm not sure, but I'll go with it meaning sustenance for now. And the older lady, means wisdom to me. The city office would mean the guys in charge."

"So now, try to impose those meanings into your dream. I've written down your symbols."

"Okay…here goes. I went to a *public gathering place* to meet my *responsibilities* to try to help find *sustenance*. When it became obvious my help wasn't appreciated by *extra responsibilities*, I dropped them, and went to find some *sustenance* in the *public gathering place*, but got lost. It took meeting up with *wisdom* to get the advice that it was indeed difficult to find things, and it was the *guys in charge* that would be able to help me out. I was determined to continue my search, with my *responsibilities* tagging along. I don't know - it sounds kind of convoluted to me. What do you think?"

Malcolm had excitement dancing in his eyes. "Don't you think it's telling you that you've been searching too, just not knowing what for, or where to look, feeling responsible for more than is necessary? And now you're close to finding wisdom from the *guys in charge* to give you some assurances about continuing?"

"Actually, I do see what you're saying, and I think it does explain how I've been feeling. This is really cool! Maybe we should start writing our dreams down so we can use them like this. It's comforting to get our own messages from a place we used to ignore. I'm quite proud of us." I reached for our wine glasses on the coffee table, and handed Malcolm his. "Let's toast to our first successful dream interpretation!" We clinked glasses and took a sip. "Now, how are we going to put our interpretations into practical use?" I asked as I put my glass back on the coffee table.

"I'm not sure," Malcolm started, but before he could go any further, I interrupted him.

"What's our belief about life?" I blurted out, surprising even myself.

Malcolm looked challenged, but he wasn't backing down. "That's a huge question. I don't even know where to start."

"Well, we have to start somewhere," I wasn't backing down either. "Maybe let's tackle that question sideways. Where do you think we get our beliefs from in the first place? I mean, it seems pretty obvious that we're not born with them. They must assemble in our minds as we're growing up. Surely a great deal of them have to come from our parents and our upbringing, as we certainly have different beliefs than people in other countries. So, society and culture have to be big influences." I was on a role and wasn't about to stop.

"But when we finally become adults, are we forced to keep our childhood beliefs? I don't think so: I don't believe in the boogeyman anymore, but I sure did when I was a little girl. I'm glad I let that one go. He was a scary dude – even though I never actually saw him."

"My parents didn't use the boogeyman to keep me in line, but some of my friends were certain of his existence!" Malcolm added with a laugh, but I was still concentrating on my newly evolving theory, so I continued.

"As we become adults then, we are free to develop our own beliefs about the world. But we actually have to *think* about it, and understand that we can make our beliefs be whatever we want them to be. Otherwise we'll just carry on with little improvement. We don't need to get rid of the good stuff; like being respectful of other people, and the difference between right and wrong, and don't take stuff that's not yours. We grew up believing in all that – or at least a lot of kids did," I added, thinking of Crow. "But we have to become aware that we are the ones who get to choose what our beliefs are! Is that not mind blowing? Did you ever think of that when you were growing up?"

"Heck no! I was taught that the *proper* way to live was to get a job, get married, get a house, have some kids, and maybe a nice car in the driveway. And to find some good friends to socialize with. It wasn't just our parents and neighbors that thought that way – we saw it on TV and magazines too. Society in general headed in that direction, so why would anyone think to question it or change it? It was the golden life we all aspired to." But then he eagerly added, "And guess what? Thirty-five years later that's what we have! Do you think we held that belief so close to ourselves that we didn't even know we had it – and bingo – here we are?"

"I think you're right, Malcolm." I felt like we'd stumbled on our first big discovery. "I would never have even thought of it as a belief. It was more like an accepted fact of life – like breathing. It's just the way it was. Wow! This is sneaky stuff. So, in order to create something different for ourselves, we have to spend time discovering what our current beliefs truly are. Once we know that, then we can somehow change how we think and decide what we expect from our new beliefs – and isn't that exactly what Bluedon was telling you?" I pointed out.

"Exactly!"

We sat there for a while, both feeling like something in our brains had been blown wide open. We knew our world was going to change from this one understanding - just not how.

"Julie, you know what else this means? It's not only about creating our own reality but also about creating our own happiness, or peace of mind. I guess it all goes hand in hand. But wait a minute - I've got an idea forming on the edge of my mind that sort of keeps slipping away. Just give me a minute."

I kept quiet. Malcolm got up and started to pace back and forth.

"I'm going to pick it apart, so bear with me. So many people find themselves unhappy, or resentful, or ill, and they can usually identify an outside source they feel can be legitimately blamed for their problems. But if we think about that in terms of what we've just learned...you know, about how *our* beliefs affect *our* reality, then it goes for this too, don't you think? Like we talked about when we were camping – there is no one to blame for our own unhappiness. The source of our problems doesn't come from outside of us, but from the inside. Life is not out there to get you. Life is there for you to go out and get, in whatever form you desire. You're the one driving the car. If we keep blaming others for our situations, then obviously we will wonder why life is treating us so badly. But the truth is that we've created it for ourselves, and probably for a reason. Life isn't doing it to us. And by not understanding this one simple idea, we keep ourselves in that unhappy situation. We'll stay stuck in our problems until we quit blaming others and work to discover our own beliefs. We have to start to realize the power that we have *inside us*. We are the ones that can do whatever is necessary to get ourselves back! We are the ones in control!"

I was still a bit confused. "If I'm hearing you right," I ventured, "then not only do we create our own reality, but we also create our feeling towards the reality we find ourselves in. And if we find ourselves in a reality that we don't actually care for too much, but can't change immediately, then at least we have control over how we feel about it. We can relax and not get upset with where we're at because we know we have the ability to create something different for ourselves going forward. A good example is your commute. Instead of blaming congestion, or being upset with yourself for getting into that situation, you can relax and realize that you have chosen to be there. No one is forcing you. Choice...there's always a choice that can be made in any predicament, don't you think? You might not like the other choices, but you still have to acknowledge their existence."

It was a revelation for us, as we worked it out in our own way, and verbalized it. We felt like we GOT IT from the inside out, and we planned to put it to use. It was a thrilling moment.

"Yeah, that works for me if I sit back and imagine it. I like it," Malcolm said. "It's really a matter of changing our perceptions of where we're at in the world, and no one has control over our perceptions except ourselves. Or at least that's part of it. But I think it all goes hand in hand with discovering our beliefs, creating our own reality, and choosing *how* we want to perceive things. Man, I feel like we've opened up a massive can of worms. I can hardly wait to talk to Crow about this, but for now, I'm tired, and I'm going to crawl into bed and hopefully drop off into instant sleep."

"I'm with you, but I'm not sure I'm going to be able to shut my mind down enough to sleep," I said. But I did, and surprisingly quickly too, only to wake up in a cold sweat, adrenalin still pumping because of the fellow who was chasing me in my dream. I knew his intent was rape if he ever caught me, so I ran like a crazy woman down the mountainside, jumping over rock cliffs, running for my life, darting here and there as fast as I could. He never seemed to be far behind me, though. I jumped over a giant boulder and then decided to stop and hide behind it, hoping he'd run right by me. That's when the thought crossed my mind that this would be the perfect time to leave this dimension and go to another one. And with that thought, I woke up in my own bed, still panicky. I was scared to even attempt to go back to sleep in case I went back there, and he found me. But it was a dream, wasn't it? It sure didn't feel like it, I was that terrified, but I kept telling myself that it was okay because I was safely lying in my bed with Malcolm snoring beside me...and how did I know about going to another dimension in my dream, I wondered? That kind of idea had never entered my head until I'd met Omar. I lay there awake till morning came, and when Malcolm woke up, I told him all about it.

"You're still scared, aren't you?" Malcolm asked, putting his arms around me and pulling me close. "I have no idea what that kind of dream could possibly mean, nor do I know if every dream is trying to tell us something. Maybe we can ask Omar about this one."

"I think that might be a good idea," I answered. "I can't seem to get it out of my head, it was so real. I'm hoping I'll be able to see it in a different light as the day goes on. I know one thing, though - I was never so glad to be right here, right now, in this house, in this dimension, and living *this* life!"

9

CROW'S FIRST DAY BACK

"There is an unending conversation going on throughout the universe, and a most meaningful one." **Seth & Jane Roberts**

After our newfound discoveries, work looked totally different to me the next day. It was like someone had slipped a new pair of reality lenses over my eyes; ones designed to change the way I saw everyone. It was similar to the drive back from our camping trip, where everything looked so surreal. I saw the lives, the dramas, the problems, along with the strengths and challenges of each of my co-workers, and not just the surface level of their working life. It was fascinating! One young woman had the challenging reality of having a full-time job and being a single mom with two small kids. The manager had just been diagnosed with cancer. Imagine what his existence must be like! He doesn't even know if he'll be able to continue working, and he has a wife, kids, and a mortgage too! And my partner in reception has elderly parents who have taken ill and are no longer able to cope at home by themselves. She spends a lot of time helping and worrying about them. A wash of understanding and empathy swept over me. Why hadn't I noticed this before? Was I so self-absorbed by my own life that I failed to realize the enormity of what was happening to others around me?

Then I got to thinking, that if we all create our own realities, then they were creating theirs too. Did they know this? Would it help them if they did? Would it give them the same sense of power to change it that it gave me? It struck me that if I could figure this whole 'create your own reality' thing out, then maybe I could help others make more sense of the situations they found themselves in, which should help make their lives better. I liked that idea. So did Malcolm when we discussed it after work. We decided to talk to Crow about it that evening when he came over after supper. That was our intent anyway, but it was close to midnight before we even had a chance, as what Crow told us that night was astonishing, as you shall see.

"I went to work Monday morning, same as you guys," Crow told us. "But before I even got two feet inside the door my boss rushed up to me and pulled me aside. He said he'd hired a new guy, and wanted me to train him! Can you imagine? I was pretty surprised, but then my boss whispered that he was equally surprised, as he hadn't actually planned on hiring anyone!"

"Well, how'd he get hired then?" I asked.

"Apparently, this guy had been sitting beside my boss in the pub one night, and they struck up a conversation. Before the evening was over, my boss hired him – just like that! It was for a trial period mind you, but nevertheless, he gave him a job! What really worried me, though, was how familiar this guy seemed, so I wracked my brain trying to figure out if he might be from the *troubled* portion of my past that I told you about."

"I can certainly see how that would be a concern for you," Malcolm admitted. "What did you do?"

"Nothing at first. My boss introduced us, and I found out his name was George, which didn't ring any bells. But he kept looking at me with this big smile on his face, as though he knew a secret, which definitely made me nervous. So, I asked him if we'd ever met before because he seemed so familiar. But he just smiled pleasantly and said he didn't think so. There wasn't much else to do then but go ahead and train him, so that's what we did for the rest of the day, but the whole time I kept thinking that something's very fishy here."

"That had to make for a nerve-wracking day for you," I offered. "What happened today?"

"Last night I'd been hoping it was all a dream and that he'd be gone this morning, but no, there he was waiting for me, with that same smile on his face. So, we spent the morning together working and talking, and after a while I quit being suspicious and actually started to enjoy his company. I asked about his past, you know – where he'd come from and all that. He told me he was single, and came from a small town in Alberta, which is nowhere near where I grew up - either time. That helped me relax even more. He told me he had no interest in getting married or involved in a relationship as he really wanted to delve into his own life, as deep as he could go, and to discover himself *this time around*."

"This time around? That sounds rather interesting, don't you think?" Malcolm declared. "Sounds like he might believe in reincarnation,"

"My feelings precisely. I wanted to talk to him more about this, and since it was lunchtime, we headed over to a quiet spot in the coffee room, where he proceeded to tell me what he was all about. He had my full attention, to say the least. I'm going to try to repeat it to you guys as best I can. I think you're going to like it as much as I did. It's a fairly long tale, though, so get comfortable."

"Wait a minute then. Sounds like a good time for me to get a few munchies before you start. Hang on while I grab a few things," I told them. I went into the kitchen and found some nuts and some chocolate in the pantry, which I combined in a bowl. I also brought another beer for each of us. When we were all settled again, Crow took a sip of his beer, and then started into George's incredible tale.

"When George was young, he always felt as though he was different from the other kids. He had what we'd all call a 'normal' childhood – pretty much the opposite end of the stick from mine.

But he always felt there had to be *more,* not even sure how to describe it any other way - just *more.* So, when he graduated, he decided to go travelling and see what he could discover in the world; thinking that maybe this would help him find what he was looking for. He travelled all over Europe, Asia and even South America, always going where he felt drawn too. And he met a lot of other people who were also searching for something. Some had turned to drugs, but they seemed to get too stuck in it for his liking. It was like quicksand, he said. Some became completely engrossed in religion – whatever the religion of the region was. But he found that too limiting and demanding, with way too many rules to follow. He met up with people that thought more meant more money, and that became their focus, but to him, that was too shallow - he likened it to a stagnant pond whereas he was looking for a vibrant ocean. After ten years of travelling around like this, he decided to come home. He still hadn't found what he'd been looking for and wasn't even sure where to look anymore."

"That had to be incredibly disappointing for him!" Malcolm said as he grabbed a handful of nuts.

"Yes, it was to begin with. But he didn't sit still for long. For some reason he kept feeling an undeniable pull for the BC coast. He'd get this vision of being in a location that had a great deal more to do with raw nature than people, or production, or drugs, or religion. He knew to follow his impulses, so he did a bit of research and came upon the *Great Bear Rain Forest,* and couldn't believe what he was seeing. It matched his vision exactly, so he knew he had to go there."

"But that's a huge area! How did he know where to go?" I asked, interrupting Crow's story.

"He didn't know. That was one of his problems. But he thought if he hitchhiked up to Kitimat, he could start from there. Money was something he never had much of, and that never worried him. Still, he was a realist and knew he needed some money. So he stayed in Alberta for a few months working at whatever jobs he could find, and once he felt he had enough to go to the coast, off he went. To shorten this story up a bit, I'll skip some of his many trials and tribulations and just tell you about his big discovery. Otherwise, we'd be here all night."

"Sounds like a good idea, as we do all need to go to work tomorrow, now that we're back in our 'self-created reality,'" I said, and we all laughed.

"This is going to blow you away," Crow continued. "One day, on one of his many hikes, George found himself beside the ocean at the end of an inlet. There was no one around – just George and nature. He'd come upon a good sitting rock that had been warmed from the sun, so he sat down and got comfortable on it. He was watching the eagles circling in the sky - enjoying the wind and the sun on his skin when all of a sudden, he felt a change coming over him. He described it as *melting into everything*. He could not feel a distinction between himself and the eagle, or the rocks, or the ocean. It was all the same thing, and he was a part of it all. At first, this scared him, as he didn't seem to have any control over it. But then another part of him took over, telling him it's okay, and to be calm. So, he relaxed into it, and away he went. He flew with that eagle, and he felt the water wash over the rocks, as though he was the rock *and* the water at the same time. It was like nothing he'd ever experienced before – he was completely in awe. As he looked around, he started to see particles everywhere - little tiny particles. It looked like the air was made up of particles – like a painting done with dots. He saw how those particles also made up the eagle, the ocean, and the rocks. And when he looked down at himself, he saw that he was made up of the very same particles!"

"No way!" I exclaimed.

"You gotta be kidding," Malcolm gasped.

"That's what he told me, and that was my reaction too. But that's not all. When he looked up again from his particle body, he saw a really large bear coming out from behind a bush not too far away from him. The bear ambled over and sat itself down, not more than ten feet away. Normally, this would have really frightened George, as you can imagine, but not this time. Instead, he felt a wash of love come over him. He looked at that bear, all made up of particles, and the bear simply looked back at him for what seemed a very long time. Then the bear asked him what he was doing there - but the bear didn't actually say anything - George just heard it in his head. So, he thought he should answer, but to do that, he first had to ask himself that question: just what was he doing there, anyway? He came to the conclusion that he'd brought himself there in search of the very *more* he'd been looking for ever since he left school. As soon as he thought this, the bear nodded. It was like the bear knew what he was thinking. Sound familiar?"

"Boy, does it ever," I agreed. "Go on." I didn't want Crow to stop telling this fascinating story.

"After a while, the bear asked him if he was finding what he was looking for. Again, George had to think about it: what exactly was it that he'd been looking for? And then it came to him, like a long, lost answer that floated down from the clear blue sky above and fell perfectly into the empty space in his heart: he was searching for a connection - for a way to feel at home in his heart, connected and supported and loved, truly loved, by everything that really mattered in this world. He was looking for that feeling of being a part of something so universal and eternal that it encompassed everything that existed, known and unknown. The bear smiled at that and then asked him if he'd found it? George started to tell him about all the places he'd looked without finding anything. The bear listened patiently and then asked again if he'd found it. George thought this odd, as he felt he'd just answered that question. He was about to say something to this effect when *whack* – something snapped at the back of his head. Before he could turn around to see what had hit him, he found himself flying in the air and looking down at himself, sitting on the rock below. All he could think of was, 'No way – what's happening?' And with that, off he flew."

"He flew? Like in the sky?" I questioned Crow. I'd been lifted up when I jumped over the crack, but I hadn't actually flown on my own accord.

"Yep, he flew. It seems unbelievable, doesn't it? It gets even better

– just listen. At first, he seemed to be on the eagle's back, but after he got comfortable with flying, he found himself all on his own zooming from here to there, doing flips and dives. He heard the bear's voice in his head again, 'Why not fly over the mountain range over there?' And as soon as George thought, yeah, that's cool, away he went - no hesitation at all. Again, the bear's voice came to him and said, 'Now, skim over the ocean surface and feel the spray on your face.' And down he dipped. It was all so amazingly real as George actually felt the spray on his skin! Can you imagine? But then the bear told him to dive into the ocean and swim with the fish, and before he knew it, he found himself under the water swimming amongst a pod of killer whales. He discovered he could even breathe! Swimming with killer whales was an experience he said he'd never forget. He spent quite a bit of time underwater, checking out whatever caught his attention. It was unbelievably beautiful and serene – like a whole new world. George got to thinking about how striking everything was, how connected it all was, how insignificant people were compared to all this natural grandness. And how much more there was to life than he'd ever imagined. He was seeing it all from such a different perspective. He'd felt so limited before, and here he was so free and connected to everything he saw. He never wanted to stop this experience, but the bear said it was time to return to his body as he had now discovered his connection and place in the world, and that he'd never lose it again unless he allowed that to happen. 'There is much to be discovered while in a body, so do not regret where you are,' the bear told him. 'But always remember that you are a part of *all* there is. No more and no less.'

"And with that George found himself back in his body, sitting on the warm rock staring out at the world, feeling separate again and somewhat disoriented. He looked around for the bear, but it was gone. The particles were gone too. But the eagle was still circling, and the water was still washing over the rocks with every wave. He remembered what he saw, but he was struggling with whether or not it really happened…and if it did happen, then what exactly was it that happened, he wondered? He ended up staying at that beach for the rest of the day trying to sort it out. But one thing he knew for certain was that he did indeed feel connected in a way he never had before. He felt it in every cell of his body. He realized he could finally stop his searching as he'd found his home right inside of himself, and it would go with him wherever he went or whatever he would do. And that left him free to figure out just what that would be."

Needless to say, Malcolm and I sat there gob-smacked! Crow said he could hardly wait to go back to work to talk more with George, and I couldn't blame him. I wanted to talk to him too. What an experience that must have been - swimming under the ocean! But then again, our experience was just as amazing, and just as unbelievable.

It was already past midnight, and we really did need to get some sleep for work the next day. However, we were all actually looking forward to going to work. None of us thought of it as a dreary inevitability anymore. Before we said good night, we made plans to get together again on Friday. Crow said he'd ask George if he'd like to come and join us. Now that would make for an exciting evening, we thought.

10

OUR NEW FRIEND GEORGE

"If you change the way you look at things, the things you look at change." **Dr. Wayne Dyer**

Malcolm walked into the house very excited one night after work. "You know, Julie, I'm really liking all the time I have to just relax and think on my commute now. I don't get uptight and I don't feel like complaining about the traffic, or the drivers in the other cars. I look over at them and realize that hey, we're all in this together. It's like a type of kinship we have."

"That's interesting, because as far as I can see the only thing that's changed is your own attitude. Those are the same intersections, the same roads, the same cars going at the same slow speed, aren't they?"

"Yeah, but I'm looking at it differently – like Bluedon said. I've changed my perception of the situation, and man has that ever made a difference!"

As we talked more about it over supper, we came to realize that changing one's perceptions was a tremendously powerful tool, and tried to think of where else we could put this to work.

"What about changing our attitudes towards our jobs?" I asked Malcolm.

"I wouldn't mind a change of attitude there at all. I do my job to the best of my ability, but I always feel like I'm working within someone else's rules, which leaves me feeling quite stifled most days. I don't seem to have a place where I can develop my own creativity, and I know that I have some. I want to make a difference, but I've never felt like I had any time to even think about what difference it is that I want to make, or how to go about it." Malcolm looked quite frustrated as he cleaned the last bits off his plate. "However," he added, looking up at me with a smile on face, "I think it's high time to start."

"But Malcolm," I countered, "don't you see? You're *already* making a difference - we all are. What we're doing right now *is* making a difference. Our actions already affect the people around us, so I'd say we need to be more mindful of what our actions are because they'll always have an effect – good or bad. The system has been working all this time, we just didn't realize that there was a system. Nor did it dawn on us that we could consciously decide to change our attitudes in order to make it better for us and everyone around us. That's part of getting out of the victim's way of thinking. We are where we are, so while we're there – let's make a positive difference."

Malcolm looked surprised. "I'd never thought of it that way before. You're right. I've got to become more mindful of what I'm doing. In fact, tomorrow at work I'm going to be as positive as possible, and to make a *conscious* effort to spread joy to those around me, and no more judgment – I'm going to try to just be kind. I wonder if it'll change things for those around me?"

"I don't see how it can't. I'm going to try the very same thing," I said, handing Malcolm a delicious bowl of raspberry ice cream I'd dished up for dessert.

The next day I got another idea of how to be nice to those

around me. It was Omar that pointed it out. While walking home Friday night, I heard his familiar voice in my right ear, "Hello, again, Julie. And just how've you been this past week?" I turned to say hello, but even as I did, I knew I wouldn't see anything; he'd left his body at home. I was so happy he came to visit that I couldn't stop myself from telling him everything that happened to us since returning. Good thing I didn't need to be verbal to communicate; using thoughts was so much easier and quicker. He had the good grace to let me go on and on – kind of like George's bear, I thought, which instantly made me realize that this was a skill I should learn to develop too – not interrupting, that is.

Omar readily agreed. "Yes, to simply listen is a great skill, and makes those around you feel respected, and valuable. Interrupting doesn't help anyone - speaker or listener, and really, what's the rush anyway? I believe you'll feel more present and relaxed, as will those you're talking to."

"I think that's a great idea," I told Omar. "I'm going to try to do this as much as possible and see what happens."

"I can guarantee you it'll work like a charm. In fact, I can foresee others following your lead. That is the power of changing one person's attitude! Think of yourself as an epicenter at all times, because that is truly what you are!"

"Oooh, I *like* that idea." We continued to walk and *talk*. It was strange to have this conversation only in my mind, but then again, I realized that I often have conversations going on in my mind, but they're usually with just me.

"Both you and Malcolm have done an excellent job of taking your everyday experiences and examining them to see what you can discover. It's not that different from studying your dreams, actually," Omar pointed out. "That's why I stopped by. I wanted to congratulate you on your desire to put the lessons you've learned to work, and not just say to heck with it, as many do. There is no need to be afraid of being isolated from so-called *normal* society, since you can't please everyone anyway - nor should you even try to."

"That's so true, but I find I still worry about stepping away from the norm," I quietly confessed.

"Everybody does. But what's more important is to discover *yourself* and not deny who you are - two things that have nothing to do with conforming to other's expectations. Take George for example..."

"How'd you know about George?" I asked before realizing that Omar knew most things that were going on. "Sorry, no need to answer that." I was pretty sure I heard a little chuckle from Omar.

"As I was saying, you'll notice that George is an excellent example of someone who doesn't care what others think of him. Instead, he cares very deeply about what *he* thinks. I'm very glad you'll be meeting him. And speaking of George, I believe you have some preparations to make for your visit tonight, so I'll say good-bye. Perhaps, we'll see you soon."

I wanted to ask him if he was going to drop in tonight, but I could feel that his presence was gone. And I needed to get supper made as Crow and George were coming over right after work, which was pretty soon. Ever since Crow told us about George, I looked forward to meeting him. I had a mental image of him being a clean-cut, tall, lean, outdoorsy type.

As soon as I got home I started to prepare the evening meal; curried chicken and rice, marinated tomatoes, a green salad, and for dessert, a scrumptious apple and blueberry crisp made the day before. I always tried to make the meal special when someone new came over for supper. It was my way of being hospitable, I guess.

I was in mid-prep when the door suddenly opened and Malcolm came in. "Hi honey! Wow! It smells good in here!" he announced as he walked up behind me and wrapped his arms around me. "I had a great day."

"Me too," I turned and said, "but Crow and George should be here shortly, so I need to keep going if we're going to eat soon. Could you pour me a glass of wine when you get your beer?" I asked as I continued on with my prep. Malcolm went to do just that when we heard the doorbell ring. "Oh-oh…sounds like they're already here," I said. "Can you get the door?"

When Malcolm opened the door, I was shocked. George was innocently standing there beside Crow, looking nothing at all like I'd pictured him! Instead of the clean-cut look, he had shoulder-length curly brown hair – and a substantial mustache! Plus, he was short – not much taller than me in fact, and I'm only a titch over five feet! He was lean, though - I got that part right, as there didn't appear to be an ounce of fat on him. My instant impression was one of contentment oozing out of every part of him.

Crow introduced everyone. I wiped my hands on my apron and came over to hug both of them - George was the kind of guy you just felt like hugging. "It's really nice to meet you," I said. "Crow's told us all about your experience, and we're truly looking forward to finding out more."

"It's nice to meet you too," he replied with a wonderful smile spread over his entire face. "Crow's been telling me about your experiences too. I have a feeling we're all going to get along just fine, especially since the smells from your kitchen are making me salivate and my stomach rumble. It feels so homey in here," George acknowledged, glancing around. "That's a feeling that's always appreciated by a bachelor."

"Can I grab you a beer?" Malcolm asked them both. They took their beers and settled themselves on the barstools on the other side of the island. I listened to them talk while I kept preparing the supper. I couldn't help but wonder how it was that Crow's boss had even talked to George in the bar, let alone hire him. His boss made no effort at all to hide how he felt about *those lazy long-haired hippies!* But the more I listened to George talk, the more I began to understand. He was extremely charismatic, and I too felt inexplicably drawn to him. His brown eyes had an unmistakable twinkle, and it seemed impossible for his face to do anything but smile. I'd have to say he wasn't what I'd call good looking or handsome, but there was something about him that was even better than that. He was just so himself, with nothing whatsoever to hide. He seemed to be completely present in the moment too. Not only that, I got the feeling that he was *willingly* and *intentionally* present wherever he was. I could see what Omar meant - here was someone who knew himself, and liked himself. I wanted to be more like that.

It was plain to see that Crow and George had become good friends over the past week, and I was really happy for Crow. He was a little bit different than most others and consequently did not have many close friends other than us. But he certainly did now, and this seemed to lighten his face up considerably. He now looked like a happy Crow with a constant smile that played around the edges of his lips. The three of them made quite the picture in the kitchen - Crow's unruly black hair, dark beady eyes and crooked nose, and George's mustached smiling face framed by those long brown curly locks, and then there was Malcolm's shaved head, sky blue eyes and piercing gaze. Yep, they were quite the group!

Supper was finally ready. We eagerly sat down at the table to eat, and helped ourselves till we were stuffed. Great friends, great conversation, and great food certainly makes for an enjoyable meal.

After the dishes were cleared, we took our wine glasses, along with the bottle, and headed to the living room to relax before dessert. I don't remember how it got started, but we ended up swapping stories about our unforgettable experiences, and their striking similarities.

I wanted to know what happened to George after his experience at the beach. "How did you come to be here in Vancouver," I asked him, "and landing a job in the postal service, of all places?"

"I will tell you anything you want to know, but first I think I'm going to join the rest of you in stretching out a bit. That supper was so delicious that I think I might have eaten more than I should have." He rubbed his stomach as he put both feet up onto the coffee table, alongside the rest of ours, and made himself comfortable before he began his answer. "Initially," George explained, "I wasn't really sure what to do. I still had enough money to last most of the summer if I was careful, so I decided to just take the time and camp up and down the BC coast. I wanted to get truly anchored in the stunning nature of the coastline, which I discovered was not difficult to do at all. It didn't matter where I pitched my tent, it was *gorgeous*. Although I don't believe it was the scenery that'd changed. I think it was my eyesight, or to be more precise, I believe my brain had changed the way it *interpreted* what my eyes saw. Colors were no longer just colors - they were like shimmering rich velvets, or shiny smooth satins, or iridescent silks flowing with the wind. It was absolutely incredible!"

"That's what we discovered too when we drove back from our camping trip!" I exclaimed. "At first we thought we were going nuts, but since we all saw it we knew it was for real. Everything took on such a different vibe than when we drove out there."

"Exactly," George replied, and then continued on. "After a few days of wandering around, gazing in awe at everything – probably looking like I was stoned to anyone who noticed me – I started hearing sounds attached to these vibrant colors! Like you, I wondered if maybe I was losing it. On the one hand, my ever-present rational brain kept telling me a green tree is a green tree and nothing more, and most definitely, they did not make sounds. But when I looked at that tree, I saw shimmering green particles - and they were singing a beautiful melody. I simply could not deny it, not even when I tried. And it wasn't just the trees I'm talking about – it was everything I looked at. I was immersed in a kaleidoscope of color and sound. I couldn't seem to shake it, so I made the decision to let my rational mind take a back seat, and to go with these new abilities. I wanted to see where they would take me."

"What did you find? Where did it lead you?" I was beside myself to absorb everything George said, like a sponge. I wanted to know it all - right now, but I was forced to patiently wait for it to come out syllable by syllable.

George looked at me with that wonderful smile of his before going on. "I started to receive messages," he said and then paused. "You know, I'm selective about who I divulge these particular details to as many are not ready or even capable of understanding it. However, it's obvious to me that you three know exactly what I'm talking about."

"Yeah, we understand completely," Malcolm confirmed for all of us. "We feel exactly the same way about our experiences so we know what you mean. We're eager to hear everything you have to tell us. No need whatsoever to be concerned about our response."

George smiled his thanks, and resumed his story. "As I said, I started getting messages. But they didn't come through the usual channels we use for hearing. Instead, I heard the words in the *middle* of me. I'm not sure how else to describe it, as that's where I heard them. I was told, over and over, that I was loved, cared for, and watched over by my own entity, and other personalities in places that we're not currently familiar with. As it was repeated, it seemed to sink further and further into my very cells until I knew it was part of my physical being. And it felt good – *really* good – to know I wasn't alone and that I was connected to something that was obviously much larger and with more capabilities than I had. I couldn't help but smile all the time. Then a few days later, another message came through to me – again, I heard it in my gut. This time it said *there's more to me than the me I see*. Over and over again, until it sank into my cells the same way as before. But this time, I asked this voice exactly what else there was to me - what part of me was I not seeing? I wanted to know."

"What did it say?" I blurted out. "What did you learn?"

George laughed at my enthusiasm. "I never actually got an answer. However, I had the most amazing dream that night. I know I was asleep, but the dream was so real that I could have sworn I was awake. I dreamt that I was flying - not just flying like a bird, but soaring like a daredevil stunt pilot – only it was my body I was flying with, not a plane. I was dipping and spinning and shooting off in all directions, and absolutely loving it. At one point, I found myself looking down on a circle of teepees, and in the center, there was a fire with a lot of men sitting around it. They were all dressed in feathers and decorated with paint – a rather imposing-looking group. They were talking in great earnest, but I couldn't hear what they were saying. For some reason, I zoned in on one of the younger fellows who seemed very impatient. I got the feeling that he really wanted to jump on his horse that was tied up behind the teepees, and to take off like the wind, but he had to stay at the meeting. Even though I couldn't hear what they were talking about I seemed to understand exactly how frustrated and agitated this fellow was feeling. Then the next thing I knew, I was off flying again. This time, I found myself flying around and around a New York skyscraper, which was fun. But then I stopped in mid-air by a window on one of the higher floors and looked in to see a woman crying. What was she crying about, I wondered? I saw a letter in her hand. I couldn't read it all, but I saw enough to know that her husband had just left her. So much pain, anguish and anger were flowing through her – and I could feel that too. It was as though it was happening to me. Then two small children came into my vision, and I saw them consoling her. All of a sudden, this wasn't so much fun anymore. And with that thought, I found myself bolting upright in my tent, breathing heavily and covered in sweat. I thought to myself that that was quite the dream. I looked around, yes, I was in my tent, zipped up in my sleeping bag. I laid back down and tried to go to sleep again, but I couldn't get the images of the restless young man and the sad woman out of my mind. I'd never really paid much attention to my dreams before, but this one stuck with me for days. It was rather unsettling. Then a couple of days later, I heard that voice again. It repeated what it said before... *there's more to me than the me I see*. But this time, it added that I should look to my dream."

"Did you see anybody that went along with that voice? Or was it only a voice?" I asked. I thought perhaps George had a *friend* that was visiting without a body, the way our *friends* sometimes did.

"No, it was just a voice coming from my gut. That's how I knew it wasn't me talking to myself. But Crow's told me about your transparent friends, so maybe there is a body attached to my voice too. If there is, I'd really like to meet it."

"I have no doubt that you will at some point," I assured George. "So, what happened next?"

"Well, I knew that what the voice was telling me was important, but I also somehow understood that it wanted me to try to figure it out myself. So, I walked and pondered and pondered and walked. I went back to the first rock I'd been sitting on when the bear visited me. I'd felt drawn there, and as I said before, I've learned to listen when I feel drawn to something. After I got settled, the bear actually came out of the bush again. It startled me at first, but I quickly recovered, as I knew it was not there to harm me, but to help me. That bear looked straight at me and told me it sees so much more than what I allow myself to see. Of course, I asked what it is that it sees - to which the bear replied that there are many parts to me, many different personalities or aspects of myself. They're all making different discoveries in the situations they find themselves in. But I still couldn't figure out what it was talking about and told the bear so. It was a while before the bear spoke again, but when it did, it gave me a long narrative, or description, of the way things work. I'm going to shorten it up for you because I want to hear about your experiences too, and not just be the one doing all the talking."

"That's probably a good idea," Malcolm said. "I can tell already that we've got a lot of things we're going to want to talk to you about, but there's only so much we can get into one evening."

George reached for his wine glass and took a sip before answering. "I get that feeling too. It's really nice to have found some like-minded friends. They seem to be few and far between. I think we should toast to new found friendship." We all took our glasses and met each other's eyes as we clinked them together. It was indeed the birth of a great bond.

George put his glass down. "Here's what the bear told me. Basically, we're born into this life with a body, complete with senses, emotions, and a consciousness. Before we were born, however, we chose a particular frame of reference for this life, such as the year, location, social climate, and so forth. This unique framework also uses time, which gives us the ability to have a past, present, and future. Everyone has the same understanding of our structure, without question, as it is the framework we've all chosen to be born into. So far, so good?" George asked us.

"Yes," I answered. "We've been learning something quite similar."

"Good. To continue then, as our life progresses inside this chosen framework, certain situations or experiences come about; different problems or challenges to take part in and hopefully learn from. Having a past, present and future helps with this as they allow you to look back, and forward, to decide if you like the consequences of a particular action. It's important to understand that within this grid there really is no end to the possibilities we can create for ourselves. This kind of structure allows us to learn, discover, and better ourselves while in a physical body. However, we will not be alive in our body forever. The more we grow here, the more we develop who we are after we die."

"Isn't that such a cool idea?" Crow cut in. "Doesn't that just give you a sense of the importance of everything you say and do, and even think?" He'd heard George's story before, so had some time to reflect on this.

"That was indeed my first thought, and I'm pretty sure we're going to come up with more ideas just thinking about that concept," I admitted, looking over at Malcolm, who seemed to be deep in thought. "What are you thinking about?" I asked him.

"Hmmm...I'm thinking about how there is no end to any of us. I get the feeling that this life is not what we grew up thinking it was."

"Too true," George agreed. "But hold on, I'm not done with my story. At this point I was thinking to myself, WOW, I really hope I'm able to remember all of this. I thought maybe the bear was done as he'd been staring at the ocean for a long time. But then he turned his large head towards me and began to speak again. He said there were other types of grids, or frameworks, that existed in other dimensions, and in some of those there is no such thing as time, or space. The senses we have now get replaced with other senses that work in that environment. Different grids are set up to help us understand various aspects of ourselves when we go there."

"That is so cool!" I was astounded.

"Isn't it though? I was wondering to myself why I was being given this knowledge. The bear gave a slight nod of his head at my mental question, and said that it was trying to give me a basic overall picture of how everything works so that I'd be able to understand the fact that time didn't actually exist anywhere else other than here. In fact, it said that all time was simultaneous! It acknowledged that this concept was next to impossible for me to comprehend, but comprehension or not, that's how it is. We are living several parallel lives at once! And that, the bear said, is where my dream comes into play. Apparently, I am both the restless young native man and the distraught woman. They're different aspects of my larger identity, and together we're all working on learning different things – at the same time. I was speechless as I tried to fathom what I'd just been told. The bear got up and ambled around a little bit, sniffing here and sniffing there, and then he slowly walked back into the bush."

"Isn't that an incredible experience? Crow asked Malcolm and I. "Can't you just picture yourself in George's shoes?"

"I suppose so," Malcolm answered cautiously. "I'm still trying to add it to what we've learned to get a sense of the bigger picture. This is a lot of information to absorb in a short time period."

"It is for sure. But I think it'll all fall into place with some contemplation. Tell them what you discovered over time George," Crow requested excitedly.

"Well, needless to say, the bear left me sitting on that rock feeling rather dumbfounded – sort of like you're feeling right now. I spent days examining what the bear told me. After a while, it started to make sense – in fact, it made perfect sense once I learned to park my pre-conditioned rational mind somewhere else."

Crow looked at me and winked. "Sound familiar?"

George ignored our little exchange and kept on. "You are born. You have a body. Your body comes equipped with five senses and definitely no shortage of emotion. And yes, the world we're born into has the appearance of time. It's truly a perfect setting for us to play out our dramas in. But – we will die, and then what? I mean, you have to think about it. It's part of the bigger picture. We're still going to exist after we die, but in a different way. And for me, that's the exciting part. What will we be – where will we be – what will it be like – did we learn what we came here to learn – what will our next challenge be?"

"I think that's so right. We do need to think about that," I said. "But our society really doesn't like the idea of dying. We're scared of it. I know I am. But if it's like your bear is saying, then we don't actually die anyway, so then maybe we don't need to be so scared of it, and really use our time alive to do some good."

"Exactly," George readily agreed. "I believe there's a much larger version of myself on the *other side of life,* and my current life is only one aspect of what the larger me wanted to experience – the native fellow being another aspect, and the same for the distraught woman. We're all part of this bigger self. When that realization swept over me I felt an enormous sense of kinship and support from both of them. I also felt a new sense of purpose – I wanted to help them, and I felt so connected to them that I knew they were helping me in some way too."

"What you're describing sounds similar to reincarnation, but the fact that all time is simultaneous, and that different lives are running in parallel really puts a new spin on that concept, don't you think?" Malcolm mentally tested the theory. "I kind of like that idea."

"I do too, actually. I think you'll find the more you think about it, the more it seems to make things fit better. Anyways, let me finish my story, and then maybe we can have some of that good-looking dessert I saw in the kitchen for a much-needed break?"

"For sure!" I'd been so absorbed in George's story it totally slipped my mind.

"Great. I'll make it real short then. You asked how I came to be in Vancouver, so after all that, I can finally answer you. After my last encounter with the bear I stayed at the coast for another week or two. I wanted to make sure I had it all sorted out in my mind, and to make sure my new concepts about life were strongly entrenched in my mind so that I wouldn't lose them when I went back into society again. I recognized that feeling of being pulled in another direction, so I went with it. I felt I needed to insert myself back into the reality of the world and discover how my new concepts affected my life. So, I packed up and headed for Vancouver, and here I am."

I marveled at how relaxed and at ease George looked right then and there. I also did not want to get up to get the dessert - I wanted to sit and think. But just then Malcolm jumped up off the couch and said, "Okay – break time. Julie, why don't you get the dessert and I'll get another bottle of wine." And that's what we did. I served ample portions of the crisp I'd made, and Malcolm topped our wine glasses up, although we hadn't actually drunk very much – we'd been too absorbed in George's astonishing story.

"Don't you find it interesting that Malcolm and I also started having dreams lately?" I asked no one in particular as I put my empty plate on the coffee table. "Could this be some sort of coincidence?"

"I don't believe in coincidences anymore," George quickly spoke up between bites, using his fork as a pointer. "Everything in life is so intertwined. It may look like a coincidence on the surface, but that's merely because we don't know how to delve into the way everything works."

"You're probably right, George," I said. "I know Crow's told you about our camping experiences and all the discoveries we've made because of them. I have to say that it's really a treat to be able to include another understanding person in our discussions. Most of the people we know would declare our experiences to be rubbish. Or they would distance themselves from us, being adamant that their way of thinking was the proper way to think, and that we must be going nuts."

"Yeah, but don't forget there's plenty of people who *do* get it and *do* want to hear about it. Those are the ones to talk to. There's never any need to justify yourself to anyone else. If someone doesn't get it, then just move on to someone who does."

"Good point," Malcolm confirmed. "I'd sure like to find a way to spread the *create your own reality* idea. That one concept has truly changed the way I look at my life now. Realizing I can't blame others for where I am gives me a real sense of power and desire to change my own situation, should I want to. What a tool to give someone! Can you imagine a world where there were no victims? Where everyone took ownership of their own predicaments, and then worked to make their own life better, without expecting anything from anyone else? What a different world that would be!"

"Isn't that the truth!" George agreed. "I wasn't told those exact words, but that's a concept I've come to believe is at the heart of everything. I look around at my life and see what I like, and pat myself on the back for creating it. And when I see things I don't like I search for a solution that I can bring about. We *do* live in a practical world after all, and I think there are lots of solutions out there – we just need to recognize the problem and then go find and implement the solution. We're only ever stuck if we let ourselves be stuck. Plus, I don't expect anything from anybody, and I know I have a lot of power to bring about what it is I want, but first I have to know what it is that I want. I think a lot of people have never really thought about what it is that *they* think, or even want – instead, they listen to what society thinks, or friends think, or what the expectations of the family are. You need to know what it is that YOU think and what YOU want, and then go for it, never mind all the noise we're bombarded with every day."

"That can be tough to do, though. I know I needed some help from Bluedon to help me sort out my feelings towards my commute. He helped me realize how simply changing my perceptions can alter the way I feel about my life too. It was such helpful information, which I've been putting to good use."

"Life is really such a rich tapestry once you can begin to look at it like that," I mused, tucking my legs up under me on the couch. "Especially when you start to add in your other lives living in other dimensions – all at the same time apparently! And then there's what happens after you die!" All of our attention was completely immersed in the terrific conversation we were having about our discoveries and the ways in which they could change our lives, and the lives of others. As the evening progressed we lost complete track of time – and the solid reality of our living room, which made it very easy for our transparent friends to sneak up on us!

11

GEORGE MEETS OUR FRIENDS

"Don't worry if people think you're crazy. You are crazy. You have the kind of intoxicating insanity that lets other people dream outside of the lines and become who they're destined to be." **Jennifer Elisabeth**

"It's simply so nice to see you all together like this! We felt drawn to drop in and join you for a bit!"

"W-h-o-a!" George exclaimed wide-eyed. "Is that your friends I just heard?"

"Yes, it is George," I laughed. "Let's do the introductions," although it was obvious who was who since they looked so similar to each of us.

"Your robes!" George gasped. "They almost look like the particles I saw that day on the beach; except they're like long strands instead of particles?" George couldn't take his eyes off the three of them. I could understand why: they truly were a magnificent sight.

"You like our robes?" Omar questioned, but didn't wait for an answer. Instead he took up a piece of the fabric in his hands and held it out for George to have a closer look. "You see, it's not really fabric at all – it's simply strands of light energy all woven together using electromagnetic forces to hold it in place."

George reached out to touch it, but his fingers went right through! "No way!" he exclaimed. "My fingers are tingling!" He looked up at Omar for an explanation.

"Yes, it would tingle to you – but not to us. In no way is it harmful; only beneficial. Do you feel its energy?"

"I do! There's this gentle wave running through me."

Omar smiled at George. "Perhaps you will wear a robe such as this one day. I think it would suit your personality just fine."

"Holy!" was all George could say, but his face took on a glow of pure bliss.

I told Omar, Bluedon, and Griffin to come and sit down, which they did, gathering their brilliant robes about themselves so that they wouldn't take up too much room. Ours was not one of those large polished magazine-type living rooms, so there wasn't a lot of space. But what we did have was a very intimate and cozy setting, so we all felt relaxed and comfortable once our friends were seated – even though they were sitting on nothing but thin air!

I was wondering if I should offer a glass of wine to each of our newcomers, but then decided I wouldn't, as I didn't think they could drink anything. I'd forgotten, once again, that Omar knew exactly what I was thinking.

"I would love a glass of wine," Omar said, much to my surprise. "When I was in physical form, I truly savored the taste of a good glass of wine."

I think all four of us must have wondered in bewildered mental unison if he could actually eat and drink.

"Sadly, no, to answer your questions. I can portray a body to you, but as you already know, it's not really the same as the solid physical body the four of you have, complete with all the workings of taste buds and a stomach. But I do have a memory – that has never left me, so I remember the taste, and will now enjoy my glass of wine vicariously, through you," Omar said as he looked straight at me and smiled.

It suddenly dawned on me that these three were privy to whatever we were doing in our lives – at *any* time. And there were definitely things I felt I'd rather keep private, as you can imagine. That had never occurred to me before. But before I could ask my question, Omar helped me out.

"Don't worry, Julie. I respect your privacy very much and do not eavesdrop unless I feel either your strong desire to have contact with me, or a certain vibrational level, such as you've achieved tonight. That is what draws my attention to you. I do have a life too, you know. It's not like yours in many ways, but there are similarities in that we all want to learn and develop."

That certainly made me feel better.

"I have a question I'd really like to ask you guys, now that you're here," Crow began. "Since you see everything from such a different vantage point than us, are you able to explain in a simple and understandable way how everything works? We've been trying to work it out on our own, but hearing it from you guys would go a long way to giving us more of a solid platform to land ourselves on, or take off from. I think I'd find that *really* helpful?"

They didn't look at each other, and they never spoke, but I was certain they were communicating. It was Griffin who finally answered, rather well, I might add. He definitely had our undivided attention. Crow was asking for something we all needed: a solid explanation that we could anchor ourselves to.

"That is an excellent question, and a really big one as you suggested. We have conferred with each other and feel we should be able to give you a basic structure to start with. Think of what I'm about to explain as an unadorned Christmas tree. Once you can first establish that vision solidly in your minds, you'll be able to hang as many lights and ornaments on it as you want."

"Oooh, I like that idea. I can picture it already," Crow said.

"I think the best place to start is with your birth, because you were all born into a physical body. No one will dispute that. This body comes complete with the five senses you are so very familiar with, a vast array of emotions to draw from, and the ability to grow older in time. However, in order to grow, a body requires certain things, such as food, as without food, it will die. Bodies also like to be warm. A body cannot survive exposure to freezing temperatures for very long. So right away, certain requirements must be met, simply because you have a physical body. And this sets the stage for life, as you know it. Are you with me so far?"

Yes, yes, we were all following along quite nicely, we eagerly told him.

"Now, obviously, a baby cannot get its own food, or wrap itself up in a nice cozy blanket to keep warm, so a caretaker must be given to this baby. And that's where the whole drama begins. You see, before a personality is born as a baby, it chooses who it wants for a caretaker. I'm sure you remember us telling you that you choose the family you're born into. Those choices are not made willy-nilly, but instead with a distinct purpose in mind. One of the things your personality does in between lives is figure out what it wants to work on – what it wants to develop. Coming to live in the world you currently find yourself in, is like entering a huge theatrical company that has every prop imaginable. Any play you wish to create or participate in is yours for the making – and I mean *anything*. You might even choose beforehand a few events to happen in your life in order to help you with your development. However, there is *always* free will, so those events may happen, and then again, they may not."

"But what if our parents don't want us?" Crow blurted out. "I'm pretty sure mine didn't want me."

"Ah, yes...well, parents actually have to agree to the birth too; this is not a one-sided affair, you see."

"Then how can such an agreement be made when the 'baby to be' and the prospective parents are on either side of life?" Crow asked, somewhat confused.

"That's a good question," Griffin said to Crow. "The answer is that the negotiations take place in your dreamworld, a place you both go to for such discussions. The contract must be freely agreed upon by both parties, so there is no place for *woe is me* in this bond. You chose your parents, and your parents agreed. Period."

"Wow! I guess that answers that question," Crow acknowledged.

"You can also come back here with personalities you've known before, and been through many plays with. You agree ahead of time to help each other out, in whatever way that's needed. But remember, as we said before, there are no karmic debts to be repaid. It's simply a matter of experiencing a situation from all angles. That's how you come to truly understand a situation. There's a great deal of accuracy to your saying of *do unto others as you would have them do unto you,* because at some point, in one of your existences, it will indeed be done unto you."

Griffin was doing a great job of laying this out, but I was experiencing some doubts about what he was saying. He was so matter of fact about it all, like it should be easy to grasp, but it was quite different from what I'd learned growing up. A part of me felt skeptical, and even wanted to deny the possibility of the information he was giving. I glanced at Malcolm and wondered if he was feeling the same way, but I couldn't tell. Crow and George looked like they were with Griffin all the way.

"I'm going to interrupt here, Griffin," Omar said kindly. "I feel Julie is experiencing some doubts, which is understandable given the society you live in. Would you care to voice what you're feeling, Julie?"

"You're right! I do have some doubts, and I feel bad that I'm having them because I fully realize that you guys know what you're talking about. And it's not like I want these thoughts either, but I have to admit that they're there. A part of me wants to say there's no way, or ask you guys to prove it, but another part of me knows you can't prove the stuff you're talking about. I've got a real tussle going on inside that will not quiet down."

"I'm actually glad you've been able to voice that concern. It's very common upon first hearing this sort of information," Omar replied. "Your worldly personal ego wants to take care of you, and it's scared to let go of the norm that it's worked so hard to perfect all these years - so it rises up inside you to tell you to 'forget that crap and let's continue on as we were before, as that was working just fine.' However, there's another intuitive part of you that wants this information because it knows that carrying on as before will not turn out okay further down the road. So, you end up with two battling portions of yourself."

"So, what do I do?" I asked, feeling quite frustrated with myself.

"You can start by having your intuitive side reassure the ego that it will not get thrown aside, but instead will be greatly needed for incorporating this new way of being into your daily life. How quickly you manage to comfort your ego depends on how entrenched it is in commanding your life. In truth, it might indeed be overworked and would appreciate a little help from other parts of your *whole self*." Omar explained. "Try to keep that in mind as Griffin continues on with his explanation. It won't happen immediately, but you can work on it, and eventually I have no doubt that your concerns will subside."

"Thanks, Omar! I hope it works."

"Are we good to continue then?" Griffin looked at us, but didn't wait for an answer. He already knew what we were thinking, so he dove right back in where he'd left off. "With the negotiations completed, you are born into a rough sketch of the play you've decided to take part in. Your dense, fleshy body has certain requirements and demands that must be addressed. As I said before, you must eat, and you must keep yourself warm. How are you going to accomplish these two basic requirements? Everyone is extremely different, as you'll see if you let your imagination go - some eat food that supports the body, some eat food that has no nutrition at all, some build huge houses for their protection, some live in tents, some have closets full of enough clothes to keep a hundred people warm, and some have only the clothes on their back. I'm sure you get the drift of what I'm saying. Those two things alone offer no end of choices a person can make - or beliefs a person can develop.

"And that takes me to the next point. As you grow, you develop your worldly beliefs: you're not born with them. The knowledge you had before you were born gets left on the other side of birth. That way, you get the complete experience while living *this* life."

"Julie and I were just talking about our beliefs the other day," Malcolm interjected. "We came to the conclusion that we layer them on as we grow without even realizing we're doing it. Were we close to getting that right?"

"I'm glad to hear that you've been thinking about it! Yes, that is what I'm saying. To start with, and *generally* speaking, you usually end up believing what your parents believe. As you grow, you pick up the basic mass beliefs that your civilization has. You then get taught many different ways of thinking in your schools, plus you pick up ideas from television, magazines, and let's not forget your new tool – the internet. Experiences that you have growing up will be perceived through *your* growing beliefs, which will either strengthen them, or make you question them. By the time you're an adult you are one walking mass of beliefs and expectations. You venture into your adult life invisibly surrounded by them, like a transparent safety net."

Once again, Griffin paused and examined each one of us individually. I liked the way he was layering the information on – one layer at a time – like an onion. It was making a lot of sense to me too, now that my ego seemed to be less up in arms.

Griffin had a big smile on his face as he looked over at Bluedon and Omar, and happily said, "I think they're getting it! I believe I shall continue on. Now, if you don't realize that the situation you currently find yourself in - right now, right where you are - is because of your own beliefs, then you will not think to question them. You won't even realize you have them. You would continue to jump from one unhappy situation to another, never truly understanding why your life seems so screwed up. Then the blame game starts, creating a downward spiral that can be difficult to emerge from. That's the part we'd truly like to see change, as it's so unnecessary."

Oh dear. I knew people like that. In fact, I was one of them until we went on our holiday and met our new friends and discovered a new way of looking at things. It would be so great to be able to help others out of any cycle they might feel trapped in, I thought to myself.

"As a society, what are the beliefs? As an individual, what are your beliefs? I have no time for that, some would say. I have to eat. I have to keep warm. I have to make money. I have to answer my messages. I have to have a house, a car, a boat, lots of friends. I have to keep up with the neighbors. I have to go along with the norm because, after all, doesn't everybody?" Griffin was very wound up. He paused for a breath. This was obviously a topic that was very dear to him.

Then more calmly, he carried on, "But, we are delighted to see the three, and now four of you, starting to question your beliefs, or at least acknowledge their existence and consequences. This means more than you could possibly know right now. We will always be right beside you in your endeavor. I want to make a suggestion - write down your beliefs as they come to you, and then challenge yourself to decide if you want to keep them or not. It might not be a bad idea to start a *belief book*. It's my *belief* that you will be quite surprised at what you discover about yourself and how it will change your life. By writing things down, you can always come back at a later date to see your progress. In other words - get to know yourself as you are the only one who can."

Then Omar added, "Just because we've chosen to no longer reincarnate in your dimension, doesn't mean we're done working with our beliefs. However, we understand the true power of thoughts, emotions, beliefs, and expectations. Basically, we're working on similar issues, but at a different level and at a different speed. Our beliefs create instant realities, whereas a time lag has been built into your existence on earth. Your civilization might also want to broaden its definition of reality so that these ideas can become accepted conscious knowledge, and not frowned upon. Then you can start to knowingly use them, like we do in our dimension, to create the type of magnificent world that I'm sure you all want to live in."

"I'm thinking that could take a while," Malcolm sighed. "Do you think you could explain to me how this actually works? How does what we believe in actually end up creating our reality? Is there some sort of physical mechanism for this?"

"That's an excellent question," Bluedon answered. "I think we can add that bit to what Griffin has already told you as it will end up giving you an even broader base to stand on. Unfortunately, most of your scientists have not figured this one out yet. They're going in many different directions – all hoping to be the one who discovers the golden key to *how it all works*. However, some are on the right track. Certain experiments have shown that how the observer thinks about something affects the attributes of what's being measured: now that's a very big clue.

"You see, your scientists like to measure this and measure that, always recording their measurements and drawing conclusions based on those measurements. But they're working with the *physical* world and their *physical* senses, and *physical* instruments that measure *physical* parameters. However, look at us – we're definitely not physical." Bluedon held out both arms to the side. "How would you measure us? What would you use?"

None of us had any answers, and he obviously wasn't expecting one as he carried on. "But we do exist - don't we? Let me ask you then - where is our dimension if it's not physical? Current scientific beliefs, or religious beliefs, for that matter, currently have no accepted place for us. But you know that we're indeed here talking to you. We're not a figment of your imagination. Like I said, your definition of reality is ripe for a major overhaul. Allowing consciousness to actually have a place in your sciences is definitely a step in the right direction, and I know there are some who are seriously considering this, but they're like a small snowplow pushing against a large bank of sodden old snow that does not want to give way. Consciousness has been safely tucked away in the psychological or spiritual realm, which has always been regarded as a place to stay well clear of if you want to be taken seriously by your intelligent scientific peers. Well, guess what - it's time to let it out of the closet, and set a place for it at the table, as it's not going away!"

"I find it exciting to know that consciousness is actually being acknowledged by some scientists!" George said. "I wasn't aware of that."

"It is exciting indeed. But let's get back to Malcolm's question of *how* it all actually works. For now, let's just say that there are many types of extremely tiny objects, or particles that have not been discovered yet by your present civilization. Actually, let's use the word *units* instead, simply because they have the ability to be whatever they want to be; particles or waves. You must also understand that they are all *aware* of each other. In your terms, you would say they're telepathically connected. It's these tiny units that do the work of taking your thoughts and turning them into specific patterns. Your thoughts are not just airy-fairy illusive things – they're physical; they don't just float away and disappear. The patterns created by your thoughts trigger certain electromagnetic mechanisms, which also have not yet been discovered. Utilizing the universal law that like attracts like, these mechanisms do the work of bringing about physical reality. So, you see - you truly do create your own reality. Now, that's an extremely simplified short answer. The long answer would take a great deal of time and understanding of knowledge that you don't possess at the moment. You're simply not ready for it yet. Does that answer your question well enough, though?"

"Yes, you definitely answered my question and gave me a lot more at the same time!" Malcolm replied. "But I actually do get the gist of what you're saying, and it does make sense to me at some level of my being. So, thank you!"

I'd never told anyone before, but I always had the feeling that so-called *empty space* was full of *something* that was busy making everything happen, and that it just hadn't been discovered yet. I felt vindicated! It would appear my hunch had been right all along. However, I had no idea how I seemed to *know* this, nor could I even pretend to explain how it worked.

"I have a question," George piped up.

"Ask away," Omar offered.

"Do I have a look-alike helper as well? Does everyone?"

"I guess we could have brought your great furry bear along with us, but we didn't think Julie would like to find a bear in her living room - even a well behaved one."

"You got that right!" I exclaimed. As I said before, our living room is small and we were already kind of squished with the seven of us.

"But in all seriousness," Omar continued, looking at George, "everyone has help from more than just themselves. We appear to Julie, Malcolm and Crow as their look-a-likes because that's an image they can believe and accept. It has credibility for them. Your helping energy essence came in the form of a bear, because that's something you have deep respect for. I'm not so sure you would have listened as well to a mosquito in your ear, for example. It's different for everyone. But all of us, including your bear, can appear in any shape or form we want to. And we often do, depending on the person we're trying to get through to. But, and this is an important but, we cannot appear to someone who doesn't believe that we exist, or that we can help, or that we have the ability to reach them. It can be frustrating for us...like talking to a wall, sometimes. Actually, the wall would probably hear us sooner than some people. Again, it's all in one's beliefs, you see."

"Are you saying that I'll only get helping energy from the bear image? Or could that energy show up differently?" George asked.

"What do you think? What's your belief?" Omar questioned.

"Well, I'd like to believe I could find that helping energy in many other forms, as I'm not always in a place where it's convenient for a bear to appear."

Suddenly, a rather large caramel colored bear with a massive head did indeed show up in our living room – on the coffee table of all places! But only briefly as it quickly morphed into a woman with a beautiful face - although after a few moments, she also looked like she could be a handsome man; both features were definitely there.

This new helping energy slowly became cloaked in a light energy robe that was as violet as that word can describe that color! It was a color so delicate and fresh that you could sink right into it!

"Do you like this image better George?" she asked…or was it a he?

"I'd have to say I do, at least while I'm in the city," George answered slowly, somewhat in awe as he watched her jump down from the coffee table. "But you know, when I'm in natural surroundings, I kind of like the bear image better."

"Does that mean we can change the looks of you guys, too?" Crow asked, looking over at Griffin.

"It's all in your beliefs - remember?" Griffin countered with a big grin. I think he knew what Crow was about to say.

"Okay, so I believe that my helping energy can come in any form - and I'd really like it to be a beautiful woman – no offence Griffin," Crow said, closing his eyes to make his wish.

"Maybe next time, buddy - be on the look-out for it," Griffin laughed. "But for now, we're going to leave you to absorb everything we've told you. We'll be back another time, but all of you should have learned from this little display to keep your eyes peeled, and your minds open for us. We may appear at any time, and as anything – with a body or without a body. It's the *feeling* that will always be there. Learn to trust the *feeling*."

And with that, they all vanished – leaving just the four of us sitting in the living room, feeling a bit perplexed - especially George.

"Man, I wish I could have talked more to my helping energy, even if just to thank her, or him, for all I've been taught. I don't even know how to address such a being. I can't say *he* or *she*, and I certainly don't want to say *it*!"

"You're right," I added. "I can't think of a word that fits either. Maybe you'll get a name the next time we all meet."

By now it was well into the wee hours of the morning. We talked for another half hour or so about what we'd just experienced, but our heads were going numb from what felt like information overload. So, we made a plan to meet up with each other every Friday night at our place, and to start a belief book for things that happened during the week. Then we said our good-byes. As soon as the door closed behind Crow and George, I headed straight to the bedroom to climb into bed, and hoped I'd drop off instantly to sleep. I kissed Malcolm good-night and promptly turned over to get comfy. That's when my mind woke up and started thinking; not in any orderly way, unfortunately. It jumped from here to there and back again. The more I found out, the more I wanted to know, but I felt like I couldn't keep up with the steady stream of new concepts that paraded before me. I was experiencing a great deal of confusion right along with my enthusiasm. I hoped that if I did fall asleep, which I knew I eventually would, that my night brain would help me insert this new way of thinking into my old standard life patterns, which seemed to be hanging on for dear life. The old paradigm was obviously very ingrained and stubborn in me. I was going to be a work in progress, for sure.

12

BELIEFS & INNER SENSES

"I love keeping an open mind. It's liberating to know the universe and our existence are not limited to my understanding."
Izey Victoria Odiase

When you begin to take notice of your daily experiences, and then dissect them, you discover that *life* happens every minute of every day. There are countless opportunities for reflection if you care to look for them.

Malcolm and I spent a great deal of time discussing an incident he was drawn into at work during the week. One of his co-workers had made a computing error and tried to cover it up with a little white lie by blaming technology and those *darn computers.* But Malcolm knew it was the co-worker that had knowingly made the error. Malcolm kept working, but he could hear the fellow tell their boss his little white lie.

"I'm telling you, Julie, I couldn't get it out of my mind," Malcolm confessed when he got home. "You tell me - are white lies okay? I mean this one didn't hurt anyone, so why can't I let it go?"

"If it was me, I know I'd have told the truth. Afterall, what's wrong with owning up to the truth anyways?" I hoped my thoughts on the topic would help Malcolm sort it out.

"That's exactly what I was thinking. I discovered I've got this *thing* or this *feeling* inside me that tells me if something is okay or not. My body seems to know if something's right or wrong. I think everybody has this ability, but some people choose to ignore it, or think that as long as they don't tell anybody else, who would know? But of course, *they* know, and *they* are the ones it affects the most. Maybe not today, maybe not tomorrow, but eventually it's going to surface in some form or the other."

"Yeah, it's like Griffin said," I added. "You have to experience all sides of an event – the one doing, and the one done to."

"So, what do you think I should do? That's my dilemma now. Am I supposed to forget about it, which seems to be impossible at the moment, or should I tell my boss?" Malcolm asked as he turned to go sit down on the couch, but then quickly turned back to me and added, "But why would I want to get the guy in trouble? I grew up under the *don't tattle* rule, so I don't know what to do!" Malcolm flopped down on the couch looking rather worn out over this one tiny incident. I came over to join him, not at all sure how to console him.

Before our trip, Malcolm would most likely have told me about this event in passing, as it was one of those things that gets mentioned when two people share what happened in their work day, although I know we would not have spent much time talking about it. But we found ourselves still discussing it in the evening – trying to sort out all the ramifications of something that at first seemed so insignificant. Stepping back and examining an issue from all sides was something we were learning to do. We both felt it was wrong, and if we do create our own reality, why would we allow ourselves to be part of something that we thought was wrong? Then we started talking about the many things in life we do not agree with and feel are wrong. However, most of them are things we seemingly have very little control over – like wars. But this one was something Malcolm could take action on, so we kept trying to work it out.

"You know what I'm wondering?" I asked, as something important just dawned on me. "This seems like such a minor incident, but as we've discovered, it actually isn't. So, who draws the line between what's classified as a *major* or a *minor* incident?"

"Hmmm...that's a great question. I'd have to say that there isn't any difference - it's *all* important. But maybe if it affects a lot of people we think of it as something major? I don't know, but I'm starting to see how all events can create positive change if you're willing to look at them."

"I'm going to get our belief book," I said as I jumped up to grab it from the kitchen counter where I'd left it. "I think we should write some of these discoveries down for our Friday discussion." I brought it back and got comfy on the couch again, leaning up against Malcolm's warm shoulder. "This is so exciting! It's our first belief! What should we say?"

"Let's start with *lying is not okay*. We don't want to lie to anybody, and we do not want to be lied to. It's not being respectful of others or ourselves."

"I like that!" I wrote it down. "I'd like to add how important it is to act in a way that we are proud of, which definitely means not lying in my books. How we feel about ourselves is more important than how anyone else thinks of us. That's a great belief too, don't you think?"

"It is for sure, and it's what Omar was telling us as well, if you remember. I do have another belief," Malcolm said as he reached back and put his arm around me. "I believe it's time to go to bed as my tired head needs to figure out what kind of action I'm going to take tomorrow at work. I'm actually hoping for some advice or direction from a dream tonight. Now that's something I never thought I'd hear myself say!"

We snuggled in bed for a while and then Malcolm began a night of tossing and turning. At one point I could tell he was definitely dreaming as he was talking about something, but I couldn't make out what he was saying. Whatever it was, it must have worked because he did indeed wake up knowing exactly what he was going to do! I was beginning to realize how important our sleep time is. It would seem that a mind does not need to sleep, and with our bodies out of commission, it can get some real work done.

As soon as Malcolm woke up he told me he'd found his answer. He was going to have a little private talk with his co-worker about the whole situation. "I'm going to tell him that by telling his lie the only one he's adversely affecting is himself. And then I'll ask him if he really wants to do that."

"Oohh...I want to know how he reacts to that," I said, rolling over onto my back and stretching from head to toe. "You know, that's really cool that you just woke up knowing what to do. That's a resource we'll definitely have to use again.

Then we both got out of bed, got ready, and headed in different directions to work. But that night, as soon as Malcolm walked in the door, I wanted to know. "What happened with your co-worker?" I asked excitedly.

Malcolm laughed and came up to me, engulfing my tiny body in his strong arms. "I need my hug first!" he said. I was impatient, but first things first. So as soon as he released me, I asked again.

"Okay, okay, I'll tell you," he replied as he went to the fridge to get a beer, and then reflected on the event a bit before answering. "Actually, he looked surprised as soon as I took him aside, but when I started telling him that he was only hurting himself by lying to our boss about his error, I think he was too shocked to even try to dispute the fact that he'd lied. I think he knew he'd been caught. He basically just stared at me, not knowing what to say. So, I nodded at him, turned and went into my office."

"Wow! Did he say anything at all to you during the rest of the day?"

"No, he didn't. But I did notice him looking at me differently a couple of times. I thought I saw a look of respect in his eyes. And I have to say, that felt really good. But you know what felt even better? After I told him, I had such a wonderful feeling of ease inside me that lasted the whole day. I *knew* it was completely the right thing to do. I really liked that feeling."

"Remember the feeling! I think it was Griffin that said that. This is getting to be fun!" I declared triumphantly.

Friday night came surprisingly quickly. Crow and George came over after supper, and we headed straight into the living room to get comfortable with a glass of wine, and our feet up on the coffee table. After a bit of small talk, we started talking about the experiences each of us had during the week. Malcolm talked about the lying incident, and how we'd worked it through and then put it into our belief book. Everyone easily agreed that lying was out of the question, no matter the consequences of telling the truth. So, Crow and George put that particular belief into their books too. We'd found a belief that didn't need changing, so we clinked our glasses in celebration. However, we were soon to discover that not all beliefs were so easy to discover, or work with.

Crow brought up the unusual topic of homeless people living and begging on the street. Whoa! I immediately knew this issue was not going to be as simple as truth versus lies. It took us all aback at first. "Why this topic? I asked.

"Well, I was driving to work one day, and had to stop for a red light. Right beside me on the intersection was a homeless person holding a sign asking for money. As soon as I glanced at him, we made eye contact. What I saw in his eyes really grabbed me in the gut."

"I've had that happen to me too," Malcolm reassured Crow. "Did you give him some money?"

"No, I didn't. Actually, I'm not proud of this, but it's the truth, and the truth has to be acknowledged. My first thought was c'mon light, turn green so I can keep going, and I told myself not to look at him again. The second thought I had was that the guy probably wasn't as bad off as he made himself look, and quite possibly made as much money as I did in a day. And the third thought that crossed my mind was that this guy shouldn't be getting in the way of traffic like this – couldn't he read the sign he was standing in front of that said panhandling was illegal? The last thought that crossed my mind, just as the light finally turned green, was that I should remember to give some money to the shelter to help out," Crow paused and hung his head in guilt. "Let me tell ya', I don't feel very good about my reactions when I look back at them."

"Yeah, but I've had some of the very same reactions, Crow," Malcolm sighed, hoping to give him a bit of comfort. "I think a lot of people do, so I don't think you're too far out of the ordinary here. Homelessness is a really big, and really complicated matter."

"Well, I certainly haven't come to terms with it in any way, shape or form, so I'd really like it if our little group could figure something out about it to help ease my mind. I think it brought back some buried memories of when I was homeless. Those were tough days. And maybe since I managed to pull myself out of it, I figure others should too? I don't know, but I do know that I'm not happy with my reaction, and I'm especially not happy with feeling guilty, which I most definitely do."

"I understand how you're feeling Crow," George said encouragingly. "Now that we've pulled this issue out from underneath the rug we've all conveniently swept it under, I have to say that I feel guilty too. I've travelled all over the world ever since high school, as you know, and I never had to beg. I always managed to find a job. But then again, I always believed I would. It never even occurred to me to stand on a corner and beg for money. I never expected anyone to give me something I didn't work for. And I made sure I stayed away from the drug scene as I saw way too many that developed problems because of it. Consequently, I've never felt much empathy for the homeless either. But maybe that's wrong. Afterall, who hasn't had some bad luck in their life? A helping and caring hand is always appreciated. I think I've been a bit callous in this area."

"I'm going to join the club too," I confessed, raising my hand. "I have to admit that my reaction is to basically ignore the whole issue, which does not make me proud of myself either. Whenever I go by someone on the street asking for money, I try not to look at them. I walk by as though they're not even there, and then feel bad for the next block, until I manage to justify my actions by saying I'll give more to the missions in the area, but then I don't. I usually run into these guys on my break when I don't have much time to stop and talk, so I just walk by. Maybe I could at least nod and say hello as I go by, but that doesn't seem to be much of an answer either. I'm glad you brought this up Crow. It's obviously a sensitive issue for all of us."

"Wait a minute here," Malcolm cut in all of a sudden. You could tell from the look on his face that a lightbulb had switched on in his head. "Haven't we just been learning about creating our own reality?"

"Well, yes, we have. What have you got?" I answered, looking at him expectantly. I recognized that look of discovery on his face and I knew he'd come up with something good.

"Clearly that must pertain to others too – not just to us. As I understand it, if you are a human being living on this earth, then that rule applies to you too. I don't believe there can be any exceptions. Which means that the homeless must have created their reality too, and for a reason, don't you think?"

"I think you're right," Crow admitted as he eagerly sprang up off the couch and started pacing – head down and hands behind his back. "Let's expand on this idea."

Malcolm had more to say to he quickly continued. "It's like Griffin was explaining to Crow about how he grew up in an abusive family. Everyone has free will, but there are some situations we *choose* before we're born - specifically to have those experiences. Being homeless would undoubtedly create an opportunity to either overcome that type of life – like you did Crow – or to learn something from living in that type of environment. They must have chosen it! If we can think of it this way, we don't need to feel sorry for the homeless. In fact, I feel a great deal of respect now for anyone who's in that environment. Those can't be easy challenges to have. I wonder if in a previous life they were ridiculously rich, or looked down upon the poor. Then in this lifetime they chose to experience the other end of wealth versus poverty. What do you think?"

"My first thought is that your explanation is a bit too simple and a bit too hard-hearted," I replied thoughtfully, "but as I think about it, I believe you could be right. In fact, I think you are right. And you know what? I think the homeless life would allow for a great deal more understanding and knowledge of humanity than being wealthy. Talk about opposite types of experiences!"

"That's for sure," Malcolm agreed. "Not just for the homeless, but for everyone they meet – including us."

"You know, the next time I go by someone looking for a handout, I'm going to do my best to see them from that perspective, and look them in the eye and show some respect and empathy for them," I vowed. "What they're going through can't be easy, and only they know why they chose it. Next lifetime, it could be you or me. How remarkable! I'm actually looking forward to crossing paths with them now. And that all stems from examining our beliefs about homelessness, and changing our perception of that type of situation!"

Crow was still pacing, looking very much deep in thought. All of a sudden he stopped short, and turned to face us excitedly. "You know where this is leading, don't you?" But we all knew him well enough to know that his train of thought was sometimes difficult to follow, so we let him continue with his breakthrough. "This means that poverty is not going away – no matter what we do to get rid of it! How could it go away if we need to be able to experience this type of situation? It's a script that needs to be available for those that choose to act in that particular play. And if that's the case for poverty, then it has to be the case for any kind of seemingly unhappy situations we have on this planet of ours!"

"*Very* good," we heard. "You've discovered a significant and far-reaching truth."

We glanced around the room but could see no one.

"Sounds like Griffin, but I don't see anybody. Where are you?" Crow asked looking around.

Out of the blue we saw four bodies slowly materialize out of shimmering particles, bit by bit, starting at their heads all the way down to their feet, which happened to be standing on our big coffee table! Holy cow, I thought to myself! It was one thing to have them simply appear in our space and talk to us, but to watch a sparkling body materialize in segments was another thing. It was like a very colorful science fiction movie unfolding in the middle of our living room. How did they do that, I wondered? And of course, they answered my thought as easily as if I'd spoken it out loud.

"Just a little display to broaden the mind, Julie," Bluedon said. "We can dematerialize and rematerialize any portion we want to. It's actually not difficult at all, considering we're made up of tiny particles. You'll understand after you pass over to this side because you're made up of the same thing. But until then, I have a feeling you'll want to keep your bodies intact and solid. Not to say that you couldn't do this if you wanted to, but I think we'll just leave that for much, much later."

We knew these guys, so it shouldn't have been a shock, but it was anyway. They nimbly jumped down from the coffee table – their light robes shooting out rays of color in all directions as they did so. "Can we sit down and join you?" Omar innocently asked.

"Yes, yes, of course you can. You guys never cease to amaze me with your capabilities and your knowledge." I said, shaking my head in awe.

George was staring at his new friend, who appeared as a human instead of the bear. Thank goodness too, as they would never have all fit on the coffee table. "You're every bit as beautiful and majestic as the bear," he quietly said. "Do you have a name too?"

George was answered with a blissful glorious smile. "My chosen earth name is Kodiak. I like that name as I think it suits me – so that's what you can call me," Kodiak replied, continuing to look directly at George. "And thank you for the compliment. I like to show the best characteristics of males and females. I hope that doesn't confuse you. I'm not an 'it' either, so thank you for not calling me that. The English language is really quite limiting, as you can see."

"That makes sense," George acknowledged with a grateful smile. "Kodiak – like the special bear up in the arctic. I like that name! I'm assuming you can read my thoughts as well?"

"I certainly can - and have been doing so for a long time. I must say, you have figured out a great deal over the years, and I'm delighted to finally be an acknowledged presence to you, as there is much more to discover. It will be exciting to do it together."

"I'm thrilled about it too," George eagerly declared, and then continued talking as though he'd never stop. "And I'm happy to know I have a true source for guidance when I need it. It's a bit scary, but also quite exhilarating. I wake up looking forward to every day. I find I'm optimistic most of the time, and I look at people differently too. After all, we're all playing the same game and following the same rules, don't you think? We've all got a physical body, so why not explore what comes with this type of life, especially since we chose it to begin with. I find it fascinating to reflect on the multitude of attributes we, or others, might have chosen to work on this time around. And since it appears that it's only our body that dies, then why would we be worried about dying? That fear runs very deep for most of us. But the part of us that goes on living is who we truly are, so why not use this life to thoroughly experience what we came for - isn't that what it's all about?"

Kodiak laughed. "For someone who is typically fairly reserved, you certainly have a great deal to say!" We could actually see George blush. "Don't worry George, our meeting has been a long time coming, so it's understandable. And what you have said is accurate indeed. No one needs to be fearful of dying. It's going to happen to everyone who was born, which is all of you. However, the you that *is* you cannot possibly die, so why not try to let the worry go and enjoy living? It's really very freeing. There's always change, and that's a good thing. This is something we'll talk more about at some point, but for now we are getting somewhat off-topic, as you had an interesting conversation going about poverty. I believe you had just 'hit the nail on the head' as you say."

Crow had quit pacing and was back sitting on the couch. He started right back where he'd left off, his voice still filled with excitement, and eyes bright as ever. "It seems like a big thing to me. It's not just about poverty, but about any kind of unhappy existence. If those situations didn't exist, how would we be able to experience and learn from those conditions? Our civilization would like to get rid of poverty, but are we trying to get rid of something that can't be gotten rid of? I mean, I'm not saying we should quit trying to help someone in need, but maybe we need to see that situation for what it really is. It's not just the people who are poor that are learning something from it. It's those who have enough to give that are also learning, and people like us having this discussion tonight. I feel like I've learned a lot, but I think there's more I can't quite get to. What do you guys think?" Crow looked at our new friends. We were all curious as to what they would say.

"You've come upon an important discovery for sure," Griffin answered. "But it does kind of hit you in the gut once plainly stated in the open. Just because you know these situations will exist for a long time, doesn't mean you can simply turn your head and say *they chose it - it's not my problem*. Every person on your planet is part of everything else. There is nowhere to walk away. There is no room for thinking *too bad for you, buddy,* and on your own whistling merry way. Poverty affects the poor and the rich, and *everyone* in between. If you know about it, it's affecting you. It provides lessons for everybody to learn from."

"Griffin is right," Bluedon added. "To have a discussion about how you feel about the homeless is a very good start. Now you can appreciate that they chose this situation for what they could learn from it. But you must also understand that they are in *your* life for *your* learning purposes. Maybe it will be you living that life next time, or maybe you already have. Empathy is extremely important. Now I am not saying you need to sell your house and give all your money to the poor. But I am saying that you can't ignore the situation and pretend the homeless don't exist. Do what you can, but more importantly, do it from a position of equality, respect, and understanding. Heart always recognizes heart."

"I like that - *heart recognizes heart*!" I burst out. "It's so simple!" Bluedon had wrapped it up for us in such a nice neat package: it's not going away - it was chosen for learning and developing - do what you can - heart recognizes heart – we're all in this together!

Omar was smiling. "I think you've got it, Julie. But there is more, should you want to carry it further."

"What do you mean?" Crow was curious. "What else is there?"

"Simply that it actually is possible to completely end miserable conditions in your world - no more poverty, no more violence, no more wars, no more grief, no more fear. Wouldn't that be a lovely place to live? But, I don't foresee this happening any time soon when I look at the current state of your world. I do want you to know, though, that it *is* possible. Once everyone has felt and understood all sides of any problem, then that situation will no longer be needed." Omar paused. "Hmmm…I see bewilderment on your faces. Let me give you an example." Omar stood up and walked towards Crow so aggressively that Crow jumped back! We all felt an instinctive sense of fear. "If I walk up to you and punch your lights out, then at some point in one of my lives, I am going to have someone do the same thing to me, as I will need to know how it feels. After each of us experiences both sides, we are done with it. It doesn't have to happen to either of us again, unless I go and punch another guy," Omar turned quickly and looked directly at Malcolm as though he was coming after him next. Man, he was really bringing the point across as it was impossible not to react with fear. Fortunately, he switched to his calmer voice as he continued to explain. "It's really quite simple - once you start treating others the way you'd like to be treated, which I'm assuming is not being punched," he said, glancing quickly at Crow and Malcolm, "then the world will change dramatically. These unhappy situations will no longer be needed for the purpose of learning. Those particular stage plots could be thrown away and replaced with something of better intent. However, this would require *everyone* understanding and accepting this concept, and acting accordingly. But from what I've seen of human behavior, that could take a while."

"You had me going there," Crow admitted. "I don't think I'll ever forget that lesson. I'm going to make double sure I treat other people better. It sounds a bit selfish, but it's not actually: yes, I want to be treated better, but I also want to help end suffering in the world. That's powerful stuff! Plus, it's something that *I* can actually do in my day to day life to make a difference."

"You got that right," Griffin affirmed solemnly, looking around at each of us to make sure we'd all understood the importance of what had been said.

Looking at the others, I'd say there was no doubt that we'd all gotten it. I felt like I had sparks shooting out of my head, just thinking about the possibilities. And I could feel a sense of *rightness* inside me.

"So much thinking going on! I'm impressed," Omar joked, looking at us all. "It's not just Julie that has a feeling of rightness inside – I see it in all of you. That's a good feeling, and whenever you get it, let it tell you that you are on the right track."

"How do you see inside us like that?" George asked.

Kodiak decided it was time to jump into the conversation too, especially on this particular topic. "Your solid-looking body is not solid at all, as George has come to know. You are a bunch of particles all put together to form a body – in much the same manner as we are, and as you witnessed with our appearance tonight. Understandably, these particles are extremely tiny, but they are still particles. It's easy for us to see through them. Once we're in there, we just open the closet door where you keep your emotions and voila – there you are. As I said, it's not difficult for us as we know how everything operates. There will come a time when you will start to realize that you have these types of inner senses too, and to a certain degree, you'll be able to develop them while living. But for now, your outer senses are all you believe you have. Don't get me wrong. I am most definitely not minimizing them, as they are exquisitely intricate and beautiful. If you're interested in developing yourself, you can start by learning to use your outer senses more fully. Learn how to really *see,* and appreciate the fact that you *can* see a sunset, or how to *feel* a tree, or enjoy a bird's existence by *hearing* its song."

As much as the words *inner senses* intrigued me, I was feeling overwhelmed again.

"It can be overwhelming in the beginning," Omar replied to my thoughts. "I can see that all of you are thinking the same thing. Let me assure you that as the days and weeks go by, it will not feel that way. This new information will sink in and become a part of who you are. Just the thinking and discussions alone open up parts of you that allows your inner senses freedom to grow. Doors that were sealed shut in your mind will spring open as you examine new concepts, and only good can come of that."

"It's actually much easier than living the way you have been living," Kodiak added. "There's a kind of free and exciting vitality to a life lived in this manner. Wouldn't you agree, George?"

"It definitely changed my life. And it does become somewhat automatic too. I'd never thought of that before, as it just sort of happened. Sometimes, I even have trouble explaining to others what I've experienced, and I'm not sure why that is. I've wondered about that, actually. Words never seem to capture the depth of what I *felt.*"

Griffin had a ready reply. "This is a topic that involves your inner senses. I'm wondering if you guys are maybe too tired or overwhelmed to get into it?"

"I'm not tired, but I am close to information overload. But if all this information will find its own place inside us in time, then why not go for it now? What about you guys?" Malcolm asked us, looking quite eager I might add. "Tomorrow's Saturday, and we can sleep in, plus how many people ever get the chance to learn what we're learning?"

"I guess you're right," I conceded. "Why not get it while we can?"

Griffin had a mischievous grin on his face. But before I could ask what he was up to, I felt a tingling wave go through my entire body.

I looked at everyone else to see if they'd felt it too, and sure enough, we all looked surprised. "What was that?" I wanted to know.

Griffin chuckled, like it was no big deal. "Merely an infusion of energy that I sent to each of you through your inner senses. A gift from me to you. The fact that you all consciously felt it means your inner channels are making their presence known. I believe none of you can possibly deny it happened? And I also believe every one of you would have a hard time verbalizing exactly what it was, how it felt, and how it is making you feel." He was looking at us with a very smug, challenging look.

Crow was about to try, but hesitated, and then said, "It was sort of tingly, and prickly, and it's making me feel really, really good." So good in fact, that he started laughing.

I took a stab at it. "It did tingle, didn't it? And I do feel good, but I can't really explain to you in what way. I feel sort of light and happy, but that description certainly doesn't do the feeling justice at all. I think you made your point Griffin. Are you going to tell us more?"

"Certainly. Anytime you want this, you just have to ask for it," Griffin teased "It's good stuff – just a bit of universal vitality, that's all. Definitely better than any of your drugs or alcohol or energy drinks, plus it's free, has only beneficial side effects, and comes from a never-ending universal supply - no prescription required." He sounded like a TV commercial. "It should keep you keenly aware for my entire presentation on the nuts and bolts of outer and inner senses. I will, however, try to keep it as short as possible."

I wondered just how short it would actually be. I got the impression that their sense of time and our sense of time were two different things. "Sorry, Griffin." I held up my hand to stop him before he could get started. "I'm going to interrupt for a few seconds, if that's okay. Does anyone want more wine?" I asked as I got up to fill our glasses, and then quickly went to the kitchen to grab some more nuts to munch on, just in case we were going to be awhile.

Griffin patiently waited until we got ourselves settled again. "Is everyone ready now?" he asked, looking straight at me before turning to the others. "And is everyone still feeling energized, because if you're not I could zap you again?"

We're good, we told him. I had my wine to sip, some nuts to snack on, and a great bunch of energy bouncing around inside me. I was ready!

"Okay, here goes then. Pay attention! You see your outer senses, and I'm assuming you know that we're talking about sight, sound, smell, touch, and taste, are designed specifically to work well on your plane of existence, and to help keep you focused on the here and now. You see, every plane, or dimension, or reality, or framework, or whatever you want to call it, has its own set of rules, and its own modes of operation – even its own purpose for existence. In other words, things work on your plane the way they do because they were designed to work that way – but only on your plane. Time is a good example. It exists here because it needed to be here, but only here. So far, so good, I believe," Griffin said as he paused to examine us individually.

"Let's continue then. Your outer senses help you function on this plane. They help you experience, and hopefully learn from, your day to day challenges and adventures. They feed information to you. Then using the past, present and future setup, which are all compliments of time, you can make judgements about what worked and what didn't. You might even decide in your *present* to make some changes in the *future* based on what happened in the *past*.

"But, as we've told you before – there is more to you than the person you see in the mirror. There is a bigger you, and I'm not talking about size. Let's call it the *greater you* as that will paint a much better mental picture. Let's spend a bit of time pondering what the greater you does all day long. One thing for sure is that it isn't confined to just your plane, the same way the physical you is. It would find it way too restrictive. But neither is it divorced from your physical existence. In other words, it's with you, but is simultaneously in many other places as well; places like other dimensions or realities. When you dream, or even daydream for that matter, you are more connected to the greater you than the physical you, and when you return your focus back to the physical you, oftentimes lessons learned while travelling *abroad* are brought back to this reality. This happens whether you know it or not, or even whether you believe it or not. The greater you uses inner senses, and the physical you uses outer senses, *but*," here Griffin paused for dramatic effect, "*you* are one and the same. Therefore, you all have a complete set of inner senses. It's just that physically, you do not knowingly use them...yet."

"That makes sense!" I could actually understand it perfectly the way Griffin explained it. I took a sip of wine, then asked, "What do you guys think? Do you get it too?"

"I think I had it all along," George clarified. "I just didn't know what it was I had. It was all a jumble, and my human brain was having trouble sorting it all out. But yes, I do get it now. So, that's why I was able to fly like an eagle, and swim underwater, and see particles everywhere. Those were my inner senses I was using!"

"Bingo!" Griffin looked so triumphant that he actually did a little happy dance around the living room, and let me tell you – that guy had moves, especially with his golden cloak shooting out light rays everywhere! He was like a disco ball! "Now, let's give you an example, and I want all of you to close your eyes and visualize this with me," he instructed as he sat down again. "Let's take a tree – maybe a pine tree...I always liked a pine tree," he said wistfully. "Crow, I want you to tell me what this tree looks like to you."

"Ah, okay. I see a tall beautiful healthy green tree standing off by itself, but the other trees in the forest are not far away either. Its needles are giving off a lovely pine scent. And I see a couple of birds perched on the higher limbs. The bark feels quite smooth, and the needles are prickly. Oh darn, I've touched some sap and now my fingers are sticky." Crow actually rubbed his fingers. Then he opened his eyes. "How'd I do?"

"Very well, for using your outer senses. Get ready for this now, as I'm going to take all of you on a journey *into* the tree using your inner senses. Stay with me.

"Close your eyes again and everyone join Crow around his tree.

Take a few steps back so that you can take a good look at this tree – and as Julie says – go park your rational brain somewhere else for a while. You won't need it here. Let your mind free itself up so that you can look inside the tree. Don't be afraid to use your imagination. Visualize how the sap is easily, and happily, flowing up and down the trunk. Feel how gracefully the wind is massaging its branches – making the needles tingle. The wind is its friend. Can you hear how the tree is beckoning birds to come and sit and sing in its branches," Griffin stopped for a few minutes.

I found it was quite easy to do this, and once I was inside that tree, I didn't want to leave. It was such a peaceful world. I wondered if the guys were feeling the same way, but I didn't want to open my eyes and end this magical moment.

"Alright," Griffin slowly began again. "I can see that you're all there, and feeling very connected to that tree. Now, wish it well and tell it that you will visit again sometime soon, and slowly come back to your living room."

I did as he said, and after a few minutes we were all looking at each other in an incredibly connected sort of way – one that certainly defied verbal description. It was very calming.

"That journey used your inner senses," Griffin proudly explained. "I think we've found some very good students here! Wouldn't you agree?" he asked, glancing at Omar.

"Excellent indeed. They are more than ready for the discoveries that lay ahead," Omar replied, smiling.

"So, let's hear you verbally explain what happened. Julie, you go first."

"Well…I could feel the peaceful feelings the tree had…and the connectedness of everything around it, but it's like I wasn't an observer – instead, I was a participator," I looked hopefully at Griffin, hoping I had it right.

"Exactly!" Griffin exclaimed. "Was it the same for the rest of you?" he eagerly asked.

"It was for me," Malcolm answered slowly, obviously still in awe. "That's a totally different world. I didn't even realize it existed!"

"Yes, yes yes! Oh, but this is good!" Griffin was obviously very excited. "The world of the inner senses is indeed a different world. It deals in emotions that are *felt*. Words can never reach the depth that emotions can go. Nor is it possible to find an emotional location using a verbal road map. Inner senses bring you *direct* knowledge, for which words are not only inadequate, but quite unnecessary.

"Is that what happened to us after our first meeting in the tent with you?" Crow asked. "We all commented on how different everything looked the next day – like the world had suddenly gained more depth or feeling. Was that our inner senses picking this up?

"Precisely! And I know you had a hard time describing those feelings even to each other. You all *knew* what it was because you all *experienced* it – not because of how you described it. That was direct knowledge at work," Griffin explained.

"But we didn't consciously try to do this. It just happened," Malcolm pointed out. "I'm wondering if more things will happen the same way, simply because we're interested? Or do we have to work at developing these skills?"

"Yes and no," Omar took over from Griffin. "Many new experiences will come your way once you're open to them. First, you must acknowledge the possibility *and* then be on the lookout for them. If you will remember, beliefs create your reality. Water rushes out of a dam once the gates have been opened, but not until then, so you might have a few beliefs that need to be discovered and re-worked in order to open those gates. There are, however, certain skills that can be worked on, should you decide you want to pursue this avenue. I'd like to get to that another time, though. There is just so much to tell you. We don't want to present it all in one sitting in case it would be too overwhelming."

"But here's a hint though – empathy," Kodiak added. "Empathy is a great place to start. When you look at a bird, or a flower, or an ant scurrying about on the sidewalk, or another human being for that matter, try to find your empathy first. Get into their shoes, so to speak. Don't worry about losing yourself, as that's actually not even possible. You'll come back to yourself enriched. All involved will benefit. Trees like to be visited in this way, as does everything else. And you will benefit by learning to view the world from their eyes. What you see might surprise you, indeed."

Crow grabbed a handful of nuts. "Is that the only inner sense there is?" he asked, as he starting munching.

"No, there are many more," Griffin replied. "Your society knows of them, but usually downplays their importance. In fact, they're oftentimes even frowned upon by some. To name a few, there's intuition, instinct, clairvoyance, and telepathy. But we're not going to get into anything more tonight. However, during the week, keep your simple tree adventure in mind and try it out for yourself and see what happens. We'll join you again next Friday. It's simply been *so* much fun watching your progress!"

We were about to say good-bye when we noticed they weren't there anymore, which left our living room feeling quite empty. Their energies certainly knew how to fill a room. We talked about getting a tape recorder so that we could go back during the week to what they said. It was hard to remember it all after the fact. We got out pen and paper and jotted down everything we could recall while it was still fresh in our minds. We still felt a tingle of energy, or vitality, as they called it, so we stayed up a while longer, just talking.

Malcolm was shaking his head. "You know, it's only been a few short weeks since we went on our camping holiday and met these guys. I can't believe how much we've changed since then, and how our lives have changed as well. I still have to pinch myself sometimes. It's so different from the everyday life we were leading before, and the life that most people around us are still leading."

"I feel the same way," Crow said. "What they're saying makes complete sense to me, but I feel like I'm living two separate lives – the *new* way and the *old* way. I hate to admit it, but deep down I am somewhat afraid to be ostracized from society."

"You can be ostracized from society, or ostracized from yourself – which one do you choose?" an invisible Griffin suddenly bellowed from the ceiling. We just about jumped out of our seats! "If you choose to trust in yourself, you will not feel ostracized from society, but will, in time, become a solid beacon that others will be drawn to. Remember, heart recognizes heart, and there is no intellectual, reasoning, or logical brain involved in that recognition! It's a *feeling*!"

There was silence for a few minutes. We waited to see if he was done, but he seemed to be gone.

"That was a bit of a shock! He certainly got his message across loud and clear, didn't he? It gives me more self-confidence and resolve though," I discovered. "Changing directions could be challenging, but there really is no going backwards, is there?"

"Nope, I don't believe so," Crow declared.

"Well, forward it is then!" I said with as much resolve as I could muster. Who knew what the next week would bring, but I was certain that it would be no less exciting than this last one.

13

THE POWER OF NATURE

"Why are there trees I never walk under but large and melodious thoughts descend upon me? I think they hang there Winter and Summer on those trees and only drop fruit as I pass." **Walt Whitman**

We headed straight to bed after George and Crow left. Once again, our minds were on overload. Exhausted, we turned towards each other to say goodnight, but were immediately overwhelmed by a seducing depth of emotional desire, the likes of which we'd never experienced before. Our love making that night transported us to places beyond imagination. It would seem that our new found knowledge was capable of making changes in *every* aspect of our lives!

Afterwards, lying there, relaxed and calm, an experience from my teenage years popped into my head - and it was about a tree. So, I shared with Malcolm how I'd discovered these three trees one day in a park during a bike ride. I'd gotten off my bike and was walking along the path by the river when I came upon three magnificent fir trees. They were so beautiful that I had to stop and gaze at them in wonder; they held such commanding majesty. I sat down on a nearby bench and continued looking at them. They had my complete attention. Suddenly, they started talking to me! I heard them as plain as day inside my head. I'd had some sort of problem I was trying to work out, and these three trees were giving me the answers I'd been searching for. Eventually, I got back on my bike and went home, but not without sincerely thanking those three trees for their advice. For the rest of the year I always went back to them whenever I had a problem, and they always helped me.

"That's an amazing story, Julie," Malcolm tenderly said when I was done. "Why didn't you tell me about this before?"

"Good question. I'd forgotten all about it until tonight. But why would I forget something like that? I guess I just became very busy after moving away, trying to create a new life, find a place, get a job, and make some friends. Plus, no one else ever mentioned anything along those lines, so I guess I let it slip. What a pity, don't you think? Imagine if I would have continued to develop that sort of ability – who knows where it would have led."

"Well, at least you remembered now, so maybe you can pick up where you left off. But right now, I'm feeling very sleepy, so I'm going to roll over and close my eyes. Good-night, honey," Malcolm gave me one last kiss, then rolled over. Within seconds he was lightly snoring. Oh, how I loved that man!

That night I had an interesting and vivid dream. I was amongst a lot of people milling about on a wooden platform. We were all going to go up to the mountains on some sort of train. We were waiting to board this train, and we were all very excited. We were the students and teachers of a particular school. I was one of the teachers. When the train pulled in everyone scrambled to get on. I managed to find a spot in the very last car. Once I was on I immediately saw that there were coffee and cinnamon buns for us, which, for some reason, filled me with an absolute sheer delight. I thought to myself, with great anticipation – almost to the point of drooling - that I was going to have one of those delicious smelling cinnamon buns. The train was really nice, and there were good vibes everywhere, but it was the cinnamon buns that really topped it off for me. But I never actually got to taste one as I woke up at that point.

I told Malcolm my dream over breakfast. I was still feeling good from it. Malcolm thought it was a very positive dream and even a good sign that I was on the right track, no pun intended. I had to agree. Cinnamon buns remind me of comfort, as they were my mom's specialty. When I close my eyes and return to my childhood, I can smell the aroma filling the entire house, making life seem wonderful. I'd been working more and more with the dream book learning to decipher my dreams, and couldn't help but marvel at how I came up with symbols that were so individual and meaningful to me. I was looking forward to talking with our *friends* about dreams. Still, I also knew I didn't need any additional information to sort out for a while. Plus, this dream seemed very easy for me to interpret on my own. Onward and upward, teaching and learning, just get on that train and have a cinnamon bun! It's all good stuff.

Overnight I'd hatched a plan to see if I could actually connect with a tree again. There was this particular Japanese Maple tree in a small park that I passed every day on my way to work. I'd always found it to be quite beautiful in passing. I realized, now that I actually stopped to think about it, that I silently acknowledged that tree every time I passed by it; always feeling a little *tinkle* in my mind, but not in a way that ever rose to my full attention - just sort of in passing and then filed away beneath the stuff of life during the day that always seemed to take over.

On my way to work on this particular morning, I didn't have much time, but as I passed the tree, I directed a focused intentional thought of appreciation and admiration towards it. I also *told* it I'd be back in the afternoon, and maybe we could chat. I know this sounds like something in the movies, but just then, a little wind blew through its branches, and the tree seemed to whisper a friendly acknowledgment of me. It shouldn't have, but it scared me a little. "No, no, no, Julie," I whispered to myself. "It's okay - just accept what happened for what it might be. Quit pushing it away and let it come. Believe it. Jump on your dream train for heaven sakes!" Yes, yes, I felt I could do that. So, with the best of intentions I continued on my way.

Work was work that day. No catastrophes to take care of, so I was able to snatch bits of time to think about my dream and the tree, and what I was going to do on my walk home. I knew it was just a little experiment, but I was excited about it – much more excited than about what was happening at work.

Interestingly, during my lunch break, I came across a panhandler, and this time I found I had no sense of wanting to avoid him at all. Instead, I found I was curious about what his life must be like, and what he was before, and why he chose poverty now. As I passed him, I looked him straight in the eye. Surprisingly, I saw a twinkle there. Then with a smile and a nod of his head, he said, "Have a nice day, ma'am."

"I hope you have a lovely day too, sir," I replied. I felt good afterwards, not ashamed of myself like I used to. A strange thought popped into my head that maybe next time I could bring him a cinnamon bun and a coffee!

At the end of the workday I began my walk home, wondering what would happen. When I was close to the park, a fellow carrying a take-out coffee and clutching a brown paper bag passed me on the sidewalk. If I had to hazard a guess, I'd say that he had a big warm cinnamon bun in that bag as I smelt cinnamon for the rest of the block. What was it with these cinnamon buns, I wondered? It can't be a coincidence as I hadn't thought about them since I was a little kid, and ever since my dream, they've been showing up everywhere. If it isn't a coincidence, then what is it, I questioned? Maybe you get symbols in your waking life too, the same way you do when you're dreaming. That sounded like a possibility, all things considered. That would be sweet if that was the case. Maybe I'd been shown these symbols all my life, but never took note of them? I jotted this down in the notebook I'd put into my purse for just such *ah-ha* moments, as I wanted to remember this for Friday's get together.

Finally, there in front of me, was my lovely Japanese Maple tree.

Too bad there wasn't a bench. I stood still for a while, sending it thoughts about how beautiful it was, and asked if it had anything it wanted to tell me. But I didn't hear a response like I had when I was younger, which I found disappointing. So, I concentrated on the gracious shape of its branches and tried to *feel* what it would be like to be inside that tree, like Griffin had said. I parked my rational brain, let go of words, and focused very intently on that tree. Then, with no warning at all, I felt a sudden *whoosh* inside as some part of me actually left my body and flew rapidly towards that tree - which scared the dickens out of me! Almost instantly, I was back in my body, wondering what the heck had just happened. But I'm sure I saw the tree smiling, looking even more beautiful than before. I stood there, trying to recuperate. I had no idea what had just happened, but it appeared that it was me who'd made it happen. Was this what Griffin had been talking about? If so, it was much more physical than I'd imagined. I thought I would just hear the tree talking to me, like before. It never once occurred to me that I'd get sucked out of my body and transported within inches of the tree. But then it hit me that indeed, it had happened before - when I got sucked up into Omar's plane of existence on our camping holiday. No need to be worried, I once again assured myself as I slowly started walking home again, still in a bit of a daze. I figured instant fear was understandable the first time, but if I managed to have it happen again, I vowed to try to keep calm and see where it would lead. Wow! I believe this is what you would call progression. I took my notebook back out again and jotted the entire incident down. I definitely wanted to share this experience with everyone.

Crow and George wanted to do their tree experiment in nature, not a suburb full of houses and cars, so they decided to go for a hike. There were several to choose from, but in the end, they picked one that would take them far into the backcountry. Being summer, it didn't get dark until at least ten, so they figured they had enough time if they were ready and left right after work, which is exactly what they did. Both thought of themselves as being physically fit, so no concerns there.

The hike was relatively easy in the beginning, but then it began to get steeper, and the narrow path took them along the edge of tall cliffs. "Let me tell you – it was straight up on one side, and straight down on the other!" Crow told us on speaker phone while driving home after the hike. "Talk about needing to be present in the moment. If we hadn't been, one small mis-step could've spelled disaster."

"We came upon a fairly flat rock with a view, so decided to stop and have our supper," George added. "And what a view it was too – sparkling blue water below, rugged mountains all around, and a golden sun warming our faces. We looked around for a tree to talk to, but there were so many trees that none stood out. So, we decided to pack up and head for the top, hoping to find our tree up there."

Crow cut in, "Yeah, we thought the path had been bad before, but now it grew a bad case of loose rocks and gnarly roots to trip us up. It took a lot longer to reach the top than we'd anticipated so we didn't really have a great deal of time to search for our tree. But what we did see was an absolutely stunning mountain top view, which seemed to overtake any trees we did find. So, we decided to head back down and see if we could find something on the way."

George took over now. "I'd say this is where we ran into trouble. It seems we are not as fit as we think we are. Turns out that going down was way more difficult than coming up. And our legs were already tired after the climb, so trying to control our speed and where we stepped on the steep narrow descent was a bit more than we were ready for. We panicked a bit, didn't we Crow?" George asked.

"Yep, we did. Hate to admit it, but there was indeed some panic. We were both worried about time becoming an issue too, as we ended up going even slower on our way down than on our way up."

George continued on. "It was Crow's idea to take a five-minute break every now and again so that our legs could rest a bit. On our first break I sat on a rock and thankfully leaned up against a nice sturdy tree trunk and closed my eyes for a bit. You probably know where this is going, don't you," George asked us.

"No, we don't! What happened?" I demanded excitedly.

"Why, I heard a familiar voice talking to me in my head. It was Kodiak saying '*don't worry, you'll be okay, just open your eyes and check it out.*' My eyes flew open, and I'm telling you, I could not believe what I was seeing. I elbowed Crow and told him to open his eyes too. I asked him if he was seeing what I was seeing."

"Well, what were you seeing? C'mon, you gotta tell us," I pleaded.

"Yeah, spill the beans," Malcolm added.

"A glow," Crow answered simply. "We saw a glow that was coming from everything – the leaves, the trees, their branches, the rocks, the bushes, even the air – everything was glowing! It was magical," he said, obviously still captivated by the wonder of it all.

"Not only that," George added, 'it was pulsating, and we could hear a low hum, similar to an electrical hum - that type of sound. And the colors changed too – especially on the leaves – they'd go from a luminescent green back to a golden glow – always pulsating. We were stunned to say the least. After a bit we could hear Kodiak's voice coming from somewhere inside this pulsating glow too. He told us we were being enveloped in a form of energy, and that we should use this energy to help us get down the mountain. But get this – he said we could tap into this energy any time we needed it, because even the tiniest of leaves were made of it!

"Wow," Malcolm declared, "that had to be quite the experience. Did it help you get down?"

"It really did," Crow answered enthusiastically. "From there on we seemed to know exactly where to place our feet, and our energy returned too. We still had a few hours of hiking to go, but we knew we'd be okay. But here's another weird thing – we stopped on the way down to watch the sunset, which was gorgeous by the way, however, we knew we'd better pick up the pace as it would soon be dark. We figured another half hour or so and we'd be down, but when we reached the parking lot it was still quite light outside, so we looked at our watches and saw it had only taken us fifteen minutes, which simply was not possible, plus it should have been much darker. We were scratching our heads about this when we heard Griffin's voice! You know, I'm beginning to realize that he's a bit of a trickster, as he said he was playing a little time trick on us, just to demonstrate that clock time doesn't actually exist."

"Apparently," George broke in, "both Kodiak and Griffin had come on the walk with us as they wanted to enjoy the scenery! Imagine that! But I gotta say that I really like the idea of having someone *on the other side* being around and watching out for me.

"Me too," I said. "I'm really glad you two are okay, and I'm equally glad that you had such a great experience. I had one too, but I'll tell you about it on Friday night as it's getting way too late now. Maybe Malcolm will have one by then too."

"I'm on the lookout, that's for sure. Have a good sleep you two, and we'll see you on Friday."

After we hung up, Malcolm and I talked about how time does exist, but then again, it doesn't exist. It's hard to wrap your head around it really. Could we somehow make it not be close to midnight? Could we expand or shrink time to our advantage? And what about getting to work on time if everyone was manipulating time - or how do you meet someone at ten, if ten can be extended? That's how we fell asleep that night; with all these questions rolling around in our minds, and no answers for them. I thought we might have intriguing dreams because of it, but we both slept so soundly that we hardly managed to wake up to our insistent alarm clock, saying for sure, there was such a thing as time, and it was reminding us of this fact, over and over again - so get up!

It was Malcolm's turn for an adventure now. He genuinely wanted to connect with a tree too, but he couldn't seem to find one. In the heart of the city, where he worked in one of the tall skyscrapers, there was more glass and steel than green trees. Plus, the ambience surrounding the downtown trees was too chaotic to allow for the quiet time he needed to delve into a tree. "It's so frustrating, Julie," he told me the next day when he came home from work. He threw his briefcase onto the chair in disgust – something I'd *never* seen him do before! "I feel miserable. You had such a powerful encounter with your tree, and look at the incredible experience Crow and George had! I walked around in my lunchbreak today looking for the right tree and all I found was frenzied, noisy energy everywhere I turned. Why am I doing this to myself?" He was leaning on the island holding his head in his hands.

Feeling somewhat alarmed at Malcolm's sudden sense of desperation, I dropped everything. "Let's grab a beer and go sit on the deck, hon," I gently suggested. We'd managed to create a peaceful sanctuary in our backyard and I hoped it would help calm Malcolm down and bring his normal sunny disposition back. As we talked, I tried to take his mind off his worries. After a while my plan seemed to be working, as Malcolm sunk deeper into his reclining deck chair and closed his eyes.

"I'm going to rest for a bit, Julie," he told me. "Why don't you finish supper, and call me when it's ready, okay?"

"Okay. You have a good rest," I said as I quietly closed the screen door behind me. "Take as long as you need." Quite frankly, I was a bit worried about Malcolm. He'd always been the solid and self-assured one. I wasn't entirely sure what to do to help him.

Malcolm let his thoughts go. He figured it must be anxiety that he was feeling – which was a new sensation for him. His thoughts were zooming here and there with a hurried energy all their own. But all of a sudden he thought he saw, in the far corner of his mind, if he didn't look straight at it, a little patch of green – like a tiny green leaf. He tried to focus on it without actually focusing on it, which he found was a feat in itself. The patch of green grew brighter and larger, and he thought he glimpsed, or felt, or heard – he wasn't sure how – that he should open up. Open up what, he wondered. He felt he was being told to open himself up, but didn't have a clue how to do that. *Just open your eyes,* he was finally told point blank. He was expecting to see what Crow and George had seen when Kodiak told them to open their eyes, but instead he found himself looking straight at the mountain ash tree that was currently shading him from the hot sun. A bird had planted this tree close to the deck a long time ago. It had grown into a big, beautiful, healthy tree.

Malcolm felt a sudden sense of disappointment, but then the tree spoke to him! Not in words everyone could hear mind you, but in words Malcolm could *feel* inside. "I'm your tree, Malcolm. I've wondered how long it would take for you to discover me." Malcolm found he didn't know how to reply or what to even say as he stared at the tree, and the tree stared back at him.

But he did feel something stirring in his heart, so he decided to try to put those feelings into words. "I had no idea you were such a beautiful tree!" he told it with a depth of emotion he'd never really captured before. "Why have I never noticed you?"

I thought I heard someone talking, so I looked out the back window to check on Malcolm, and found him staring intently at the mountain ash tree. Something was definitely going on inside his head, as he looked like he was talking to the tree. I decided to watch, mesmerized by the look of pure rapture on his face. He continued on in this manner for several more minutes. He was definitely on a different wavelength. Eventually, I could see the old Malcolm return in his face, so after a bit I called out that supper was ready.

When he came in, he plunked himself down on a kitchen chair, still looking somewhat mesmerized, and said, "Julie, I've just had the most incredible experience. And I've found my tree! Look, there it is," he said as he triumphantly pointed out the window to the mountain ash tree. "It told me to look at it, and when I did, I saw it in a manner I never would have believed possible before. And when I focused in on one of its leaves – just one tiny green leaf – something happened." Malcolm stopped talking as he seemed to get transported back to that moment.

"What happened? You have to tell me, Malcolm!"

"Yes, yes I will. It's just that I can't find the words to describe it."

"Just try, and I bet it'll come to you well enough for me to understand. Remember, heart recognizes heart."

"Okay. Well, as I was staring at this one leaf I felt my knowledge expand. I understood the meaning of *everything* in the universe – all the how's, and the why's, and the reasons for being – and that every single thing is connected. There is no less important or more important; there is simply *life*!"

"You mean like seeing the universe in a grain of sand?" I asked.

"I'd say it's probably something like that. The complete meaning of everything was in that one tiny leaf, and for a moment my entire being truly understood what that was, even though I can't repeat it to you now. It was glorious."

"It certainly sounds glorious. Plus, you've found your tree! Congratulations!"

"Yeah, I do believe I have." Malcolm turned to look out the window at the mountain ash again, and felt that it was smiling at him. In fact, as I glanced at the tree over his shoulder, even I could see that it was smiling – however it is that a tree smiles. He turned back to face me. "I feel so much better than when I came home, but now I'm wondering what I'm going to do about the toxic environment downtown that I work in every day. I've just discovered simple beauty where I never knew there was any, and chaos where I always thought there was order."

Oh-oh. That was a big dilemma. We discussed the ramifications and possibilities during supper, but came up empty-handed. We hoped our Friday night get together would give us some direction. Maybe we just needed a different belief or perception of the situation – like with the commute. It would have to be pointed out to us, though. Neither of us could find a way around the fact that noisy cars spewing exhaust, horns honking, people rushing, endless glass, steel, and dirty buildings crowding out the sky were probably not good for anyone.

This was the start of an itch that needed to be scratched. It was not going away.

14

THE HELPERS

"Organize your reality according to your strength; organize your reality according to your playfulness; according to your dreams; according to your joy; according to your hopes – and then you can help those who organize their realities according to their fear."
Seth & Jane Roberts/Sue Watkins

"I'm so excited about getting together with Crow and George this evening," Malcolm told me as we were getting ready for work Friday morning. "And I sure hope our transparent friends show up. I've got a lot of questions for them."

"Me too," I replied. I'd been sipping on my cup of coffee and thinking about how the evening might turn out when something dawned on me. "Malcolm, do you realize how much we've changed? I mean, I feel like I want to know *everything* they can throw at me now, whereas before I often felt overwhelmed. And I must admit that what I used to think of as a healthy dose of skepticism on my part seems to have completely vanished. What about you?"

Malcolm sat down beside me at the kitchen table to stop and

think about it for a minute. "You're right. I feel like I've truly accepted the core of what they've been saying, and now I want to grasp it all and implement this new way of being. In fact, I feel like a thirsty sponge that wants to know more and more. Good pick-up Julie. I think we've come to a turning point."

We left for work that morning feeling really proud of ourselves and feeling as positive and full of energy as we'd ever felt. Throughout the day thoughts of the evening kept creeping in. I could hardly wait.

Crow and George came over around six-thirty. We all got cozy in the living room, where a bottle of red wine, wine glasses, and several snacks had been set out. We helped ourselves and then got comfortable in anticipation of a great evening.

"I've been looking forward to this evening all day long," I told everyone. "What about you guys?" I asked Crow and George.

"Couldn't get it off my mind," Crow agreed. "I was thinking that if our friends do show up, I'd like to find out more about them. I'm pretty sure they'll know all about our experiences as they seem to know everything. But what about them? I keep wondering *who* they are in relation to us. And *where* they are when they're not here? George and I have been talking about this a lot, and we think it would be really interesting to find out. What do you think – is that something you guys want to know too?"

"Actually, I have been wondering about that too," Malcolm answered. "They've dropped a few hints along those lines, but I've never really understood what they were trying to say. But after everything we've been through lately, I think I could grasp it now. I want to know *who* and *what* they are, and *where* they go, and *how* they..."

"Whoa! That's a lot of questions, you guys!" Griffin protested out of nowhere.

Suddenly, there they were - all four of them. They appeared faster than I could snap my fingers. Their abilities never ceased to amaze me.

"I can see you are all in fine form this evening," Griffin proudly announced. He looked at us – one by one. "Just look at all the eagerness on these faces will you, and not only eagerness but interest as well! I don't see a hint of disbelief lingering anywhere at all anymore. What about you, Bluedon?"

Bluedon took a good long look at us too. I felt like I was being subjected to x-ray vision. "I agree completely," he finally said. "I believe a big hurdle has been crossed. We are facing four eager beavers tonight instead of four confused doubters! I have a feeling your tree experiments were a beneficial eye-opener for all of you."

"Yes, yes, I think so," Omar added. "I'm sure you realize that any of you could have experienced the same thing as the others. Definitely a positive step forward for all of you. And please - don't stop experimenting in this way. It cannot be harmful – only helpful."

"There's a lot of energy out there that can help you, as you've discovered," Kodiak said as he looked around for a place to sit. "It's there for the asking, but you *must* ask. And don't forget that you can help others as well using your own energy, but you'll get that figured out all in good time."

They'd all found a comfortable spot to sit. At least they looked comfortable, hovering a few feet off the floor with their colorful cloaks sparkling away. They certainly added a great deal of color and energy to our living room!

"So, what's the first question?" Omar asked.

Crow jumped right in. "Just who are you in relation to us? We all want to know, and I think it would be helpful to have this knowledge now. Like you said, we all feel like we're in a different headspace than we were a few weeks ago, and I think we could actually understand the answer now – and even believe it!"

They didn't even hesitate. Obviously, they knew what we'd been discussing, and their answer was prepared.

"You're right," Omar nodded, "you are ready. And it's actually not even hard to explain or comprehend. Believing can be a problem, but apparently not for you guys anymore.

"Basically, the four of us belong to a group of entities called *The Helpers*, so clearly what we like to do is help. We exist in a dimension that has a very different set of rules than yours. As you know, we don't deal with time, or space, or even gravity. We don't have a body that requires food or sleep either. Our mechanisms of existence have more to do with consciousness and electromagnetic energy and..."

"Wait a minute here," Crow interrupted. "I'd think there is no shortage of people on earth that need help, so why did you choose us? What made you think we needed your help?"

Omar laughed. "We became aware of your group because of the type of thoughts and energy you were projecting. You see, thoughts are far more important than your current civilization realizes. Nothing ever happens without it first being a thought, even for us. Your thoughts, individually and as a group, were quite probing and emotionally charged, which produced a very noticeable signal in our world. That's what drew our attention to you. And yes, we do help others. You are not alone in searching for a new way of *being*. Helping is what we do – it's what we've *chosen* to do. There is actually a large group of helpers in our dimension. We work in other dimensions as well though, not just yours."

"That seems to make sense," Crow conceded. "But hang on – how'd you hear thoughts I didn't even know I was thinking?"

Omar looked at Griffin. They didn't say anything, but I thought I could *hear* Omar say that Griffin should be the one to answer. I didn't hear with my ears, and it wasn't even words I heard - just an instant understanding that arrived in my mind. Incredible! Omar looked at me with a smile and a nod of approval. Apparently, I had actually managed to *hear* them - telepathically!

I'd been correct too, as it was indeed Griffin who answered Crow's question. "Let's see," he slowly began. "The simple explanation is that we have access to a part of you that your species has not universally acknowledged yet. It's called your *inner consciousness*. You'll have to agree that that is certainly no household phrase in your society...dare I add the word *yet*? You see, the consciousness you are familiar with can look both to the outer physical world *and* the inner nonphysical world. I'm sure you remember us telling you that there's more to you than what you see in the mirror? Perhaps now you can see that there is *a lot* more, and this is only part of what you are. But for now, we'll keep it simple. The total package of YOU lives in an outer world *and* an inner world simultaneously. We, as helpers, have access to both worlds. The thoughts that attracted us to you came from your inner self, which is why you didn't physically know you had them. However, we certainly did – loud and clear. And once we were able to establish an acceptable connection with you in your physical world, we were good to go. Since then, we've been giving you tidbits of knowledge in a way that will hopefully be helpful to you."

"Helpful!" I burst out. "That's an understatement. Our life is nothing like it used to be. And I have a feeling we haven't seen anything yet."

"I'm curious to know what my inner self was saying so loud and clear that it got your attention?" Crow asked.

Griffin suddenly jumped up and yelled in desperation, clutching his chest, "Help! I'm stuck...I can't get through to them...they aren't where they want to be...they don't even know where they want to be...this was not the plan...I'm going to need some help...Anyone out there?"

"Okay, okay - I get it," Crow replied laughing. "It's funny because I was feeling like that. I think we all were, which is why we took the trip to begin with, but I didn't realize I was pleading for help that urgently."

"Neither did I," I added. "But maybe our combined desperation for *getting away from it all* made for a stronger message. None of us were ecstatic with the way our lives were going, so I'd think we probably did know what our inner self was saying, we just didn't know we had an inner self that was pleading on our behalf – and that someone was actually listening."

"I think I've got a great analogy to help us understand this better," George cut in excitedly. "I have this mental image of a two-story house, which I see as a symbol for *me* in this lifetime. The main floor deals with my outer world, and the top floor deals with my inner world. There is a big door on the main floor that opens out to the physical world, and I am free to come and go through that door. On the top floor, there is a glass dome that connects with the, ah – the universe, for lack of a better description. The top floor, or the inner world, only gains access to the outer world through the main floor. And the main floor, or the outer world, only has access to the inner world through the top floor. Does that make sense?"

"That's an excellent analogy," Kodiak acknowledged. "I'd like to add to it if I may. You see, there are inner and outer *egos* as well. Obviously, the inner ego would reside on the top floor, and the outer ego would reside on the main floor in your analogy. These egos know about each other, and they also know they're meant to work together – not to shun one another. Clear communication between them is of prime importance, and I'll tell you why. The outer ego encounters day to day physical events. Its job is to process and assess the experiences it encounters, using the beliefs, intentions, and desires it has come to have. It uses its reasoning capabilities, makes its deductions, and feeds this information to the inner ego, whether it knows it's doing this or not. The inner ego takes this information and works within its unrestricted medium of infinite possibilities to bring about the desires and intentions of the outer ego. You see, the inner world's structure is quite different than the physical world you currently find yourself in. It's part of a much, much larger organization, where the knowledge of everything that is, is known to it. Its abilities are without boundaries. Plus, it is what gives energy to the outer world. In fact, the world as you know it would not last ten minutes without support from the inner world."

"That sounds incredibly powerful, but what I'm wondering is how do the two egos connect, or do they?" I asked.

"Good question," Omar answered. "This may come as a surprise, but eventually it will make sense. You see, they connect, and often merge, in the dream world. In George's analogy of the house with two floors, there would also need to be a connecting staircase. Let's use that to represent the dream world. The outer and inner ego are designed to meet to discuss your experiences and what to do with them. The inner ego has a great desire to ensure your survival and to help create a fulfilling life. It does its best work when it's acknowledged by the outer ego, and fed all the facts, hopefully from an *open-minded* bottom floor ego. When it's ignored, or misunderstood, or its very existence denied, trouble will ensue. And let me tell you, trouble can come in many different shapes and sizes in your dimension, as I'm sure you already realize. The bottom line is to not deny your gut feelings, your sudden intuitions, inspirations, impulses, or even feelings of déjà vu. Those are the methods your inner ego uses in its effort to be heard, and to help. Try to remember that the inner ego is *always* of good intent, and tries to urge you towards the best path for yourself. Be open to hearing those messages, and thank that part of you for sending them."

"In fact," Griffin jumped in excitedly, "it's a good idea for your outer ego to make it a habit to invite your inner ego down for tea regularly!"

"But why?" George looked confused. "Why is it like this? Why do we even need to live in an outer physical world, when our inner world seems to have access to all the answers? It seems a bit cruel, actually. Why put us out in this world with no idea as to what's going on, and say - here, let's see what you can make of it?"

"Growth," Kodiak was quick to answer. "Growth of the personality is the goal. Even existence in our dimension is for growth - for a bettering of ourselves - for an understanding, for knowledge. The desire for growth is built into all of us, and I know you feel it too, so I think you can comprehend what I'm saying. As for why you chose to spend time on earth in your physical body, the answer is the same. You are looking for personal growth, for a sense of fulfilment, for knowledge and understanding, and this is a good place to work on that. You've come here many times. In some of those lives, it's possible you were involved in matters detrimental to your personality, rather than beneficial. Violence or cruelty toward others is never good. Greed is not helpful either. If that's the path you took, then you need an opposite path in another lifetime, simply to experience the other side of the situation. Or there may be a re-balancing that needs to happen. Without knowing this, it can be hard to understand why certain events happen to you in your lifetime, but when you keep in mind that there have been many other lives where perhaps you were not always the good guy, then you can maybe make more sense out of events in this life. Learn! Always learn from whatever happens to you. And I guarantee there will always be something happening to you. It's how you learn. Life was not meant to be a bowl of roses from beginning to end. So, if you can view situations and troublesome events in life from the bigger picture, you'll be able to see them for what they actually are – an opportunity to learn."

"I'd like to add another rather important point," Omar spoke up. "We have told you many times that there is more to you than you realize, but now I'd like to add that this does not only pertain to you four, but to everyone else as well. So, don't be too quick to condemn or praise yourself, or others, as you are all wearing a costume in the same play. When the play is over, the costumes come off. Then everyone goes to the pub to have a beer and discuss how the play went. The one who acted as your adversary could actually turn out to be your very best friend. In fact, if you think about it, who would want to take on the role of being your adversary other than a true friend? You may find yourself congratulating him or her on how well they were able to portray the villain!"

"This is absolutely fascinating," Crow exclaimed in amazement. "It puts such a different spin on things. When I look back at my life, I see it completely different now. How could I have ever blamed anyone? Why did I ever feel sorry for myself? It was all there in the script. And it was me that wrote the script! Wow, this is going to be so empowering going forward. Thank you for getting us to this point."

"Yes, thank you," was about all I could say as everything we'd been told started to sink in.

"This is just the tip of the iceberg," Bluedon answered. "There is so much we could explain to you – like some of the other universal laws for example, but it all has to come at the right time for you to understand it, and now is not the right time. In fact, I believe it's time for us to withdraw and leave you to your discussions as we've given you a great deal more to contemplate. Good-night to you all."

Poof! They were gone! I felt like I wanted to go with them. I wondered what it was like to be them. Who were they going to see now?

"This has been an evening I'll always remember," Malcolm confessed. He had a very peaceful look on his face as he continued. "They've laid down such a beckoning yellow brick road of discovery for us. All we have to do is follow it. We even get to have their help along the way. It seems we were never alone or lost before, even if we thought we were. They were always there hovering about, trying to get through to us, wanting the best for us. Not to mention our inner selves wanting to help as well. And it was nothing but our own pigheadedness that stopped us from getting that help."

George was shaking his head. "All those years I spent searching for something! I went all over the world trying to make sense of everything - only to discover that what I'd been looking for was actually right inside of me!"

"But you couldn't have known that at that time, George," Crow argued. "None of us could have known this kind of stuff growing up. Did any of your friends or relatives ever tell you something like this? Did the media talk about it? Were we ever given any books that might lead us in this direction? In fact, we were given the opposite message. I remember a girl in grade one that said she could see colors around some of the other kids - and being young, she wasn't shy to tell us what she saw. But another kid, I can't remember who it was, said it was weird and told the teacher. Well, that girl got marched into the principal's office right away. When she came back to class, you could tell she'd been crying. She was a lot quieter after that, and she never said anything about seeing colors again. I can only imagine what she was told in the principal's office. And on top of that, when we told our parents, they told us to stay away from her and her family. They didn't want us associating with anyone that was considered *weird*. Being kids, we listened and took away the belief that anything out of the ordinary was off-limits and would get you labelled with a condition similar to the plague. As a kid, you always want to fit in, so I think what you experience in those formative years can really affect you for the rest of your life. Imagine how different that scenario would've been if she'd been supported and admired for her abilities - and even encouraged to develop them. There would have been thirty students that would have believed it to be admirable and might have even tried it on their own. Who knows where that could have led?"

"Isn't that the truth," I agreed. "I had a grandma who was able to *see things* and *know things*, and she would talk to me about it when I visited her, but only if we were alone, and always in a hushed tone. She said she'd get carted off to the crazy house if anyone found out she felt like this, so I was not to tell anyone, especially Grandpa. He was a stern type of man, and as a kid, I made a point of steering clear of him. These days it's definitely more acceptable, but in her era, you were considered a nut case if you talked about those kinds of abilities. I loved hearing her stories, though. And, obviously, she somehow knew it would be safe to talk to me. She must have sensed something in me when I was a little girl. I never did tell anyone either. I felt very close to her. But when I look back at that now, I can see how that taught me from the get-go to keep my thoughts and ideas to myself. No one wants to be labelled as odd - even today."

"This has me wondering about the aboriginals and some of the ancient cultures," Malcolm added. "We've all heard stories about unusual happenings within these groups. For some reason, it's okay for us to speculate about how they managed to know things, or do things. Look at Stonehenge and the Pyramids, or the Mayan and Inca ruins, and all the other astonishing megalithic structures on earth. We're still wondering how they were built to such immense size and perfection; science has yet to give us a plausible answer in my opinion. It seems to me that our current civilization must have lost certain abilities it once had. We developed along a different path, and forgot a certain type of knowledge we used to believe was important. I wonder what life on earth would be like today if civilization had taken a different route and developed our inner world more? Imagine if telepathy and tapping into free universal energy was a common event amongst the human population. Imagine if we knew this whole thing was a play being acted out for our own benefit - and that our enemies could turn out to be our friends - and that no one ever really dies!"

We couldn't help but feel sad about the state of the world when we could see that it could be so much better. We envisioned a world where people didn't feel that they were in charge of nature and the animals, but instead lived in co-operation with them. One where wars had become obsolete and useless because *everyone* knew violence kept the global society from advancing in a positive direction. One where the earth itself was revered and not raped daily for man's profit. One where people were genuinely interested in each other, no matter their size, color, or age.

"It's such a pity," I gloomily pointed out. "I think you're right, Malcolm. It would seem that civilization veered off on the wrong path somewhere. We've got so much to learn yet. We're definitely not the smart ones we think we are. In fact, I'd say we know less of the important stuff now than the people that lived thousands of years ago did. I'm not so sure technology has been our friend. We're all so reliant on our cell phones and the internet for human interaction when all we really need to do is look up and smile at each other. And connect with each other internally – not through a handheld device!" This was getting depressing.

"You're probably right, Julie," George said. "But this *is* where we're at. Right here, right now…in your living room, working at digesting an abundance of information. And if we're going to make any difference at all going forward, then we have to start with where we are right now. So, I'm thinking that lamenting the issues isn't going to help us other than pointing out the importance of changing things around in our *own* lives first. If anything is going to change in the bigger picture, it's got to start with the individual –

with me, and with you. Let's ask ourselves the question, *where can we go from here?*"

That was the jolt we needed. No need to stay stuck in poor-me mode. What were *we* going to do? We exchanged ideas for the next couple of hours. What kind of changes, if any, were we going to make?

"I think we've got to start talking to other people about the new information we've discovered," George suggested. "Look how it's changing our lives."

"I don't know about the rest of you, but I still don't feel all that comfortable about doing that," I admitted. "I think it's easier for you to do something like that considering your childhood, George, but I think my upbringing of always fitting in is getting in the way."

"I could see where that would make you uneasy, but you've got to start somewhere, don't you think? Not everyone is going to get it, and you have to expect that. But there's plenty of people who would understand and want to know more. Those are the people you talk to, and then hopefully they'll talk to others too."

"I think George is right," Malcolm agreed. "We have to conquer our fears and simply start – even if it's just baby steps. What do you think? Shall this be our goal for the near future?"

What could I do? I had to agree, but the very thought of it made my heart palpitate.

15

LIFE EVENTS

***"To avoid criticism, say nothing, do nothing, be nothing."* Aristotle**

I thought I'd make my first attempt at sharing my new knowledge with my co-worker, Jodi, who I'd always thought very highly of. We were usually quite busy at work and didn't have much time for talking, but I thought maybe I could just throw a few thoughts out during the day and see how she reacted. I was surprised to discover that it was not difficult at all once I reassured myself that it was perfectly alright to think the way I did. Comments seemed to find their way out of my mouth all on their own. For example, we had a woman in her fifties march up to our reception window just after lunch, and you could tell she was stressed to the nines. In fact, I could feel her frenzied, nasty energy washing in as soon as she forcefully flung open the main door. Both Jodi and I immediately tensed our shoulders. We knew this conversation was not going to pleasant. And it wasn't. This woman had many things to vehemently complain about - and in a twisted sort of way, we were apparently to blame for most of them! There was no way of calming her down, although we gave it our best effort. After ten minutes of blistering, she declared that she must now rush off to another meeting, which she was already late for - and apparently that was our fault as well! When she left, Jodi and I looked at each other in shock, and then burst out laughing.

"I think a tornado just touched down!" Jodi declared. "I know how the rest of her day is going to go, and I'm really glad it isn't going to intersect with mine."

Go, Julie, go - I silently urged myself. Now's the time. I took the leap. "I could feel her negative energy as soon as she walked in that door, couldn't you?"

"Feel it? It was so foul I could smell it!"

Keep going, Julie, I said to myself. "Too bad she can't see how she's affecting everyone around her, and more importantly, what she's creating for herself. I don't think she realizes that she's the one creating her own reality. Blaming others for what's happening in her life isn't going to get her anywhere either, except more negativity and unhappiness."

Jodi looked over at me. "You know, that's interesting. I've always felt that people should do less blaming and take more responsibility for their own happiness. But I've never heard it expressed so precisely."

This was good, I thought. So, I kept on with baby steps. "Well, I've been thinking a lot about this lately, and it's really changed the way I look at things now. It's put a positive spin on my life. I feel a good deal more in control of what actually happens to me, and it helps me understand events like the one that just took place in a totally different light. Instead of internalizing that woman's negativity and letting it ruin my day, I was able to see it from a perspective of observation - not participation, and to even have a laugh at the end of it. And you too. That's what made me think you might feel the same way."

"I do believe that we're all responsible for our own happiness and that happiness is not a state, but more like a choice or an action. But I've never considered the possibility of actually creating my own reality. I find that to be a very empowering statement, and I'd certainly like to know more about that."

Jodi was about to say more when the front door opened again, and our attention was diverted to the customer walking towards us. This time it was an elderly man. He didn't move too fast, so we had time to notice his kind eyes and contented smile that seemed to have forever etched itself into the crevices on his face. We had no trouble helping him take care of the minor concern he had, and then we started to chit chat. His vibe was so agreeable that I could feel the plants behind me dancing. When he left, Jodi looked at me in amazement.

"I believe you," she said. "Those two people were polar opposites. It's obvious how that woman was creating, and attracting, a very negative life for herself; all the while blaming everyone else for her frustrations. And that man had created a calm, easy-going, content, and happy reality. It was so clear! I wonder if she'll be able to turn herself around by the time she gets to his age?"

"I have no doubt that she could, but only if she realized, and accepted, that she was doing it to herself and that it wasn't being done to her from outside influences. A lot of people are simply not open-minded enough to even consider such an idea as creating your own reality. It's far easier to play the victim and the blame, blame, blame game."

I was going to continue, but just then the phone rang, and someone else walked in the door. Quickly, I told Jodi that we'd talk about this later, and I grabbed the phone, while Jodi took care of the customer. I glanced at her though, and thought I saw a look of curiosity on her face. Maybe she was already looking at other people differently - wondering what reality they were in the process of creating for themselves. And I knew that was only a hop, skip, and a jump away from examining what she was creating for herself. This was good, I thought...this was very good!

The rest of the day remained busy, and we really didn't have any more time to talk. However, Jodi was a thinker, and quite similar to me in many respects. I knew she would be thinking about this in her own time, and that we'd be continuing this conversation in the future at some point. I felt good about myself too, realizing that if I hadn't said anything, nothing would have changed. But because I did, something good might come of it. It dawned on me that in my own little way, I had just changed the world for the better - and that was a nice feeling!

When Malcolm got home that night, I told him all about my experience with Jodi, the bitter lady, and the content man. We talked about the ramifications all throughout supper - liking the results very much. Then he let a bombshell drop. "I also had an extraordinary experience at work today – in fact, it involved our entire office. It's still got me bamboozled!"

"Why didn't you tell me that right away when you came home? I thought you seemed a bit preoccupied."

"Yeah, my mind's preoccupied for sure. What's in there needs to come out. Let's go sit in the living room and I'll tell you the whole story."

My curiosity was certainly roused. The world of business, along with suits, status, and climbing the corporate ladder, with other men and women elbowing each other out of the way in their race for the next rung, was quite different from where I worked as a receptionist. In Malcolm's office, it was all business - and don't screw up if you want to keep your job. It was easy to imagine so many different things going wrong.

Malcolm put his feet up on the coffee table and rested his head on the cushion behind him as he slouched into the couch. I tucked my feet up under me and looked at him in anticipation. "Okay, you have my full attention," I urged. "What happened?"

"Well, you know how my boss is always so 'by the book' on everything, and always watches us with eagle eyes even when you think he's nowhere around?" Malcolm asked as he stared straight ahead.

"Yeah," I nodded. I'd certainly heard this sentiment on more than one occasion over the years.

"So, today he slowly walked into our office with a noticeably dazed look on his face. He never even looked at anyone - just walked straight into his own office and shut the door behind him. We all looked at each other completely astonished. None of us had ever seen him like that before. I wasn't sure what to do next, and I don't think anyone else knew either. So, we all went back to work, but the whole time I was racking my brain trying to figure out what the heck was going on. Half an hour later, he opened his door and walked straight into to my office, closed the door, and sat down, rather wearily."

"No way! Into *your* office?"

"Yep. You can imagine what was going on in my mind. I figured I was about to get fired, but then realized he'd have done that with a lot more pomp and vigor than he was showing. I had no idea what was going to come out of his mouth...and when it did, it shocked me."

I was beside myself with curiosity. "What did he say? Tell me."

Malcolm calmly turned to face me. "He said that his youngest son had just been in a car accident and was in the hospital. It was a bad hit and had left his son a paraplegic! And then he started to cry!" Malcolm was tearing up just remembering it.

"Oh, no!" I whispered. I started to tear up too. "What did you do then?"

"I didn't know what to do. I think I was in shock myself. First at the news, and then at the fact that my cold, distant, hard-nosed boss was in my office, crying! But something came over me. I've had this feeling before, but it was really powerful this time. I felt like a different version of me swept into my body and took over. Somehow, I knew it was all going to work out fine in the end. But of course, my boss wasn't at the end - he was at the beginning and had no way of knowing that anything like this could ever work out okay. Without really thinking about it, I got up, went over to him and knelt down beside his chair and wrapped my arms around him in a big hug, which really opened the floodgates. He cried uncontrollably while I held him. I believe he needed to do that for more reasons than just his son. We must have made quite the picture, but I somehow knew it was what I had to do." Malcolm paused for a bit as he sat up and reached for his beer.

"Yeah. I'm trying to envision it, but it seems so unbelievable considering your bosses personality."

Malcolm took a sip of beer and continued, "After a while, he was able to compose himself somewhat, so I stood up and went back to my chair. Then he started to talk. He told me about everything flashing in front of him at the hospital - the way he'd led his life and his stone-cold attitude towards everyone, including his family. Really, he asked me...what was it all for, this life we find ourselves living? *Why*, he wanted to know? *Why* are we here, *why* do bad things happen, what are we supposed to make of this thing called life?"

"Those are huge questions, Malcolm! What on earth did you tell him?"

"I didn't know what to say. Like you said, those are big questions, and they were coming from a man that doesn't usually ask that sort of thing. Many thoughts came to mind, and that was peculiar too, because it seemed like I had them all at once, but I was able to consider them individually - like time was somehow stretched. I wondered why he'd chosen to come into *my* office, when there were many other offices he could have gone to. I wondered where to start when you had someone in such a vulnerable position asking, and what to say so that it would remain with him after the vulnerability wore off. I wondered how I was going to put into words ideas that I wasn't even sure I could explain to myself. I wondered if I was up to the task, and I was horrified to think that I might make a mistake and say the wrong thing and make things worse, or miss the opportunity that was sitting right there in front of me.

"I was working myself into an emotional tizzy with all my wonderings. But if you remember, our helper friends told us that they are always there for us, especially when we have a strong emotion or need for them. Well, I have no doubt about that now, as all of a sudden I heard Bluedon - somewhere inside me. I couldn't even tell you where. But I know the thoughts didn't come from my brain."

"Malcolm, this is fascinating! What did he tell you?" I asked, anxiously. I tried to picture myself in Malcolm's shoes.

"He told me to make sure my boss knew he was loved, not just by me, but that there were many that loved him. I have to admit that when I heard that, I wondered who actually did love my boss because he wasn't all that loveable. But I decided I would tell him anyway as it seemed right emotionally, if not intellectually. I was to tell him that his son was also loved and that he was going to be okay. Life, Bluedon said, could be lived well on many different levels. His son was going to flourish and actually become well known for his bravery and accomplishments. He was going to be a great help and inspiration to others, but he would need the love and support of his family for that. My boss was to understand that the supporting role was what he needed to do in this life if he wanted to find the meaning he was desperately searching for.

"Now you can imagine that was a lot to tell my boss, and I had no idea how he was going to react to it. But it was coming from a source that knew a lot more than I did. So, I told him. Maybe not word for word, but I got all the ideas across, and then waited to see what the reaction would be."

"Man, I hope it was a good one," I said.

"It actually was." Malcolm had that far-away look again as he stared at the ceiling. "I'm still somewhat shocked by it to tell you the truth. He listened to everything I said. He never interrupted me once. I couldn't read what was going on inside his head at all, as he never reacted to anything I said until I was finished. His response seemed to take an eternity." Malcolm looked over at me again. "When he finally spoke, he turned his head to look me straight in the eye, and without so much as even blinking he told me that *that* was exactly what he needed to hear. He reached out and shook my hand very firmly, then stood up and walked out the door!"

"No way!" I burst out. "He just walked out?"

"He just walked out – and not just out of my office, but out of the building too. I have a feeling he was heading back to the hospital, or maybe he was going home. Who knows? But I could feel that he was going to be on the right track from there on."

"That's a phenomenal story. Its life changing. What did the others say?"

"Of course, everyone wanted to know what happened. I didn't tell them everything, as that felt like it should be kept between my boss and me, but I did tell them about the accident and that he might be a bit different for a while, and to give him his space. That seemed to answer their questions well enough. We all went back to work, but I couldn't concentrate on anything for the rest of the day. I've still got all sorts of thoughts roaming around my head that are looking for somewhere to land."

Malcolm and I stayed close on the couch for hours that night, quietly chatting about the experiences of the day. They gave us plenty to talk about. What happened to Malcolm was undoubtedly more dramatic than what happened at my workplace, but we came to the conclusion that the magnitude of an event doesn't really make that much difference. Big or small, every experience provides the opportunity for examination, reaction, and emotion. And because no one lives in a bubble, others are always affected too. Without a doubt, our lives were changing. And the lives of the people around us were changing because of that.

I'd heard it said before that one person can change the world, but I always thought that was a bit far-fetched. Now, however, it seemed as plain as day because we had both just done that in our own way. In fact, as Malcolm and I examined this point further, we came to realize that that's actually the *only* way the world gets changed – by the actions of one person. What one person starts, others pick up, and who knows where that could lead. We all need to feel that our actions are important – and guess what...*THEY ARE!*

The next few days at work did not allow a lot of time for Jodi and me to talk at any length. But we were building a new type of bond - bit by bit. We could both feel it. It was especially beneficial for me. I discovered that thinking internally about concepts and actually verbalizing them are two different sides of the same coin. Working out how to put my thoughts into words was a continuing challenge for me.

Malcolm's work environment ended up changing quite a bit after his boss's breakdown. Empathy seemed to replace tension, which made for a more pleasing environment for everyone. His boss was relatively quiet and kept to himself a lot. Malcolm thought he could hear the comings and goings of his boss's thoughts – sort of like a warm fall wind that would brush past you heading one direction and then coming back again in the other direction. Everyone wondered where it would all lead, but without a doubt, they knew it was going to be for the better once the dust settled.

Crow, on the other hand, had a completely different sort of experience to share with us. He phoned late Thursday night, and Malcolm answered. "Hi Malcolm. Look, I really can't figure out what's going on inside me and wanted to talk to you guys if it's not too late." Malcolm motioned for me to pick up the other phone, which I did.

"Hi Crow. I'm here too. What's up?"

"Hi Julie. I don't know if you guys remember me telling you about Cliff at work – you know, the guy that doesn't seem to like me very much? We certainly don't think of each other as friends, but over the years we've learned to tolerate each other, and to avoid each other. But then a couple of nights ago at the bar, he sat down at the same table I was at, which really surprised me. Next thing I know he's throwing sarcastic little jabs in my direction, of all things!"

"Why would he want to do that?" Malcolm asked surprised.

"I don't know. As far as I could tell he had some sort of bee in his bonnet, because it got worse, to the point where his intention to discredit my work ethic in front of everyone else became blatantly obvious."

"Talk about being put on the spot! What did you do?" I questioned.

"After my initial surprise, I decided to just let it go and not react.

I know I do a good job at work, and so did everyone else at the table. Cliff is the type of guy that needs to put others down to lift himself up – you know the type, so I actually even found myself feeling sorry for him and the kind of life he must be living."

"Then why are you so upset now? Obviously there's more to this story." I knew there had to be more for our positive out-going Crow to be this bothered.

"You got that right – way more. When I woke up the next morning I was shocked at how upset I was at the whole situation. In fact, I was *really* pissed off, to the point where I was uncontrollably bitter *and* angry at the same time. That's not an emotional state I want to be in – but there I was. I couldn't seem to shake the feeling or get any kind of control over it. I was plain old mad! And I remained that way the entire day at work. I knew the solution lay with me, and not Cliff, but I couldn't get myself to think rationally because my emotions kept getting in the way. They were not about to be ignored."

"Are you still angry then?" I gently probed.

"No, at this point I'm more stumped than anything. You see, as I lay in bed that night after work, a thought came to me that this was actually a useful experience – one that I could use to examine myself. Then I remembered that this was all a play we were acting in anyway, and that the guy who plays the jerk could end up being your friend in the end. That's what allowed me to get beyond my emotions and to start thinking in a reasonable manner again. So, I started to wonder about the buttons this guy pushed. I thought I'd gotten over those kinds of issues as I grew up. In fact, I was pretty sure I didn't have buttons to push anymore, but apparently I was wrong, and this experience was showing me there was a bit more work to do in this area. And I know I need to figure it out or it's going to get repeated until I do."

"I bet we all have buttons we don't know about," I offered. "Did you manage to figure it out?"

"That's the funny thing. As I started to get into it, I realized that the self-confidence I had in myself might not be as strong as I thought it was, cuz if it was, then what the guy said wouldn't have bothered me. So obviously, there's more to it, and that's what I can't figure out. I must have some sort of belief deep down that I haven't worked through yet. That's actually why I called you guys to begin with. I wanted to ask you if it was okay to talk it out on Friday to help me out. It would be great if Griffin would show up too and give me a clue, but even if we could all just talk about it, I think it would help."

"That actually sounds like a great topic for Friday night. We've both got stories to tell too," Malcolm replied. "Friday's going to be very informative."

"What about George?" I asked. "Did he have anything interesting happen to him?"

"Oh yes, he did," Crow announced. "But I'm going to let him tell you all about it on Friday."

Now that sounded exciting. We went to bed after we hung up, hoping for a good night's sleep because we were pretty sure Friday night was going to be a late one – there was just so much to talk about – even if our helpers didn't show up.

16

THE POWER OF THOUGHT

***"Thinking is the hardest work there is, which is the probable reason so few engage in it."* Henry Ford**

Friday evening finally came. We'd managed to settle ourselves down comfortably in our living room. You could feel the anticipation in the air. We started off with Crow's experience, but we'd barely begun when we were interrupted by a bellowing voice saying, "Expectations!" It was Griffin. "What are your expectations?"

"Where are you guys?" I asked looking around. "Are you going to appear, or do we need to talk to thin air?"

I heard them laugh. "We've been here listening since you first sat down. You're all starting to understand the way life works, so it's nice to hover about and hear what you come up with."

At the word *hover*, we all instantly looked up, and sure enough, there they were – floating horizontally in various relaxed positions a few inches below the ceiling, looking down at us!

"Very funny," I said. "Do you think you could come down to our level and join us? I don't want to get a kink in my neck."

They gradually floated down with slightly rambunctious smiles on their faces, and found places to sit. It would be so neat to have the kind of freedoms they have, I thought to myself.

"What are your expectations?" Griffin questioned Crow again, but in a much softer tone.

"I'm not sure what you're getting at?" Crow confessed.

"Everyone has expectations. As a child, you automatically develop them and rarely think to question them, let alone attempt to change them. Think of some of the situations you experienced as a child, and you'll see how innocently expectations can become ingrained in you. But they create your reality, just as much as your beliefs do. Actually, it's the only way your reality gets created. Understand your beliefs, understand your expectations, and you will discover why your reality is what it is."

"Okay," Crow replied slowly. "I think I get it. But I believe I *did* change my expectations about myself from what they were when I was growing up. I do expect to always be an honorable, hard-working, honest type of guy - and so far, I think I've achieved this. That's why I don't understand why I became so upset from that whole incident the next day. I thought I was past those feelings."

"And what is your expectation of others? How do you expect the world to be, and how do you expect to be treated by the world?" Griffin continued gently probing.

"My first thought is that I expect to be treated respectfully by others, as that's how I would like to think I treat them. Am I being short-sighted with that expectation?" Crow asked Griffin.

"I wouldn't say short-sighted, but maybe too constrictive. You cannot control others, or how they think, or how they act. You cannot expect them to be this way or that way just because you are this way or that way. Everyone, and every*thing*, sees the world from their own personal perspective - even an ant, or a tree, or a star. They see life from their perspective – not yours, and as you can imagine, what they see is very different from your way of looking at things. You see, your control lies within you, and that is all you have control of. But don't get me wrong when I say *that is all you have,* as you are powerful beyond imagination. Now, there will always be others who have different opinions than yours - even a different view about you as a person than the one you hold about yourself, and some don't mind being vocal about it either. So which opinion are you going to value the most? If you value others' opinions over your own, then indeed, be concerned about what they're saying about you. But why would you give them that power? Why not spend your time learning more about yourself and give yourself that power? No one has authority over you unless you allow it. And no one will come into your life unless you've invited them."

"Hmmm - sounds to me like I unwittingly handed Cliff my power on a silver platter for fine dining," Crow said. "I think it would have been better if I'd tried to diffuse the situation when it first started instead of acting like a thick-skinned martyr. That did nothing to help, did it?"

"To diffuse would have been a better choice for both of you," Griffin acknowledged. "You could have asked him how it is that he manages to perform so well at his job, and would he mind if you came around to get some pointers. I mean, really, what's he going to say after that? You would have snuffed out the spark on the fuse before it hit the dynamite – kaboom!" We all jumped sky high when Griffin suddenly threw his arms up and exploded vocally. "Relax, guys," he said laughing. "Just trying to get my point across, which I believe I did quite well, if I do say so myself. Yes, diffusion would have been the best option. But, that brings me to another point. What is your definition of good? What is your expectation from the very idea of good?" Griffin questioned Crow staring intensely at him.

"Good is, uh - good, isn't it? Good things, happy things, fun things, interesting, positive things, right things. I'm not sure how else to describe it, but I have a feeling there's more to it than I'm seeing because my wheels are spinning."

"Your definition of, and expectation of, good might be something you want to look at too," Griffin explained to Crow. "Good can come in many forms. Something that does not look good at first sight could end up being the best thing that's ever happened to you, once you've worked it all the way through."

"Are you saying that what I might initially term as negative could actually end up being positive? Cuz I can see that making sense."

"Exactly. Your expectation of *good* needed an adjustment for you to grow as a person. Your co-worker offered you the opportunity to do this. It's not a button inside you that needs fixing, it's a different perspective that you need to think through, develop, and adopt as a belief. You cannot stipulate how the world should operate - trust that experiences will come your way in whatever manner that best benefits you. In other words – it's *all* good. You do live in a safe universe, even though it can often appear to be quite the contrary."

"I think that's what's happening to my boss," Malcolm added. "I think the tragedy that's befallen him and his son is going to make better people out of both of them. It'll probably help a lot of other people too. So then, it's not really a tragedy, is it?"

"That's exactly right, Malcolm," Bluedon agreed. "Things happen when you live a physical life. It's part and parcel of living in a body in this reality. What you make out of those happenings is what's important. You don't die. You will change form and leave the physical body behind, but *you* will never die. While you're alive, you'll be presented with opportunities to help you learn about yourself, and hopefully improve yourself. Some were even planned before you came here. Then when the day does come to leave your physical realm, you get to take your new and improved *self* with you - so that's what you should be concentrating on while you are here. Remember – if you are alive, then *BE* alive!"

"Well said, Bluedon!" Kodiak added, looking rather impressed. "Get your vitality going! I like it. I wonder if that could become a catchphrase?"

Griffin chuckled, "That is good, I have to admit. Now, Crow - I'd like to give you a bit of insight on your co-worker." Griffin turned his attention back to Crow. "I think it'll help everyone get a better understanding of the dynamics possible behind emotional interactions with others. Your co-worker's personality does not possess the type of self-confidence you do. He's not yet figured out how to take responsibility for his current position in life. In other words, he's an active participant in the blame game. Of course, he hides this by being somewhat outspoken and obnoxious, which does not help him make friends - but friends are what he would truly like to have. Instead of attracting friends, his attitude distances others from him. For self-protection, he's developed a shield that states there's nothing wrong with him. In his mind, he's superior and others are inferior. It's a vicious cycle, and very difficult to step out of. When I look at his childhood, I see that it's fairly similar to yours, except that he did not leave as you did. Instead, he stayed around for many more years of abuse, which put a big chip on his shoulders. He was quite the bully in school. He was trying to create protective armor from the poisoned arrows his classmates and family directed at him. Why would he expect anything different as he grew into an adult? Poisoned arrows were all he'd known since childhood. His armor is still intact. Only now he eggs people on to shoot their arrows so that he can demonstrate his superiority in being able to deflect them. It's rather complicated for him, but you can see that getting upset with him will not help either of you. If you can find a chink in his armor and throw something positive at him - catch him off guard - now that would be the best solution for all concerned. If you can get in there with good intent when he's not looking, you would be doing him a big favor. As I said, what he really wants is to be accepted by others, to have a friend, and to one day be a friend to himself. That is his challenge this time around."

"I had no idea! It sure changes things when you look at situations from the big picture. I'm gonna see if I can help him. I'll need to wait for just the right moment - but you know what - I *expect* that moment to show itself! How's that for putting your advice into action?" Crow was quite excited by the opportunity. What a switch to go from being pissed off to be eager to help.

"Very good, indeed!" Griffin affirmed. "Keep in mind too, that as you help him, you also help yourself. It's a big win all the way around."

"What about you, George?" I asked. "We haven't had time to find out what happened to you yet, and I know something interesting did. Why don't you tell us?"

"I'd like to hear it again, too," Kodiak added.

"Sure. It's not as dramatic as what happened to Malcolm, but it's still extremely interesting. I haven't been able to get it out of my mind, actually."

Kodiak interrupted, "Just remember, there is no such thing as good, better, and best when it comes to interactions and learning. They all have the same value whether it has to do with a bug on the sidewalk or a person of authority. I just wanted to clear that up before we continued, as it's important to understand that concept."

"Cool!" I interjected. "Malcolm and I came to that conclusion all on our own a few days ago. A pat on the back for us, honey!" I said, looking over at him.

"Got it. I was actually at the pub with Crow and saw the whole thing with Cliff. And I have to say that I agree entirely with what Griffin's been saying. It was a good experience, and I can see it expanding to become even better as time goes on," George raised his glass to Crow and nodded before continuing with his own story. "So, after I left the pub, I started walking home, and in fact, I was deep in thought about why Cliff had acted like that towards Crow. I wasn't really paying attention to my surroundings, which is unusual for me. Suddenly, I heard a noise, and when I looked up, I found myself face to face with a young woman that looked every bit to be a *woman of the night*. She seemed quite desperate as her eyes locked onto mine. She didn't even glance away. It was me that looked away. I was going to shake my head to say that I wasn't interested in what she appeared to be offering, and continue walking home, but then I thought, you know what, she's a person that has put herself right in front of my path. Maybe there's something I can learn here. So, I asked her if she'd like to just talk for a bit. Her eyes got that frightened animal look to them, and I didn't know what to do as I thought she was going to break into a run. I quickly told her that I had no trouble paying for half an hour of her time, but all I wanted to do was go sit down on a bench and talk - nothing else. That seemed to calm her down. Forty bucks, she said, quite assertively, and held her hand out for the money. Fortunately, I had forty dollars in my wallet. So, I gave it to her, and she pointed to a nearby bench that was under a lamppost. We sat down, and she said, okay, what do you want to talk about? I told her I wanted to talk about her. I wanted to know her story. Why she came to have the occupation she did. She stared at me for quite some time at that request. I think she was trying to assess if I was a weirdo, a cop, or an angel. I'm not sure what her final conclusion was, but at least it was good enough to have her start talking about herself. She said she'd had a happy, normal early childhood - wonderful parents, lived in a good neighborhood, had lots of friends, and all was well until she turned seven. That was when her Dad was in a car accident and passed away. In the blink of an eye, her life changed. One day he was there laughing with her, and the next day he was gone. I could see her eyes moist up as she told me this. They never really got over it. Her mother had been a stay at home mom, and now she was left with all the bills, no job or training of any kind to bring in any money. Plus, a ton of grief to deal with, and a seven-year-old daughter who rebelled at the loss. Unfortunately, it was too much for her Mom, and she turned to alcohol to drown her pain. She was not able to get a job, so they ended up on welfare. They had to sell the house and move to a more affordable neighborhood, which was okay for a while. But since a lot of the money went to alcohol, they eventually couldn't afford to stay there either and left their house for the street. She was ten when that happened. She stopped talking for a while after that statement. I think she was reliving that part of her life. I felt so sad for her, but at the same time, I realized that her story happened all too often. She told me she didn't want to get into the details of street life at the age of ten, trying to support an alcoholic mother, but needless to say, she said it was not ideal. It wasn't long until a fellow saw a lucrative situation in front of him, and took both of them in, in exchange for both of them turning tricks. I felt like throwing up when she said that."

"Good grief, that makes me sick to my stomach too!" I gasped. "She was only ten for heaven's sakes! What kind of man would even want to take part in something like that?" I found it completely disgusting.

"Believe me, Julie, that's exactly what I was thinking and pretty much what I said to her."

"What did she say?" Malcolm asked, feeling quite concerned as well.

"She looked at me with such weary old eyes that told me without words that there are lots of those men around, and they're the ones that keep this sad wheel greased. I asked her how old she was now, as it was tough to tell with all the makeup and the type of clothes she was wearing. Sixteen, she said, going on thirty - and your time is almost up. You're either going to have to give me more money, or I'm going to have to go back to work, she told me. Apparently, her so-called 'caretaker' kept watch on his prized property so that she wouldn't run away. Why do you stay, I asked her, while I was looking to see if I could scrounge up more money from my pockets? For my mother's sake, she said, with a pained look on her face. She isn't well, and I can't leave her. I don't think she'll live much longer. I'd found five more dollars in change in my pocket and handed this over to her so that the fellow watching would see that she was getting more money, but I knew it wouldn't buy me much time. I told her she could change this - it would take courage, but I felt she'd be able to do it because I could sense a powerful personality underneath all the rubbish thrown at her. I asked her what her name was, but she looked at me like I was a fool, as there was no way she was going to give me her real name. I told her I would give her my name and phone number and if she ever wanted to talk again, she should call me. Again, that look. But then she softened a bit and said I should tell her my phone number and that she would remember it, as she'd always been able to remember numbers. So, I told her, and she repeated it and then that was it. Our time was up. She got up and walked over to another street corner to continue on with her life. I watched her walk away and sent her every bit of help and healing and good wishes I could muster. She's been heavy on my mind ever since. I find it all so incredibly sad."

"That story knocks the stuffing out of me," I said, still feeling sick inside. "I don't even know what to say - other than that my heart breaks for her and all the others in that situation. Is there some way we can help?"

"It is sad. I have to agree. And so unnecessary," Omar slowly began. "The first thing to remember is that good can always come from something like this. It was chosen, and it can be turned around, but it is an uphill battle. I don't see your current civilization wanting to change it quite yet. Or maybe I should say, I don't see a certain segment of society wanting to change it yet, and I am talking mostly of a certain type of man, although to be fair, women are not totally excluded here either. But remember - all of you," Omar emphasized, pausing to look at each of us individually, "you cannot fix the entire world. You can only work with what comes to you in your life, or what you concern yourself with in your life. What you work on in a positive manner is indeed helping in ways you cannot even imagine right now. Do not let yourself become depressed because you can't fix everything. Just keep working on what you can do, where you are, and with who you know. Be assured that your actions will indeed change the world for the better."

"I'm not sure you realize what you've done for that young woman George," Kodiak added, looking over at George. "She's been thinking of finding a way out for a while now, and your talk with her has reinforced that idea at an important point in her life. It will take some time yet, but your sincere interest was the trigger that'll start the shift into a new life for her. It was no accident that you ran into her. It was her own expectations that brought you to her. She is indeed a strong personality and has a good chance of turning her life around, but she will not leave her mother. However, I also do not believe her mother will be alive much longer. And I agree that her situation is unfortunate, but it was necessary as she is repaying a debt from a life when she was a very abusive male. That debt is almost paid, and she will soon have the opportunity to break free.

Whether or not she takes it is up to her. There is always free will. But you have given her a nudge in the right direction."

"I'm happy about that, but I don't understand why I can't get her out of my thoughts. Are we connected somehow?" George asked Kodiak.

"It's really quite simple when you can see the whole picture," Kodiak answered. "You see, you were the wife she abused when she was a male in that lifetime. It would seem that you wanted to let her know the debt was paid, and now she should get on with her current life in a better way. Yes, there is a connection between the two of you, and so you see, it was no accident that you ran into each other."

"Her wife! Wow!" George exclaimed as he put it all together. "That actually explains a few things. What about her mother? Was she connected to me too?"

"Her present mother was your daughter in that life. Some incest took place, and now your young friend is making up for it by taking care of *his daughter* till her dying day in this lifetime. As I said, there is always free will. What you do in this lifetime affects your other lives, and what you've done in other lives affects this lifetime. We don't like to use the word karma, as it has too many improper connotations attached to it. However, harm done to others is not forgotten, and debts do need to be repaid in some way, at some point."

"Man, I can see a lot of debts being repaid all around me, and a lot of debts that are going to need to be repaid," Crow acknowledged. "I, for one, do not want to create any of those for me going forward."

None of us did, that's for sure. Now that I knew how it worked, I planned to be much more aware of how I treated others, and the choices I made in this life. It seemed like there was so much to learn, and that we were only scratching the surface of truly living life. What had I been doing up to this point, I wondered? Living life for sure, but not with this kind of purpose or understanding. I wished I could just project the knowledge I'd gained into every person's brain that I met. It would be so neat if they could simply assimilate what I knew without me having to explain it first.

"They actually do, Julie," Omar said.

Right. I'd forgotten once again that these guys know what we're thinking. But Malcolm, Crow, and George did not have a clue what was going on in my mind, so I explained to them what my wishful thinking was about, then asked Omar to explain further.

"It's inner reality at work. You don't know it, and your society definitely does not accept it, but telepathy is at work constantly on your plane. Your thoughts don't stay in your brain. It's not even your brain that thinks your thoughts – it's your mind that comes up with thoughts and ideas. They are not encapsulated forever in your bony skull. Thoughts and ideas are composed of energy that flows outward from you. And that energy can be felt by other people's inner senses. Like tends to attract like, and that goes for positive and negative thoughts. One day your scientists will realize this, but I believe that could take a while as that type of energy hasn't even been discovered yet. Many aspects of your civilization will definitely change once this discovery is made, however, and of course *proven*, as we know how much your civilization needs proof before there is acceptance."

All four of them were looking rather intently at us. "I have a feeling this concept comes as a surprise to you all," Griffin announced.

"I remember you telling us about thoughts not staying in our heads, but I never took it much further at that time," I conceded. "I'm actually not sure where to put this information in relation to everything else."

"Same for me," Malcolm added.

"I can see where it would be confusing for you, as it's certainly not common knowledge in your society these days. But there were previous civilizations on earth that understood the power of thought and knew how to utilize it. Your skin is not a bag that keeps everything locked inside. It does hold in your physical parts, but as you are learning, you are so much more than a physical body. There is that top floor inner self we've talked about. Not everything is physical and solid. You can't deny that you think thoughts, and you know that everyone else does too. Many people, including your selves, have ideas. Are those thoughts and ideas physical? You can't see a thought, or taste a thought, or touch it, or hear it. It's not physical the same way the tree outside your door is. So where is it then? What is it then? I'll tell you. It's a form of energy that you create, and once created, it radiates outward. It's drawn to live in the realm where all energy lives."

"I'm almost afraid to ask, Griffin, but I need to know. Where is that realm?" Crow asked cautiously.

"You see that space between you and Julie - or the space between the couch and the coffee table - or the space between all the particles that make up your rug, or the space between the earth and the stars, or the space between your cells? Well, *that's* where it exists. It exists everywhere. It's where you exist too. It's where everything exists. *Everything* is made of energy," Griffin triumphantly finished, flinging both arms out to indicate the enormity of his answer. Golden rays from his cloak were flying everywhere!

At first, I was bewildered, but there was a tiny bit inside me that felt vindicated. For I'd always believed, in the back of my mind somewhere, that the world worked using an undiscovered type of energy. From what I was hearing, that is what we were being told by our helpers. Wow! Maybe I could bring that belief to the forefront now. How come I *knew* this? Where did that knowledge come from? Where was this all going to take me, I asked myself?

"Many people know more than they allow themselves to acknowledge," Omar told me. "You're not unusual in that respect, Julie. The rest of you know a lot of things too; otherwise, you wouldn't be the close friends you are. It's good to start unlocking some of your knowledge and sharing it as well. Knowledge doesn't do anyone any good if it's hoarded. But, I think we've said enough for tonight, and we will leave you to your discussions and the living of your exciting physical life. You are all doing well in that area.

There are many changes taking place within you. We will be seeing you again at some point soon."

They'd vanished before we could even say good-bye. When they were there, the living room seemed so alive, but now it felt normal again. We all looked at each other, not really knowing how to even begin verbalizing what we were thinking. We decided to call it a night. We wanted time – that thing that's not even supposed to exist – to absorb what we'd just learned before beginning a discussion about it.

George and Crow left to go home, and Malcolm and I went to bed right after they closed the door.

"What do you make of this, Malcolm?" I asked as we climbed into bed. "I'm afraid to even think a thought. I don't want to send anything negative out into this realm of energy surrounding us."

"I feel the same; like I need to be very careful what I think. Maybe careful is not the right word. Maybe we need to be more *aware* of what we think, and the power that thoughts have. And I can see now why changing a belief would indeed change reality - how could it not, really, if you follow their logic. Your new belief would send out different thought energy that would set into motion...ah, whatever it is that it sets into motion. But I believe it would all lead to a different result in the physical world. It actually makes perfect sense if you think about it."

"You're right. I like that idea. And you know how they were saying that like attracts like – so then positive thoughts would join up with other similar thoughts, and that can make for a whopping mass of good energy."

"Yeah, but don't forget the same goes for negative thoughts," Malcolm cautioned. "They would build up their own mass too. I wonder which mass is larger right now - the positive or the negative?"

"I sure hope, for the sake of the world, that it's the positive one, but it could be neck and neck, especially when you think of the news stories. There's not a lot of positive in most of them. I know when I read about all the disasters, crime, racial unrest, drugs, not to mention climate change, it doesn't make me feel good inside. But I don't believe I think negative thoughts after reading those stories. It's more like I feel sad about the state of humanity. So maybe if I try to send out a positive thought, it would help. What do you think?"

"I think," Malcolm slowly replied, "that for many situations, sending out positive thoughts is the best we can do to help. I mean, you can't pretend these issues don't exist. And it's plain to see that you and I can't fix everything that is going wrong in this world. Still, at least we can send out something positive, especially now that we know that thought is an energy that gets attracted to other helpful energies. Maybe, just maybe, by adding to the positive side, rather than the negative side, we truly are helping more than we actually know."

"You're right. We can't fix everything. That's what they said, and I definitely agree. But I think we have a responsibility to do what we can in our own little sphere, like we were saying before. Spreading the idea of open-mindedness and positive thinking will help a lot. We may never know how much, but at least we know it's actually doing something in a good way."

"Yeah, I think you've got it, Julie. It's no joking matter, is it? I'm going to try to do my best to put out positive, helpful, understanding thoughts," Malcolm assured me as he turned over to get his pillow just right for sleeping.

"Me too, although I'll be surprised if I don't slip up from time to time, but at least I'm going to consciously try."

It took a while to fall asleep that night. My last *thought* before I drifted off to sleep was that we were so lucky to be learning what we were being taught and that we needed to do something with this knowledge.

17

A DAY AT THE OCEAN

"You are here to use, enjoy, and express yourself through your body. You are here to aid in the great expansion of consciousness. You are not here to cry about the miseries of the human condition, but to change them when you find them not to your liking through the joy, strength, and vitality that is within you; to create the spirit as faithfully and beautifully as you can in flesh." **Seth & Jane Roberts**

We woke up to one of those glorious sunny, but not too hot, days. You know the kind I'm talking about; when all you want to do is get outside and let that blue-sky soak into every cell in your body. The forecast said the whole weekend was going to be like that.

Malcolm and I were enjoying a relaxing breakfast on our deck when I suddenly had a great idea. "Too bad for housecleaning!" I declared, sitting up. "Let's get out of here today!"

"Great idea, Julie! I'll call Crow to see if we could climb into his van and head out to the ocean; maybe pack a lunch, and just sit back and enjoy a natural vista for a change."

Malcolm took his coffee with him into the kitchen and called Crow. I could hear them chatting but couldn't make out what they were saying. It didn't take long, though, and Malcolm came back out on the deck grinning from ear to ear. "Crow had an even better idea. You're gonna love this. He said we should take tents and sleeping bags and spend the night at the ocean. In fact, he'd just been on the phone with George, and they were making plans to go out there, and were about to call us. What do you think? Should we do it?"

"Heck, yeah! Let's get packing. I'll do the food and you get the other stuff together."

An hour later, the van pulled up. We threw everything in and took off like a bunch of excited ducks heading for water. George had recently discovered this place on one of his bike rides. It wasn't even far away!

When the van came to a halt, we jumped out and ran to the ocean. What a view! Gorgeous - absolutely gorgeous, as far as we could see. The powerful ocean waves crashing on the shore were relentless. They had the kind of energy that drew you in until you were completely mesmerized; swaying back and forth in their rhythm. We checked out the entire area, trying to decide where to set up camp. We had lots of choices too, as we were the only ones there! I voted for a place that was a little quieter than right close to the shoreline. Those crashing waves were loud, and I actually found the sound a bit threatening after a while. The others didn't, but I did, so we found a nice secluded spot a bit further back for our tents; a small clearing surrounded by tall cedar trees and large boulders that cut down some of the sound. It was a rather cozy campsite - quite different from the situation we had in the dinosaur park, where everything was wide open. Without a doubt, immersing myself in nature was something I needed to do more often. I loved the feeling of freedom it was giving me.

With our campsite set up, we had the latter half of the afternoon to wander around. The shoreline was beckoning insistently. Walking along the beach is something you just have to do when you're at the ocean, so off we went. I think everyone feels that pull, whether it's the ocean, or a lake, or even a river. Water just seems to hold some sort of magic. Same as when you have a campfire, and everyone is drawn to stare at the fire. Must be some sort of primal instinct, I figured.

We didn't get very far when we came upon a large driftwood enclosure made by someone who'd been there before. It would have been relatively easy to do considering how much useable driftwood was on the shore. We went to investigate and saw that it was made reasonably well. We figured that whoever made it planned to come back to spend time there, but we didn't see any signs of recent habitation, so we thought we could maybe make it even better and add to it with whatever joint expertise we could muster. Then when the original builder came back, he'd be in for a pleasant surprise, and we'd have left our mark. A type of pay it forward, I suppose. Plus, who doesn't like building a fort?

The guys set to work on the roof. They found more pieces of driftwood and secured them with some rope we'd brought along. I worked on making a rock stove. There were so many flat rocks along the shore that it was a relatively easy thing to do. I'd watched my father do this on one of our camping holidays. Now it was my turn. First, I started on the firepit area. I didn't want to have to lift the grate off to add more wood, so I made an opening in the front of the firepit for stoking the fire – kind of like a wood stove. I wanted to make sure I could get the fire going easily, so I made a hole at the back for draw, over which I built a chimney. I was able to make it tall enough so that the smoke didn't blow all over us. Then on one side of the firepit, I laid a big flat rock for a warming area, and over the firepit I put the grill we'd brought along.

When the guys were done with the roof, they went to work on creating a table and benches close by the fire. They found some ocean worn planks further down the beach that were perfect for this. The placement of their table presented us with a stunning view. They were finishing the table off, while I was putting the final touches on my stove.

"Man," Crow exclaimed, plopping himself down on their newly made bench, "I have not had this much fun for a very long time!"

"Ditto for me," Malcolm added, wiping the sweat from his bald head. "I feel like a kid again."

"Julie, I have to say that I've seen a lot of camp stoves in my years of travel, but I've never seen anything as wonderful looking as yours!" George said, whistling. I was so proud of it I think I must have blushed!

We all sat down on the new benches and surveyed our handiwork. A sense of group pride came over us. Here we were - playing at the beach, with not a care in the world. If you've ever done anything like this, you know exactly what I'm talking about - and if you've *never* done anything like this, then you're missing out big time!

"Who wants coffee?" I jumped up. "I want to try out the stove."

Of course, they all wanted a cup, but more so, I think we simply wanted to play a bit more. The guys went to gather driftwood for a respectable fire, plus enough for the evening too. I went back to our campsite to get the stuff needed for making a fine cup of coffee.

The stove worked brilliantly. It took a little bit of work to start the fire because the driftwood seemed a bit damp, but once we were able to get some heat, everything worked like a charm. It didn't take long at all to get the coffee pot percolating – one of the best sounds and smells you can have when camping - and I was able to put the pot onto the rock slab to keep it warm, just as I'd planned. We all sat on the bench facing the ocean and very contentedly sipped our brew.

"Don't you think we've all become too serious in our lives?" Crow asked after a while. "Look how much fun we had working on this fort - it's so freeing somehow."

"I was thinking the same thing," I added.

"Me, too," Malcolm sighed a very long peaceful sigh. "I feel weightless and completely energized. I think it's a momentary release from responsibilities and concerns, not that they won't return Monday morning, but for now, I'm soaking up every ounce of this freedom." Malcolm was silent for a while before continuing. "But why is that? You have to ask yourself that question. All we did was build something, quite co-operatively I might add, to the best of our ability, in a very creative way with whatever materials we had around us, using our own minds and hands. I have to say that I feel a greater sense of satisfaction sitting here at this table than I do in our own home - and way more than sitting at my desk at work. Plus, the view is, without a doubt, far superior."

"I'm sensing a create your own reality belief sort of thing going on here," I said. "What do you think? I can feel a nugget of truth slipping around beneath the surface, but I can't quite grasp it."

"I feel it too, Julie," George acknowledged. "I think we all just experienced, or maybe it's better to say that we all just *allowed* ourselves to experience, pure natural creativity - no strings attached. That's something we don't get the chance to do in our day to day lives very often. But, then again, is that a requirement of the society we live in, or is that simply our *belief* about our day to day reality?"

"Hmmm...good question," Crow answered. "It's certainly a requirement at my job, and I would think for all of you too. I have to go by the book if I want to keep my job, and because I need the money to live, I want to keep my job. But...hang on a minute here. It just hit me that I only work eight hours a day, and there's a lot more than eight hours in a day. Why not allow my creativity to surface with some of my other time? I'm sure I could find something to do that I could put some creative energy into. Why did I not think of this before?"

"I don't know Crow, but I think you're on the right track," I agreed. "How I felt building that stove is very similar to how I feel when I'm out in our backyard tending to the flowers and the trees. I think I've got a bit more creative leeway at work than the rest of you, but it still wouldn't be enough for me if I didn't have an imaginative outlet of some sort at home. Being creative always gives me more energy, which helps make work more positive, I find. I have a good idea - why don't we all become gardeners? The world definitely needs more people to learn how to grow things."

"I like your beautiful backyard, Julie, but I have to admit that I'm not much into growing," Crow answered sadly, but then perked up. "I've always liked working with wood and with my hands, though. I don't suppose you'd want some birdhouses for your backyard, would you?"

"I'd love some birdhouses! That's a great idea. But they'd have to be funky ones – kind of like the structure you just added to, only more waterproof. When do I get my first one?" I eagerly asked Crow.

"Maybe not too long from now. Let me play around with it for a bit."

Malcolm and George decided to come up with something they could do too. It had been a revelation to discover that our current life didn't entail much creativity, nor the kind of personal satisfaction we gained from working on the ocean fort. We'd forgotten that sensation, which brought us face to face with a buried belief that said *life is mundane, and we must grin and bear it.* That's what we believed, what we expected, and what we got. Sad, but true. However, we knew it didn't have to be like that at all, and planned to change this belief going forward. I was really looking forward to Crow's first birdhouse, and seeing what the other two would come up with.

We were all thinking about various creative ventures when a massive golden eagle flew past our vision. It's not that uncommon to see these at the coast, but this one was especially impressive, and we had a front-row seat to its antics. At first, we thought it must be fishing. But it soon became apparent that it wasn't looking for anything, but was simply enjoying playing with the wind currents. What a display of perfection! It would fly up high and hover for what seemed an eternity. Then it would drop straight down faster than our eyes could follow it, only to go right back up again in a spiral motion. Then another eagle showed up. They locked talons in mid-air and did cartwheels across the sky! We'd heard they did this as a mating ritual but none of us had ever seen it before. What a show they put on! Eventually, they flew off to another area, and we lost sight of them.

"I could feel their energy - their spontaneity, and the pure joy they exude in being alive," Crow exclaimed, craning his neck to see if he could find them again.

"I felt it too. They're beautiful and so majestic, and so much who they are. They ooze confidence." I closed my eyes trying to remember their beauty. "You know, I don't think they're worried about what the newspapers say every day. They don't know about the dire straits the world is in like we do - because if they did, they couldn't possibly be so free." Where did that come from, I wondered as soon as I said it? I opened my mouth and out it came. I heard myself saying it, but hadn't heard myself thinking it. Weird.

When I opened my eyes, six astonished eyeballs were looking at me. I didn't know quite what to say. I felt like I had someone inside that was speaking for me, and told the guys so. We wondered what to make of it, but after all the crazy things we'd experienced lately, we were more curious than concerned.

"Well, just think about it." I decided to play further with these thoughts. "Those eagles don't know about the wars being fought in the world, or the social unrest and crimes we have in our society, or the consequences of climate change. They don't worry about any of that. They only make sure they take care of themselves, which includes a bit of playtime. And look at what their personal enjoyment of their own aerial abilities has given us today. We all feel their joy, their vitality, and isn't that a better thing to spread around the world than worry and negative thoughts?"

"You're definitely right," Crow agreed, nodding. "That's what those guys were telling us, remember. Energy is everywhere. Positive attracts positive, and negative attracts negative - and that your thoughts are a form of energy that doesn't stay inside your head."

"So," George began, "when we fill ourselves up every morning with the negative news the media seems so eager to pump into us, and then commiserate with others about it during the day, we're actually adding to the cloud of negative energy. But, I'm thinking that the animals must know in some way what's going on in the world, at least when it comes to climate change. I mean, they have to live in the toxic atmosphere we're creating. Take those eagles for example; they've got to know the air is not as clean as it used to be. But that knowledge doesn't seem to stop them from performing with pure joy. You know, I think I'd feel guilty being that joyful when there's so much crap happening in the world. What do you guys think?"

"You're right, George." I let my imagination go. "That eagle *must* know how polluted the air's become, but what's it going to do about it? It must understand that the only thing it can do is enjoy its life now and hopefully add to the positive side of things. Same for a tree – what's it going to do about all the climate change and greed going on? The only form of protest available to it, is to die, and hope somebody notices! Holy! Do you think nature *knows* its environment is changing and is *consciously* choosing to emit positive energy instead of negative?"

"That's a revolutionary thought," George speculated. "But I think it does! So, using nature as an example, we can listen to the news, but still make a conscious choice to put positive energy forward afterwards, not negative. Maybe it's not important what the news says, but our reaction to the news, and what we do with it definitely is. Now, that's a really cool idea!"

"And powerful!" Malcolm exclaimed. "It's something I've never thought of before. At first it struck me as being a bit callous, but I like the idea of actually having some sort of power to do something about the awful things we're told happen in the world every day. It's natural to want to help and to feel that our actions actually do count. I find it very frustrating when it seems like there's not much I can do. Not to mention how overwhelming it is as there's just so much that needs fixing. But using your logic, we *could* do something about it, just by adopting an attitude of positivity in our own lives, and spreading good vibes. Happy no matter what! That's something we can definitely learn to do. In actual fact, those eagles are helping the world more than we are when we grimly discuss all the dreadful world events with others in our day to day life. That always leaves me with a helpless feeling."

The eagles were back. The show they put on before was nothing compared to what they were displaying now. They truly out did themselves. I think they were thanking us in their own way for joining their team.

"Actually, discussing negative news with friends just doubles the negativity, don't you think?" I continued, staring up at the eagles. "You'd have two people shaking their heads about how awful it is instead of two people enjoying themselves like these two eagles are. I can visualize all those negative thoughts flying straight up to join with the negative energy side." I quickly jumped up from my seat, as the urgency hit me. "We've got to change – not tomorrow, but today, right now! I don't want to add even a smidgen of negative energy to that pot. There's too much there already. I like the free, joyful, and invigorating way nature expresses itself. I want to learn how to radiate that in my life." Arms outstretched, twirling barefoot in the sand, I turned to face the guys and said wide-eyed, "Let's be like them!" I got a standing ovation!

What was left of the afternoon was spent drinking our coffee pot dry and discussing the issue of positive versus negative thoughts and energy. It seemed like a big deal to all of us, and we wanted to work it through to a solid understanding so that we could act on it when we got back into our everyday working reality.

Eventually, our stomachs reminded us that it was way past supper time. We'd brought leftovers, so not a lot of prep was required. The fire got stoked, and we combined everything into one large frying pan. You can never recreate these types of meals. They're a one-off. Sometimes they're delicious, and sometimes not quite so. This one was most definitely worthy of mention, especially when the sausages, onions and garlic got to sizzling in the frying pan – what a delightful aroma. But the ambience and million-dollar view of our natural *restaurant* added much to the taste, I'm sure. A glass or two of red wine didn't hurt either. After cleaning the dishes with water heated up and kept warm over my wonderful rock stove, we decided to bring our lounge chairs over to the shore. Sitting at our picnic table was fine for supper, but as dusk approached we wanted to be able to lean our chairs back and look up at the enormous sky without craning our necks. We'd hoped for clear skies for star gazing, and were not disappointed. It was a spectacular evening, and we all felt overwhelmingly content.

The sun was getting close to the horizon. We knew it was about to dissolve into the ocean – much like it had at the dinosaur park, which made us wonder if we would hear from our helpers since we knew this was a sight they truly enjoyed. How could anyone not?

We watched, somewhat mesmerized, as it dipped further and further into the ocean. I was afraid to look away for even a second as it went down so fast. When you have something for contrast, it truly shows how quickly the earth is turning, which I found quite remarkable, actually. No wonder people long ago thought the sun revolved around the earth. That's certainly what my eyes were telling me. That sun was going down, and I knew I would see it coming back up directly behind me in the morning. So naturally, the sun was running circles around us. Imagine how difficult it must have been for people way back when to accept the fact that what their eyes were seeing was not how it really worked. It would seem that you cannot always believe what you see - just like our helpers were telling us before. There is more happening than our physical senses can ever know. Now, if scientists could…I was instantly stopped in my mental meanderings as I heard someone behind me say *WOW*!

"You came!" I happily shouted as I turned around. "I don't know about the rest of you, but I was missing these guys."

"I know I was," Malcolm quickly agreed.

"I think we all hoped to share this beautiful place with you," Crow added. "You've become a really big part of our lives, so we're really glad you came.

"How nice to be so wanted," Omar replied with a lovely smile.

"We've actually been here for a while, just drifting about watching you build your fort and listening to your discussions, which were excellent by the way. Your supper smelled delicious. In fact, the smell was a joy in itself, but I'm sure its taste was also first-rate."

"I enjoyed that smell too," Griffin spoke up as he patted his stomach. "I did enjoy my meals when I was last a physical human. The smell, the taste, the colors, the sound of the sizzle in the preparation…it's all an incredibly joyful experience. Or at least it could be if one thought about it that way. Food offers you a great venue for creative expression, and I heard you all talking about finding ways to bring more creativity into your life earlier on. I offer cooking as one of my personal suggestions, as it is close to my heart."

"I love cooking! I always have," George suddenly blurted out. "Griffin, I think you've just handed me my creative venture, and on a platter to boot. Thank you! I'm going to spend time coming up with my own great recipes. I'll test them out, and when I like them well enough, maybe I'll even write my own cookbook!"

You should have seen how lit up George's eyes were. He was so excited he was buzzing.

"Won't you need people to test your food on?" Crow elbowed him.

"For sure, I will. You guys would make great guinea pigs. Why don't we start with me cooking once a week? I could do it on Friday, maybe in your kitchen Julie, if that's okay. You've got a great kitchen, and I've just got a hot plate in the place I'm renting. I could come over right after work with stuff somewhat prepped and then cook up our Friday night meal before our weekly get together. What do you think?"

Who in their right mind would say no to an offer like that? I liked cooking, but when you have to come up with what to cook day after day, a break is very welcome. We all heartily agreed to this new schedule, and I have to add here that as time went on, we were extremely pleased we did. George turned into a fantastic cook, which was to the benefit of many. But I'm getting ahead of myself.

18

THE LECTURE

"And yet I know that you realize that your own progress as a civilization, in your terms, will come to a halt unless you progress in other directions. This is what your civilization is learning. That you cannot rape your planet." **Seth & Jane Roberts**

The sun was down, but the evening sky was still lit with a golden, pink, and orange afterglow. We had a bit of afterglow inside us too. It's hard to describe with words how utterly satisfied and content we felt inside and out. We were very present in the moment, and the moment was very present inside us, if that makes any sense. It was magnificent! We must have been sending out positive energy in spades.

"This is indeed a wonderful state you are all in," Omar announced. "It comes from being immersed in nature. Never underestimate the power nature can have on you and the energy it can give you. Try to get yourself into nature as much as you can. You will suffer no ill effects from it, and instead, add positivity into your life."

"That's what we were just talking about," I said. "I know you guys were listening. Did we think that one out correctly? Are we helping the dire state of current events by consciously keeping ourselves positive, joyful, and happy so that we can spread positive energy rather than negative energy?"

"We think we've got it right," Malcolm added. "But at the same time, I don't want to appear to be coldhearted and uncaring about the terrible plights of others that we're constantly being told of."

"But do you actually need to worry about what others think about you?" George asked Malcolm.

"Considering what just came out of my mouth, I'd have to say yes, it would seem that I do. I'd like to get rid of that concern, though. I appreciate you pointing that out to me."

"None of this is simple," Kodiak addressed us all. "It's often not clearly straightforward in physical human life. Beliefs, expectations, choices, free will - you always have those, but if you are not aware of what you think or how you feel, you tend to act without being aware of your actions, or what drives them, or their consequences. You just go with the flow. Most people don't want to stick their head above the crowd as it makes for an easy target for those who'd throw rotten eggs, and many can hardly wait to toss that egg. We all get it. We've been in your situation before, so we can empathize with you. But we've also been *past* your situation and can see it for what it really is - a learning ground.

"You hit upon a gem of information when you worked out the effects of positive and negative energy, and like attracting like. Now, what are you going to do with this discovery? That's the question. You *know* - in that place inside you that simply knows, that this is how things work. But a part of you is still worried about facing a public stoning if holding true to yourself and acting upon your knowledge gathers unwelcome public attention, and maybe even ridicule. And before you start to feel too holy about yourselves, let me tell you that all of you were quick to be the ones throwing stones in other lives. The tables are turned now, and you're on the other end of this emotion. How do you want to respond, now that you have the chance?"

"Throwing stones at people! How could I have allowed myself to do that?" I gasped in horror. I didn't want to think I was capable of such a thing! But I had to admit that deep down, a part of me felt that this had indeed been the case. Apparently, I was no prima donna.

"You've all had these tendencies in some of your other lives," Bluedon took over now. "It's not uncommon at all. Just look at all the violence around you. It's still happening, and it didn't appear out of the blue. You're better off to not deny this portion of yourself, but to use this life to rectify it."

"That certainly puts it into perspective," Malcolm replied. "I can see now why I worry what others think of me, and more importantly, why I need to learn how *not* to worry about what others think of me. I've gotta learn to move past it."

"I've cared a great deal about what others have thought of me in the past," Crow explained. "I had to carve an *acceptable* image of myself from a seemingly negative past. No easy task, but I believe I succeeded. However, it's no longer just an image – it's become who I am, and without a doubt, I *like* who I am. I don't feel like I need anyone's approval anymore. I'm going to forget about the dramatic and negative events that the news so faithfully searches out and brings to us. Instead, I choose to focus on the beneficial parts of the news. Some stations actually do make sure they include good deeds and actions. It's not all doom and gloom. The same goes for stories in the newspapers or on the internet – there are lots to choose from, and they're not all negative. Then when people say to me, *'hey, have you heard about such and such awful event,'* I can counter with *'no, I haven't, but did you hear about such and such,'* and make it a positive story. Maybe that will have a good effect on them too. That way, not only am I not reinforcing their negativity, I'm also turning their focus to something positive." Crow looked quite pleased with himself.

"Good for you. That will work just fine for starters," Griffin agreed. "And you have to start somewhere. The rest of you might want to give that a go too, and then keep track of people's reactions and how you feel about yourself afterwards. I think you'll be pleasantly surprised."

I felt like I'd just learned something very powerful, and was visualizing how I could put it to work. I found I was most anxious to try this. It seemed like it would be easy to add into my life, and I couldn't see anything but good come of it. I sank back into my lawn chair to enjoy the night sky. The others joined me in this relaxing mode - even our helpers, but since they didn't bring lawn chairs, they just laid on their backs in thin air with their arms behind their heads, and their colorful cloaks gently flowing with the night breeze. What a special moment!

It was pure enjoyment. The sky was so vast and so dark. The waves were still rolling in but in a calmer fashion than earlier in the day. Billions and billions of stars sparkled in the dark sky and on the water for as far as we could see – it was absolutely breathtaking and awe-inspiring. And it was here every night putting on a show for anyone who wanted to come, and even if no one came, I realized with a jolt. It was putting on the show for itself, and for no other reason than to fully express what it was. I wanted to be like that. To just be who I am. Expressing myself fully, and not wondering if anyone was watching or what they would think or say about me behind my back. I felt extremely moved by this discovery and knew I'd hold this moment forever in my heart.

It was Crow that broke into our serenity. "Okay, I've got a question I've been wanting to ask you guys for a while now, and this seems like a very appropriate time to ask, considering the setting we find ourselves in."

"Go ahead, ask away," Griffin gallantly offered.

"Alright - where does God and religion fit into what you've been telling us?"

"Yeah, I've wondered about that too," George quickly added. "It's pretty hard not to when religion has played such a huge role in our civilization and the way we think. But I haven't heard you guys ever mention anything about God, and I'd sure like to know what you have to say on that subject."

For the first time ever, I actually heard Omar sigh. "This is such a touchy subject for humans. I'm glad you didn't ask about it before. But we can indeed start the discussion tonight. I believe you've all had enough firsthand experiences to trust that we do indeed have knowledge from a place beyond your current sphere of reality. And that what we're telling you does actually work. We do not want you to throw the baby out with the bathwater."

We got ourselves comfortable for what we were sure would be an interesting and lengthy discussion, but after we settled in, all we heard was silence for what seemed like a long time. In fact, I had to look over to see if they were still there, which they were - just quietly looking up at the night sky, so I laid my head back down again to see if I could zone in on what they were looking at.

Bluedon finally began. "God is a word we don't like to use, simply because every single person on earth has attached their own personal meaning and history to that single word - not to mention the power some have granted it. That's why it's such a complicated and touchy subject. The very word *God* is highly charged. I hear you wondering, well, do these guys believe in God, or not? The answer is both yes and no. Let me explain this in simple terms, if that's even possible. As I said, we don't use the word God as its meaning has become too varied and volatile. Instead, we like to use the term *energy*. But this is no ordinary energy. It's an *aware* energy that's composed of a loving vitality that is continuously trying to realize itself. This energy has always existed, and it will always continue to exist. There wasn't a beginning to it, and there is no end to it. It's what made you, and it's what you're made of at this very moment. It's what the ocean waves and stars in the sky are made of. It's what the space between you and the stars are made of. It's what the wind is made of. In fact, it's what every single thing is made of. Period. No exceptions exist.

"So far, this has similarities to what you think of as God, just with a less compelling name. But there are differences. This type of energy has nothing to do with a heaven or hell, as those places don't exist anywhere other than in the minds of those who believe they exist. Nor does it belong to an actual *being* who is watching over everything, giving to some and holding back from others. That type of thinking puts this energy outside of you. But it isn't outside of you. It's not even that it's inside you. It IS you. It IS everything. There is nothing that it is not.

"It works using certain principles, some of which you are starting to learn. Its essence is of a loving vitality of enormous proportions. It cannot be contained or ended. Stop and think about that for a minute; *love's energy cannot be contained!* Remarkable, isn't it? The human comprehension of love doesn't even come close to describing the type of love this energy embodies. It cannot be understood using words either - only by experiencing it. And for anyone who has experienced it, they know precisely what I'm talking about. I will not be able to describe it to you any better, but please understand that it exists in no uncertain terms, and its power is *incredible*. I hope that one day you'll understand what I'm talking about."

"That's the energy we're feeling right now, isn't it? Nature's energy!" I asked excitedly, because I thought I could indeed *feel* what Bluedon was talking about.

"Yes, that's part of it. But this type of aware and loving energy is even bigger than nature," Bluedon answered, gesturing to the incredible display of nature surrounding us at the moment.

Before I could ask anything more, Omar took over. "Belief in some kind of power greater than yourself has been a part of human civilizations for eons. How could it not be? Just look at what we're seeing in front of us right now. People long ago would be looking at a similar sight. They'd be assessing what they saw using the knowledge of the day, which for them would have been cutting edge information derived from nature. The internet certainly did not exist then. Life was much simpler. The main focus was on learning how to survive *in* nature, just as the animals do. Those cultures saw themselves as part of nature - not separate from it. They had tremendous respect for it, as natural disasters were just as mighty then as they are now.

"All humans need to eat, and nature provided their sustenance. They didn't try to control it or harness it for their own ends. They simply learned how to live within it, and honor it, because they knew they were *part of it,* and so they became very intimate with nature. Now, let's fast forward to the civilization you live in today. You do not live *in* nature. You disregard it and feel it often gets in the way of human progress, which according to your civilization is the only progress of importance. You believe it's okay to take, and take, and take from nature, without even thinking of giving back to it. You have no respect for it and no thought of even offering it some protection or even empathy. At some point the human civilization must realize that it can only carry this attitude so far, and at risk to themselves. Humans do not stand alone, or above, anything on this planet. Now is the time to change your ways and become part of nature, not separate from it."

It was all so wrong, I thought, and I felt terrible. Omar was so right. How did we get here from there, I wondered?

"Good question, Julie," Griffin answered. "As Bluedon mentioned, there are principles that natural loving energy follows. And since everything is composed of this energy, then everything follows these principles. Our sincere hope is that humans will start to look for, understand, and accept these principles again. That should help to turn things around. What's important to understand is that this energy does not impose its ideas or wishes on anything. It's composed of a loving vitality, but it does not say '*you must say such and such*' or '*you must do such and such, or else*!' Instead, it puts no restrictions or requirements on anything. In other words, it's given everything free will, and says '*here's your free will...show what you will do with it.*' How else could it ever realize itself? Free will is free will. Humans, however, are no angels, and they do like to test the waters.

"A good analogy is the gas pedal on your car. Its purpose is to move the vehicle forward when you press on it. If the driver, which would be you, pushes on it hard without a thought for the post six feet in front of the car, the gas pedal does not say *'Oh, I better not go as it will cause damage.'* No, it's been floored, so the car rushes forward, and a crash ensues. Obviously, you cannot blame the gas pedal. It's the mind that governed the foot that's caused the crash. The energy we are talking about is like the gas pedal. It will work for you in no uncertain terms as that is what it was designed to do, but you must learn how to regulate it for the outcome you desire. It is simply an all-pervasive, good-intentioned, loving energy. It is *you* that must first begin to understand yourselves, and then, learn to understand this energy and how to work with it."

Crow sat up and ran his fingers through his crazy hair a few times. "Isn't that a great analogy?" he asked George, Malcolm and I. "It makes it so easy to understand – at least for me anyway. If I want something, then I just need to figure out how to use the gas pedal to get there. It's so simple, it's brilliant!"

"Yeah, but I'm thinking that the tricky part might be figuring out where you want to go," George countered. "Otherwise, you'd be driving around aimlessly."

Griffin was suddenly in front of us in a noisy yellow dune buggy zipping back and forth in the sand – even doing a few do-nuts! "You see," he yelled out as he zoomed right past us – his golden cloak billowing behind him, "lots of gas and nowhere to go!"

We all laughed. He certainly knew how to make a point. What a crazy guy, but in a good way! I wondered what types of lives he lived when he was a human. The dune buggy had disappeared and Griffin was instantly back calmly lying beside us again.

Bluedon got up now and began to pace in front of us. His white cloak was luminous and sparkling against the dark background. For a moment I found that he was indistinguishable from the stars – their colors were one and the same! He was fairly serious as he began talking, but in a very loving sort of way. "Now, let's check out where some of your current ideas of God came from. Humans, as you know, are equipped with a full range of emotions to draw from. The two strongest are fear and love, and each one of those emotions has several brothers and sisters in its family. Many of the emotions attached to fear, like greed, anger, and control, can completely take over the loving emotions of a civilization, to the point where a downward spiral can suck a human civilization down the drain.

"We watch," Bluedon paused in his pacing for a moment as though he was remembering something before continuing. "Many of us watch and want to help as we care what happens to humans. We know more about the way things work than you do, simple because we've lived as a human, and because we no longer live as a human. *You* are on the stage acting out the play. *We* are watching from behind the curtains trying to advise.

"Now, the play being acted out two thousand years ago needed some directing. Without additional help, the audience, the actors and the stage would have annihilated themselves. There would have been no one left to clap. It was time to introduce *a way of being* that gave people hope for a better life; something with loving qualities, something that gave a sense of purpose, something that would help them out of the hell-hole they found themselves in. Otherwise, they were going down."

"Bluedon, do you mind if I take over now? Kodiak asked.

"Certainly, you may. Be my guest," Bluedon offered as he sat back down.

Kodiak and his delicate violate colored cloak were suddenly in front of us. He was pacing quite eagerly. "But how to do it? How to present something that would capture everyone's attention? How to get people to jump ship for a tiny lifeboat? We needed to start combating all the negative energy with positive energy. A decision was made to have a man born into that crowd. I admit, it's sad to say that it had to be a man as no one in that era would have listened to a woman. And it would have to appear to be an ordinary man so people could relate to him - but of course, he was no ordinary man. He needed to maintain a clear understanding of what he was bringing to the situation after he was born and not break down under the stressful conditions of the time. We knew one man was not going to be enough, so we started to work with the dream world to help prepare the way for him."

"Whoa, whoa, whoa," Crow interrupted. "What do you mean you started to work with the dream world? I was following you up till that point, but I'm not sure I understand what you mean about working with the dream world."

"The dream world," Griffin cut in, "is nothing more than another dimension of your reality. You live in your physical waking reality, but you also live in your dreaming reality. Now, don't tell me you don't dream? You know that you do, so I don't think this should surprise you that much. Thoughts, ideas, and inspirations often come through to you in your dreams. How do you think your civilization gets its ideas for advancements?"

"Okay, okay, I get it now," Crow said. "But are you telling us that you started dropping dreams into people's minds to help this guy out?"

Kodiak continued. "It was sort of like that. We wanted to create a fertile environment for this person, and to help him with what was going to be a rather difficult task. He was going into a nasty crowd, and you guys know how difficult it is to stand out in a crowd and be the target of someone else's fear and hatred. Imagine how he felt. He was going to need help, and we helped him. One man was not enough, however. It took hundreds of years, in your time, and many more men, and a great deal more dream work, but *faith* was eventually born again. Faith in something larger than yourself. And faith in something intangible. And faith is just another word for..."

"Belief!" I shouted out. Now I was excited. "I got it! There really is no difference between faith and belief and expectations - and creating your own reality! Wow!"

"Well done, Julie," Omar said kindly to me. "You do have it. An important point to remember is that faith, or beliefs and expectations, is one of the principles this energy we've been talking about uses. It works with positive beliefs and negative beliefs in the same way - it really does not make any distinctions – remember the gas pedal. It works with beliefs. What you believe is what it will work to create for you. So, you can see why prayer works as well as it does. We needed to bring some hope back to the human civilization at that time. And I believe we succeeded. This is how your current ideas of God and religion came about. What happened from there is another story, and why we continue to watch and help."

"Are you saying it was the four of you that did that?" George asked incredulously.

"No, not just the four of us. There are many that want the best for your earthly reality. Various types of helpers work together," Kodiak answered.

"But you're talking to *us* now!" George continued, somewhat alarmed. "Is there something you're trying to get us to do?"

"Not to worry," Kodiak laughed. "You're not being singled out. There's a different method being used now. The focus this time around cannot be upon the correctness of one particular person or one particular way of being. That has caused separation in your civilization. Global unity is now the goal. We hope it will eventually become obvious to the masses that *every* individual has capabilities and tools at their disposal that are currently not being utilized, let alone recognized, understood, or believed in. We want people, *all* people, to understand that the power lies *within* them, and not outside of themselves. And that it makes no difference the color of the skin that holds your physical body together, or whether you're tall, short, large, tiny, male or female, young or old. I mean, surely, your civilization has to realize this at some point, you'd think. It's obvious in other dimensions, and can become the norm here too. That's why the shift this time around has to be of mass proportions. You must quit looking outside of yourself, and start looking at what lies inside. *Everyone!*" Kodiak answered, as he swirled his cloak around him for dramatic effect.

"Don't worry," Omar added. "You are not alone. There is indeed a shift happening globally. It's been going on for quite some time. We also work on another level with global consciousness, so that the shift can happen easier. If you remember back to our first conversation Julie, I told you that the energy that propelled you to us was happening all over the world. Your civilization needs some help if it's to continue. Many, many people in your society are being worked with in various manners. There is no one correct way. We want people to understand how things actually work. We feel that if they knew this, they would make better *conscious* decisions, and perhaps then, more positivity can start an upward spiral. Does that put you more at ease?"

"I guess it does," Malcolm answered slowly. "But it also makes me realize that these visits are more than just pleasant get-togethers. Something is expected of us. What do you think, guys? Can we deliver?" Malcolm asked us all.

"I sure hope so," I said, not feeling all that sure. "I keep thinking about all the problems the world has, especially when you look at some of the leaders that have been elected, and what they stand for. Seems to me that Genghis Khan now wears a suit and a tie."

"You're not expected to change the entire world, Julie," Omar assured me. "Do not make your circle that large, or the task will seem hopeless. Change the circle around you by first changing yourself. That's where your power lies - in your own *self.* That is where you need to start. If everyone does that, the rest will take care of itself. Think of the snowflake, or the raindrop, or the grain of sand. They each do what they do, but when added together, they can be a force to reckon with."

"That I can do, I believe. In fact, I've already discovered new ways of thinking from our talks. So, I feel like I can continue on that path - but I know," and I looked over at Malcolm, Crow and George, "that we're really going to need your guidance, so please don't desert us."

"Not going to happen." Griffin was grinning. "We are stuck to you like glue."

I felt a sense of renewed energy. I've always liked projects, and this now felt like a project to me, complete with a goal. Being somewhat of an organized person, I started to plan my route. But just as I got going on that, I was once again brought up short with the next comment.

"I'm a bit surprised that no one has brought up the subject of science and how it fits into all of this," Griffin said. "Crow, you've got a scientific mind - aren't you curious?"

"I'm very curious. But I'm still trying to digest all the other info you've given us. And now you want to throw science in as well?"

"Might as well get it all out at once, don't you think? I mean, look at where we are right now," Griffin said, as he turned to gaze out at the ocean, arms raised to soak it all in. The golden light energy in his cloak seemed to be blending in with something – I could sense a swirling energy all around him, and everywhere else I looked. Was this nature's energy, I wondered? "You don't get better surroundings than this for such fundamental weighty matters. You could be here all night without any interruptions – no sirens, no traffic noise, no cell phones ringing, nobody knocking on your door. What do you think?" Griffin teased as he turned to face us. In the moonlight I could see that he was grinning most delightfully. Then he looked directly at me and winked!

It hit me that our life was not going to be the same tomorrow after all of this, so I was ready to listen. And for some strange reason, I didn't feel tired, even though it was well past midnight.

"Sure." I took the bait. "But I've got a feeling this could take a while and my stomach's rumbling. Did anybody happen to bring something to munch on?"

Crow sprung up out of his lounger. "Hey, I've got a bag of sunflower seeds in my van! I'll just run and get them. Don't start without me though." We assured him we wouldn't, and he took off in a sprint. His van wasn't too far away, so it didn't take long for him to return and fill each of our outstretched hands with a substantial bunch of seeds. Crow automatically offered some to the helpers too, which was good for a chuckle.

"I would zap you if you needed it," Griffin announced, "but you're getting plenty of revitalizing energy from the view in front of you, and the air surrounding you. You're in a good energy zone, so I know you'll be able to take in what I have to say." Once again, he looked over at me and winked.

Energy zone! So, I'd been right when I sensed the swirling

energy! I liked the sound of that. I was going to figure out how to locate those, and use them when I needed it because I did indeed feel magnificent.

Griffin started to pace back and forth in front of us, head down, hands clasped behind his back. What was he up to? He looked like a serious professor to me, gathering his thoughts. He spun around quickly, pointing his finger excitedly at me. "You got it, Julie! We should play charades later on," he announced enthusiastically. "What I'm trying to do is set the atmosphere for my dissertation on science. I certainly like this backdrop better than some of the classroom environments I've been in.

"Hmmm...how to start, I ask myself?" He took another short pause. "Well, if you look back into your history, you'll find men and *women,* believe it or not, who were interested in figuring out how things work and why things work the way they do. Inquisitive questioning minds is what they had in common. They took into account what they saw and what their senses told them existed in the reality they found themselves in. They made good use of their high intellect and reasoning powers to decipher what their findings were telling them. However, their discoveries were not always in accordance with the ruler of the day, which happened to be the rather powerful church."

Slowly, Griffin turned to face the ocean again, looking up at the stars as he continued to talk. "Galileo is an obvious example here. His discoveries in the 1600s did not support the rules the church had stringently established at that time. After peering into the skies with his homemade telescope, Galileo discovered that the earth did, in fact, circle the sun, and not the other way around as everyone took for granted. And, he had physical proof! How exciting! But, what did this discovery earn him? An inquisition from the Church, and seven years of house arrest for heresy because he wouldn't be quiet about his discovery! Ask yourself, why was the church so worried that news of Galileo's discovery might spread to the masses? Power and fear - plain and simple. By this time, the church had become an institution that was manipulated by power brokers.

They were worried that science's discoveries might become a threat to their power, so they planned to squish these types of thoughts before they got started. No one with power willingly relinquishes what they've worked so hard to establish." He was quiet again for a while, but we all knew he was nowhere near done. He turned to face us again after a bit, and when he did, our jaws dropped. He'd turned himself into a woman!

"But," s/he continued on as though nothing had happened, "inquisitive and questioning minds cannot be silenced forever - even when burned at the stake. They're like a plant with deep roots - when you pull one out, three more come in to take its place. The world needed science and the type of mind that scientists, both male *and* female, brought to society since the church's thirst for power was once again taking things in the wrong direction.

"Griffin, you're a woman!" Crow declared.

"Why, yes I am. You did ask for this if you remember."

"Well, I know I did, but it's a bit disconcerting to have it actually happen right in front of me!"

Griffin laughed a beautiful musical laugh. "We're not going to get into it now, but later on when you're all digesting this evening's events, sort out how you feel about information coming from a man versus a woman. I think you'll be surprised by beliefs you don't even know you have. Now, I'm going to continue on as a male as I don't want to overload your brain with too many changes. Watch carefully and you'll see the change."

In the moonlight we could see Griffin's features changing ever so slightly until he was back to being the male image we were used to. It was a phenomenal experience. Regrettably, I noted that I felt more comfortable with Griffin being a male. Even I, as a woman, felt that I could trust information from a male more than from a female. Hmmm...guilty as charged. Darn! I definitely planned to work on that.

Griffin started to pace again. "Many important discoveries were made over time. Eventually it became apparent that the church had been wrong on several fronts, and was consequently questioned by many. In due course, even the church realized it had been wrong. The scientists had actual physical proof. The church did not. *Proof* versus unquestioning *faith*. Now, there's nothing wrong with either of those, but one couldn't seem to accept the other, and sides were drawn. You either wanted solid proof of something's existence before you believed it was true, or you went completely on faith and believed what you were told to believe.

"Do you see where we're going with this?" Griffin stopped pacing to ask us, but I didn't think he really wanted an answer, and I didn't want to interrupt his flow. We all kept our mouths shut in anticipation of what was coming next. He had us hook, line, and sinker.

"Well, I should think it's obvious! They both went to their separate corners, quite happy to intentionally ignore each other. Science started to earn a great deal of respect, and the church started to have its power questioned, which of course led them to try to find ways of gaining followers back. Science and religion grew so far apart that it was impossible to think of ever bringing them together. Unless...unless some new scientific minds were born - scientific minds that were open to religious ideas previously snubbed. And some new religious minds that were open to scientific ideas that had been held in contempt. Imagine! Imagine what they might come up with if scientists *and* religious leaders could ignore previously held taboos and be brave enough to look at what's *actually* happening around them!!!! There are a few of these minds living right now, and I find that extremely exciting. My fingers are crossed."

"All of our fingers are crossed!" Kodiak suddenly thundered from where he was sitting. I almost fell out of my chair. I'd been so entranced with Griffin's speech that I'd forgotten about the others. "You can't prove *anything* if you don't take *everything* into consideration. You can't ignore certain types of occurrences just because they don't ring true scientifically or religiously, or because they don't happen to fit into a particular theory, or due to a fear of being laughed at by your colleagues. *If it exists, you have to include it in your theory*! Period! End of story!"

Griffin nodded courteously to Kodiak, "Well said, and too true! Thank you for that."

I saw Kodiak nod back to Griffin as he settled himself back into a lounging position. "Proceed, my friend."

Griffin thought for a bit. "Let's use an example. Where do you go when you dream? Where are your thoughts? Where are your ideas? Where are your inspirations? Where is that voice that talks to you inside your head? You're not going to find physical locations for these sorts of things. You're not going to be able to measure them with your scientific instruments. Your outer physical senses can't help you here because it all belongs to the inner world - the one that is inside you. The inner self is connected to everything. It's the self that lasts forever, and the one that is directly linked to that aware, creative, loving vital energy we spoke of earlier. The inner world follows all the universal principles we've talked about, and many we haven't. It's what creates the reality you're currently trying to sort out. The new frontier is not outer space – it's inner space! And it doesn't even require a ridiculous amount of jet fuel to get there.

"Your civilization has done wonders with its technological advancements. Still, it's in the dark ages when it comes to the inner world. Aboriginals were far more advanced in this area than your current society. Yet, you think you're superior to them because you've managed to invent vehicles of transportation that suck oil and gas out of the earth and pollute the atmosphere to boot. In case you didn't know it, that's the very air you breathe to stay alive! Your oceans have become your garbage can. But think about the animals that have to live in the ocean – do they want to live in your garbage? And now you're doing the same thing to outer space - filling it with your waste! When will your society learn? You're slowly killing yourselves *and* others, yet you mindlessly continue on. This is lunacy in my mind, not the signs of an advanced civilization! The combination of increasingly complex powerful technology, and mis-directed stagnant minds can be dangerous - a recipe for disaster, as I'm sure you all must realize at some level of your being. Surely it must be obvious that continuing growth is not sustainable. Maybe it's time to change your ultimate goal to one of *fulfillment* in a lifetime, instead of steady growth." Griffin was quite worked up.

"It may sound like we're berating you, but that is not our intention," Omar said calmly as he went to stand beside Griffin. "We're simply trying to point out to the four of you, and your intelligent minds, that the paved path the masses are gleefully traipsing down may not take you where you truly want to go. Don't wait till you get to the end to find this out. If this is ringing any sort of bells inside you, then you might want to take some time to sort out where your beliefs are in this respect. Then change them to reflect a situation more to your liking in your everyday world. Learn to think for yourself. You'll be surprised at how the changes you make to yourself will affect those around you. And in this manner, things do start to turn around. You might feel you are too insignificant, but you are more powerful than you think. Truthfully, it is the only way to create change."

"We're going to leave you alone with these thoughts now," Bluedon said. "Have your discussions and do your homework. We'll check in again from time to time. Never feel we are far away. You are *very* important to us."

They disintegrated right in front of our eyes, which left us looking out at the endless sparkling ocean and star-studded dark sky, feeling quite stunned.

"Wow," I said after several minutes, still mesmerized by their lecture. "I think we've just been told!"

"But in a caring way, don't you think?" Malcolm asked. "I mean, how could you sugar coat those issues? I think it's good they were so blunt. It's going to take some serious soul searching to do the deep housecleaning that obviously needs to be done when it comes to my beliefs. You can't keep building on top of a rotten foundation if you want to have a good solid house."

"That's certainly true. Once we sort out what a good foundation looks like, then we can build away. Think how satisfying that kind of life would be. I also liked what they said about not waiting till you get to the end of the path to discover where it led," George cautioned. "I certainly don't want to get to the end of my life only to realize I'd been going in the wrong direction the whole time. That'd be a terrible feeling. I want to sort it out now and embark on a better path. What I see as being the problem, though, is how?"

Right. How do you change the way you are, the way your life is, the way everything around you is? And how do you manage to carry on when you feel like you're the only one attempting this? Do we need to move, or can we turn our life into something different right where we are? After an intense discussion we decided to try to change our lives staying put in the city. Although, we didn't rule out moving at some point if that's where our beliefs eventually took us.

"We're free to create our own reality. That's what we're learning," Crow declared at the end of our discussion. "So, let's get on with it!"

"Count me in," I announced wholeheartedly. Malcolm and George agreed too. "Remember how they said they worked with the dream world to help the masses change the thoughts of the day? I bet they're doing that again. I know dreams have helped me gain some insights since we've known these guys. Since it's getting pretty late, why don't we go to bed and all request a helpful dream, and then tomorrow we can compare our dreams."

"That's a great idea," Crow agreed. "Let's try it and see what happens."

19

ELADIO

***"The significant problems we face in life can not be solved at the same level of thinking we were at when we created them."* Albert Einstein**

It was finally time to get some sleep. I hadn't been tired until I stood up, and then I wanted nothing more than to lay my head down on the pillow and let sleep overtake me. Energy is such a peculiar thing. It would be nice to learn how to work with it knowingly, I thought. As I lay all cozy in my sleeping bag, I made suggestions to myself about the dream I wanted to have. But right after that, I got the idea that I could also suggest that I'd have an abundance of energy tomorrow. That would be really cool if that worked - and then I drifted off to sleep.

Next thing I knew, I was in my kitchen making cookies. I had a nice old log home in a country setting. It was getting dark outside. A short flicker of light in the sky caught my attention, and when I looked out the window to see what it could have been, I saw more and more lights showing up. I knew instantly that they were flying saucers – *lots* of flying saucers – and I also knew that they were coming for me. I was scared, but only for an instant, as the next thing I knew, I was inside one of the smaller saucers! As I looked around, I was surprised to see that the people operating the spaceship looked the same as humans, except that their hair was somehow stiffer and very silvery. A man was driving, and a woman was helping to organize things. They were looking for a particular tree they were supposed to meet the mothership at, and they couldn't find it. They were worried they'd be late, and the woman was frantically going from window to window trying to find it. I was amazed that they were lost. I'd thought people in spaceships would be more advanced in their technology than that – but they were just like us, looking out the window trying to find out where they were. Then, without knowing how, we were inside the big spaceship, which was a lot bigger than the first one. Definitely a saucer shape judging from the inside and the large flat, spherical floor we were standing on. The driver was rather stocky and wore a black type of bodysuit, and his pure silver hair flowed like a lion's mane past his shoulders. He looked very serious as he concentrated on the substantial instrument panel in front of him.

There were many people in that saucer, and all of them were lying down in rows on the bare flat floor. They were crammed in side by side and head to toe like sardines. I realized as I looked at them that all of these people had been taken, the same way I had, for various reasons. Some were obviously Olympic athletes; two swimmers in their speedos and swim caps, and many more in different types of dress attached to their profession. I was told that I was brought there because of my exceptional ability to make good cookies! Then I looked outside a window and saw a lady on the ground that I knew in real life as a reporter. I didn't particularly like this lady in real life and in the dream, as I thought she was pushy and phony. She was standing beside a small tree, which she was watering with a hose held in one hand; in her other hand she was holding a microphone and was describing how she was watering the tree. The next thing I knew, I was falling out of the spaceship, and I knew my fall was on target to land right beside her, which I desperately did not want to do. All the time I was falling I kept thinking *'no, no, I don't want to go there, I don't want to talk to her, I don't want any part of what she represents!'* But plunk - that's precisely where I landed. She looked at me, absolutely startled, and was about to start asking me questions so she could do a report when I noticed that a big tunnel had been lowered down to me from the spaceship and that if I wanted to, I could climb up it and get back into the spacecraft. I wanted nothing more than to get the heck away from that nosy woman reporter and back into the ship. So, I climbed with all my might up that tunnel, with nothing to hold on to, just to get back in. It took a great deal of effort, but I was successful! When I looked back at what I had just climbed, I could see that my effort had been miraculous indeed! That's how much I wanted to be with the spaceship and not with the phony reporter back on earth. That's when I woke up. This dream was so incredibly vivid and real that I didn't even have to write it down. It was imprinted on my mind in permanent ink. I could hardly wait to tell the others. Then I fell back into a deep sleep.

When I woke in the morning, I heard nothing but quiet. It was so peaceful. Malcolm was not in his sleeping bag, so I knew he'd be up making coffee. I wondered if the others were up too. I left the warmth of my sleeping bag and quickly dressed in the crisp morning air, and then went in pursuit of coffee. It was quite foggy, but you could see that the sun was about to break through and dissipate the fog. I could see Malcolm leaning against the shelter they worked on yesterday – gazing out at the ocean - so I went to join him. He gave me a warm heartfelt hug, and then he got me a wonderful cup of steaming coffee and a chair close to the fire he'd made. The others were not up yet. I asked Malcolm if he had a dream that he remembered, and yes, he had. I was excited to tell him about my dream, but we decided to wait until the others were up before we discussed our dreams. I wondered what Crow was going to come up with. He had a fascinating mind.

Malcolm and I quietly sat there together, looking out at the ocean and the fog. Small bits of mountains started to show through here and there, and occasionally the sun. It was going to be a stellar day. I could tell. I started to tell Malcolm about how peaceful I felt, and how great life was. We were part of the beautiful vista in front of us, we had each other, and we had great friends to share our lives with.

"I'm feeling the same, Julie. In fact, I've been rolling a few thoughts around in my head the last few weeks that I haven't told you about. Mostly because I'm not really sure what may come of them."

I looked over at him. "You've got my undivided attention. You're going to have to spill the beans now that you've told me this much."

"Yeah, you're right." There was a long silence. "I guess it started on our camping trip to the dinosaur park. Just being out in nature made me feel so relaxed and present. It's hard to describe actually, but I felt calmer and happier - more like that's where I *wanted* to be. I felt centered. Then when I got back into the city and the commute and the busy bustle of everything, I lost those feelings. But now that we're out here, I have them again. I like feeling that way, and I can't seem to find that feeling in our city life, and I've tried, believe me."

Ooh...I liked where this was heading.

"Now, I'm not saying we should jump up and do this, but I think we should consider it for somewhere in the future. How would you feel about eventually moving to a smaller community? The sort where traffic jams are relatively unheard of, and nature is really close by, no matter which direction you go?" Now Malcolm looked over at me.

"Wow! We do think alike. I've had similar thoughts too, but didn't want to say anything just yet - mostly because it means making such major changes in our lives. We need to be really sure before we embark on such an important decision. Reality is still reality after all, and no matter where we go, we're going to need jobs. That's a big consideration. But, on the other hand, we may be able to downsize in a way that would mean needing less money from a job."

"What's this I'm hearing?" Crow suddenly butted in. "You guys are thinking of moving? Well, don't think you're going to get rid of me that easily. Wherever you go, I'm coming too!"

"Me, too!" George added.

"Were you guys standing there listening the whole time?" Malcolm asked.

"Pretty much," Crow replied. "You were so engrossed in your conversation that we were able to sneak up on you."

"Well now that the cat's out of the bag," I said, "what do you think about eventually - and I do mean eventually - moving out into the country, or a small community somewhere – wherever that ends up being?"

Malcolm handed Crow and George a cup of coffee and topped ours up. Then we all sat around discussing the possibilities of a move. Should we, shouldn't we? What to do about jobs? Where to find a place? What would life look like if we did? And what would life look like if we didn't? You've got to think of that too. After a few hours, we were all most definitely leaning towards moving, which was scary, but more so, I found it extremely exciting. I think we all did.

"Hey, we almost forgot about discussing our dreams," I said. "I had a doozy! Malcolm said he had a dream too. What about you two?" I asked George and Crow.

"I had one of the neatest dreams I think I've ever had! It was one of those dreams you never forget," Crow declared.

George said he didn't have one, and Malcolm said he didn't feel his dream could match Crow's enthusiasm, so Crow got to tell his dream first.

"I was flying!" Crow exclaimed. "It started out with me being in some kind of a field…or a farmer's yard with low cut grass. I don't remember seeing any trees or mountains, and up above me was an enormous clear dark night sky. I was looking up at all the stars, and suddenly I became one of them! I turned into a speck of light, but no ordinary speck of light. I had endless energy. I was zipping this way and that, and doing loops and summersaults, and going at Mach speed up to the other stars, and then back down again, and loving every minute of it. It was flippin' amazing! I had so much fun and felt so much freedom - and talk about unlimited energy! I don't remember how it ended; I was flying, and then I was awake, recalling it all. But even as I was remembering it, I felt happy and energized. You know what I should have done was gone outside the tent to see if I could have flown while I was awake. I don't think my body would have flown away, but my mind would have taken off for sure…just like it did in the dream state. It was such a cool dream!"

"That is a fantastic dream for sure," I agreed. "But guess what - I was flying too, only I did my flying in a spaceship!"

"No way!" Crow said. "You gotta tell us about that one."

I told them my spaceship dream, and how I was given a choice to either be back on earth with the phony reporter or go back into the spaceship to who knows what. And that I chose, with all my desire and effort, to be back with the spaceship. It appears I was up for the adventure into the unknown, but more than that, I felt a type of kinship with the spaceship people, and was repulsed by the phony earthly reporter.

"You know," George pointed out, "I don't think your dreams are telling you much about science and religion, but they're definitely telling you what's important to you in life. And that should help with the decision to move or not - don't you agree?"

"I want my freedom, that's for sure," Crow said. "And to be a light in the sky full of energy and joy is a feeling I want to pursue."

"And I think I made my choice last night before I even knew we'd be discussing moving this morning. I definitely do not want to be part of a phony, boring, false existence. I scrambled for all I was worth to get back into that spaceship. I didn't even know what was going to happen from there on, but I wanted in on it. That helps me sort out a few things in my waking life. I'd sure like to learn more about dreams and how they work." I turned to look at Malcolm, "What about you? You said you had a dream too."

"My dream sort of left me as I woke up, but I had the gist of it imprinted on my mind. It was a simple statement that said I should *feed my health*. That's it. And even though I can't tell you the story behind it, it still feels like a profound statement to me."

"That's for sure, buddy," Crow acknowledged. "I think we all need to listen to that one as I don't think it's talking about just your physical health."

"Yeah, you're right. I got the feeling it was talking about the big picture, but not to forget our physical health either. We are in physical bodies after all, and I'd say it's up to us to *feed our health* in that area as well."

"I wonder why I didn't have a dream," George said. "I must admit I'm a bit jealous of your discoveries."

"But remember the neat experiences you had when you weren't even dreaming?" Crow reminded George. "None of us ever had anything like that happen, so maybe you didn't need any extra persuading like we did."

"I suppose you're right. That was a pretty neat experience. I do hold on to it rather dearly."

"Let's change the subject!" I abruptly announced. "I'm famished." My stomach was growling. "What about some French toast?"

We'd been talking on nothing but caffeine for hours. Everyone pitched in and soon we had an absolutely delicious brunch of French toast slathered in maple syrup, with bacon on the side. When we were finished, we decided to pack up the van and then go exploring on the beach before we had to head back to a reality we weren't too excited to be heading back to.

I have a habit of admiring and collecting rocks, especially at a shoreline, so as we walked my head was down looking at the rocks. That's why the others saw him before me.

"Hey, look who's here," George happily declared.

I quickly looked up and saw Omar, or at least I thought it was Omar, sitting cross-legged on top of one of the large flat rocks about fifty feet ahead of us. He looked like he was meditating, gazing out to the ocean. But something seemed odd. As we got closer, we discovered we couldn't see through him, and knew it wasn't Omar. But who was it then? Even with our noisy approach, he still did not acknowledge our presence. Finally, he spoke to us, just as we'd walked past him.

"Greetings, my friends," he said, and slowly turned his head, like an owl, to look straight at us.

My heart skipped a few beats at his intense gaze. There was something about him that was mesmerizing. I think it was his eyes, and yes, maybe his smile. We all must have felt the same, as none of us could get a reply to come out of our mouths.

"What's the matter? Cat got your tongues?" he calmly asked, smiling.

After a few stammers, Crow answered. "I-I think we're all surprised by the way you look. You remind us of someone we've come to know over the last few months, but you're way more solid than he is."

Now that's the sort of statement that could cause great confusion if not said to a like-minded individual, as most people are indeed solid. Fortunately, this fellow understood exactly what Crow meant.

"You must be speaking of your four friends that visited last night. And, yes, I do indeed resemble one of them. I enjoyed your conversations very much."

"You were there!" Malcolm exclaimed. "We didn't see you. Where were you?"

"Let me explain. First of all, my name is Eladio. I'm the person who built the enclosure you so nicely added to. And a good job too, I must say. You're all skilled and quite inventive." Eladio nimbly jumped down from the rock. "I actually came here last night to spend some time and found that my little getaway was in use. Surprisingly, this is the first time that's ever happened. I didn't want to disturb the wonderful time you guys were obviously having. And when your friends showed up, I most definitely wanted to listen to your discussions, as that was indeed *very* interesting to me. So, I sat further back, and when you went to bed, I simply went quietly back to my truck to sleep. Your friends knew I was there, however, and sent me the occasional nod."

"Sorry about taking over your shelter. If we'd known you were coming, we'd certainly have left it for you," Malcolm offered before introducing us all by name.

"Very nice to meet all of you. And don't worry about the fort. You made great improvements to it, and I thank you for that. I especially like the new fire pit. At one point, I had thought about making my presence known, but I was afraid it would change the dynamics of your interactions with your friends. Who are they, by the way?"

"That's a long story," I said. "They appeared a few months ago, and our life has not been the same since. We've changed for the better, no doubt about that, but we still feel a bit lost about where we're going from here."

"Well, that's not unusual when you think about it. Change is a constant. Always has been, and always will be, and thank goodness for that. Otherwise, our lives would be stagnant and boring. But, what I'd like to ask is if you have anything planned for the rest of the afternoon? If you don't, then I'd be extremely interested in hearing your story."

We quickly came to the same conclusion that we had nothing of greater importance to do. So, we each found a comfortable rock to sit on and proceeded to tell our story to Eladio. Even though this took several hours, he never interrupted us once. He just let us go on and on, nodding from time to time. We took turns telling him everything, right from the dinosaur park camping trip up to the lectures delivered last night. We also told him about requesting dreams to help us to understand the concepts behind science and religion but instead received amazing dreams on different subjects.

"I find dreams fascinating myself," Eladio finally spoke. "Trying to understand them is certainly worth the effort. At least it has been for me. I think that if you continue asking for that type of dream, you'll indeed receive one, probably when you're ready for it. Perhaps the reason you didn't get what you asked for last night was that you really have not spent much time considering these topics in your waking life."

"That could be," I nodded. "Dreams can be very helpful in solving dilemmas, but right now, we don't have a dilemma because we don't even know what we think." Then a thought occurred to me. "I'm curious to know what you think about these topics? Do you mind telling us?"

"You mean science and religion?" Eladio asked.

I nodded. He took his time answering, but then he agreed to tell us what he thought, which of course, led to another lengthy discussion. I'll paraphrase it here. He felt that what our friends were saying was true. Religion and science needed to put their grievances and lofty ideals aside and start to listen to and respect each other. Religion had something science did not possess, and vice versa. Religion was based on faith – a belief in something that could not be measured or seen, but powerful none the less, and not to be disregarded. And science brought a searching and inquisitive mindset, which encouraged discoveries into the nature of reality. Now, if those two attributes would marry, imagine what the offspring could be! We wouldn't have people put under house arrest for their discoveries, and we wouldn't have people crucified for their faith or beliefs. Sooner or later we all have to face the fact that no one truly knows how the world works, he said. Sure, we have lots of theories, but they're only theories. We can't come up with one theory that takes *everything* into account because no one actually knows *everything*. Scientists discovered a world they never even imagined existed before they stumbled upon the quantum world, and who knows where that will lead. Religion, on the other hand, can't seem to incorporate these discoveries into their firm belief system, so they ignore it. He definitely agreed with Griffin that the two sides need to meet. And he'd also heard of a few scientists who are currently looking at the world from a completely different scientific viewpoint - almost from a spiritual point of view, where consciousness plays the biggest role. For Eladio, this was very good news. His gut instinct told him our civilization was approaching a crossroad, and anyone who could help steer it in a beneficial direction was a good thing. I, for one, couldn't agree more.

Such an interesting *coincidence* that we would run into someone like this today. But we knew better than to believe in coincidences any more. Eladio was very interesting and exceptionally well versed on topics we'd rarely thought about before meeting our helpers. We wanted to stay in touch with him, but he didn't want to exchange contact information as he liked being more on the alone and free side. However, he told us that he comes to this beach often, and if we ever wanted to reach him, we'd find him here from time to time - so we left it at that.

We had to get back to the city and our regular life, which was not all that regular anymore. We said our good-byes and thanked Eladio profusely for giving us his excellent views, and wished him well. Then back into the van, and the traffic, and the hustle and the bustle, and the job in the morning, which we must get enough sleep for so that we can do it well enough to get the pay cheque to pay for the house and the car that we were not really sure we even wanted anymore. It's pretty obvious where these thoughts were taking us...

20

ENERGY BUNDLES

***"Climb the mountains and get their good tidings. Nature's peace will flow into you as sunshine flows into trees. The winds will blow their own freshness into you, and the storms their energy, while cares will drop away from you like the leaves of Autumn."* John Muir**

Monday morning found two very different people in our house than the ones who'd left it on Saturday. How can a person change so much in just two days? Malcolm and I had merrily driven off to the beach Saturday morning, just to enjoy some one on one with nature, and had come back completely transformed in ways we'd never have imagined. We really had no idea what to expect next.

Work was work, and life was life just as it always had been, but *we* were not the same. We'd changed with every discovery made in the last few months, but this time it felt different as the repercussions of moving to the country started to sink in. It hit us that we'd be leaving behind all we'd created in our present lives, and what an enormous shift that would essentially be. Would we end up missing some aspect we currently took for granted? We didn't know.

It was one thing to simply say *'hey, let's move,'* and another to actually do it. We'd be giving up our current group of friends, our present financial stability, our routines and our comforts, our little spot in the world really - and to go to what? That was the crux of it; we didn't know what we would be going to. There were just so many reasons why we should stay put. On the other hand, we discovered some very good reasons for moving too; big reasons - like discovering our potential, developing independence, feeling good about ourselves, conquering our fears, thinking for ourselves, relying on ourselves, and most importantly, room to be creative. You couldn't ignore the benefits of those sorts of intangibles. Interestingly, they didn't have anything to do with physical possessions. I knew I was going to make the move, and I knew the others were as well; it was one of those things you simply *knew* at some level. But that didn't diminish the enormity of the decision.

As Friday approached, we happily remembered George's plan to start cooking meals at our place. We'd all given him some money for the necessary food for his first feast. He wouldn't tell us what it was going to be though, so we waited in anticipation for the day. We were not disappointed. The three of us sat around the island with a glass of wine, watching George prepare the meal, and guess who was going to be cleaning up this time! But I didn't care. I rarely got to sit on the guest side of the island. First, George brought out the steaks he'd been marinating. Then all the fixings for a salad with homemade dressing – I love salad – and a bag of quinoa, which I'd never made before. There were also several bits of things that had destinations I couldn't determine. He wouldn't reveal dessert yet, and we were warned to not to look in the fridge either.

Sitting there in our kitchen like we were, made me realize how close our little group had become. Truly, there wasn't anyone I'd rather spend my time with than these guys. A tight bond had been created after all we'd discovered and shared over the last while. I raised my glass and told the guys that we needed to have a toast to our group - a toast for everywhere we'd been, everything we'd discovered, and everything we were yet to learn. Here, here to that, they all said.

"Don't you get the feeling that we've known each other a long time?" Crow asked. "And I don't mean in this lifetime, but in previous lifetimes. I think we've been together before, and in important ways. At least that's the feeling I get."

"I certainly do," George piped up. "Until I found you guys, I'd always felt the need to keep searching - since high school really. But ever since I've hooked up with you guys, that feeling's gone. I am where I want to be. Although, I must admit I'm happy we agreed to think about moving to a smaller community. I feel like that's going to be a good move for all of us."

"Malcolm and I have been talking about this a lot. Thinking about moving has made us realize how good some of the things we currently have are." I could see a worried look in their faces that maybe we'd decided not to move. "Don't worry, we still want to move eventually. It's just that it's put a different twist on how we see what we currently have. I guess what I'm trying to say is that we often don't appreciate what it is we have because we're so busy looking at what we don't have, or what bothers us in our lives. The idea of moving is allowing us to see the positives we have now, and that's a good thing."

"We know we're going to create even better things wherever it is we go," Malcolm assured everyone, "but I think we're going to find a heightened sense of appreciation for what we now have, until we do go. Don't you guys find that too?"

Surprisingly, or maybe it wasn't that surprising after all, neither George nor Crow felt that way. They would have picked up right then and there, climbed into the van and driven to wherever it took them, ready to discover whatever there was to find. It seems their roots had not been set as deeply as ours. But then again, they were renting small apartments, and we owned a house. They were single with next to no attachments to anyone, and we were married and had other friends who were also couples. All of our jobs were just jobs, working for someone else, so there wasn't a lot of difference there. However, Malcolm had worked himself up the ladder at his job, and to step away from that seemed like a bigger leap than leaving George's job, where he only recently started. There were differences, for sure. Not everyone has the same situation. As we talked, we realized it would also be okay to stay right where we were and still lead a life that was very worthwhile and interesting – it wasn't necessary to move to make discoveries. I mean, the whole city can't just leave and hightail it to the country. But for the four of us, there was an undeniable pull to move to a quieter existence closer to nature. This engaging conversation took us right up to supper being ready. I envied George's ability to cook and participate in the conversation at the same time. That was certainly not something I could do.

Without a doubt, George had a knack for cooking. What lucky guinea pigs we were! The steak melted in our mouths. The salad was full of all sorts of bits that made it not only extremely tasty but very colorful as well. His secret salad dressing was so delicious that it could make millions if he decided to market it. And I found I really liked the quinoa. Why had I never tried making that before, I wondered? Too stuck in my cooking box, I guess. We were all stuffed and felt we would need to exercise caution with George's cooking, or we'd all end up needing stretchy pants. "Dessert," George proudly announced, "will follow later."

The clean-up crew went to work while George sat on the other side of the island watching. We quickly discovered that he was not a clean cook! There were dirty dishes and pots and pans scattered everywhere. But we were only beginning, and we figured he'd get better at this as time went on. Besides, there were three cleaners to one cook, so no complaining from us. Once the kitchen looked normal again, we moved to the living room where we could relax.

"So, has anyone come up with an epiphany about religion or science?" I asked.

"I've certainly been thinking about it a lot this past week," Crow said. "Those are big topics; how could you not think about them? To summarize my thoughts, however, I'd have to say that I agree 100% with what our helpers said. I think they hit the nail on the head. I mean, scientists have discovered so much. You can't deny that. But the scientific minds I've known seem to close their eyes when it comes to something intangible like intuition or dreams or even the power of prayer. Unusual things really do happen to people – to normal, sane people - things that can't be explained by science as we know it. But scientists either ignore this or shrug it off. Why, I ask you, does science pooh-pooh anything to do with a psychic, spiritual, or religious flavor? They accept anything to do with chemical properties or electrical types of energy, but when it comes to psychic energy, they look at you as though you're nuts."

"I couldn't agree more," George added. "I think scientists have really missed the boat on this. Not allowing the psychic component into their theories is like painting a picture without having access to *all* the colors. You need to examine everything, not just the things you *want* to examine. After all, they're supposed to have open minds and look at the world objectively and then try to figure out what it is they're seeing. They can't just say they'll disregard a particular aspect of reality. And besides, they admit that they have ideas that just *come to them*. Well, where do they think they come from? And don't you think they'd be interested in discovering how that type of intuition works? I remember a poster my mom hung at the bottom of our stairs; it was a larger than life portrait of Einstein's head, with his wild crazy hair – kind of like you, Crow!" We all laughed. "Anyways, the saying on the poster was *Imagination Is More Important Than Knowledge*. At least he admitted the existence, and importance, of something that wasn't concrete. Still, so many deny the very thing they use all the time."

"Yeah, but let's not be too hard on them," Malcolm cut in. "I've heard it's real tough to get funding for research, so maybe they're forced to investigate the so-called 'safe' areas of science."

"Okay, so we all agree that scientists somehow need to enlarge their focus a bit. But what about the religious people? And let's not forget spirituality, or other religions, like Buddhism, for example. Don't they need to change too?" I asked.

"From what we've learnt from our friends the last few months, I'd say that *everyone* needs to change," Malcolm pointed out. "I don't think there are many who'd fully get what these guys have been saying, including us. And I'm pretty sure that we've only been shown the tip of the iceberg. But from the little we know so far, I'd say that people, in general, need to open their minds up a bit - including the ones who think the only thing that matters is the size of their pay cheque. And then there are the people who are certain they *know* how things work. I think they're in for a big surprise when they pass over to the other side, especially the ones who think there is no other side to pass over to. Seriously, if you truly think about it for a while, how can anyone honestly know how it all works from our perspective as a tiny speck living on this hunk of rock, spinning around in a universe filled with millions of other hunks of rock? Its mind boggling really. And I'm not convinced that you'll automatically be in the know once you die either. I'm beginning to think that you just continue on, almost as you are now, only without a dense body, and probably feeling as bewildered as a newborn coming into this world."

"You could be right, Malcolm," I said. "That might be something we should talk to our friends about, but I think I'd agree with you. You and I used to fit into the category of never really thinking about this sort of thing either - just too busy living our lives the way we thought we were supposed to, without actually reflecting on what it was all about. But it matters, don't you think? It matters what you think and what you believe in, and what you want for the future, and not just for yourselves, but for the world. I mean, we don't have children, but for those who do, they have to want a better future for them. Why would we knowingly pass on a world filled with pollution or diseases so bad that you have to wear a mask? Or a world where the glaciers have all melted? No one wants to live through catastrophe after catastrophe. You're right Malcolm! We *all* have to start opening our minds and realize what it is that's important to us, who we are, who we want to be; basically, what we stand for and what we believe in. What do you think, George?"

"Well, after my travels around the world and the different cultures and mindsets I've lived alongside, I'd have to say that the human civilization could be in trouble. If you were from another dimension looking down on the world as a whole, you'd be shaking your head, wondering how people could be so blind, and so arrogant. You'd be asking yourself, how is it that one species has managed to screw up so much for so many others? I wonder about that too. I'm not sure what the solution is, but an open mind and acceptance of reality is a good start. But right away, you run into the problem that reality is different for everyone. And everyone is adamant that their way is the right way - and if you don't agree with me, then I'll come over and bomb you. That tactic is short-sighted for sure and hasn't exactly worked well if you take a look at our history. So, what is the answer? I don't really know, but I'm for sure going to keep trying to figure it out, as something has to change if we want to keep from annihilating ourselves."

Our discussion was getting very serious and somewhat gloomy, which gave us all that familiar feeling of helplessness. It just seemed to be too much - too much to clean up and turn around - too much to make us even want to start.

But no, no, no! Wait a minute. We'd been here before, and we remembered what our friends told us. You can't change everything - you can only change yourselves. Don't make it so big and daunting. Just do what you can with yourself, and the ripple effect will be astounding. Whew! That reminder made us all feel better. Crow added a great analogy about one of those huge bumblebees he saw the other day. It was doing its thing, slowly buzzing from flower to flower, simply trying to get some pollen to help out the whole beehive. And the first thing he thought of was how diligently that bee did what it could to help out, never mind anything else. It was driven to do what it was meant to do. That was a great perspective to adopt: just do what you can, but do it wholeheartedly. So okay, we were going to get back to looking at what *we* could do and where *we* could go with it, and what *we* thought and believed. We knew it was all going to fall into place. We just had to let it.

"I think this is a good time for dessert!" George said to everyone's quick agreement. "Wait here."

It was definitely a good time for a break. Sometimes our conversations got very heavy. A good hearty belly laugh would do us all good, but second best would be indulging in a culinary delight. Not too much, but a little taste of something delightful would balance it all out in my opinion.

And what a level of delightfulness it was! George carried in a tray displaying four pieces of cheesecake. Did he know that cheesecake was my most absolute favorite dessert in the world? He even had different sauces he could pour over his mom's secret recipe! "Would you like blueberry, strawberry, lemon, or chocolate sauce?" he asked, teasing me.

"Oh, for heaven's sake," I told him impatiently. "I want a piece of cheesecake with each sauce on it!" But even I knew that would be too much. "I'll try blueberry this time, but I want to try the other sauces in the next few days too."

"As you wish!" George declared, looking very pleased with himself.

That cheesecake was heavenly. We'd only had one supper from George, but after savoring dessert, we knew he truly had a special gift. I lightheartedly told him he should think about opening up a restaurant someday - and bingo, the light bulb went on in all of our minds at the same time. "Maybe not a restaurant," George announced excitedly, "but a little Bistro, in a little town, in the country, close to nature. Now that would be very possible and extremely exciting!"

"And that's where we're headed!" Crow exclaimed. "I could be your helper; you know, someone to wash the dishes, take the orders, clear the tables, chat with the customers, while you created your masterpieces."

I got in on it too. "I could learn how to grow a vegetable garden and supply you with produce for your Bistro – maybe I'd even learn how to preserve food you could use in the winter."

"I don't know much about growing food, and it sounds like you guys got most things covered. How about if I get a job that gives us a steady monthly pay cheque, just so we have some cash if we need it for, you know, things like bills, emergencies, and all the other things life might throw at us?"

We might have been on a cheesecake sugar high, but this idea just kept growing and growing in our minds, and we talked about it for a long time. We let our imaginations go. It seemed like it was actually doable, and not some fantasy. However, on the other side of the coin, we realized it could fail for various reasons that we might not be willing to look at in this moment of positivity. Reasons like moving to a community that was too small, or to a community that wasn't known for dining out, especially if something like quinoa was on the menu! I could hear the locals saying '*who are these guys and what the heck is quinoa anyway*?' We thought it best to let the idea simmer, like a savory stew, and see what would come of it. It did, however, allow us to start to formulate some sort of plan going forward. We decided we would not move anywhere until next spring or summer. This fall and winter would be a time to explore ideas and possibilities - and to all save up as much money as we could. That was going to be important because we knew that whatever we ended up doing, money in the bank was going to be a good idea.

It was getting late, and I knew I shouldn't do it, but I couldn't help myself. "So, George," I started slowly, "do you think I could have one more, little sliver of your cheesecake?"

"Of course, you can." George laughed. "Although I can see that learning how to cook healthy food that won't bulk us up is going to become a priority."

"I'm going to join you in that sliver as well, although somewhat vicariously, unfortunately." Omar delicately floated down beside me on the couch. "There are some noteworthy perks to being physical, you know, and cheesecake is one of them!"

"It's so nice to see you. How long have you been here?" I asked, looking around. "And where are the others?"

"Oh, they're off visiting another group right now. They're not a fan of cheesecake to the degree that I am. It used to be my favorite too, you see, so I simply couldn't resist this opportunity." George handed me a sliver with chocolate sauce. "Go ahead and savor," Omar urged me. "I'll easily pick up on your emotional delight, which will be very enjoyable indeed for me."

We all had another little piece, which left Omar surrounded by savoring emotions. The heavenly look on his face definitely enhanced our own enjoyment too. It was an interesting experience. One that we hadn't had with these guys before, but one that was to become more common as time went on.

"How do you pick up on our emotions for your own cheesecake delight?" Crow asked.

"It's really very simple from my position of existence, but understandably difficult to comprehend from your point of view in that limited physical body of yours. Especially given all the rules you've been taught to adhere to since a young age. You know that there's more to you than your body. It's those other parts that are well connected to emotion. Does that help you?"

"I still don't get the big picture," Crow said, shaking his head. "What exactly are we when we're not in our body?"

"Why, you're a bundle of energy - that's where your whole personality and your emotion reside."

I guess Omar thought it was obvious, but it wasn't to us. We'd been taught so many new things lately that we hadn't actually been able to arrange all the info in an understanding sort of way yet. I found it hard to go past being primarily a physical body, as that's what I'd been for three plus decades now, along with everyone else I knew. But I really liked the term *energy bundles*, and wanted to learn more about them.

Omar understood and patiently continued. "When you go to sleep at night and dream, does your physical body go with you? No, of course it doesn't. It lays on the bed and snores. So, what part of you is it that's off galivanting in your dream, I ask? It's your personality in the form of an energy bundle. Sometimes you find yourself daydreaming during the day - your body stays put, but your mind is off somewhere completely different. In fact, you often don't even realize you're daydreaming until you come back to your body, sitting on the chair, or a rock wall, or driving the car, heaven forbid. I know you've all experienced that feeling. Your body is driving along, but some part of *you* is elsewhere. Well, that's your energy bundle off doing whatever your daydream was about, leaving your physical body to deal quite effectively with its physical reality. This is not an uncommon occurrence, and has attracted all sorts of labels, such as astral body, dream body, or spirit body. But these are just names. It's actually a bundle of immensely intense and aware energy. At its center is your larger self; the *more* that we've often spoken of. All energy is aware of all other energy, and if you remember, *everything* is made of energy. The composition and intensity of your bundle has been built up by everything you've been, and all you will be."

"Are you talking about our past *and* future lives?" Malcolm asked.

"Correct," Omar replied. "As you live your life, this one and other ones, everything you think, say, do, and feel affects your *entire* personality. It all gets added to your energy bundle. Your lives, your experiences, the abilities you master, and your perceptions all end up adding to the identity of your very own bundle. However, there's no one way, or right way, for everyone to be. It's all a work in progress. The underlying desire for betterment is built into everyone. But you must be careful as to what *bettering* means, as all is not what it seems at times. And don't forget that *better* means different things to different people, and that *all* emotions affect the bundle. For example, Julie likes cheesecake to an enormous degree, and the emotion she feels is strong in regards to George's cheesecake. This strong positive emotion is part of Julie's energy personality bundle and increases its intensity. Now, a strong negative emotion to something would also become part of her bundle - and that is one of the reasons why it's so important to sort out what your beliefs are and what your reactions are. Your perceptions are also vitally important. *Never underestimate the power of any single moment or emotion*. You may shrug it off and think it has disappeared, but now you know that is not true. It resides within the source of you, and can color other incarnations."

"Can you see our energy bundles then?" Crow asked.

"Of course, I can see them. In fact, that's mostly what I do see, as that is predominantly what you are. Your current body is a physical manifestation of a portion of your energy bundle, and your personality is an expression of the intensity of your energy bundle. I think the main piece of information you can take away from this discussion is that you are the ones in control. It is you that adds to your bundle. The way you live your life, and the way you perceive your life, determines what gets added. And that, my dear friends, is a fundamental statement to remember."

"And a very powerful inspiration!" Crow nodded. "Could I see my energy bundle? Are they like auras?"

"You could, and yes, there are colors involved to a certain extent, but it would be more like feeling it, or sensing it with your inner senses - a goal worth taking on in my humble opinion. Learning to recognize and connect with your own energy gives you the ability to truly work with it – which allows your entire personality to become more integrated and fulfilled. Nothing is static. There is always change. But remember, *you* are in control of the change that happens for you."

"And my energy bundle!" Crow said excitedly.

"Yes, I believe you understand now. When you have excursions into ideas like you had tonight about the little Bistro and all the connections surrounding it, you are all expanding your possibilities. Your energy is there to help you. Do not minimize the amount of help it can give you. Remember, everything is energy, even when it comes down to the smallest smidgeon or particle. Energy knows how to work with energy. In fact, there is really very little difference between energy and action. Connections are being made as we speak. So, my advice to you is to fly at it! Feel free to use your imaginations and see what you come up with; be mentally spontaneous and impulsive. I think you will surprise yourself as to how creative you all are."

"Can you see what we'll end up doing?" Malcolm asked, hoping for a tip in the right direction.

"I can see probabilities," Omar thoughtfully answered. "Actions in your so-called present can change any of them though. And before you ask, no, I cannot give you the winning numbers for a lottery ticket either," he said with a smile. "However, I can tell you this: I believe you will indeed move to an area of great benefit for your growth, and to the development of those currently living in that area. I cannot tell you where that is, however. There has indeed been an expansion of all of your energy bundles tonight, as well as a deepening of their intensity. You're on the right track, but keep in mind that the track never ends. Now I believe I have said enough for tonight, and I'm going to leave you to digest your cheesecake and your thoughts. Maybe next time we'll all come for a visit." Omar vanished as effortlessly as he had come.

Energy bundles! Imagine! In fact, that's precisely what I did. I looked over at the other three, who were deep in conversation, and tried to see them as a bundle of energy. I focused hard, but with no success. I wondered what our energy bundles looked like to Omar. I couldn't imagine that we'd be anything near to what theirs must look like. I wished I would have asked Omar about that before he left.

All of us were quite excited about this new concept. It gave a great deal of rationale to everything that happened in our daily lives. And a lot more reason to be sure of who we were, and any changes we wanted to make in order to become who we wanted to be. Not to mention how important it was to *consciously* choose situations in our life with the full intention of doing what benefitted our energy bundle. It put a whole new spin on things for me. I knew before that it would be good to move and challenge myself, but now I knew why.

"Well gang," Malcolm announced at the end of the evening, "I believe cruising along in neutral is over for us. It's time to consciously put ourselves in gear and discover what our full potential is, and what direction it lies in. Wouldn't you agree?"

Crow stood up to make a toast. "Here's to fearlessly stepping up to the edge to see what lay beyond!" We all stood and clinked glasses. It was definitely time to look for our full potentials. That simple decision gave us all a tremendous burst of energy, which carried well into the night. I didn't get much sleep – but I did get a lot of thinking done. Surprisingly, the energy was still there in the morning and even continued into our weekend chores.

The plan was to get some of the yard work done before winter rolled in. The trees were shedding their leaves, so we started the process of raking and bagging. Malcolm and I have always found yard work to be very pleasant and meditative, and both of us caught ourselves daydreaming several times during the day. Maybe we were supposed to stay focused, but that was hard to do considering the repetitive job at hand. I often caught myself flying along on my newly discovered energy bundle as though it was my own personal magic carpet. And boy, did we go - first to the backyard of the house I grew up in. I could see myself as a little girl on the swing hung from a big old tree. I felt the same abandoned joy and exhilaration I had when I was that little girl, all dressed up in my Annie Oakley outfit, complete with six-shooters. Then back to raking leaves. Okay, that was neat, and as I started to think about it, I was off again. Only this time, I was gliding a few inches above a lake that was smooth as glass, not a ripple in sight. It was like floating in mid-air with the soft blue color suspending me. Then I was back raking leaves again. And as I started to think about how nice that feeling was, off I went again. This time I was standing at the side of my dad's bed in the care home. We were talking, and he told me how he was living inside himself now and didn't care to see the external reality anymore. I didn't completely understand what he meant but left it at that. Then I was back raking leaves - however, this time I didn't go off flying again. I thought about what my dad had said, as now I *got it*. I bet he'd taken many interesting inner trips with his energy bundle as his body lay on the bed. Was he trying to communicate with me now, I wondered? I told Malcolm about it, and together we came to the conclusion that since all energy is connected, then there is nothing to stop my dad's energy from communicating with mine, even though he's on the other side of life. The only issue would be if we were aware enough as physical human beings to allow it to happen, and recognize it when it did. That sounded very reasonable when you looked at it from an energy standpoint, so I took it as that. My dad and I had connected, and that left me with a warm glow inside and a smile on my face for the rest of the day. Life was good!

People who rent are not tied to property maintenance the way homeowners are. That meant Crow and George were free to follow their hearts desire, which turned out to be a hike along a river, or I suppose at this time of year one would call it a creek. They figured that if their walk ended up anything like the last one they took they'd have plenty of experiences to share with us. However, it turned out to simply be an easy pleasant hike. The leaves were a gorgeous gold and red mixture, and reminded them of impressionist paintings. The sun burst through chosen bits of spaces between the shimmering leaves, and brilliant green moss grew in patches on dark grey rocks below. The crystal-clear water babbled along in gentle cascades. The air was cool, crisp and fresh. They sauntered along and found themselves stopping often to sit on the rocks and just breathe in as deeply as they could. Such peace and tranquility! Their bodies became so relaxed that they felt themselves expanding in all directions. Instead of trying to stop and comprehend it, they just let themselves go.

"While we were sitting in this one particular spot," George told us when they came over later, "I looked over at Crow, and told him how nice it would be to see his energy bundle sitting there instead of him. Not that I minded seeing his crooked nose and black beady eyes, mind you, but I wondered what his energy bundle would look like - would it be all different vivid colors, would it be swirling around, would it be as large as Crow, or would it be tiny, but dense, like a marble? Ever since Omar told us about energy bundles, I keep wondering about them."

"Did you get any answers?" Malcolm asked, looking up from the bag he was stuffing with leaves.

"No, I didn't actually. I think I'm used to getting the answers from our friends, so I felt disappointed that they didn't come to the rescue and enlighten me."

"But that got us thinking about how much we've learned from them. And how much we've come to rely on them," Crow quickly added. "They're the ones who've taken us to this point. And if you remember, Omar was surprised that we hadn't figured out yet that we were energy bundles. Maybe he felt we would have sorted that one out for ourselves by now."

"So, you're saying we need to think some of this out for ourselves now and rely less on them?" I asked.

"That's exactly what I'm saying, Julie," Crow assured me, twirling a red leaf around in his hand. "They can't babysit us all the way through the rest of our lives. We already know enough from them to really start working on ourselves - and adding to our energy bundles. We should be able to learn how to work with that energy to create something we feel good about, don't you think?"

"Yeah, I do see your point, Crow," Malcolm agreed, methodically tying up the leaf bag with a piece of string. "We've got a lot of information to put to use, and we've got each other to talk things out with. And I know we'll still hear from them as they wouldn't simply abandon us, but I think they might be trying to nudge us out of the nest to test our wings. And I, for one, think we're indeed ready to fly."

"It's like it's time to emerge from the cocoon, put the seed in fertile ground and get it growing, birth the baby and nourish its soul..." I declared, twirling around the yard, ready to continue on with my descriptions, but Crow stopped me with a sidelong glance.

"Yeah, something like that. I think we get the picture, Julie. Hey, do you guys need help with your yard work tomorrow? I was thinking it might be neat to hang out together, and who knows what we might come up with?"

"I think that's a great idea," Malcolm said. "What do you think, Julie? Can we find some work for these two?"

"For sure! You see all those weeds that have grown in the rocks over there - well they need to be pulled, so the more people on their hands and knees doing that, the better."

"I still have leftovers from our Friday supper, so I can whip together something to eat when we're done," George offered.

"Great idea!" I said.

We were spending more and more time together, which ended up being a good thing when you consider what happened to us next. But I do not want to get ahead of myself.

21

DISCOVERING CARBERRY

"You get what you concentrate upon. There is no other main rule."
Seth & Jane Roberts

N*ever undervalue any single moment.* Now that's a truth I'll always remember. All four of us were on our hands and knees in our backyard pulling out weeds, when out of the blue Crow innocently said, "Hey guys, I got a great idea. Why don't we cohabitate?"

We stopped and stared at him. I was actually quite taken aback as it literally felt like a marriage proposal. Did he mean all four of us living together in a house - like a commune?

"Why're you all looking at me like that?" Crow asked, surprised. "Did I say something wrong?"

"It's not wrong, buddy," George chuckled. "It just sounds like a huge step. I'm pretty sure Julie and Malcolm want their privacy as a couple, and you and I have only known each other for a few months, and from what I've already seen, there could be the odd annoying habit that would irritate the heck out of all of us. Do you really want to try living together?"

Crow ran his hand through his hair, leaving it even more disheveled than before. "Yeah, I guess I hadn't really thought it through. It was just a notion that popped into my mind, and out it came. Let's just forget I said it."

"That's pretty hard to do now, Crow," I countered. "And you never know - maybe it was something we needed to hear. Who knows what kind of living situation we'll end up with when we actually move? And if you think about it, buying one piece of property would be a lot cheaper than buying or renting three."

Malcolm grabbed his pail of weeds. "You get what you expect to get through your thoughts, expectations, beliefs, and intentions. Isn't that what we've been taught by our friends?" he asked as he stood up to go dump the bucket. "So maybe all four of us should talk about what it is *we* expect to get, as a group. If we're all on the same page, then we have a pretty good chance of turning it into a reality, I'd think."

We spent the rest of the afternoon on our hands and knees, slowly pulling weeds and describing to each other what we thought our imagined place would look like. It made for a really neat afternoon. Topped off, of course, with a cold tasty beer on the deck at the end of it all. The yard looked good, and we'd arrived at a few conclusions.

Crow still envisioned us all living together, but the rest of us did not. Malcolm came up with an idea that I really liked. We'd pool our money and buy one piece of property; somewhere close enough to a small city so that driving wasn't too daunting, but far enough away from the city so that we felt like we were part of a natural surrounding rather than a housing development. Plus, this property would either need to have some outbuildings that could be turned into living quarters, or enough land that we could pull in some mobile homes for Crow and George. Being the only couple, it was decided that Malcolm and I would get the house. That suited me fine, but I also wanted enough land and sun on the property for a garden. I really wanted to learn how to grow vegetables. To me, being able to provide food for yourself, and maybe even others, was an extremely important skill to learn. George liked this setup too but thought finding something so specific, not to mention affordable, could prove difficult.

"Okay, okay, I agree!" Crow threw his hands up in the air. "I think you're right about needing a healthy separation in order to stay friends. But I'm *not* going to be talked out of building an outdoor fire pit where we can *all* congregate."

"That's more than fine with me!" I laughed. "It will remind us of our ocean fire-pit."

Next came paper and pencil. We each drew a picture of the type of house we wanted to live in. Even though none of us were great at drawing, it was easy to see that we were quite similar in our expectations; only I drew an older two-story farm-type house, with a big tree at the back, of course with a swing tied to a branch, while the other three drew fairly modern homes. After some discussion, we decided to meet in the middle and focus on a modern home that had character; maybe some dormers in the roofline - that kind of thing. And if there was a tree – great, and if there wasn't, we'd plant one. Done deal. We spent a bit more time perfecting just one picture that everyone was satisfied with. We also wrote down exactly what we were looking for and what kind of surroundings it needed to have. Then I did a photocopy for each of us so we could put it up where we'd see it every day, just to help hold it in our collective thoughts.

"Omar said he saw us moving. And we've been taught that we create our own reality. So, okay guys," I instructed, holding my beer forward for a toast, "time to get serious and put this concept to work!" We all clinked on it. It felt like we were making a pact.

We now had full intentions of pursuing a move to the country. It's all we talked about for the winter months as we saved every penny we could. I don't want to portray this as a fairytale, however, because it wasn't. In the backs of our minds a niggling thought developed that maybe this was all Pollyanna, and we were being gullible fools for allowing ourselves to think the way we did. Were we being naïve? Weren't we supposed to be pushing and shoving to get ahead; you know, survival of the fittest and all that? Was it really as simple as stepping away from the rat race and have our dreams fall into our laps simply because we wanted it too? That seemed way too easy; after all, wasn't life supposed to be hard? Having *faith* in our new way of thinking was a struggle that we constantly had to help each other with as we waited for spring. Some sign of success was what we needed to quiet that insistent little voice inside that kept telling us we were crazy.

However, as spring approached, our anticipation did indeed grow. It was difficult to sit still. We started checking property listings, but since we didn't know what area of BC we wanted to live in, it meant a lot of checking. But we kept at it as we had ninety-five percent faith that something would turn up. Pollyanna firmly retained the other five percent though, and try as we might, we couldn't seem to make it go away. I would love to be able to tell you that bingo – there was our property, just waiting for us. But it didn't happen that way at all.

"I don't get it," I said miserably to Malcolm one morning over coffee. "We keep checking and checking, but nothing turns up! I hate to admit it, but my faith in our success is dwindling. Maybe we're not supposed to move after all." Voicing this sentiment allowed the heavy weight of disappointment to settle down on my heart.

"I feel that way too sometimes, Julie, but I think we have to overcome that thought and at least try to stay the course," Malcolm sympathized. "Doubt is such a weed - we can't let it take over."

And then out of the blue we heard Griffin's familiar, but startling, voice booming all around us in our kitchen. "Anticipated fear is a great impediment, you know!"

"Griffin," I gasped. "You scared the dickens out of me!"

"Sorry about that, but you two both needed to be shaken up a bit. What's this about doubt and losing faith in your abilities?" Griffin, and his fabulous golden cloak, materialized in one of our kitchen chairs. The kitchen took on an instant glow.

"Well, we think we're doing what you guys taught us – you know, about creating our own reality using our expectations and intentions, but it's not working. We haven't found a piece of property yet, and believe me, we're trying," Malcolm explained, somewhat gloomily. "This is new territory for us, so I guess I have to admit that we're floundering a bit. What do you mean by anticipated fear?"

"Yes, I see it needs an explanation. I believe that's where you're stuck." Griffin put his feet up on one of the chairs and made himself comfortable. "You see, when you envision yourself doing something in the future, you also open yourself up to imagining all the things that could go wrong. Think of it this way: your second-floor inner self is working away at getting your intentions organized, but your main floor ego is putting the brakes on because it sees too many possible dangers ahead. It thinks it's protecting you from that crazy spontaneous inner self, but in actuality it's creating fears over something that may never even come to pass. And so, you worry. But it's these *anticipated fears* that hold you in limbo."

"That makes sense," Malcolm acknowledged. "I have to admit that I am worried about quite a few things: like having terrible neighbors, or not finding jobs, and basically regretting the change."

"Yes, yes! You see," Griffin continued excitedly, sitting up and pointing his finger at Malcolm. "You are worried. All of you are. You should get together and get these fears voiced and out in the open so you can deal with them because that's the only way you'll get past them. You can't know what you'll be up against until you're actually up against it – in the now, not the future. You can't fix something in the future, only the present, as the present is all you *ever* have to work with. And you can't fix something that doesn't even exist. All of you are more than capable of dealing with *any* issue that might come up once you actually have your property. Plus, there's a very good chance that none of your fears will even materialize."

"That's great advice, Griffin," Malcolm acknowledged. "It

certainly makes me feel better. We'll call Crow and George over tonight and get this all sorted out."

"Good idea. Quit worrying about any anticipated fears, and start to realize and appreciate your capabilities - as singly, and combined, you guys are powerhouses! Remember that! I'll be seeing you soon." He stood up, waved good-bye, and disappeared.

So, that had been our block - our immobilizer! We talked endlessly with Crow and George that night. It's easy to say get rid of your fears, but it soon became obvious that it was not so easy to actually do. However, eventually we made the discovery that what feels like a big fear can become very insignificant once it's been voiced. But first you have to figure out what your fear actually is.

I went first. "What I'm worried most about is that the garden I attempt to grow will turn brown and die. That would be such a failure, and you know how much I don't like to fail at something," I slowly confessed. I must admit that it almost sounded silly as I said it out loud.

They actually laughed at me! "Julie, food grows – it has for centuries," George kindly said to me. "You just need to learn how to help it. And you have the internet to help with that, which is way more than our great grandparents ever had. And with any luck maybe some neighbors would be willing to teach you too. I think that's a worry you can definitely let go of."

That certainly took the wind out of that fear. "You're right! I think I was blowing it out of all proportion. This is cool! Malcolm, what about you? What's your fear?"

"That's easy. I'm worried about quitting my job and then not finding another one in our new place, and that would let everyone down financially. We're going to need money, and it's got to come from somewhere."

This took a bit more figuring out, but we did come up with a great solution. We realized that Malcolm could stay in the city at his old job and rent until he found something suitable wherever it was we were going. There didn't have to be any pressure put on any of us.

"I like that idea. Maybe it won't even need to happen that way, but just allowing for it certainly does take the stress away. Thanks, guys! I'm truly not worried about it anymore."

George was used to believing that the universe would unfold in a beneficial way for him, so he didn't really have any fears. But surprisingly, Crow did. "This might sound weird, especially coming from me, but I'm actually worried about being too loose and free. I'm not sure how well I'm going to handle not having the structure of my job." He actually looked a bit sheepish.

"Crow," George began, "you are one handy fellow with an extremely inventive mind that never quits. You're what I would call a jack of all trades, and if you think you're going to have time to just swing on the swing, then think again, buddy. We're going to keep you and your talents busy from dawn to dusk."

We had a good laugh at that as we knew we'd all be kept pretty busy once we found our place. With our biggest fears out in the open and dealt with, we were able to rid ourselves of them. Not only that, we learned to voice any new ones we discovered as the days went by.

A new sense of excitement took over. We started looking once again at listings - but still to no avail. Then one night, Malcolm and I turned the TV on to watch a program someone had recently told us about. It looked at small communities in Canada, and their struggles. It showed that despite, or maybe because of their troubles, community spirit always seemed to surface and keep the town going. We thought at least it would give us an idea of what was out there, so we'd been taping it and watching it occasionally. On this particular night they were focusing on two small communities in BC. When they started talking about the second community, both of our hearts began to pound at the same time. I grabbed Malcolm's hand tightly. Something was happening here. I could feel connections clicking in the air around us; dots connecting to dots. It was almost electric. And that feeling of *knowing* was starting to take over our living room. Malcolm and I were side by side on the couch, leaning forward, listening very intently to the rest of the program, trying to soak in every detail about that community. We didn't even want to take the time to call Crow and George to tell them. We'd found our place, and we *knew* it.

Our town was situated in the BC interior. Mining had always sustained it, but now the mines were shut down. Consequently, a lot of people had been forced to leave for work. However, some old-timers remained, vowing to leave only in a coffin. A recent insurgence of young people was helping to keep it alive, as it had become a bedroom community for the two larger towns nearby.

The scenery was absolutely stunning. The mountains were high, and there was a fairly large lake on one side of the town. The best part was that property was still affordable. The town mayor, who happened to be a woman, voiced the hope that people would start finding their way to their small town. There was nothing about it we didn't like. But - was there property with a house available, were there jobs, could I grow a garden, was there going to be enough to do for all four of us? Of course there was!

As soon as the show ended, we quickly called Crow and discovered George was there too, so Crow put us on speaker phone. "We found it, you guys! We found our town!" I happily and assuredly stated, feeling very matter-of-fact about it all. We told them all about the show and how we just knew it was the place.

"What's it called?" Crow asked.

"Carberry," I said, letting the word roll deliciously off my tongue. As soon as I said the name I heard a sharp intake of breath from both of them - pretty much simultaneously! Turns out just hearing the name was enough for them to know it was the place too. Yikes, but this was getting exciting! We checked the map to see where it was, and since it was only about a seven-hour drive, we decided to go there on the weekend to check it out in person.

"Gas up the van, Crow – we're going on an adventure!" I declared, feeling very excited indeed.

We left Friday right after work and took turns driving until we couldn't anymore, and then crashed at the closest motel we could find. We got up bright and early Saturday morning, had breakfast at a local diner and off we were for the final few hours. I don't think any of us will ever forget that trip. The closer we got, the more anticipation we felt. I could have jumped right out of my skin.

We turned a corner, and there was the carved wooden sign we'd been aching to see: *Welcome to Carberry*. Crow was driving, but he started shaking so bad he had to pull over. I just stared out the window. I knew I'd come home. And what a magnificent home it was too! There was still a bit of pure white snow on the tops of the tallest and steepest mountains. The trees everywhere around us were dotted in fresh new leaves that must have just burst open, displaying their brilliant spring green. You could see the lake in the distance; it was an inviting gorgeous turquoise color, the likes of which I'd never seen before. Of course, the sun was shining – how could it not be at a time like this. This was our special moment and we drank it in.

Once we got over our initial awe, Crow started to drive again. Carberry was not a big town; only about 1200 people, but it looked and felt like a town with promise - or maybe we were just projecting that onto it from our hopeful hearts. We parked on what appeared to be the main street and got out to walk around. We walked the five or six blocks up one side of the street and then back down the other side. There was a hardware store, a drug store that doubled as the liquor store, a post office, two banks, a small library, a grocery store, a couple of churches, a small coffee shop, and an eye-catching pub that looked like it belonged in an old movie set. On one of the side streets, there was a fire hall complete with a fire engine. Next to it were the RCMP headquarters. Then off the other side of the main street, there was a rather large building, all things considered. The TV program had talked about this facility because it was so unusual for a small community. It was a care home for the elderly; all the way from minimal care to full care. It was also a big part of why Carberry was still a functioning town rather than a ghost town.

Everyone we met on the street looked at us in passing and said *Hi*. What a difference from the city where you rarely look at, or say hi, to people you pass on the street. No eye contact seemed to be the rule in the city. I think the locals must have been somewhat curious about us wandering around their town, but they certainly didn't show it. I figured they thought we were just visiting someone. So far, so good. None of us had lost a smidgen of our initial euphoria. We decided to go to the coffee shop and have a coffee and see what we could find out about this place.

Now, I like strong coffee, as do the rest of us. But apparently, the people that visited this coffee shop did not. It was nothing more than flavored brown water. They didn't even have cream – only skim milk! Most of the people in the shop were older men. It looked like a gathering place for old-timers. Who better to ask questions of? So, we started to talk to them about Carberry. What an outpouring of stories! I'd thought they might be more guarded with complete strangers, but that didn't seem to bother them in the least. They'd have told us how many teeth they still had in their heads and how many gallstones they had removed if we'd asked them. It was a delightful afternoon that gave us a fascinating history of the town. These guys had lived in Carberry most of their lives; some had moved there early in life to work, and some had been born there. But all agreed, with eyes a-light, that in its heyday this was one hopping place. There were saloons, theatres, ladies of the evening, preachers, merchants, mining developers, hotels, and even a hospital!

"What happened?" I asked.

The fellow with the silver hair tied back in a long thin ponytail spoke up. He was my favorite with his tanned, wrinkle-worn face, and calm solid manner. I remembered him from the TV show. "Well, you see," he drawled, leaning forward and resting his elbows on the table, "it's like this. There'd been a large vein of high-grade silver running through the mountain over there." He pointed behind him. "Seemed like it would never come to an end. The whole town was built on the wealth from that silver, but as the vein got smaller, everything slowed right down. Silver prices dropped at about the same time, and what you see out the window is pretty much the result."

"That's so sad," Crow sighed. "I've heard of that happening to lots of small towns, and now they're ghost towns. So, what makes Carberry different? I realize it's less than it was in its heyday, but it's definitely not a ghost town." We knew the answer to this from watching the TV show, but we wanted to hear it from the locals.

This time the shorter fellow with one arm answered - the result of a mining accident, I figured. "It's all because of the hospital and Dr. Fell, ya' see. He's the one that took care of my arm when I had my accident. And thank God he lived in Carberry too, or I-da lost more than my arm, let me tell ya'! He had a heart of gold, that man did. He wanted to help everyone that needed his help. He didn't care if ya' had money to pay him or not! Many a surgery was performed on kitchen tables too, by golly." He paused to take his crumpled hanky out of his pocket to gently dab his forehead before continuing. "He became a local hero, ya' see, and everyone wanted to support him in whatever way they could, so we all started to donate money towards a hospital, and by golly, it got built!"

"You mean you guys raised enough money to build that huge building over there?" I asked in disbelief.

Another one of the fellows answered now. It was actually the first time he'd spoken since we sat down. "No, not quite. You see, when the silver ran out, the population dwindled. Dr. Fell stayed on, but he was ageing too. About twenty-five years ago he died of a heart attack, bless his soul. It was sad...very sad. He'd been so well respected that the funeral had to be held outdoors just so's all the people could attend." You could tell these guys still missed him. "Anyways, we tried to get another doctor to take his place, but the new ones don't wanna come to a little place like Carberry."

Silver pony-tail finished the story for us. "We couldn't get a doctor, but the next best thing happened when the government decided to buy the building and add on to it – turning it into a care facility. It's the finest one around," he said proudly. "Folks come from all over to stay here, which is why it's always full. It's really well run, and gives the locals some jobs too. I think it's the real reason that Carberry managed to stay alive. And now lots of younger people are starting to come, just so they can raise their families in a safe community, where your keys can be left in the car and your door unlocked. You don't get that too many places anymore. They live here and commute for work."

"And just how far would that commute be?" Malcolm asked cautiously.

"Oh, anywhere's from forty-five minutes to an hour depending on where you were working," one arm answered.

"Would that be an hour of bumper to bumper traffic, or just an hour of normal highway driving?" Malcolm asked with fingers crossed.

It was one arm that answered again. "Now jus' where do ya think we'd get enough cars for an hours' worth of bumper to bumper out here?" He looked at Malcolm like he had a hole in his head.

Malcolm laughed. "That's the answer I've been dying to hear! Thank you!"

We said good-bye to our new friends and thanked them for filling us in on Carberry's history. We made sure to tell them how great we thought they all were. There were toothless smiles and warm handshakes all around. They wanted to make sure us *nice city folks* would come back to visit. Not to worry guys, we will, we will.

Next we went looking for a real estate office - but there wasn't one. We asked around and discovered that whatever real estate there was for sale would be up on the bulletin board in the post office. It seemed that technology hadn't really hit here yet. Off we went to the post office and started to peruse the board. There were actually quite a few listings, but mostly of houses in town. Halfway into our search, we came across some acreage with a house on it a few miles out of town. Then we saw another listing that looked good too, but it was a bit farther out of town. Both places gave us a good feeling, but not one more than the other. So, we took down the addresses and off we went.

We checked out the first place – the one closest to town - and it would have been okay, but it didn't cause our hearts to melt. The next place however, did, and in a big way. We all knew it as soon as we drove down the tree-lined driveway that opened onto a grassy yard with a stately older two-story house firmly situated on a slight rise at the side of the yard. *That* was my house! I need look no further. We scrambled out of the van to check things out: the house being first. We knew from the listing that no one was living there at the time, so we were free to respectfully roam around.

It was not a large house, but the upstairs floor had two dormers sticking out, which gave the house such a homey look! I loved the covered screened-in veranda on the side, and all the shrubs in the rock garden, just waiting for a few more weeks of spring to get them really growing and blooming. The windows were generous and seemed to be smiling at me. With a sigh, I turned to tell Malcolm that I wanted this house with all my heart and soul, only to discover that the three of them were nowhere around. They'd all taken off to see what else there was besides the house. I found them standing beside the barn deep in conversation. Could they fix this up and make it livable? Or could they make the workshop into something livable? Or maybe we could pull a mobile home in over there? I left them to their discussions and went back to the house trying to figure out where the garden could be, and lo and behold, there already was one behind the house! It was perfect.

We gathered together in the middle of the yard and excitedly declared that this was the place. We knew we needed to find out much more about the property; the price being a good place to start, but also how many acres, cost of taxes, was there water, and on and on. But that all seemed like nothing more than preliminaries at this point. We spent a bit more time walking around in discussion, but then headed back to Carberry, in a truly excitable state, to see if we could find out more.

After several phone calls, we were able to get in touch with the real estate agent, whose name was Brian. He had an office in his house in town, so that's where we met.

"What can you tell us about this property?" Malcolm asked. We'd decided to let Malcolm do most of the talking as he was able to maintain his calm better than the rest of us.

"It's a nice piece of property, that's for sure," Brian began. "It belongs to a couple that lived there for most of their lives - Barry and Rose Jones. In fact, Barry grew up on a neighboring property, and when he met Rose, they bought this place and raised their family of three there. But Rose passed away a few years ago, and Barry just didn't have the heart and desire, or health, to keep it up the way he felt it should be kept up, so he recently decided to sell. Heck of a nice guy."

"You can tell they had a lot of pride in the property. It's so well taken care of," I said.

Brian eyed us closely as he next said, "There is a catch, though."

"What kind of catch?" Malcolm asked. I could feel my heart drop.

"Well, you see, like I said, Barry is a heck of a nice guy, and he doesn't want his property to go to someone he doesn't like. It's got to be someone he considers worthy. He wants to meet them first."

Worthy! Hmmm...were we worthy? We thought of ourselves as good human beings, but we weren't sure how Barry would feel about four newcomers from the city moving onto his beloved property. "Well, we've come this far," Malcolm said, "so we've got to follow it through."

Brian set up a time for us all to meet the following day. It was exciting, but nerve-wrecking at the same time. All we could do was be ourselves and hope Barry liked us. But now we needed to find someplace to sleep for the night. Carberry didn't have any such thing apparently, but Brian told us that an hour away we'd find a motel in Fresco. Or we could try Cusick, which was only forty-five minutes to the north.

We flipped a coin and headed for Cusick, hoping to maybe check out Fresco tomorrow before heading back home. We found a motel on the highway leading into Cusick, so we booked in, asked for two extra cots in the room, and then drove around looking for a café. The town was triple the size of Carberry with a lot more amenities.

It seemed like a nice enough place. We found a restaurant and sat down to a delicious home-cooked meal while we discussed what was happening to us.

We were so wound up we didn't know where to start. We hoped our dream was about to turn into reality, but it hadn't actually happened yet, so we tried to keep each other calm, which was quite the task. We tried to think of all the things we needed to be wary of, and to not forget that the deal could still go sideways. That night at the motel, it was hard to get to sleep - all I achieved was a few snatches here and there. When the alarm clock rang, I'd been wide awake for hours already – turns out the others were too.

We made ourselves as presentable as we could. The first impression had to be a good one. Was Barry going to like us, or laugh at us? Really, who in their right mind would want to sign over the property they built up over their lifetime to a bunch of beginners who knew nothing about farming? But we had optimism, and heart and desire going for us - not to mention youth. Actually, we didn't feel all that young, but to someone who's seventy-five, as Barry was, the thirties would seem very young. The price wasn't going to be an issue as we could afford what Barry was asking. We just needed him to *like* us.

With fingers crossed, we sat at the table with Brian in his real estate office, nervously waiting for Barry to come. When the door finally opened, and I saw him for the first time, I was able to relax a bit. This was obviously a *nice* man - you could see it in the smiling lines of his face. He certainly did not look seventy-five either! His hair was more blond than grey – and none of it was missing! He was of medium build, and had on a pair of worn blue jeans and a red checkered flannel shirt rolled up at the sleeves. His arms and face were well tanned, and his hands looked like they'd seen a lot of work in their time. I couldn't say for sure, but I thought I noticed that he was a bit bow-legged. He sat down and looked intently at us, one at a time, as Brian made the introductions.

"So, you four wanna buy my farm! Tell me, just what are your intentions anyways?" Barry challenged us right away. His voice was low and sort of raspy.

I started. I couldn't wait. "I've discovered a burning desire to become a gardener. I want to learn everything I can about it and how to preserve what I grow. I'd even like to sell my produce – maybe to a farmer's market, or a restaurant, or even the care home. I was so happy to see that you already had a good size garden area developed. That's where my attention will be. And I just *love* your house. I'd treasure living in that house for the rest of my life." I thought I saw his eyes light up at that.

"And the rest of you?"

Malcolm spoke next. "Our collective plan is to move out of the city and immerse ourselves in rural life. We're all looking for a change of direction, and feel we could be a positive influence more effectively in a small community, rather than a large city where everyone goes their own way. We can't really give you any hard and fast specifics other than we simply *know* this is something we must do. In the same way, we also know opportunities will appear that will immerse us in this community in a beneficial manner. It's the way we believe things will work for us."

"Plus, we *really* like your place," Crow quickly added. "You can tell it's always been tended with care and love. We'd carry that on – fix up anything that needs fixing – adding to it in ways that will bring continued care and love. I'm fairly handy and can hardly wait to sink my teeth into the maintenance of such a wonderful piece of property."

"I see," Barry nodded, then turned his attention towards George. "And what about you?"

"I didn't know it until I saw your property yesterday, but I'd like to bring some animals onto your farm. I get along really well with animals, and I think it would bring such a nice bit of life to the place. I'm not sure which animals, but chickens are always a good place to start, I would think. Then I'd go from there. I've also developed some skill in cooking, and I'd like to work that ability into our new way of life here in Carberry. I just don't know exactly what form that would take yet."

"Hmmm...," Barry said, eyeing us up. I was on the edge of my seat, and my heart was in my throat - what was he going to say? "I get the feeling you guys are pretty much in tune with your surroundings." We nodded eagerly. "I guess that's why you wanna get out of the city then. I can't imagine anyone wanting to live in that kind of commotion, but I know some thrive on it. Let 'em have it, I say. Rose and I lived on our farm for over fifty years! There's a kind of peace I get when I look back at what we've done with our lives. We built a nice place...heck, what am I saying...nice doesn't even begin to describe the orioles singing in the clear morning air, or the sun shining peacefully through the trees we planted and nurtured with our own hands, or the ducks and their ducklings proudly swimming on the pond every spring, or the taste of the spuds we grew ourselves and kept in the root cellar we built ourselves. Money doesn't buy those things. Many city slickers don't even know enough to appreciate those things." And then he paused and looked straight at us - his eyes were moist. I believe we may all have been close to drooling at this point. "But I know, when I look at each one of you, that you do understand what I'm saying and would appreciate those things too. I can see that you're all eager, and probably a bit foolhardy simply because you haven't got the slightest clue what you're gettin' yourselves into. You look like good folks with good intentions in your heart, but I'm not sure you're up to the task." Oh no! My heart sank at that statement! But it soon buoyed back up as Barry continued. "So, I would like to make a proposal."

"Yes, yes, we'd love to hear your proposal," we said in some sort of fumbling unison.

"Here's what I'm thinking. I will sell you my property. However, I don't want to see it deteriorate with the likes of four greenhorns trying to run it. So, I will offer myself to you as a consultant on any matters you have concerning this property. I'll be moving from my daughter's house into the care home in Carberry soon, so I won't be far away. Now…I won't charge you money for my guidance, but I would occasionally expect payment in the form of a home-cooked meal, complete with desert – an' I like pie." Barry looked directly at George and winked.

What blabbering idiots we must have seemed after he said that. We were all talking over each other and gushing with good intentions – shaking Barry's hand, shaking Brian's hand – hugging each other. Yes, yes, yes, we said. We accept that deal. Where do we sign? What kind of pie?

That was a momentous day - one we never forgot. Barry turned out to be one of the most helpful people we've ever known, and we came to be very fond of him. He really became one of the family. But you will see for yourself if you read on.

22

THE MOVE

***"The energy of the mind is the essence of life."* Aristotle**

The real estate transaction went as planned: we were to take possession May 1st. Collectively, we had more than enough money saved up for a very healthy down payment, but we needed to sell our house to have money to live on while getting settled in, and turning the barn into living quarters for Crow and George. Lucky for us, housing prices where we lived had gone through the roof in the last few years. There was a bidding war for our place, which gave us three times as much money as we paid for the house ten years ago! It seemed too good to be true, however, we weren't going to look that gift horse in the mouth. Our worry about having enough money was not going to be a worry after all, at least not right away, and we vowed to never catapult that worry into the future either. We'd learned that lesson and knew we'd be able to deal with whatever came up. No need for anymore anticipated fears.

There was much to be done in the next two months – like

packing - a lot of packing! As I went from room to room armed with boxes, felt pen, and tape dispenser, I kept wondering why we had so much stuff. Did we really need all this stuff, I asked myself? Well, of course, some of it we did. But there was no way I was going to cart the trappings of city life into new beginnings in the country. I was ruthless. Only the most necessary items made it into the boxes destined for Carberry. The rest went into the boxes marked garage sale. We'd decided to pool all the stuff we weren't taking and have one big garage sale and use that money to buy something useful for our new place. We figured that once we lived there for a while, we'd know what that would be. It was to be our symbol for rebirth, if you know what I mean. Something that would always remind us of our brave shift from city to country, or from being followers to free thinkers, learning about ourselves instead of learning how to fit in. A large sculpted Phoenix kept coming to mind - maybe on a perch by the fire pit Crow was going to build. Hmmm - back to packing, Julie – enough daydreaming.

When all was said and done, we had way more boxes for the garage sale than for Carberry. Barry had told us that he didn't want to have a garage sale, nor did he want to do much in the way of packing. He wasn't going to have much room in the care home anyway, he said, and most of his needs were going to be met by the caregivers. He told his three kids to come and take what they wanted, and then he left the rest of his stuff to us; he felt like it kind of went with the place. His kids mostly took small mementoes, as they already had a houseful of their own stuff. That's how we ended up with most of Barry's furniture, which was still in excellent shape even after all those years. His creed was to *buy once and buy good*, and then take care of it. He left us his tractor and all the implements - not that we knew what to do with them, but our *consultant* was going to teach us all about them. He also left most of his tools. Imagine, if you can - fifty years' worth of tools! And then there was the bookcase full of various books gathered over time. They must have had an eclectic taste. To say it was a treasure trove of information and interesting reading was definitely an understatement. We thought ourselves very, very lucky at first – but we soon came to realize it wasn't luck at all. We'd created a spectacular reality for ourselves, and we all felt that we might have had a wee bit of help from our friends up above, if *up above* was an appropriate description of where they lived.

Our helpers hadn't shown up for several weeks. We weren't sure if this was because we were so consumed with the new life we were embarking on, plus all the details of the sale and packing and on and on - or was it because they didn't want to interrupt a good thing going in the right direction? Not hearing from them hadn't worried us, as there was a feeling of *rightness* about everything. Plus, our energy and vitality seemed endless - always a good sign. But still, we thought it would be comforting to share our experience with them. We'd finished packing and were sitting down to share a pizza we'd ordered when we started to discuss the fact of their absence. As I said, we weren't concerned as we knew we'd always have them to turn to for the rest of our lives, but we were missing them. And that's when they showed up.

"Last time in this living room, I'd say," Griffin piped up from behind us. "I'm going to miss it, I think. We've had lots of great discussions here."

"Me, too," Omar agreed, standing a few feet in front of us. "All of you have come such a long way since we first joined your awareness on that wonderful camping trip in dinosaur country. Now, instead of us taking you on a journey, you're taking us on a journey. We're all going to enjoy watching your personalities flourish as you learn about country living, and more importantly – about your potential."

There wasn't anywhere for them to sit as all the furniture, other than the couch we were sitting on, had been put into the garage for tomorrow's sale, so they took up various floating positions all around the living room.

"I will definitely enjoy visiting you in the country much more than the crowded city. Cities have their advantages and some personalities seem to really like them, but my inclination is toward the freedom and open spaces of the country," Kodiak said. He was leaning against the wall, but his feet were six inches off the floor! "So, George, what kind of animals are you going to get for the farm?"

"How'd you know about that?" George asked.

"Just because we don't make ourselves known to you doesn't mean we aren't with you," Kodiak replied. "A portion of us is with you most of the time. There was no way we were going to miss your historic meeting with Barry, so we were there too. Such a fascinating person."

"Did you guys influence that deal?" Malcolm asked straight out.

"Maybe a little nudge here and there," Bluedon said, "but not much, as you guys were so on the mark. If only you could have seen the brilliant fields of electromagnetic energy shooting out from your group! It was quite the light show - plus, we all liked Barry the minute you met him. We know his larger self on this side of life. There is kindness, happiness, helpfulness, intelligence, and a wee bit of mischief mixed into his personality. You're dealing with an exceptional human being, as you already know. You'll have lots of good moments with him going forward. Treasure him, as he is indeed a treasure."

Kodiak asked George again what kind of animals he'd like to bring onto the property.

"I'm not sure actually, but I thought of starting with chickens."

"And why is that?" Kodiak questioned George.

"I think there's a lot of benefit to them - like laying eggs for starters. And they run around eating bugs. And I like the sound they make – it has an undercurrent of domesticity and peacefulness. Except for the rooster, that is. That early morning crow won't be so peaceful at daybreak when we'll still be sleeping. But on the other hand, it is the sound of a farm and rural living in my mind. So that's why I'm choosing chickens to start off with."

"And what are you going to do with them when they're old and no longer producing eggs?"

"That could end up being a problem," George answered. "I've been thinking about that. I don't know how to butcher, and I don't even think I could. I have a picture in my mind of those chickens becoming my friends. So how could I just up and kill one? I don't have the answer."

"Everything dies, George," Kodiak said. "Chickens, too. Death is not the end of anything, really. All life continues on somewhere, so you needn't feel too dramatic about it. You weren't concerned at all about the death of those bugs you envisioned the chickens voraciously eating, were you? And I can assure you, the chicken did not suffer a moral dilemma before gobbling one up alive and whole. I have a feeling Barry will be able to help you out in this regard. He raised many animals on his farm, and yes, some of them were raised for the specific purpose of becoming food for his family. But he gave those animals the best of care, and before they died, he thanked them profusely for helping to feed his family. This is really no different than what the indigenous people have done for centuries. And it's something that you, Julie, will need to do in your garden too."

"In my garden? What do you mean? I don't plan to kill anything there."

"Well, is a carrot not alive? It wouldn't grow if it was dead. All the plants in your garden have a purpose in mind: to grow to the best of their ability and produce seeds to help with the continued existence of their species. And what do you do? You walk out there, grab that carrot by its hair and yank it right out of its home. Or you pluck those beans, also full of seeds destined for propagation, right off the stalk, and eat them. It's the same for all the plants. Never doubt that they are alive. They just aren't capable of running away, or screaming at a frequency your perceptive mechanisms are able to hear, or you'd all be hearing a great deal from them."

"I'd never thought of vegetables like that before. But I can see what you're getting at. I'm going to have a lot more reverence for them from now on. That's a really good way to look at it."

"It's more than just a good way to look at it," Omar jumped in from his cross-legged position two feet in the air, "it's the way it is! Everything is alive, and everything dies. Birth involves death. It's your perceptions about it that matter. Your society is fooling itself by having all the unpleasant dirty work of killing done in factories behind closed doors, and then packaging everything attractively for the public to buy in grocery stores, as if that's where it comes from. That hamburger meat sitting on the foam tray wrapped cleanly in plastic wrap came from a butchered cow, and I can guarantee you that that cow was not shown any appreciation or understanding before the deed was done to it. The customer is so removed from the act of butchering that they rarely think about the hamburger's origin. The way your society is currently set up has made it convenient for people to wash their hands of the killing, pretend it doesn't exist, and in so doing, they're missing out on that aspect of gratitude and pure connection with nature. But on your farm, the middle man is gone, and you will not escape having to come to terms with it in some manner. And that's a good thing."

"Man, there's going to be some serious discussions about this till we get it right in our heads," George said.

We had no doubt that life was going to get a lot more *real* for us. We felt we were up to the task, but this one was an eye-opener. We create our own reality - no one to blame - taking responsibility for one's life does not always correlate with easy and fun. This one was going to be tough. But as the guys said, Barry could probably help us out with getting our thinking straight in our heads, so we decided to shelve this issue for now. We had so many other things to deal with in the present moment; like the garage sale first thing in the morning.

"Are you guys going to come to our garage sale?" I asked, changing the subject.

"Not only will we be there, we'll also be helping your buyers feel good about their purchases. We don't want any bad vibes attached to anything you leave behind," Griffin said as he floated on his back around the room, as though he was in a swimming pool.

That was something we'd never even thought of. We wanted everything to go to a good home but didn't realize we had a choice in the matter. Apparently, we did. They told us we could send out an intention that all goods were going to find a lovely home and fulfill a useful purpose - and then forget about it and just know it will happen. Our guys would be there to help if something went wrong. How neat is that!!

They all left when the pizza was done, and we decided to call it a night. The garage sale was going to open at eight the next morning, and we still had lots to get ready before that. Sleep actually came easy that night, but the six o'clock alarm bell was still a shocker. I've always felt alarm clocks to be necessary, but very annoying. I was thinking a rooster might be better - at least you never have to set them, or change their batteries, but then again – you can't shut them off either!

We got everything outside just before people started showing up in droves. Cars were lined up and down the street as far as we could see, and lots of people from the neighborhood came on foot. We were inundated. Best thing was that everyone was buying. I don't remember seeing anyone leave without something in their hands. By noon we hardly had anything left, and the frenzy had died down. That's when I felt the sadness creep up on me.

"Everything's gone, Malcolm," I sighed, looking around our empty driveway. "I'm feeling a bit lost and unsure. Do you feel it too?"

"A little bit, but I think it's normal. A great deal of what we've gathered up to this point in life has just left us, and we don't have our new stuff yet. So, it's got to be normal to feel like this," Malcolm assured me, hugging me close.

"There's no need for so much *stuff* in a lifetime," Omar whispered inside my head. "It's a new page – just let go and enjoy your temporary feeling of freedom."

Okay, I could do that. I stepped back and told Malcolm and the others what Omar had just whispered to me, and that seemed to replace their looks of concern with smiles. We gave the last bits away for free to anyone who showed up, and by the afternoon it was all gone. This chapter was done!

"Let's go out to eat," Crow suggested. "Let's celebrate our last supper in the city."

Great idea since we had nothing to eat, nor anything to eat with left in the house, so off we went. The next morning we'd be heading out to take possession of our newly purchased farm. Our vehicles had been packed with whatever we kept. We had full tanks of gas, and hearts and minds ready for our new adventure. We'd done it. Well, actually, we hadn't really done anything yet except make the shift happen. But that was a big one, we figured. And we were going together - all four of us.

Malcolm did not have to continue working in the city, as we thought he might. In fact, when he gave his notice to his boss, they had a great discussion. Probably one of the most meaningful conversations they'd had in all the years Malcolm worked there.

"Tell me, Malcolm," his boss asked, "why is it that you're leaving, and just what do you plan to do in the future?"

"I guess what we're hoping for is to lead a more productive, creative, and meaningful life in the country. And we're definitely looking forward to a more peaceful setting, surrounded by nature instead of traffic. Truthfully, we're not entirely sure what we'll end up doing as time goes on, but we feel pretty confident that the right things will come along."

Malcolm's boss didn't say much at first. He seemed to be gazing at something over Malcolm's head. "You know," he finally began, "I've realized so many things about my life after my sons' accident, and I've always felt it was you who steered me in the right direction. My life has become very satisfying – even peaceful. I want to show you my appreciation for all the help you've given me." He opened his desk drawer and took out a cheque book and proceeded to write a cheque payable to Malcolm for ten thousand dollars! He handed it to him across the desk.

Malcolm looked at it, and then looked up at his boss. "Ten thousand dollars!" he said, shaking his head, trying to hand it back. "I can't accept that!"

"Look Malcolm, this is only money, and money is nothing

compared to what you gave me. I wish I could repay you in kind but I don't see a way to make that happen. This is something I can do, though. So please accept it and allow me to enjoy the pleasure of giving and helping others too. I'm sure money will be helpful in the situation you're heading into."

There was nothing for Malcolm to say after that, except, "Thank you from the bottom of my heart." They stood and warmly shook hands. It was a rather meaningful and emotional moment for both of them. It was also very fortunate for us, as that money would provide a nice cushion of safety until Malcolm found a new job in Carberry, which we all *knew* he would.

23

BARRY STARTS EDUCATING

"Argue for your limitations, and sure enough, they're yours."
Richard Bach

Barry was there waiting for us when we drove up. He was about to hand over his life's work to city greenhorns; *his* place was going to become *ours*. I was expecting him to be a little sad about the whole thing, but instead, he had a warm and welcoming smile on his face. There were heartfelt handshakes all around as soon as we got out of our vehicles. We gushed with promises that secretly we hoped we could keep.

"Now, I'm gonna show you a few essential things you need to know about this place, and then I'm gonna get outta your way and let you move in." For the next few hours we attentively followed Barry around the yard like baby ducklings following the mother duck. When he felt satisfied with what he'd shown us, he climbed back into his very shiny, cherry-red, old pick-up truck and waved good-bye out the window as he drove off.

We stood there, silently staring down the driveway where the truck had been. My heart was pounding. How do you make something your own when it's so fresh and so new and still so much someone else's? I felt like I was trespassing, but there was nothing for it except to move in.

"Start carrying those boxes, guys. You carry, and I'll unpack," I instructed. And that's how we got over the big lumps in our throats. We just started. Baby steps - one after the other - and after a while it became somewhat normal, and even acceptable.

We'd moved into the house in what we felt was a temporary situation, with Malcolm and I taking the larger bedroom on the main floor, and George and Crow each taking one of the smaller bedrooms upstairs. We worried that one bathroom for all four of us could be a challenge, but there was also a really neat log outhouse in the backyard, so that helped. The sunny, bright kitchen was a delight, and cooking there was an absolute treat. We even attempted an apple pie for when Barry planned to come out. The smell permeated the entire house and really made it feel more like a home. Funny how smells trigger certain emotions.

After most of the unpacking was done we started to wander around outside. When you have five acres and several buildings full of paraphernalia, you end up with a lot of discussions and wandering. Barry said he'd answer any questions we might have, so we hoped to compile a list of intelligent ones for him. That meant getting things clear in our citified minds first, so we kept at it, trying to decide what to do first, and what would be the best way of beginning our lives on a farm we knew nothing about.

We wanted to streamline our thoughts into one direction to make it easier on Barry, so after supper one night, we took pen and paper and got cozy in our new homey living room. Barry's furniture was all made from a dark maple and upholstered with luxurious, deep red, patterned material that felt like velvet. No matter where you sat, you felt like a baby sinking into a mother's arms. Our city living room had been comfy, but this one, with all its history, was leagues above ours.

I set my glass of wine on the small table beside my chair, and tucked my legs up underneath me. I had the notebook, so I began. "Let's make this really clear for Barry. What *I* want to do is learn how to turn that garden out back into a highly productive piece of land. And once I learn how to do that, I'm going to need to figure out how to preserve everything I grow. Now what about you guys – what're your plans?"

"I want to build my fire pit," Crow piped up right away, "but first things first. I think us guys should tackle the barn so that we can turn it into living quarters for George and I - *separate* living quarters, I might add." Crow elbowed George, who was sitting beside him on the couch.

"Good idea," George said, "cuz you snore!"

"I do?"

"Yep, you do. I'm thinking maybe sound proof walls even, if we can afford that."

"Sounds like we should work it into the budget, because I've heard him snore too!" Malcolm teased. Crow pretended to be offended, but we knew better: he didn't offend easily. "Seriously though," Malcolm continued, "I agree with Crow. I think the first thing we need to do is get that barn cleaned out so that we can start to work on it. There's a lot of critters calling it home right now."

"Critters!" I said. "Malcolm, you're starting to sound like a farmer already!"

"Hmph...I am, aren't I? How about that. Anyways, like I was saying, first we need to clean it up, and then probably figure out how to do the plumbing and wiring and construction. Crow, you're pretty handy at building so we'll be your laborers and you can be the foreman."

"I like that. Don't worry either, because I'll be a kind foreman to you two."

"Someone's going to need to do the cooking, don't forget, and since you'll be busy building, George, I think maybe I should do the cooking for now," I offered. "Maybe when we have the barn project done you might want to take it over, or we can do it together. We'll work it out then, but for now, I'll be the chief cook."

"That sounds like a great plan," George agreed. "But what about when we're done these projects? What're our long-term plans? Let's give Barry the whole picture when he comes tomorrow."

"Like I said, I'm going to build that fire pit first opportunity I have. Then I think I'll see what opens up in the way of work around Carberry, if I'm not too busy doing maintenance around here," Crow explained.

"I don't want there to be any pressure on any of us," Malcolm said, "so let's take it one season at a time. We have enough money to live on and build if we're resourceful, so I'm not going to even look for a job until we've got that barn done. And if for some reason we don't get it done before this winter, then let's all just keep living in this house until we do."

"I like the no pressure part," George said. "I do want to start honing my cooking skills though. Hopefully everything will go well enough to stay on track, but like you said, Malcolm, if it doesn't we can just stay together in this exceptional house. No pressure."

I jotted everything down in my notebook for tomorrow. "I wonder what Barry's going to say when we tell him about our plans?"

"I don't know, and we won't know until we tell him. It's getting late," Malcolm announced, standing up and stretching, "so maybe we should call it a night. I think all this fresh air I'm getting is making me sleepy."

After a final nightcap with a wee bit of our favorite brandy served in Barry's very decadent crystal brandy glasses, we went off to bed, feeling very pleased with ourselves.

Barry's red pick-up came slowly down the tree-lined driveway at noon. Looking back, I'd describe that meeting as one between young eager beavers, bubbling over with heart and desire but next to nothing in the way of knowledge, and the wise old owl who has seen it all, is in no hurry, and finds that sometimes the best answer in life is to leisurely blink. As soon as Barry got out of his truck we swarmed around him and began to talk. He listened patiently, leaning up against the side of his truck, as we went on and on about what our plans and intentions were. When we were finally able to clamp our mouths shut so that he could reply, he just swallowed, blinked, took a big sniff of air, and asked if that was apple pie he could smell? Talk about a 180-degree turn!

"Well, yes, yes, it is apple pie," I told him, somewhat impatiently. "Would you like a piece?" I asked him.

"Oh yes, I would," was his slow, serene reply.

"Right now?" I asked.

"Yes, that would be very nice," Barry replied, almost licking his lips. So, we all changed direction and trundled off to the kitchen to sit around the table while I quickly dished out a piece of pie for everyone.

Barry carefully tasted his first bite, then he turned towards me and said, "You've made a most delicious pie, Julie, but I'm wondering if you have any vanilla ice cream to go with it, as that really sets an apple pie off nicely?"

I stared at him. He had such an innocent look on his face. Was he fooling with us, or what? But I got up and got the ice cream and plopped a good-sized dollop right on top of his pie. He nodded his thanks, and smiled at me, and then went back to finishing the rest of his pie, obviously savoring every single morsel while we sat and watched, as by this time we'd gobbled up every last bit of our own piece of pie.

When he finally laid down his fork, he complimented me once again. "You have the knack for making a good pie, Julie, which makes me realize that I just made one of the better bargains of my life. Money is not everything, you know," he told us as he wiped the corners of his mouth with his napkin. And then he put his feet up on one of the empty kitchen chairs and leaned onto the back legs of his own chair, folding his hands over his belly. "You know, one of the things I've always loved about living on my own farm in the country is the pace of it all. I never liked the fast-rushed pace; always felt like it belonged in the city. But out here, you can set whatever pace you like. It's a mindset really, as of course, you gotta get those potatoes in before the snow flies, so there's still deadlines.

But you can develop an outlook that goes along with nature, rather than be a city whizzer. You can take the time out of your day as you're going about your chores, walk over to those roses and take a good whiff of their perfume, maybe talk to 'em and tell 'em how beautiful they are. Or you can stop mid-track to listen to the oriole sing. If you've never heard that birdsong on a clear sunny day, then you haven't lived."

Just where was he going with this, I wondered?

"Now, you just bought this place. You come outta the city all hot to trot, let's fly at 'er sort of attitude. You haven't lost your city rush hour traffic mentality yet. I could see that the minute I opened my truck door this afternoon when you all couldn't talk fast enough. So, I thought you could use a little help in learning how to slow it down a bit. You're on a farm now - you're on *your* farm now - you're living in the country, and you're working with a time element that you'll create yourselves." He paused and looked at us rather mischievously, "You do realize you create your own time structure, don't you?"

My first thought was: how does he know about this time stuff? I didn't think older people would know about something like that, which made me realize I'd just discovered a belief that needed to be examined and obviously changed, and made a mental note to do so. "We actually do know that," I said, nodding, "especially since time doesn't really exist anyway."

Barry allowed himself a tiny smile before continuing. "You're gonna discover that you'll get more done in a day if you go about it calmly rather than with a frantic attitude. Don't rush - savor the moments, and never, ever, underestimate the value to be found in any single given moment. They are what's important, as they're the building blocks of your future moments."

Hmmm, Barry was starting to sound like Omar. This definitely needed some investigation. But now wasn't the time, so I patiently waited for him to continue. I found it tough to calm myself down, but I knew he was right. It was going to take effort to get out of city mode and trickle into the slow but steady country approach.

"First we'll take a look at the barn, and you can tell me your ideas, but one at a time, mind you," he continued, gently rocking back and forth on the chair's back legs. "I can't think of a reason off the top of my head as to why your plan wouldn't work, but maybe I can help you formulate it a bit better. And then Julie, I'd really like to spend some time with you in the garden, and maybe I can give you some advice and planting options there too. But remember, you guys...I don't walk fast...not because I'm 75, but because I like to enjoy the moments discovered between *here* and *there*."

I stood up to clean the table off, and to hopefully trigger a slow but definite nudge out the door and towards the barn. "We'll do our best," I explained, trying to sound easy going, even though underneath I was still ready to fire on all fronts. "But it might take a while, so I hope you can be patient with us."

"Sure, I will." Barry finally stood up, grabbed his hat and thankfully headed for the door. Off we were – like a herd of turtles. I must say, though, that I got to like that pace a great deal as time went on.

The barn had been built so well that there really were no major structural issues to contend with. Barry hadn't built it but had certainly taken excellent care of it all those years, and we admiringly told him so. He swung around to face us, "Well, why wouldn't a person take good care of something they owned?" he demanded rather seriously. "Not only do you guys need to leave your city pace behind, but you gotta get rid of that *Kleenex culture* of buy, use and toss!"

He nailed us with that one. "Man, you are quite the teacher," Malcolm sighed. "We've only known you for a short time and you've already taught us two very important facts of life."

Barry eased his firm gaze and let a smile play across his face. "Right you are. Now, where were we?" he said as he turned to continue discussing the barn project.

The plan was to leave the bottom as a barn, in case we did get animals one day, but to renovate the top into living quarters. Sturdy stairs were already there, but the loft needed walls, doors, plumbing and electricity.

"Do you know how to do any of these trades?" Barry turned to Crow.

"I know something about all of them, except electricity. But I doubt I know enough to do the job properly, and I feel like it should be done right."

Barry was well connected in the community, and well respected, we discovered. "That's not a bad start," he told Crow. "I'll get some of the tradespeople I know to come by and take a look. They could give you tips to get started, and maybe even spend some time helping you."

That was great news. We spent another hour in the barn talking about what would go where and how to go about it. The first job was to clean it all up. Some spiders, swallows, and a few bats were going to have to find a new home.

Then Barry and I left the guys in the barn and wandered over to the garden. This got my juices flowing. I think Barry could sense that I really and truly wanted to learn how to garden.

"So, tell me Julie, what do you know about growing things?"

"Not much, really. I mean I had some decorative plants in our backyard in the city, and a few house plants that I managed to keep healthy, but I've never grown vegetables in a big garden. Neither did my parents, so I don't have much gardening experience to draw on, I'm afraid." I hung my head for a second. "Am I hopeless?" I asked softly.

"No one's hopeless," Barry answered in a supportive tone. "It's just a matter of learning a few fundamentals, preferably from an old geezer like me, and then listening with your gut and your heart. You have to learn how to hear your own *insides*, not what society constantly bombards you with on the outside."

"Do you mean your *inner* self?" I asked, looking directly at him. Once again I was amazed to hear him talk about these sorts of things.

He looked straight at me...into my soul, I think, and I didn't flinch because I was looking straight into his. In that instant we connected; a bit of alchemy that bound us together and transferred an understanding between us that could never have been achieved with even a lifetime of words.

"You will be a great gardener!" he said with a nod of his head. "A gardener extraordinaire, and I will be proud to impart my knowledge to you."

That was a profound moment for me. I remembered Barry saying only a short time ago never to underestimate a single moment for they are the building blocks of your future. Well, I liked this moment, and I believed I was heading for a great future.

"Now, how are you going to till the soil before you plant?" Barry asked.

"I didn't know I had to. I'd always just dug a hole and plopped in the plant that I bought at a gardening store." When I looked at the size of this garden, I couldn't imagine doing the whole area with a shovel. "That's going to take me weeks, and a lot of sore muscles."

Barry found that very funny, and had a good chuckle. "I don't have much to do this afternoon. Why don't I till the soil over for you this time, and in the process, teach you how to do it for future years?" He had a mischievous sparkle in his eye, and seemed very excited about something.

"How," I ventured, "are you planning to do that in just one afternoon?"

"Why, the tractor, of course!"

The tractor indeed! We were to use the tractor and the cultivator to till everything over. Talk about a brain explosion for me. Even with all my planning, this hadn't dawned on me before: what a rookie I was.

We sauntered off to the shed that housed the tractor and the various pieces of equipment it pulled. I got a lesson in what all the different implements did, and then Barry started up that old green tractor and got it running smoothly. He was careful to show me what he did and explain why he did it. I hopped on and leaned against the wheel cover, hanging on to whatever I could find. I'd never been on a tractor before. He backed up to the cultivator, got down, and hooked it up. We drove out into the yard and then he stopped, got down, and this time unhooked the cultivator. Then he drove ahead a bit. I was bewildered.

"Now, you do it," he instructed.

"Me! I don't know how to drive a tractor!"

"Time to learn, my dear." He stood up, and we exchanged places. He showed me how to work the gas and the brake and off we were! I drove that tractor all around the yard a couple of times. The boys were cheering me on from the loft. It was a hoot - I absolutely loved it. But then Barry told me to back it up to the cultivator and hook it up. Uh-Oh. But I did okay after a few tries. I proudly drove to the garden, where Barry told me, "You'd better let me take over now. You've never actually done any cultivating before, and there's a knack to it, you see."

"Good idea," I quickly agreed as we changed places once again. The first important thing I discovered, was that the cultivator shoes needed to be dropped down, so that they actually plowed the dirt. As we went around and around the garden area, I could see there was definitely a method to it so that in the end the soil would be nicely tilled, the rows going the right direction and not compacted by the tractor tires. Then I did a few rounds so that I'd know how it felt for next time. Doing actual work with the tractor was different than just driving it around, but I liked it just as much: maybe even more, realizing what it could accomplish.

"I believe the running of the tractor is going to be your job, Julie," Barry proudly declared after I managed to park the tractor back in the shed perfectly on my first attempt. "You seem to take to each other really well."

"But I'm a girl!" As soon as I said it, I realized how silly it was. Obviously, it was another one of those rooted beliefs I had that needed changing. I was about to say something to that effect, but Barry beat me to it. I got his weighty lecture about how a female can do anything a man can do and usually even better than a man, and how society has spent too many centuries trying to *keep women in their place,* and did I want to know why? What else could I do but nod since I could see he was going to tell me anyway as he was on a powerful roll.

"It's because men have always been afraid of just how intelligent and formidable women were, and are, so they became bullies and made sure that women were given no opportunities for success or advancement at all. And they stuck together. Men thought they were safe with this attitude, but boy, were they wrong." He jumped down from the tractor and stood solidly on both feet; like he was grounded to the earth somehow. "Well, you can't keep that kind of power and intelligence down forever. The shift is happening. Men are gonna struggle until equality is truly reached, and respect is shown by both sides. Not just in one country, but in all of humanity." He calmed down somewhat, and then sighed. "What makes me really sad is that I don't think I'm going to live to see that day."

"I do understand, Barry," I told him softly, as I climbed down from the tractor – not nearly as nimbly as he had, I might add. "It's just one of those beliefs we grow up with. Our society still puts those messages out. Women put themselves down without even realizing they're doing it. All you've got to do is watch a few TV adds to see that. But I know there are a lot more women now who have control of their lives, respect for themselves, and the respect of men. And I know there are men, like my Malcolm for instance, that truly do hold women in high regard. What gets me is that I thought I was one of those self-respecting women, and then out popped my remark, which tells me I'm not there yet. It's a work in progress, I guess, but I'm going to be much more aware of it now and work on myself. And I'm also going to be the tractor driver of our group - and do a darn good job of it too!"

That brought a smile to both of us. "But seriously," Barry said, once again looking me straight in the eye with that penetrating way of his, "promise me you'll *always* remember what we just talked about Julie. It's incredibly important!"

I knew there was something more behind Barry's passion on this subject, but today was not the day to continue on with it. We would, though; all in good time - time of our own making! Right now, I was going to learn what to plant and how to plant it. As we slowly walked to the house to discuss seeds, I knew I would make this man a million apple pies if that's what he wanted. He was a treasure, indeed.

We spent a few hours going over seed catalogues and what he and Rose had found worked well in their garden. It was a serious business for them; they even kept records from year to year as to what they planted, when they planted, and how it turned out. They had notations beside planting dates that told of what was going on around them at the time; like *planted the beans today – lilacs are budding out*. When I asked Barry why they did that, he explained that nature had a much better sense of time than the calendar, so best to watch what nature did rather than what the calendar said. Plus, May 10th is very different in this area compared to May 10th on the coast, so you can't plant just because it's May 10th.

Then there was the phase of the moon to consider as well. Right, I told him, but he could tell I didn't know what he was talking about. The moon, he told me, has power, and anyone who knows this obvious fact learns how to use it. You always plant things that grow upwards on a waxing, or near to full moon, and anything that grows down into the soil on a waning moon. The push and pull of the moon work on plants just as powerfully as they do on the tides. He also explained how all the old geezers knew how to watch nature's signs to figure out what the weather was going to do. They could even tell by sniffing the air, or watching the swallows, if rain was coming, or a storm, or a sunny day. It saddened him to see so many farmers these days turning to the weather channel on TV to find out about the weather rather than looking to nature. It was a skill that was being lost, along with so many other essential skills.

"Would you teach me those skills?" I asked eagerly.

With a beaming smile he told me he most certainly would.

By the time we'd gone through a few years of gardening journals, we'd decided on what to plant, where and when - approximately. It was too late to order seeds from his favorite seed catalogue, so he told me of a place in Carberry where I could get good quality seeds, as good quality was important.

"Make sure you check the packages carefully," Barry instructed. "You want *organic* and *untreated* seeds. The last thing we want to condone is more of that chemical crap in our food!"

"Yes, sir! Message understood!"

"I'll show you how to make your own seeds this fall. That's the best. Just let me know when you get the seeds and I'll come back out and show you my planting tricks."

I could hardly wait. My fingers were itching to get into that nice black dirt we'd just plowed over. I got a few more tips from him on the flowers around the house, and then he headed back to the barn to see how the guys were doing while I started to get supper ready. I could tell this was going to be a lovely arrangement. We were all so suited to what we were undertaking - even Barry.

24

OUR NEW LIFE

"You do not need to know precisely what is happening, or exactly where it is all going. What you need is to recognize the possibilities and challenges offered by the present moment, and to embrace them with courage, faith and hope." **Thomas Merton**

For the first few years on our farm, life continued in pretty much the same fashion as those early days. There was so much vitality, excitement, contentment, and joy in all of our endeavors. Our accomplishments, singly and as a group, came one after the other. With every project completed, or every bit of knowledge grasped, we felt an enormous sense of pride that became part and parcel of who we were. Barry seemed to be going through a jubilant second blossoming. One morning over coffee, he confessed that in the beginning his decision to sell to us had indeed given him some concern. But once we got going, he knew it was the second-best thing that ever happened to him. And what was the first, you ask? Why, marrying Rose, of course. How could it not be?

The guys managed to finish the hayloft before winter that first year. To celebrate, we had a huge barn warming party, inviting the surrounding neighbors and all of the people who helped us build. Some of them even brought their instruments along, and out of the blue we ended up with a country jam session - and dancing! That would never have happened in the city. What a great evening that was! We were forming a tight bond with everyone in the area – young and old. Apparently, us *city-slickers* were thought of as being *okay* after all.

Since Malcolm and I ended up with the house to ourselves, there was room for guests to visit. First, my parents came for a few days, and then Malcolm's. Later on, George's parents visited too. It was so great to show them all we'd accomplished, and to explain everything we still wanted to do. It was an eye opener for them as well, especially when they met Barry and saw how vital he still was, even though he was ten years older than they were. They had no idea country life could be so rich.

Crow was never able to get in touch with his parents, even though he tried; too many years of no contact resulted in the connection being entirely lost. It was sad for him, but he handled it well. There wasn't a person that met Crow that didn't like him, so he certainly wasn't short of friends.

One day Malcolm's old boss called us – just out of the blue. He was hoping to come out with his family to see what we'd gotten up to. That visit was a celebration and a half! We would never have thought their family could end up the way it did – all full of fun and happiness - especially when we thought back to the way things were before their son's accident. Malcolm's boss beamed with pride every time he looked at his family, plus he was pretty proud of what we'd accomplished too.

I've come to realize that life has a habit of taking unexpected twists and turns. You don't always get to see them for what they are until you've driven down the road a bit further. Only then are you able to look in the rearview mirror and see the past for what it is. But I, for one, preferred to look ahead. Of course you need the past, and everyone has one, but the present and the possibilities for the future always seemed to be foremost in my mind. I never wanted to get stuck in the past - I felt that would only keep my wheels spinning in the present. I liked looking to the future where the possibilities were endless, like a canvas waiting for the colors of my own choosing.

And let me tell you, my garden became a canvas like no other. With Barry's help, I learned how to garden so that my heart and soul were one with the dirt and the plants. I swear those plants turned and greeted me every time I walked through the garden gate. I absolutely loved it and spent a great deal of my time there. I even gave my garden a name: *Carberry Gardens*. Crow surprised me one day with a skookum wooden, hand-painted sign hung over the gate, and a large hand-carved Phoenix that was firmly attached to the gatepost, but with its wings outstretched, reaching for the sun! My heart skipped a beat every time I saw it.

I learned how to can, freeze, and dry my produce, and I sold a lot too. I canned sixty dozen – yes, sixty *dozen*- jars for the winter; all kinds of jams, pickled this and pickled that, sauerkraut, fruit, applesauce - you name it, I learned how to preserve it. I filled up a full-size freezer with my very own frozen vegetables, and I traded some for meat. Barry taught me the ins and outs of using a root cellar, so we had no trouble keeping carrots and *spuds*, as Barry would say, either. A neighbor showed me how to braid onions, so I did up a dozen long braids of onions and hung them in the pantry, alongside braided strands of garlic. They lasted all winter! This garden knew how to produce food – all pesticide free, I might add. It never ceased to amaze me how simple and magical it was to grow your own food; all one needed was good black dirt, water, seeds, sun, and lots of care and attention. It's a miracle we can all achieve if we're willing to try. Before, I used to have to rely on a store for my food. Now, I get very little from there, and that gives me a feeling of satisfaction that defies verbal description. In my heart I hang on to a hope that more people will learn how to do this, even in the city. Why not turn those green lawns into food? At least your water bill would be giving you something good to eat. There's a great deal of missed potential hiding in those decorative green lawns.

The second year on our farm was the beginning of many exciting developments we hadn't even planned on. For starters, Malcolm was asked if he'd like to apply for the position of assistant manager at the care home in Carberry! It had never even crossed our minds to think of them as a place of employment.

"I'm going to apply, Julie," he told me as soon as he got off the phone with them. "I know it's not the kind of work I'm qualified for, but nothing in Carberry is. I'm pretty sure I'm capable of learning a new position, so why not?" he looked at me, beaming. New adventures could be scary, but also exhilarating, and I could see Malcolm was definitely excited about this one.

I stood up and gave him a big hug. "Go for it, sweetie," I whispered in his ear. He went in to apply, and was hired right on the spot.

A week later he drove to his new job for the very first time. I was getting supper ready when he came home after his first day of work. "Hi, how was your commute?" I turned to ask him. "Hopefully not bumper to bumper," I said jokingly.

Malcolm came straight over to me, grabbed me in a bear hug and spun me around the kitchen a few times before putting me down. "Fantastic, Julie! It was absolutely fantastic! There wasn't a single car in front of me or behind me the entire way into Carberry this morning; I didn't even meet another car on the road. It was a solo commute, if you can believe it! My only company was a couple of cows in the field watching me pass by. And on the way home, I counted no more than ten cars on the road. Man, I'm going to love this."

His enthusiasm was infectious. "I'm so happy for you," I laughed. "Think of all those lovely mornings you're going to have driving to work. Those cows will get to know you. What about the job? Do you think you're going to like it?"

"I think I'm *really* going to like it. I never realized how important the older generation was before." He sat down with a beer and put his feet up. "We don't give them enough recognition for all of the hard-earned knowledge they have. I want to change that. I'm not sure how yet, but I'm going to figure something out. They definitely need more respect for all they've done in their lives."

That's my Malcolm – always wanting to make something better. He came to love that job, more and more with every month that passed. The older generation became an inspiration for him, and he became a sign of hope for them, simply because he listened and cared. The stories he brought home were priceless and full of insights for all of us. People who are not so firmly attached mentally or physically to the world as we know it, come up with the darndest things if one is willing to take the time to actually pay attention. We all came to believe that the so-called *delusional* patients were getting flashes from the other side of life, and were simply trying to share them with us. Unfortunately, not everyone could accept this as a possibility. We asked Omar and the gang about this, and they agreed. Often, these people were basically starting to prepare themselves for their upcoming shift to the other side. Understanding that concept made Malcolm feel it was an honor to be privy to their conversations and goings-on, plus it gave us some starting points for more than a few great discussions. Not only did his job supply us with a steady income, but it also provided flashes of insight. All in all, it grew into the perfect job for him.

George took the leap he'd long been dreaming of. What's life without a leap or two, he'd often say. It was certainly not the first one he'd ever taken. He managed to buy a solid old house on Carberry's main street, a bit farther down from where all the existing stores were; pretty much at the point where commercial switched to residential. Two majestic maple trees stood in the front yard, and in the back there was a small, but quaint, fenced-in area: the perfect set up to start his very own bistro! He picked the perfect name for it too: *Kodiak!* That was an easy decision for him. Many days when I'd walk in there, I'd see the filmy soft purple outline of Kodiak happily lounging in a corner, just taking it all in. Sometimes he'd even join others at their table! I could see him, but they certainly didn't; and thank goodness for that, as they'd probably have run out the door if he'd made himself suddenly visible!

Crow helped George put a covered deck onto the front of the house, and a smaller enclosed deck in the back, which he heated in the winter. He kept the feel of the heritage house with its high ceilings, worn wooden floors, original chandeliers, and deep wooden window casings, which he filled with colorful potted flowers and herbs from me! He put up a light turquoise striped wallpaper on the upper walls, with wainscoting finishing off the bottom half. All in all, the result was that of a genuine solid old-fashioned house, especially with the quaint tables Crow had made for him out of some old barnwood someone had given him. The overall feel was warm, inviting, and cheerful.

In the kitchen George went completely modern; nothing but new, stainless steel appliances, which he kept spotless. No expense was spared for what he saw as the tools of his craft. And what a skill he developed over time. First was the coffee: strong, flavorful, organic coffee for a reasonable price. That alone brought a lot of the younger people in, and even some of the more curious older ones. He spent a lot of time developing a menu that would fill a need he believed was there - using us as guinea pigs once again. There was a growing younger generation that had jobs in Cusick or Fresco, but lived in Carberry - just for peaceful living it offered. This gave them a commute that took up a substantial portion of their daily time, and George figured if he could offer the same type of food you'd find in a city bistro right there in Carberry, a lot of the commuters would buy from him just for the convenience of it all. It was to be a city bistro, but set in a peaceful rural setting. Mission accomplished! His food was delicious, healthy, and affordable. Most of his vegetables came from my very own garden! He did indeed fill a niche. Word even spread far enough that he'd get weekend visitors from Cusick and Fresco too - people wanting to enjoy the small-town atmosphere. He had no worries about being able to pay off the sizeable debt he'd taken on. He loved his job, and he loved his customers, and they seemed to love him too.

George's only problem was getting enough help. He couldn't run the bistro alone as he got busier and busier. He definitely needed someone to work with him. He'd hire young people from the town and give them proper training for when they went out on their own, but that was the trouble: they never stayed permanently.

Then one day, his cell phone rang, and when he heard who it was, he almost dropped the phone. If you remember, a long time ago, in what seemed like another life to us, George had come upon a young girl in the city that'd been working the streets and taking care of her ailing mother. George had given her his phone number if she ever needed help, which she'd memorized. Well, her memory must have been excellent because here she was, calling George a few years later. Apparently, her mother passed away a few months ago, so she decided to make a run for it, which is exactly what it would have to be to get away from ever watchful eyes. But that's as far as her plans went. She'd secretly saved enough money for a bus ticket, but she didn't know where to go. She wasn't sure where George was, or if he'd even remember her, but if it was okay with him, she asked, could she come to the place he was, as he'd been the only one she'd ever felt she could trust? George didn't hesitate one bit. He told her to come to Carberry, and he'd be able to help her for sure – no questions asked. She couldn't tell him exactly when it would be as she had to wait for just the right time to sneak away without being caught, but to expect her at some point. They said good-bye and the waiting game started.

Every time the phone rang, George thought it would be her. It took over two weeks before she called again, and when she did, she sounded terrified. "George?" she whispered. "George, I'm so scared."

"Where are you? What's happened?" He thought something terrible must have happened, putting her in serious trouble."

"I'm here - here in Carberry, like you said - but I'm so scared George - what if someone followed me?" She cowered in the phone booth, trying to hide her face. "I need to get out of here fast! Can you hurry? Please, can you hurry?"

"I'm on my way. Just stay where you are."

What if someone did follow her? He needed to get down to that bus depot right away, but his bistro was full of customers and he was alone that day. He quickly climbed up onto one of the chairs and got everyone's attention with a sharp whistle. "Hey everybody, something's come up and I've got to run out of here, but I don't think I'll be too long. If you're ready to leave, your bill is on me." Then he jumped down and ran out the door. Luckily the bus depot was only two blocks away.

He didn't recognize her at first; she was so thin and pale. Her occupation had certainly taken its toll. She looked at him with panicked, desperate eyes. What a life of hell she must have led, George thought. His heart melted. He opened his arms and she ran to him. He could feel her shaking as she sobbed and sobbed against his chest. "Look," he said, "you're going to be okay – everything's going to be okay. I'm going to help you get back on your feet so that you can finally live a normal life. It's all going to be okay now. You'll see."

With tears still streaming down her face, she managed to look up at George between sobs and say, "I want that with all my heart!"

George took a look around the bus depot. It looked like everyone had cleared out, so he didn't think anyone had actually followed her, so off they went, back to the restaurant.

Now, it's fairly common knowledge that small towns, including Carberry, like their gossip, and this young girls' appearance walking close beside George started off a great bunch of it: who was she, where'd she come from, was it his daughter, why was she crying, and why was she dressed like *that*?

When they got back to the restaurant, everyone was still there. George's unusual sudden disappearance had definitely roused their curiosity, so they stayed to see what was up. Consequently, when George and the young girl walked in, they were met with a lot of stares and dead silence. George had to say something. "Everyone, I want you to meet my young friend Tasha," which was not her actual name, mind you, but a name she'd chosen for herself while on the bus. George could feel her shaking beside him, so he put his arm around her for some comfort. "Tasha is a long-lost friend that has come to me for help, so she's going to be staying with us for a while. I want everyone to get to know her as time goes on, but right now, she's going to need some time to get over a few personal issues. I'm hoping everyone will go out of their way to treat her nicely, as she sure needs that." Then he took her to his office in the back and told her she'd be safe there.

Tasha looked around the office, and then at George, eyes still moist from all the crying. "Thank you," she softly told him. "I don't ever remember being anywhere that felt *safe*. I think you've just saved my life. Thank you!"

George brought her something to eat, and something to read, and that's where she stayed for the rest of the afternoon until George closed up the bistro. Then they drove back to the farm. He'd called ahead, so I knew Tasha would be coming home with him. I'd made one of the upstairs bedrooms ready for her. When we first found out that she might be coming to Carberry at some point, we'd decided it would be best for her to live with us at the farm indefinitely. She needed a safe haven where she could start to leave her past behind and find herself again, so we offered her that.

In the beginning she seemed to be in a constant state of fear. Since Crow knew all about that sort of thing from his childhood, he spent a lot of time talking to Tasha about what constant fear does to you, physically and mentally. They'd sit out on the swings most evenings, talking and talking. I'd say it took her about a year to get through an entire day without unwelcomed memories and fears suddenly cropping up. Crow taught her to recognize her approaching anxiety; how to allow it come out, assuring herself that it would indeed pass; and then actually letting it pass without grabbing on to it. Bit by bit it started to work. It was a great start, but there was just so much in life she had to become comfortable with.

It was baby steps, but we had no timeline, so we all did what we could to help Tasha. I found her to be a tremendous help in the garden. In fact, I'd say she liked gardening almost as much as I did.

George taught her cooking skills, as the plan was always for Tasha to join George in the bistro eventually, if she wanted to. Crow discovered she had a buried creative side as she started to show a great deal of skill and imagination when working with wood. Malcolm was able to teach her some of the business end of things - like how to do accounting. She seemed to like working with numbers. And Barry treated her like another one of his granddaughters and gave her the gift of acceptance - she even called him Grandpa, which made him beam all over the place. We all taught her as much as we could, as who knew what skill she would need as she ventured out of the safe cocoon we'd created for her. She hadn't been to school since she was ten and really wanted to get her grade 12 diploma, so we set her up with a way to do this at our farm, and she simply flourished - there was no better way to describe it. Tasha was a beautiful flower ready to blossom, and we were all very proud to be a part of it.

To make a long story short, Tasha went on to get her Grade 12 education without any difficulties whatsoever. She helped George at the bistro during the day and studied in the evening. She started up her own line of wooden crafts that she sold at the bistro too - her specialty was birdhouses. She'd opened a bank account for her newly found income, and learned the importance of saving money. When everyone felt it was safe, Crow and George built a tiny suite for Tasha in the attic of the bistro so that she could become more independent. The town people really took to her too. They quit trying to find out about her past and just accepted her for what she was *now*, which was an intelligent, strong, independent young girl turning into an equally intelligent young woman. We were as proud of her as any parent could be.

Crow also discovered his passion in life. He developed into the handyman that everyone in Carberry called if they needed help. The jack of all trades that would renovate your basement, build you a deck, fix your roof, or your plumbing, plow your snow, prune your hedges, haul away your garbage, and even walk your dog while you were on holidays. His reputation all started when he built us a fire pit/barbeque/meeting place/star gazing arena sort of thing on our farm. He spent a great deal of his first winter designing and redesigning it until he felt he had it exactly right. Then in the spring, he started to build one of the neatest additions to our farm we could ever have imagined. Even Barry had to take his hat off to him since he felt he could never have achieved anything quite like it. We ended up cooking and eating there many summer evenings, followed by great discussions, along with gazing up at that black sky lit with millions and millions of stars: no light pollution out here. It became the talk of the town, and some people even came out to see it for themselves, after which they'd hire Crow for a job at their place. His skill and honest magnetic personality were a great combination, and within a relatively short period of time he was inundated with requests. He became one busy and highly respected fellow in the community.

To say that we enjoyed the fire pit gazebo is an understatement: it became the heart of our farm. Omar, Bluedon, Griffin, and Kodiak often joined us when we were out there, too. They told us it had become one of their favorite places to be, and if you think of all the places they were privy to in the universe, that says a lot! I remember the night they showed up when Barry was stargazing with us; it was the first time they met. I'd often wondered if they ever would, and if they did, how it would go. I got my answer one warm summer night. Barry had decided to stay overnight, as it was getting late and he wasn't ready to go home yet. The five of us were lying back in the reclining chairs we'd purchased specifically for stargazing, having a great conversation about UFOs.

"I gotta tell you my UFO story," Barry said. We were all ears. "You see, it was calving season and I was out in the barn in the middle of the night. It was a clear black night, just like this one. I was keeping an eye on one of my cows delivering her first calf. When it was all over I was walking back to the house, looking up at that inviting black sky, like I usually did. But let me tell you – I stopped dead in my tracks when I saw this brilliant light in that sky - directly in front of me!"

"No way," Crow exclaimed. He sat up in his chair and looked over at Barry, who happened to be lounging right beside him. "What happened then?"

"Well, I knew it wasn't a plane because it stayed in one spot, and the brightness was tremendous, and kinda' mesmerizing. I felt like it was meant for me, somehow, but I couldn't figure out what to make of it. It pulsed from extremely bright to rather dull - then back to bright again." Barry paused, remembering that night.

"Then what?" I asked, trying to urge him on.

"I just kept staring at it. I don't think I could have pulled my attention away even if I'd wanted to. It was like a stand-off, for what seemed like a very long time. Eventually, it zoomed off to the east, leaving me wondering if it'd really happened at all – even though I *knew* it had."

"Well, of course, it happened. We don't fool around with such things, you know!"

We knew where that voice was coming from, but Barry certainly didn't. He bolted upright in his lounge chair - a lot quicker than I'd ever seen him move before. In fact, I was worried about it being too much of a shock to his system. I didn't want any heart attacks. But the guys knew how to calm the whole situation down.

Omar appeared in front of Barry with a gentle look on his face and simply said to him, "Don't you think it's time we finally met?"

But Barry was still speechless. I knew what must be going through his mind. It was the same for all of us the first time.

"I was the one driving that spaceship," Omar continued. "I wanted to give you an undeniable personal memory that would forever keep your mind open to new possibilities and unexplained wonders. And as I followed your life, I can see that it worked. You've done an exemplary job of living, and you're not done yet."

I could see some explanations were going to be needed before Barry was going to get comfortable enough to speak. "Barry, these four guys have been our friends for several years now. We've had many meetings and wonderful discussions with them. They're the reason we found our way to you and your place. Without their help, we'd still be in the city, unhappily plugging along with the rest of the crowd. Let's do a formal introduction then." I introduced everyone. Barry needed to say their names a few times – he looked like he was chewing on something to get the full taste of it before swallowing. But fortunately, I could visibly see him calm down. He relaxed back into his chair, and our guys sat down on their imaginary chairs too. We weren't going to get any cozier, yet Barry was still quiet.

"Barry are you okay?" I asked, feeling somewhat concerned as normally he's not lost for words.

"Yes, yes, I'm okay, Julie. I'm just somewhat taken aback, that's all. I've got so many thoughts running around in my head right now. Countless times in the past I was sure that there had to be more to life, but discovering what that could possibly be always lay a bit beyond my grasp. That feeling always left me wanting for more, but more what, I didn't know. It was buried in my gut, but I couldn't seem to raise it up into my mind for examination. Now everything's falling into place – it's all starting to make sense. It's truly amazing!"

"It is indeed amazing," Griffin nodded, "and somewhat shocking when you've lived your life according to someone else's rules, and all of a sudden you're confronted with something you were told was impossible, or didn't exist, like UFOs, or us. Where does that leave you, you have to wonder? Old rules say you must be going crazy, and you think that you must be because non-physical personalities like us simply don't exist. But on the other hand, you *are* seeing them. You *are* talking to them, and you feel in your heart of hearts that they *are* real, and they *are* right, and you're pretty sure you're not going crazy," Griffin explained, looking directly at Barry. "Am I right?"

"I get the feeling you already know my answer, and I get the feeling you probably know everything I'm thinking too. But yes, you are right. I know I'm not crazy, but I've never been able to put my finger on these feelings well enough to talk to anybody but Rose about it. I always felt I couldn't tell anyone else about the UFO incident for fear of being called a weirdo behind my back. I didn't want that for me, but especially not for Rose."

"Well, you now have four understanding friends you can talk to till the cows come home, plus the four of us that can tell you even more. We like to drop in from time to time, as you can see," Griffin pointed out. "We've been following you around for a long time, so we know you very well, but you might want to spend a bit of time getting to know us, now that you can see that we do indeed exist."

"You've been following me for a long time?" Barry asked, quite eagerly. "Do you know my Rose then?"

Bluedon smiled and calmly replied, "We know Rose very well - when she was alive, and now on the other side of death."

"Is she okay?" Barry's moist eyes were ready to waterfall into tears.

"She's more than okay. Rose is home, and she loves it there. She misses you, of course, but she knows you'll be joining her at some point. But no rush, she says to you. Live your life, and live it well. There'll be endless time to be together again when you're ready to move on." Bluedon stopped talking and looked as though he was listening to something. "And she says to maybe eat a little less pie so that you can still fit into your pants when you come over!"

By now, Barry was in full flood. I went to the house to get the tissue box as he was definitely going to need it. We let him empty himself out, and after he was done, he just looked at us, and we all knew. Words were not necessary. Theirs had been a relationship of gold - the kind that doesn't come around very often - the kind that was a beacon for all others who had their typical struggles - the kind we all wanted to emulate, but usually fell short of. Omar told us later that those two have been in love for centuries, and it showed.

There really wasn't much more to be added to that emotional night, so we just lay back again and watched more shooting stars until someone suggested we wander off to bed. It had been an unforgettable evening.

Barry was up bright and early the next morning, smiling from ear to ear as he came bouncing down the stairs.

"What's up with you?" I asked as I filled his coffee cup and set it on the kitchen table. "You look like you're glowing!"

"Oh, you guys - I had a dream last night - a wonderful dream about Rose!" Barry sat down between Malcolm and Crow at the table, and gazed wistfully out the window as he began to tell us his dream. "We were together again, and she explained to me where she was and how she would be waiting for me when it was my time to join her, and what it would be like when we were together again. It was heaven - or I guess it was heaven-like in my mind. She told me it would be whatever we made it to be." He picked up his coffee cup and drank a few sips before continuing. "But then she said that I have the same opportunity to do that right now, while I'm alive, but in a different way. She was very emphatic that I must live my life *now*...to its fullest...age meant nothing, she said, so I was not to try to hide behind it. There was so much more I had to give to those around me, and to myself, so what was I waiting for? She was very adamant and wanted an answer, but I didn't have one for her." Barry looked at me for help, but I had no idea what to say to him, except to ask him if that was the end of the dream.

"No, that's not the end. She told me a couple of times '*Do it now, and do it well.*' I asked what it was I should do, but she just looked at me with those soft velvety brown eyes of hers and told me that my heart knew very well what she meant. I'm on the right track – I just need to embrace it and let myself go more," Barry sighed, leaning back in his chair. "I love that woman more than I can ever say. She smiled at me one last time and blew me a kiss, and then I woke up. But as I'm telling you this, I really question if it was a dream at all – it seemed so real."

"Wow, Barry! That must have been wonderful!" Malcolm declared.

"Yeah, it truly was. I'll hold that gem in my heart until the day I pass. And I have no worries about passing over to the other side now as I know what's waiting for me. But, as Rose said, I'm still here

- sitting in your kitchen, complete with body and all - and it's gettin' mighty hungry. What's for breakfast, Julie?"

What a lovable character. I dished up a plate with bacon - homegrown and smoked by our neighbor, two eggs sunny side up - from our own chickens, two pieces of toast - from our homemade bread, and jam that was a mixture of our own strawberries and rhubarb. Barry seemed to have worked up an appetite overnight as he devoured everything in front of him and then asked for another cup of coffee.

When he was finished and I'd cleared away the dishes, I sat back down at the table with everyone and asked Barry if he was okay to talk about the relationship he had with Rose when she was alive. I thought it might have been a touchy subject, and I didn't want to bring up more memories that would start another teary flood.

"Fire away," he said with no hesitation whatsoever. "The experiences I had last night have helped me cement my thoughts of late, and nothing could ever make them waver again. So, go ahead, Julie. What would you like to know?"

"Well, for starters, how did you two meet and fall in love?"

"That's easy. We met the same way so many folks did back then – at a country dance. Man, those dances back then - they were hopping!" You could see his memory drift back there. "I was looking for someone to dance with when I spotted Rose all the way across the hall. She was *so* pretty – and I could tell she was kind of shy - I liked that about her. But I was stopped dead in my tracks when she looked up at me and her gaze met mine. Believe it or not, we both knew at that moment that we would be lovers for the rest of our lives. It was like a thunderbolt between us."

"Barry – that's incredible," I said. "And it certainly turned out to be true too, didn't it?"

"Yes, that it did. No doubt about it."

"But you must have had some difficulties in all those years together. What did you guys do to make your relationship so cherished and lasting? Or did you even have any troublesome times?" I asked.

"Of course we had some troublesome times. We were two different people, with two different ways of thinking about things: two different childhoods, two different sets of desires and goals to fulfill in a lifetime, two different ideas about raising children, money, religion, jobs, you name it. But we both wanted to live in one home *with* each other, not *against* each other. When someone manages to do that with ease, then you know they've found a winning formula, as it's not the easiest thing to do over a long period of time."

"So, how'd you do it?" I was very curious.

"Respect! Without a doubt, that's the first key. Without mutual respect, and I mean *genuine* respect for the other person being who they truly are, nothing is going to be possible. You can't expect to change the other person, nor should you even try to, so you have to get to know who they genuinely are as you enter into a relationship. And if you find you can't honestly respect their values or qualities, or they can't respect yours, then that relationship is not for you."

"That's a really good point," I acknowledged. "I know that I feel a great deal of respect for Malcolm," I said, looking at him, "and I certainly feel respected by him."

"Ditto for me, Julie." Malcolm reached over and put his hand on top of mine. "Respect has always been one of the foundations of our relationship. Sounds like we've been on the right track all along."

"That's good cuz it's the cornerstone," Barry continued. "It's equally important to know yourself too, and what you bring to the table. You can't expect someone else to know you, let alone respect you, if you don't even know yourself. And you certainly should not go changing yourself just to get someone else's respect. Know who you are and never waiver, I say. You *must* respect each other's values.

"Now, you take Rose and I - we didn't know each other in the beginning, but we did have a very strong attraction to each other. So, we spent a lot of time learnin' each other – what our goals were, what our temperaments were, what our fears were – don't forget the fears – even the unpleasant or unrecognized ones. Get 'em all out on the table for inspection. There were lots of long walks and lots of long talks our first two years together. I think we both found out things about ourselves, and each other, that we didn't even know before – strengths and weaknesses. But at the end of that time we were sure – mind you, no thunderbolts this time – but *sure* that we wanted to get married and spend the rest of our lives together. That's how we started with a very solid foundation."

"That's great advice. And I'm happy to say that Malcolm and I pretty much did what you're advising. We did spend a long time getting to know each other before getting married, didn't we hon? And for sure there were some surprise discoveries, especially after we got over the initial honeymoon period where we were both on our best behavior. But as everything gets acknowledged and worked out, a tight bond forms."

"You're right, it does. Both Rose and I had certain areas that were not negotiable, and other areas that possibly could be. They need to be talked out. Something that's not negotiable, is *not* negotiable. Can the other person respect your wishes? And are you strong enough to demand that they're valued? Make sure, and make this very clear, especially if you're the women, as they seem to be good at giving in just to make a relationship work, which only results in resentment as time goes on. Resentment is a relationship killer and a powerful magnet that attracts other resentments to it. You can't afford to harbor even one of those. But if you each start out knowing yourselves, and understanding the importance of maintaining respect for each other, and yourselves, then you have a strong foundation to build on. Troubles that arise over time, and there will be some, can be cleared up simply by coming back to the very idea of respecting and honoring the thoughts, abilities, and differences that you each have."

"You know Barry, you've got lots of good knowledge here to pass on," I said. "I think Rose was right. People are sponges for your kind of tried and tested wisdom, me included. But getting back to what you said about resentments – I get what you're saying. They do pop up from time to time. I know we've experienced them in our relationship."

"That's true, they do," Malcolm agreed.

"But we've found that if we discuss them honestly, they go away. And because I know I'll never be criticized, or made fun of, by Malcolm, or vice versa, we always feel safe to say whatever's on our minds. Wouldn't you agree with that, Malcolm?"

"For sure. I'm always interested to hear what you have to say, and I believe it keeps me from creating any bad habits as well. If you tell me what you're thinking, then I don't have to guess. Guessing is never good, as I don't ever seem to guess right." We all had to laugh at that. Malcolm truly was not good at any kind of guessing; he was more of a factual type of guy.

"That's another key! You've already discovered it. It's so important that you each feel free to discuss any issue, big or small. Lots of couples don't, you. know. They tell themselves to just sweep it under the rug, to not rock the boat, or that it's not that big of a deal, so why bother to upset him or her, and on and on. Phrases like that run through a lot of people's minds, both men and women, but in this day and age I think it's more likely to hear a woman say these things to herself, than a man. If she finally gets the gumption to talk to her partner about something that bothers her – let's say something the partner's doing, or not doing - and the partner gets defensive right away and tells her that she doesn't know what she's talking about, she's crazy, she's wrong, or it's not like that and how could she be so silly to think like that, then do you think she's gonna feel free to initiate a discussion in the future? No way. She'll clam up, and then resentment upon resentment starts to build until there's gonna be an explosion…and those are never pretty."

"So, how does one go about avoiding that kind of situation?" I asked.

"Try it out at the beginning of the relationship - before there's too much at stake, like marriage, a house, and kids. Learn how to talk to each other right from the get-go. You know…this bothers me because, or that makes me uncomfortable because…and if you're met with a defensive reaction instead of an honest willingness to learn and try, then you have a choice to make. And remember, there are *always* choices. If you're uncomfortable with your partners reaction, try it a few more times to make sure. If it doesn't work, don't drag it out. Part your ways. Both of you have to feel respected by the other one. Everyone needs to feel comfortable to be themselves in a relationship. I'm not saying there won't be disagreements from time to time - like I said, you're two people trying to share a life together, and no two people are completely alike in all areas. But you should each be granted leeway and supported for being who you are by the other person, and not made to feel that *you* are wrong and *they* are right."

Malcolm's eyes met mine. We'd talked about this several times in our marriage and have always strived to do exactly what Barry was telling us. Acceptance, live and let live, want the best for each other, to understand and support each other and never try to put ourselves up by putting the other one down. We'd seen this sort of behavior in some of our friends and didn't want any part of it, so we worked at becoming better partners for each other. And I really got what Barry was saying about resentments building up until they blew. We knew one couple that ended up getting divorced simply because they talked to their friends about their problems, but never to each other. They always tried to be civil in public, but you could see that their smiles were pasted on and their touches were forced - all designed to fool everyone around. But no one was fooled. They managed to hang on to that toxic relationship for a few years, but then it all broke loose, and a nasty divorce ensued. It seemed to me that had they had followed Barry's rules about getting to know and like yourself first, and then getting to know and respect the other person, and discussing anything bothersome right from the beginning, they either would have realized they were not going to be a good match, or that they needed to work on these areas. Blame didn't exist in a good relationship - but there was always plenty of it in a divorce.

Being single, Crow had an entirely different viewpoint to add to our lively kitchen debate that morning. "You know it's always bothered me that our society says you *have* to be in a relationship to be a proper good person. Anyone who decides to stay single is thought of as being not quite right, or lacking socials skills, or any other negative explanation that can be found. What's wrong with being single?"

"I'm with you on that one," George quickly agreed. "Like you said, what's wrong with being single? Women can be single, men can be single, and so what if they are? That's their choice. Are they any less human if they are? I think not!"

"That is definitely an outdated way of thinking, isn't it?" Barry said. "Even though things are different now, old attitudes still stick around. All sorts of old ideas and beliefs turn into unspoken understandings – it's part of being a member of the tribe of humanity. But things have changed – they always do - and there's more change on the way. Personally, I find it exciting to be part of that change. We have a lot to say about what those changes are too, just by being ourselves and not hiding behind the old rules we've been taught, and are expected to follow. First, however, we need discussions like this one to help us ask ourselves questions. That way, we can start to understand what our own beliefs are and where they came from. Then we can either get rid of them completely, or replace them with ones we want. How else can we ever create change for the better, unless we change our beliefs?"

We all turned to stare at him. It had taken us a knock on the head from our guys, plus lots of discussions to understand the concept of changing our beliefs in order to change our reality. Yet, here was this guy who lived in a generation gone by that came to this understanding all on his own! "Barry, you've got to tell us something," Crow blurted out. "How do you know about changing your beliefs to create your reality? We only learned about it recently, and it wasn't the easiest of concepts for us to adopt."

"Well, just what makes you think that younger generations know more than us old guys?" Barry challenged us. "Do you think it's because your generation invented computers and a technology that keeps everyone's eyes glued to these devices instead of looking at the life that surrounds them? How does that make you smarter? I've seen people walk straight into lamp posts – even drive into a parked car because they couldn't keep their eyes of the cell phone! That's not looking too smart, in my opinion."

He had a point there.

"Humanity itself isn't all that smart when you think about it – young or old. We've used our brains to invent enough technology to blow us all up and turn our world into a radioactive nightmare - just so we could feel powerful. Yeah," he shook his head, "let's pat ourselves on the back for that one. It's ridiculous! And don't forget how brilliant we were when we learned how to produce chemicals that pollute the very air we rely on to breathe and the very water we rely on to drink – plain old stupidity, in my opinion! We even pump the soil with chemicals to supposedly grow more food, and if that's not enough, we spray that crop again with chemicals when it starts to grow, and then one more time to keep the produce from going bad before it gets to market. Nothing about that is smart. Think about what all those chemicals are doing to your body! Everyone's liver must be so overworked and tired from trying to rid ourselves of all those toxins we keep pumping into ourselves!" He pounded his fist on the table so hard that the salt shaker fell over - this topic was obviously near and dear to his heart. "I can just see future generations looking back on this time in history, shaking their heads wondering how a so-called intelligent society could merrily go about *knowingly* poisoning itself. It's insanity, but yet we continue on because we believe we are such an *advanced* civilization. And don't even get me started on profit and how it drives everything. It's not health or well-being that runs this world – it's profit, plain and simple."

I hated to admit it, but Barry was right. Sadly, it seemed we hadn't learned that much about the important stuff as a society.

"You wanna know what I think?" Barry was obviously not done yet. He pushed his chair back and stood to pace the kitchen floor, not waiting for our answer. "Well, I'll tell ya – I think there's been many civilizations on this planet that have been way more advanced than us, way more intelligent, and way more productive;

civilizations not driven by greed, money, possessions, and fear!" Barry stopped suddenly as a thought hit him. "I would truly love to see the world return to its senses, and after my dream last night, I'm gonna do what I can to help us go in that direction. I think that's what Rose was trying to tell me: I do have way more to offer. And from knowing you guys, I think you want the same, don't you?" he looked at us questioningly with such intensity that I almost had to look away. His energy was incredible – dare I say it – for a seventy-five-year-old man! He had us young-uns all revved up!

"I'm with you a hundred percent," Crow declared. "What about you guys? We've learned so much from our helpers and we always talked about giving back. Maybe it's time now to figure out how to do that. Plus, Barry's got tons of knowledge to share, not to mention a very passionate enthusiasm."

"I'm in," Malcolm spoke up. I think we can figure something out. What about you, Julie?"

"Yes, of course I'm in. The question is, how do we do it? How do we spread these messages about? I mean, it's great that we can talk amongst ourselves, but we need more people to hear what we've discovered, whether they believe it or not."

As we continued talking at our kitchen table that memorable morning, we managed to sort out a few things: we weren't out to convince anyone, or to preach to anyone – we simply wanted to get our ideas out to others and let them do with it what they would. We hoped it might open a few minds – sort of put a crack in the nut so it could eventually open. And we knew better than to fool ourselves with wishful optimism, as the world was not going to change in an instant, but we wanted to do our part to help. We'd been taught to start with ourselves, right where we were – so okay, how do we go about this, we asked ourselves. We had good intentions and managed to throw a bunch of ideas around, but nothing felt right, so in the end we decided to sleep on it and see what would come up going forward.

A few weeks later, around our fire pit one evening, we were once again running ideas past each other as to what we should do with all of the information and all of the ideas we'd gathered over the years. What was our responsibility - or was there a responsibility? We'd all become very busy in our daily lives and unsure of just how much time we'd have to take on any sort of project, but something had to be done. Now was the time. We knew that. We just needed to find the right way. When the guys dropped in to join us, I asked them what we should do.

Omar smiled a most benevolent smile at me. "I can help you in many ways, but I will *not* tell you what to do or make those kinds of choices for you. I'm afraid you'll have to make this decision on your own."

"Darn," I said. "I was kind of hoping for an easy answer."

"However," Bluedon was quick to add, "you have the answer in your heart - all of you do. When you hit upon the right course of action, there'll be no doubt for any of you. That's my clue."

Griffin had to put his two-bits in too. "There'll always be enough time to do what you truly want to do. You guys should realize better than anyone else by now that time doesn't actually exist, so never use the lack of it as an excuse to hold you back."

Kodiak was the only one who hadn't spoken. I turned to him to see what kind of advice he had for us. May as well get everyone's opinion.

Kodiak looked over at George, like a wise old owl turning towards its target. "Do you remember when you soared in the sky and swam in the ocean?"

"Do I ever! That's something I'll never forget."

Kodiak smiled. "And Julie, do you remember when you jumped over the crack and were transported to another dimension?"

"Yeah," I said and nodded. He was up to something, I could tell.

"Malcolm, do you remember Bluedon joining you on your commute to help you change your attitude?"

"Of course," Malcolm answered. "These are all unforgettable events in our lives. What are you getting at?"

"All in good time," Kodiak calmly answered before continuing. "And Crow, our beloved crazy Crow, do you remember how you discovered shimmering energy everywhere on your mountain hike?"

"Well, yeah. It was beyond magical."

Kodiak paused and looked intently at each of us, as though we should have gotten the hint he was trying to convey without really coming out and saying it. But all he got was our blank expectant faces. "Well…don't you want to tell others about those experiences?" he asked, rather emphatically, leaving his calm demeanor behind.

"Of course we do," I answered, still bewildered.

"Well, then – how do you best do that?"

"Hmmm…I'm not getting it," George said. "That's exactly what we're trying to work out. Sorry, Kodiak."

Somewhat exasperated, Kodiak walked back and forth a few times, then began again. "Okay, let's try this angle. I truly enjoy going into the bistro, so thoughtfully named after me, and I'll tell you why. I love to watch the people come in and talk to each other, or when they take a book off the shelf and sit back and read it, or a newspaper, or a magazine. Your bistro has become a place of information sharing. That's my favorite thing about it - *information sharing*." He looked at us expectantly.

My brain had started percolating. It didn't dawn on me right away, but I knew I was close. I could feel an idea pouring itself into my head through a funnel from above, and then it knitted itself together in my brain. Once it was all there, I knew I had it. "Oh-My-God!" I jumped up. "I've got it! Yes, yes…that's it!"

"Tell us, Julie," Malcolm said eagerly. "We can see you've had a brain explosion. What is it?"

I looked at them quite excitedly. "We're going to write a book! We're going to write a book about our story - about what happened to us from the very beginning at the dinosaur park to this night itself. We're going to talk about it all and let people get what they get from it. What do you think? I can feel it in my gut. Can you guys, too?"

"Wow – that's it! That's truly it!" Crow shouted.

Everyone got up and we had one big happy group hug. It was so exciting.

Over our jubilation I could hear sighs of relief from Omar, Bluedon, Griffin and Kodiak. "Really," Griffin said to the others, "I thought they'd never get it. You did a good job of leading them in the right direction, though," Griffin nodded his acknowledgment to Kodiak.

"Wait a minute," I stopped for a second. "None of us have ever written a book before. Do you think we can pull this off?"

Malcolm held me at arms-length and looked me straight in the eye. "There's lots of things we've never done before, and I'd say they've turned out pretty good. All we can do is try our best."

"Let's do it then!" Boy, but this was exciting. "What are we going to call it? We need a title." I could hardly stand still.

Our helpers listened as we excitedly threw names back and forth, but none of them hit the mark until Barry said, "Wait a minute – I think I've got something. What we're trying to do is get our *vision* of how we feel the world works, or could work, across to others – it's like we're portraying a *new way of being* almost. Yes," he nodded, "a new way of being – that would be our vision, don't you think? It would be our perfect vision - and isn't 20/20 another way of saying you have perfect vision? So, what about *20/20 Perfect Vision?*"

Yes, yes, yes…it was just the name we'd been looking for. Cheers, and high-fives all around! That gave us a platform to start with, which we did wholeheartedly and without delay. We never looked back! It is our heartfelt wish that you have enjoyed our sincere efforts.

The End!

Or maybe it's only the Beginning???

EPILOGUE

I must confess that I have a writing helper. It hovers just above my right shoulder, and when I'm writing it seems to leap forward with ideas. Countless times I sat down at my computer to work on this book, not knowing what direction I was going to go in, only to have characters and events suddenly *appear* that were news to me. But they always worked! I learned to trust this helper, and together we have happily completed *20/20 Perfect Vision: A New Way of Being.*

What's next, my helper asks? Well, we do indeed have another book on the go. It will be Volume Two, and will take Crow to a place between lives. Do I know what happens between lives? Well, no, I don't. But neither does anyone else that's alive. I do, however, plan to use my imagination, my opinion, and fortunately, my own personal helper for assistance - so let's just see where it goes. Stay tuned!

ACKNOWLEDGMENTS

I would like to acknowledge Jennifer Sparks, of *Stoke Publishing*, for her honest and clear guidance into the confusing world of self-publishing. Cara Lockwood, my editor, who gently pointed me in the right direction with writing tips that were beyond invaluable. Billie Sparks for her unexpected, but highly valued, proof-reading skills. Julie Larsen, best described as a *Thought Energy Practitioner*, who gave me the confidence to believe I was on the right track. My friend, Barry, for first introducing me to the Seth books so many years ago - I cannot thank you enough. Joan McIntyre, my English professor, for once telling me "You can write!" Also several family members and friends for their excellent ideas, feedback, and support. And last, but definitely not least, my husband Ted, for not interrupting my writing time unless the house was on fire!

SUGGESTED READING

Bach, Richard. ***Jonathan Livingston Seagull.*** US: Scribner, Div. of Simon Schuster Inc, 2014

Dahl, Lynda Madden. ***Living A Safe Universe, Vol 1 - 4.*** US: The Woodbridge Group, 2013-15

Emoto, Masaru. ***The Hidden Messages In Water.*** US: Atria Books, Illustrated Ed., 2005

Friedman, Norman. ***Bridging Science And Spirit.*** Oregon: The Woodbridge Group, 1990

Harman, Willis, Ph D. ***Global Mind Change.*** US: Warner Books, 1990

Hicks, Esther and Jerry. ***The Law of Attraction.*** US: Hay House, Inc., 2006

Kagan, Annie. ***The Afterlife of Billy Fingers.*** US: Hampton Roads Publishing, 2013

Lanza, Robert, MD & Berman, Bob. ***Biocentrism.*** Texas: BenBella Books, 2010

Lipton, Bruce, Ph D. ***Biology of Belief.*** US: Hay House Inc, 10th Anniversary Ed., 2016

McTaggart, Lynne. ***The Field.*** US: HarperCollins Publishers, 2008

Morgan, Marlo. ***Mutant Message Down Under.*** US: Harper Perennial Anniv. Ed., 2004

Roberts, Jane. ***Seth Speaks: The Eternal Validity of The Soul.*** US: Amber-Allen & New World Library, 1994

Roberts, Jane. ***The Nature of Personal Reality.*** CA: Amber-Allen & New World Library, 1994

Roberts, Jane. ***The Individual And The Nature of Mass Events.*** CA: Amber-Allen, 1995

Weiss, Brian L, MD. ***Many Lives, Many Masters.*** US: Fireside – Simon & Schuster, 1988

Website: ***Institute of Noetic Sciences,*** Noetic.org

ABOUT THE AUTHOR

Sharon discovered her love of writing later in life, using the days of her retirement to happily explore this creative activity. Before that she was kept very busy raising her five children, who have since brought spouses and several grandchildren into the extended family. Besides writing and interacting with family and friends, you will be sure to find Sharon in her garden where she employs the green thumb she's inherited from a long line of relatives. And in the winter, she will be in her sewing room creating works of art from pieces of fabric. She is also the author of "*Stalked and Shot: A True Story of Survival and Change.*"

Sharon grew up in rural Saskatchewan, but has spent her entire adult life in British Columbia. She currently lives in a small town in the BC Interior with her husband.

OTHER BOOKS BY SHARON VELISEK

Stalked and Shot: A True Story of Survival and Change

This is not fiction! It is a true story, written by the actual victim, who miraculously managed to survive the stalkers attempt on her life.

In order to show how naively a relationship can go wrong, Sharon divulges her involvement from the very first date to the breakup. And to show how innocently stalking behavior can escalate, Sharon has put together a chronological series of events complete with everyone's participation, including the police, the stalker, the doctor, the lawyer, counsellor, and friends. This is an honest and rare birds-eye view of how stalking can spiral out of control.

This story will grip you from the very first date to the fateful night of the attempted murder. **It is a must read if you don't want to be stalked, if you are being stalked, or if you know of someone being stalked.**

Available on AMAZON.

Made in the USA
Middletown, DE
02 February 2021

32954003R00213